D1025082

Heading Home

Also available by Katie Flynn

A Liverpool Lass
The Girl from Penny Lane
Liverpool Taffy
The Mersey Girls
Strawberry Fields
Rainbow's End
Rose of Tralee
No Silver Spoon
Polly's Angel
The Girl from Seaforth Sands
The Liverpool Rose
Poor Little Rich Girl
The Bad Penny
Down Daisy Street
A Kiss and a Promise
Two Penn'orth of Sky
A Long and Lonely Road
The Cuckoo Child
Darkest Before Dawn
Orphans of the Storm
Little Girl Lost
Beyond the Blue Hills
Forgotten Dreams
Sunshine and Shadows
Such Sweet Sorrow
A Mother's Hope
In Time for Christmas

Katie Flynn

Heading Home

arrow books

Published by Arrow Books 2010

4 6 8 10 9 7 5 3

Copyright © Katie Flynn 2010

Katie Flynn has asserted her right under the Copyright, Designs
and Patents Act 1988 to be identified as the author of this work.

First published in Great Britain in 2009 by Arrow Books
Random House, 20 Vauxhall Bridge Road,
London SW1V 2SA

www.rbooks.co.uk

Addresses for companies within The Random House Group Limited can be found at:
www.randomhouse.co.uk/offices.htm

The Random House Group Limited Reg. No. 954009

A CIP catalogue record for this book
is available from the British Library

ISBN 9780099520252

The Random House Group Limited supports The Forest Stewardship Council (FSC),
the leading international forest certification organisation. All our titles that are
printed on Greenpeace approved FSC certified paper carry the FSC logo. Our paper
procurement policy can be found at www.rbooks.co.uk/environment

Typeset in Palatino by SX Composing DTP, Rayleigh, Essex

Printed and bound in Great Britain by
CPI Mackays, Chatham, ME5 8TD

For Daphne Jolly and her husband Michael, who love the Norfolk Broads as I do and have the luck to live cheek by jowl with them.

Chapter One

It was a bitterly cold January day, the pavements ringing with frost and Claudia's breath coming out as fog. As she emerged from Blodwen Street on to the Scotland Road she slowed, anxious not to slip and fall as she had done the previous day, and looked around for her pal Danny. After only the most cursory of glances she saw him hurrying towards her, a broad grin on his face and his black hair standing up in spikes. He shouted at her to run, but Claudia did not increase her pace, remembering yesterday's fall which had resulted in her crashing to the ground, dirtying her one and only school skirt and scuffing her neat button boots. It had taken her father most of the evening, working away with an old piece of rag and a tin of polish, to make the boots respectable once more and her grandmother, sponging and pressing the skirt, had told her to be more careful in future. 'Skirts don't grow on trees, queen,' Emily Dalton had said rather reproachfully. 'This 'un will have to last you a while yet.'

Now, however, Danny had reached her side, puffing and breathless. 'What's up wi' you?' he asked aggrievedly. 'Why didn't you hurry when I shouted?

1

We's early this mornin', so I thought we might go to Harper's, see if they've got any orange boxes to spare. It's so bleedin' cold it might easily snow, and if it does we wants to be ready, don't us! If I can lay me maulers on an orange box or two I could make us a decent sledge. What d'you think?'

'I'll come with you, but I don't think it's going to snow,' Claudia said, looking up at the clear sky. 'You need clouds for snow. Still, we are early; our Jenny's got a nasty cold and it's gone on her chest, so Mam got up to see to her and decided to make my butties, since she was already awake. What's in yours, eh? Mine's fish paste.'

'Margarine,' Danny said gloomily. He lived in three rooms in a tall and tottering house in Albemarle Court with a weary, hard-pressed mother and two younger sisters. His father, a seaman, had been killed when Danny was ten and now he had to cope as best he could. Danny Callaghan was thirteen, six years older than Claudia, and had befriended her when she had first started school and he had found her backed into a corner in one of the many small jiggers nearby, trying to defend herself against a crowd of kids who were accusing her of being stuck up, teacher's pet and a goody-goody.

Claudia remembered how Danny, used to fighting his way through life, had taken one look at the situation and decided that she needed rescuing. Accordingly, he had piled in with both fists and boots and from that day on no one, as he put it, who did not want to take his teeth home in a paper bag meddled with Claudia Muldoon.

2

Claudia was not only grateful; she very soon came to admire and respect Danny, who was almost totally self-reliant. He made his own butties each day, for his mother was not an early riser. Mrs Callaghan and her son struggled to make ends meet, but Claudia knew that Danny's mother 'entertained gentlemen' and that this helped the family finances, though what Mrs Callaghan did for the 'uncles' who visited whenever their ships were in port was a closed book to her, and to Danny, Claudia thought, though it was a subject that was never mentioned between them.

Claudia had tried asking her mother about Mrs Callaghan's mysterious visitors, but Louisa Muldoon had gone rather red and had said that it was none of her business. 'But Danny's a good boy; he looks after his mother and he takes care of you, so I never worry when you go off with him,' she had said. 'It's a struggle to rear a child on your own, as Mrs Callaghan does, which is why I always tell you to bring Danny here after school, rather than hanging around Albermarle Court.' She had given her daughter a hug. 'To Mrs Callaghan, you're just another mouth to feed,' she had concluded.

'Wake up, dreamy!' Danny's voice brought Claudia back to the present and she realised that they had reached the greengrocery. Mr Harper was building apple pyramids on the staging in front of his shop and looked up as Danny addressed him. 'Gorrany orange boxes goin' spare, mister? Us fancies makin' a sledge for when the snow comes, so if you could . . .'

Mr Harper balanced the last apple on the top of the pyramid and turned to shake his head sadly at the two children. He was a small man with an enormous white moustache and a pair of thick black eyebrows that looked oddly incongruous against his bushy white hair. 'Me orange boxes looks like bein' full of oranges for a few weeks yet,' he told them. 'I do good business up to Christmas, then there's a call for fruit at the New Year, but right now folks is just buyin' what you might call essentials, mainly spuds an' cabbage, so I shan't have no orange boxes until the weather gets warmer and folks start fancyin' fruit again.'

'Oh well, thanks mister, but by the time the weather gets warmer us won't be wantin' sledges,' Danny said rather gloomily. 'I s'pose you've gorra delivery lad what works weekends an' school holidays? Only me pal here an' meself could do with earnin' a few pennies . . .'

Mr Harper laughed and his magnificent moustache tilted up to reveal large, tobacco-stained teeth. 'I'm fully staffed, but I don't blame you for askin', lad,' he said. 'I know what it means to need a penny or two. When I were a lad livin' in the country, January, February an' March was always called the hungry months. We came close to starvin' several times, an' I reckon it ain't that different in a town.' He stood back to admire his handiwork, then gave an exclamation and pounced on one of the apples lying on the staging. 'Bruised,' he said briefly. 'Want it?'

The children left with profuse thanks and shared the apple, bite and bite about, as they retraced their steps along the Scottie. When they reached school they parted, with a promise to walk home together when classes finished. Danny, spotting a neighbour's child, gave her the apple core, pointing out that there were still two good mouthfuls left, if she was careful. The child, however, ate the core as well as the fruit that remained and thanked him wholeheartedly.

Claudia smiled to herself. She guessed that an apple was a rare treat for the little girl and was grateful that she and young Jenny got such things as a matter of course. Jenny was five, and worshipped her big sister, but would have looked askance had Claudia given her an apple core and expected her to be grateful.

Now, not to be outdone by her pal, Claudia plunged a hand into her coat pocket and produced a small object wrapped in greaseproof paper. It was a milk roll, baked by her grandmother the previous day and given to her granddaughter as a little extra. Claudia broke the roll in two and handed half to the child. 'Have it for your snappin' at break time . . .' she began, but the little girl, cheeks already extended by the milk roll, simply nodded her thanks, swallowed, and then rushed towards the school gates as the infants' bell sounded.

'That were nice of you,' Danny observed, following the child with his eyes as she careered across the playground and joined the line of her classmates. 'That kid gets more clacks than kisses. Hey up, that's my bell! Ta-ra. See you later!'

Claudia's own bell sounded seconds after, and she trotted across the playground and headed for Chloe, her best friend, who was beckoning her wildly, halfway up the queue. As Claudia slipped into place beside her, Chloe turned and grinned. 'I called for you, but your mam said you'd left early,' she said. 'I met the postie as I was turnin' into Blodwen Street; he gave me your mam's letters, so I went to the front door an' she came out with a bit of toast in her hand. She's ever so nice, your mam. She axed me to bring the post right into your kitchen 'cos she said her fingers was all buttery, an' she give me a whoppin' slice of bread an' jam . . .'

'Where is it? You ought to give me a bite at least, if not half,' Claudia said with an inward giggle. Chloe was a plump and smiling child and would have eaten the bread and jam long before she had turned out of Blodwen Street.

Chloe grinned and rubbed her tummy. 'It's in here, but you didn't take the post in,' she reminded her. 'Your gran were in the kitchen; she told me she's bakin' today, so you're to hurry home after school if you want one of her fruit buns.'

'Gran's the best cook in the world,' Claudia said fervently, as the line began to shuffle forward. 'I don't suppose you noticed, Chloe, but was one of the letters from Ireland? Me dad's worried, because since me Irish gran died me granddad keeps sayin' he could do wi' some help on his farm.'

Chloe shrugged. 'I didn't really look at 'em,' she admitted. 'But you'll find out when you go home after school.' By now they were in the cloakroom, and they headed for their pegs and hung up their coats. 'Wish I could come home with you, but Mam's got a grosh of messages for me, so she said to go straight back.'

'I expect Gran will have messages for me too, and I'm jolly sure Danny's mam will have some for him,' Claudia said as the two girls entered their classroom. 'I just hope that if there is a letter from Ireland, it's good news and not bad. It makes our dad unhappy when he gets a sad letter.'

Louisa Muldoon sat at the table, gazing at the envelope propped up against the jam jar. Her mother, washing up the breakfast dishes, glanced over her shoulder and shook a reproving head. 'Wharrever is the matter, queen? You're lookin' at that letter as though it were a perishin' snake, poised to bite! Why the devil don't you open it and be done? Oh, I know it's addressed to Cormack, but there never were an easier-goin' feller than your husband, that I will say. He'd tell you to go ahead an' open it instead of sittin' there imaginin' the worst. And anyway, if you don't get off, you'll be late for work. Miss Timpson's a good boss, but . . .'

'Oh, Mam, I know you're right and he wouldn't mind, but I've never opened Cormack's letters and I don't mean to start now,' Louisa said distractedly, getting to her feet. 'I'll just nip upstairs and check that Jenny's all right. Do keep an eye on her, Mam. She's that full of cold ...'

'Course I will,' Emily Dalton said. 'It's a pleasure to take care of me youngest grandchildren. In fact, don't you bother goin' upstairs. I'll nip up as soon as you leave.' She watched as her daughter struggled into her coat and arranged her hat so that it did not disturb the bun she wore low on the nape of her neck. 'You look grand, queen. Off you go!'

'Thank God it's only a short walk to the shop,' Louisa said, glancing at the clock on the mantelshelf. 'If I run I won't be late.'

7

Her mother began to remind her that the pavements were slippery, but Louisa was already halfway out of the back door and had no time to promise she would be careful. Instead, she flew across the cobbled yard, jerked open the stout wooden door and ran along the jigger, holding her hat on with one hand.

She made it to the shop in time to open up for an impatient customer, who wanted to purchase a pair of lisle stockings, since she had slipped on the ice, and Timpson's Emporium was well known for selling the cheapest hosiery on the Scotland Road. 'I've been and gone and beggared meself,' the sufferer said mournfully, pulling up her skirt to display both the laddered material and her badly grazed knee.

Clucking sympathetically and telling her that she should not have hurried with the pavement so icy, Louisa allowed the other woman to go through her stock whilst she hung up her coat and hat and tidied her hair. Then she turned back to her customer. 'Have you found anything to suit, madam?' she asked politely. 'They cost two and eleven a pair.'

'Oh! Well, I suppose . . .' The woman looked hopefully at Louisa. 'I suppose I couldn't buy just the one? After all, t'other's perfect . . . well, mebbe there's a little ladder down by the ankle, but me boss won't notice that.'

Louisa smiled, but was forced to shake her head. 'No, I'm afraid stockings have to be sold in pairs. But if you're short of money until the end of the week, you could become a member of our clothing club. You pay a shilling a week and at the end of each month you can spend three and six of it, or you can stay in credit and have a good lump sum by Christmas.'

The customer sighed deeply but shook her head, produced a worn leather purse from her shabby handbag and handed Louisa half a crown and a sixpence. 'Better not; next Christmas seems a long way off,' she said. She smiled widely as Louisa handed her her penny change, together with a neat paper bag containing the stockings. 'Thanks, miss. And if you happen to come across a one-legged woman, let me know, 'cos she an' me might get together.'

Louisa was still laughing as the woman left the shop, just as Miss Timpson came down the stairs, all ready for work in a navy dress with white collar and cuffs. She greeted her counter assistant with all her usual amiability and told her that they had new stock in the back, which Louisa might as well begin to sort and price before hanging it on one of the revolving stands. 'And I'll brew us a nice cup of tea while you do that,' she said. 'Why were you laughing when I came down the stairs? I could do with something to cheer me up 'cos it's perishin' cold in my flat and I hate the cold, so I do.'

Louisa related the story of her first customer and then went through to the stockroom and began to open the cardboard boxes. Another working day had begun.

Cormack came into the kitchen whistling a popular melody beneath his breath and found Claudia sitting at the table, frowning over her homework. 'How's Jenny?' he asked. His mother-in-law, busy at the stove, smiled a welcome and assured him that his youngest was much better and would return to school next day. 'That's grand,' Cormack said, sniffing appreciatively. The room smelled delightfully of cooking, and as soon as she turned from the stove Emily cut a slice off a large fruit cake that was cooling on a wire tray.

'I've just brewed the tea, so sit yourself down and I'll pour you a mug,' she said briskly. 'Claudia got the messages for me as soon as she came back from school, so we're ahead of ourselves for once.'

'Thanks, Ma, but I'll have a bit of a wash first. I'll enjoy me slice o' cake all the more if it's not covered in muck,' Cormack said. He headed for the sink and saw, out of the corner of his eye, the letter propped against the jam pot. He sighed, recognising his father's handwriting, but started to wash his hands. Ever since his mother's death, some eighteen months previously, his father's letters had, it seemed, contained nothing but bad news: the family pig had escaped from its snug sty and been attacked by a passing dog, and though old Fergal Muldoon had rescued it before the worst could happen, the pig had not thrived. In addition, a fox had got into his chicken run and caused considerable mayhem amongst his fowls, and the boy he had employed immediately after his wife's death had stolen eggs from the henhouse and small sums of money from the teapot on the mantel, so he had been forced to dismiss him.

Drying his hands on the roller towel which hung on the back of the door, Cormack picked up the envelope. What would it be this time? Not bad news, he hoped devoutly. Despite his fears, however, the first page of the letter was both cheerful and optimistic, causing Cormack to breathe a sigh of relief. He reflected that his father had always been cheerful; clearly he was beginning to come to terms with the loss of his beloved wife. With considerable pleasure, Cormack read that his father had purchased a sow which had been going cheap at a local market; the animal would give birth at the end of the month, his parent had written. Furthermore, he had been promised the loan of a neighbour's donkey and cart when summer came so that he might cut and carry peat from the bog, sufficient to last him for many months. He had also found a young lad from the village who was honest and hard working, and content to help Mr Muldoon with the heavy work of the croft for a few shillings a week and a couple of meals a day.

Halfway down the second page, however, the letter became more difficult to read. His father usually wrote a clear, old-fashioned script, but as the letter progressed the writing deteriorated until it became a scrawl so bad that his son could scarcely make out a word of it.

Beginning to frown, Cormack turned to the last page and was relieved, at first glance, to find the writing firm and clear once more. Then, with a lurch of dismay, he realised that it was not his father's writing at all, but that of . . . he frowned down at the signature . . . Mrs O'Hara, who he remembered lived on a croft a couple of miles back down the road in the direction of the village.

With his heart in his mouth, Cormack began to read.

Chapter Two

June 1928

'Look, Mam, it's not as though we're going for ever, me and the children,' Louisa said, trying to keep her voice quiet and even. She had no desire to quarrel with her mother, but sensed that this was becoming a distinct possibility. If only she could convince the older woman that she was not being deserted for no good reason! 'But poor Cormack just can't manage alone any longer. We've been apart now for more than two years and though his father has recovered from his stroke, he's a long way from right. And Mam, Cormack's my *husband*, for goodness' sake! You wouldn't expect me to let him down, would you? He's soldiered on there all this time – but now he needs me. There's things he's had to do for his father, nursing like, which are really a woman's work and . . .'

It was evening and Louisa and her mother were alone in the kitchen, Emily baking and Louisa ironing the girls' school skirts and blouses. Now, Emily tightened her lips and slammed her rolling pin viciously on to the ball of pastry she had just made. 'Oh, Lou, just listen to me for a moment! I said nothing when Cormack gave up his good job and went flyin' off to Ireland. I held me peace when he asked you to send him some of the money you and he had saved out of your Post Office book. I bought Claudia new shoes when you couldn't afford 'em, but now you say you'll give up your job with Miss Timpson and take my girls off to that . . . that . . .'

'Don't say it, Mam,' Louisa said, bristling. 'Cormack's the best husband in the world, which you were happy enough to acknowledge when he was living here with us.' She smiled coaxingly at the older woman. 'I know you love him almost as much as I do, and you know he wouldn't beg me to join him if it weren't absolutely necessary. And remember, when we've got his father fit again, we'll be back here before you can say Jack Robinson. Oh, come on, Mam, you've always told me a woman's place is with her husband. Don't go changing your mind now.'

Emily fished a handkerchief out of the sleeve of her cardigan and blew her nose defiantly. 'I weren't going to say anything against Cormack,' she muttered. 'It's Ireland. From what I've gathered, this place – the Muldoons' croft, or whatever you call it – is in the middle of nowhere, so no chance of Cormack gettin' even a half decent job, lerralone a good one, like he had here. As for yourself, you've been real happy with Miss Timpson, and valued, what's more. And wharrabout schoolin'? Claudia's doin' right well, and Jenny's holding her own . . .'

'Oh, Mam, stop it! You're talking as though Ireland were half a world away instead of just across the Irish Sea. Do you think there are no good schools there? Cormack went to the village school, the same one the girls will be attending, and he's better than I am when it comes to figuring, and reads every book he can lay his hands on. Besides, I keep telling you, we won't be there for more than a few months . . .'

Emily cut in swiftly, her eyes flashing. 'If you truly believe that, Louisa Muldoon, then why won't you agree to leave the kids wi' me while you're gone? Don't you trust me? If only you'd leave them, then I'd know you'd be coming back and I wouldn't be so lonely. Oh, Lou, can't you understand how I'll miss me granddaughters if you take 'em away? And Claudia will be leavin' school and wantin' work one of these days. What chance of a good job will she have over there, eh?'

Louisa sighed. She felt weary to the bottom of her soul, for this argument had been going on for the best part of a week, ever since Cormack had written, begging her to join him. 'Of course I know you'll miss 'em, Mam, and they'll miss you, as I will,' she said gently. 'As for Claudia getting work, we'll be back with you long before then. And if you came with us, then no one would have to miss anyone, but you won't leave your home and your friends, not even for the sake of being with our little family. Cormack's desperate to have his children with him and to be honest, Mam, I think it's probably a better life for the kids with all that countryside to play in. I know I've only been to Ireland once, that time Cormack took me to meet his parents just after we were married, but it's beautiful, Mam. The girls will love it, and so would you, if only you'd join us.'

Emily shook her head. 'I'll not give up me own little home and see the landlord let it to someone else,' she said. 'In fact, if you really do go, Louisa, honest to God, I don't know how I'll manage. Think on, once you're away, you won't be payin' your share of the rent. Have you thought of that?'

'Of course I have,' Louisa said, aware that the arguments were simply being repeated until her head spun. 'But you know very well, Mam, that you can get lodgers for our two rooms as soon as we move out. You're a first-rate cook, so folk will be queuing up to stay with you, and as I keep telling you, it'll only be for a few months, until we get things sorted out for Mr Muldoon.'

Emily was making an apple pie. She had sliced the apples and now lifted her pastry, covered the dish and began to trim the edges, pinching the crust into place with finger and thumb. 'I don't want strangers in me home,' she said sulkily. 'But if it's truly only for a few months, I s'pose I'll have to make the best of it. Oh, Lou, I'm going to miss you so bad!'

Impulsively, Louisa put down her iron, ran across the room and gave her mother a hug. 'We shall miss you too, all of us,' she said. 'Oh, Mam, I wish you would come as well, but I do understand why you won't. This is a nice house and the rent's reasonable, and the neighbours are friendly. But I'm sure it won't be long before we're all back home.'

'And tryin' to find work, which won't be easy,' Emily said reproachfully. 'Your Cormack's job was a real good one and no matter how much they valued him they won't employ him again on the same terms, that you can rely on. As for Miss Timpson, I know she's fond of

15

you and a good employer, but once you're replaced that's another chance gone.'

'I know, and we've thought of that, Cormack and meself,' Louisa admitted, returning to her work. 'But no sense in meeting trouble halfway, Mam. And I dare say the croft is worth a deal of money, which Cormack will inherit. When we're back in the Pool we'll find work of some sort, and for now all I can do is promise to write at least weekly, and to come home just as soon as me father-in-law can manage without us.'

Emily finished off her apple pie and carried it over to the oven. 'All right, all right, I suppose I'll have to leave off tryin' to persuade you not to desert me,' she said gruffly. 'But try to come back before Christmas, there's a good gal.'

'We'll do our best,' Louisa said rather doubtfully. 'The person I'm really sorry for is young Danny Callaghan. He and Claudia spend all their spare time together, as you know; he goes with her to get my messages, takes her off to Prince's Park to play cricket with his mates, protects her when she needs protection and jollies her along when she doesn't. Even if we're only away for a matter of weeks, he'll be lost without our Claudia.'

'I don't *believe* it! Oh, I know your dad's gone back to Ireland to help your grandpa out 'cos he's been ill, but why's you got to go? You and Jenny is only a couple o' kids; I can't see you plantin' spuds or doin' whatever they do to cows an' pigs an' that. You could stay with Mrs Dalton if your mam feels she's gorra go.'

Danny and Claudia were sitting on the wall that

separated the yard of No. 22 from the jigger. Claudia had just broken the news that the Muldoon family were off to Ireland in a couple of days to join her father, and though Danny knew very well that there had been talk of such a move he had never truly believed that it would happen. Now he stared at Claudia with real dismay, for to his way of thinking folk who went to distant lands did not return to Liverpool for many years. Some, he knew, did not come back at all.

Claudia, however, shook her head. 'We're a family, Danny,' she said reproachfully. 'We want to be together. As for working, Jenny and me will still be goin' to school. Mam wants Gran to come with us, but she won't leave Blodwen Street, and all her friends, so that's not on. But you never know; if we're a fair time away, Gran might decide to come to Ireland after all. So staying with her just wouldn't be sensible.' She smiled at him coaxingly. 'Do try to understand, Danny. Me and Jenny would much rather not go off to Ireland leaving Gran and all our pals behind, but I'm sure it won't be for long. Anyway, it's all arranged. And I bet we'll be back in Liverpool before Christmas.'

Danny shook his head dolefully. 'You won't come back, not to live you won't,' he mumbled. 'Folk hardly ever do. Oh, Claudia, I don't know what I'll do when you're gone. It ain't just that you're my bezzie, it's 'cos I spends all me spare time with you. In fact, I'm in Blodwen Street nearly as much as I'm at home in Albermarle Court.'

'Well, that needn't change,' Claudia cut in. 'Gran will want someone to get her messages, so you can pop in two or three times a week and offer to give a hand. Then you can ask her if she's heard from us, and get all our news that way. Or you could write to me yourself – I promise I'll reply – which would be fun, don't you think?'

Danny, however, shook his head decidedly. 'No it wouldn't, it would be like doing extra bleedin' school-work, and I get enough of that now I'm at the Institute,' he said gruffly. 'And come to think, you've always give me a hand with me English essays and that. What'll me teacher think when me work goes downhill faster'n a runaway horse down Havelock Street?'

Claudia giggled but gave him a playful punch on the arm. 'Stupid! You're clever, you know you are – much cleverer than me. You'll simply have to work harder. And honestly, Danny, you really should do just that, because your exam results will affect what sort of job you get, and you know your mam relies on any money you bring in now, so a proper wage will be a real blessing.'

Danny had opened his mouth to answer when Claudia cut him short with a sudden exclamation. 'Danny! I've had a brilliant idea, honest to God I have. You'll be leaving the Institute and hunting for work quite soon, and if we really do have to stay in Ireland Dad's bound to want hired help on the croft, so why shouldn't you come over to Ireland and work for him? I'm sure you'd pick it up quick as quick. I don't suppose it would pay much, but you'd have all your meals and so on, and oh, Danny, it would make me so happy if you could come to Ireland and be with us.'

'Oh, very funny,' Danny said sarcastically. 'And what's my mam going to do whilst I'm swanning off to a foreign country? You say you Muldoons are a family and want to stick together. What about us Callaghans? Aren't we a family? And we don't have no dad to bring in a wage. There's just what my mam gets from her bits of jobs, and anything I can earn. So that little scheme is a non-starter.'

Claudia reached for his hand and grabbed it, whilst tears formed in her eyes and trickled down her cheeks. 'Oh, Danny, I was wicked and thoughtless, and I'm ashamed of myself,' she said huskily. 'It was selfish, too, because you're the best pal a girl ever had and I can't bear to think that we might not meet for years and years. But I promise you I'll do my very best to come back to Blodwen Street and until I do I'll write whenever I can, and I won't expect you to write back because you'll be far too busy. Please forgive me for what I said and tell me you'll be my pal for always.'

'I will,' Danny said fervently. He put his arm round her and gave a squeeze, then kissed her cheek. 'But oh, Claudia, promise me you'll do your best to come back, 'cos I'll be lost without you, honest to God I will!'

It was a warm spring day and Claudia was sitting at the rough kitchen table, writing her weekly letter to Grandma Dalton. It must be admitted that the letters between herself and Danny had gradually ceased, but since Gran always handed Claudia's letters over to her old friend to read she knew that Danny was not kept in the dark about her doings. The family had now been in Ireland for nearly a year, and though Claudia enjoyed keeping her grandmother up to date her mother had told her gently that she must not over-enthuse. 'Your gran loves us all very much and naturally she wants you and Jenny to be happy, but it won't do to let her think you prefer life in Ireland to that in Liverpool,' she had said.

But that advice had been given when they had first arrived at Connacht Cottage and since then many things had changed. Cormack had improved the croft out of all recognition; he had built on two extra rooms as soon as he had realised that Grandpa Muldoon would never again be able to manage the hard physical labour the croft demanded. Claudia had been sorry for Grandpa, knowing that he fretted at his uselessness, but for her own sake she was glad. She adored everything about her new life and knew that Jenny felt the same. When her father spent his savings on a donkey and cart so that they no longer had to borrow if they needed transport she had been delighted, because it was another sign that they were to stay in County Kerry. They had been happy enough in Blodwen Street with their dear gran, but it could not compare with the glorious countryside by which they were now surrounded. Rivers, streams, woods, meadows, moors and its nearness to the sea made Connacht Cottage a paradise for children, and Claudia and Jenny knew themselves blessed.

They had made many friends and loved the village school, and the two teachers who reigned there. The three-mile trek each way presented few problems, for city children without money to spare became great walkers. Claudia's friend Dympna, who lived further away from the village, called for them each school day and the three girls collected children as they went, making Claudia think of the Pied Piper. In cold and snowy weather, they left home earlier, throwing snowballs at one another, creating slides and snapping icicles off any convenient branch to suck as a city child might suck an ice lolly. In summer, they beguiled their way by playing tag, collecting wild flowers and hunting for birds' nests. In a part of the country that was almost completely rural, birds' eggs were a useful addition to one's diet and many a child sucked the contents to augment the soda bread that they took for their dinners.

Claudia had been a little afraid that the children might consider her and Jenny to be outsiders; might pick on them simply because they were different. This did not prove to be the case, however. It was a small school, and both teachers had taught Cormack when he was young. They greeted the girls with warmth and told them they expected great things of their father's daughters, and so far Claudia had not disappointed them.

Things had changed in Liverpool as well. Grandma Dalton now had permanent lodgers who appreciated both her cooking and her cheerful company. When Mam had first asked her to come over to Ireland for a little holiday, Gran had refused, regretfully but firmly. *Me lodgers are in regular work and keep their rooms as nice as you could wish*, she had written. *I give 'em breakfast and evening meals during the week and make 'em butties to take to work. They go out for a bite of a Sunday, but they rely on me and I wouldn't let them down. If it's holidays you want, then you'll have to come to me.*

But there was no question of that as yet; animals could not simply be told to fend for themselves. The house cow had to be milked twice a day, hay had to be cut, potatoes had to be dug up and clamped so that they would last the winter long. Hens would go on laying and someone had to collect the eggs, and even the wild tabby cat would look for her saucer of milk whether one were in Ireland or visiting Liverpool. So Mam had had to explain these things to Gran and for the moment at any rate only the letters kept Emily Dalton and the Muldoons in touch.

'Have you nearly finished, Claudia? I've found a bit of slate, like you said, and I've marked out a piggy bed, but there's no one to play with until you finish writing that letter. Do come out; it's a nice day, so it is.'

Claudia turned to smile at her sister, framed in the doorway that led into the farmyard, a hopeful expression on her small freckled face. She was not a pretty child, with lank, fawn-coloured hair and rather small blue eyes, but Claudia loved her little sister and thought that her sweet expression made up for her lack of obvious good looks.

'Claudia? Do come out,' Jenny repeated hopefully, now shifting from foot to foot. 'I've done me work, so now I can play; Mam says so.'

Claudia glanced at the page before her. 'I'm nearly

done, queen,' she said cheerfully. 'Give me ten minutes and I'll join you.'

She turned back to her letter, meaning to read it over and correct any mistakes, but instead found herself seeing, in her mind's eye, her grandmother's neat house in Blodwen Street, with its big kitchen, nicely furnished parlour and small courtyard leading on to the jigger. In a previous letter, Gran had told her how the little boxroom on the first floor had been made into a bathroom and lavvy – imagine that, an indoor lavvy! – so that her lodgers no longer had to cross the yard to the privy in all weathers.

Then, naturally, she thought of her present home. The long low cottage, single storeyed of course and thatched, with whitewashed cob walls and a sweet-scented yellow rose climbing up until it touched the roof. Most of the ground surrounding the cottage was given over to growing vegetables, but her mother had asked Gran to procure flower seeds – the locals had looked askance when she had tried to buy such things in the village – and Gran had posted off a mixed bag. Now, though their cabbages, carrots and peas flourished, each bed was surrounded by a delightful mixture of colourful flowers. Marigolds, forget-me-nots, pansies and pinks formed what amounted to a hedge around the vegetable beds and were much admired by the local children, though their parents said frankly that whatever grew on a croft should be either eaten or sold, and to their way of thinking, flowers, though pretty, were useless.

Flowers were not the only things that made the Muldoons a little different from their neighbours. Both householders and small farmers thought nothing of leaving their doors open in hot weather, so that hens, ducks and even pigs wandered in and out of the cottages. Grandpa Muldoon had been astonished and rather affronted when his daughter-in-law had refused to allow animals or poultry to roam indoors at will, but he had soon grown accustomed to what he called Louisa's finicking ways and had actually admitted, in Claudia's hearing, that the cottage smelt a good deal sweeter now that the creatures were banned and a large bowl of flowers stood on the kitchen windowsill.

Claudia heaved a sigh and finished her letter off, as she always did, with the words: *Much love, dearest Gran, from your own Claudia.* She always left space at the bottom of the letter for Jenny to add a few words, and now she beckoned her sister to come into the room. 'I've done, Jen,' she said as the child arrived beside her. 'Tell Gran you collected eighteen hens' eggs and half a dozen duck eggs this morning. Tell her Mam will take them into town in the donkey cart and she'll give us sixpence each, 'cos we've worked hard this week. Then you can sign off "With lots of love", same as always.'

'Can't I just say I collected lots of eggs?' Jenny said plaintively. She was not fond of writing and was frequently in trouble at school for untidy work. However, Claudia considered that her sister would one day make someone a good wife, for she was a practical child and already, though only eight years old, she could bake a batch of scones or a round of soda bread as good as anything her mother could produce.

Now, Claudia got off her chair and let Jenny slide

into her place. 'You can glance over what I've written if you want,' she said. 'I know you only write to Gran once a month, but it'll be your turn in a couple of weeks and if you read my letter it might give you some ideas.'

Jenny, laboriously printing the words *Deer Gran*, shook her head. 'You know I'm very bad at reading real writing,' she said reproachfully. 'I'm not clever like you are, Claudia, and I want to play piggy-beds. If you make me read all this . . .' she flicked over the five pages of her sister's neat, closely written script, 'gracious, what a lot you've writ . . . I'll be here half the night. There ain't room to put hens' eggs and ducks' eggs, and stuff like that, so it'll have to be just "lots of eggs". Did Daddy tell you he's taking the donkey cart down to the shore tomorrow, at low tide? He wants seaweed to fertilise the new field what he and Dónal have dug over. I'm going with him; are you coming?'

'Of course I will, if Mam can spare me,' Claudia said slowly, after only a moment's thought. Dónal was the trustworthy lad from the village their grandfather had employed, and was highly regarded by Louisa and Cormack, who had kept him on. Claudia, however, tried to steer clear of him, for the moment he had set eyes on her he had made no secret of the fact that he thought her the prettiest girl in all of County Kerry – probably in all of Ireland, come to that. Claudia had been amused at first, even a little flattered, for Dónal was four years older than she, and a handsome enough lad with curly black hair, dark brown eyes and a sturdy body. But though he could read and even write a little, he was not quick-witted and his dog-like devotion sometimes made

Claudia want to scream. Being a kind-hearted girl, however, she tried not to embarrass him by letting her feelings show, and instead avoided his company whenever she could do so.

'Well, I thought you would,' Jenny said, beaming. She finished writing and handed the page to her sister. 'Will that do? I swear to God I can't think of another word ... can't we go now? Only Dónal and Dad will be coming back for a bite to eat in about half an hour and Mam will want us to slice the loaf and lay the table and so on, and we've not played so much as one round of piggy-beds.'

Claudia smiled to herself. She knew that her sister would not want to miss a moment of Dónal's company when he came in with her father for the mid-morning snack her mother always provided; there's Dónal thinking himself in love with me and Jenny tagging at his heels like Dad's collie dog, and that weird little boy Sean, who always comes bottom of her class, who thinks Jenny's the bees' knees because she's English . . .

'Claudia Muldoon, will you stop staring into space and grinning like a Cheshire cat,' Jenny said wrathfully. 'You're mean to me, so you are! You promised to play piggy-beds if I finished off the letter and I've done what you said and now it's near on time me dad came in from the fields.'

'I'm sorry, I'm sorry,' Claudia said quickly. She picked up the letter and pulled a face as she saw her sister's ill-spelt and uneven writing, but she folded the pages and pushed them into the envelope she had already addressed. Then she licked the flap and stuck it down, and pushed the letter into her skirt pocket. 'All right, all right, I did promise,' she said. 'But if I play piggy-beds now, will you come into the village when we've washed up and cleared away? I'll take my letter to the post and we'll deliver a dozen eggs to the grocer. We can certainly spare them this week 'cos the hens have been laying really well.'

As she spoke, the two girls approached the piece of smooth flat earth upon which Jenny had traced the outline of her game. Claudia examined it critically, then produced a ha'penny piece from her pocket. 'We'll toss to see who goes first,' she said briskly. 'Hens or harps?'

Emily Dalton picked up the letter from the mat and felt the usual little stab, part excitement, part dismay, when she realised it was from Claudia. The excitement was because she loved reading her granddaughter's letters, thought them good enough to be put in a book, and the dismay was because she had not seen her family for such ages and missed them all, even Cormack, who was none of her get but a good young man nevertheless. Although she had fought against the move to Ireland, she had not really blamed Cormack because family meant as much to him as it did to her and she knew that she could not expect him to abandon his father. One day the croft would be his only inheritance and from what her daughter – and Claudia – had told her, the place was already as good as his own. He and Louisa had spent their savings improving both land and cottage, and from the sound of it it was beginning to repay them for their trouble and hard work.

As she examined the letters in her hand she wished that she could have accepted her daughter's invitation to visit. Perhaps one day she would, but not yet. Right now she was too dependent on the money her lodgers paid her; later, perhaps . . .

As she headed for the kitchen she heard footsteps descending the stairs and turned to smile a good morning to Mr Payne, in his navy blue pinstripe suit and dark tie. He had a job in an insurance office on Exchange Flags and now he glanced meaningly at the letters in her hand as he joined her in the narrow hallway. 'Anything for me?' he asked hopefully. 'I haven't heard from my brother for several weeks, but of course when he's at sea, where there's no post box at the end of the road, he has to wait until his ship docks to despatch his letters.'

He went ahead of Emily to open the kitchen door for her but Emily, riffling through the letters in her hand, had to disappoint him. 'No, there's nothing for you Mr Payne,' she told him. 'There are two for me, both from my family in Ireland, and two for Mr Clarke.'

They entered the kitchen to find Mr Clarke already seated at the scrubbed wooden table. He had helped himself to a bowl of porridge, which he was sprinkling with brown sugar, and grinned cheerfully as his fellow lodger and his landlady entered the room together. 'Mornin' both,' he said breezily. He turned to Emily. 'Hope you don't mind me helpin' meself, missus, but I want to get in early. There's some jobs I didn't finish yesterday what I could do wi' workin' on whiles the office is quiet. It's always the same at this time o' year,

28

when the timetables change because it's summer, and school holidays.'

'No, that's fine, Mr Clarke,' Emily said at once. 'I've made your butties; they're in your tin on the bottom shelf in the pantry.' She tossed two letters on to the table in front of him. 'There's your post. You can read 'em while you tackle that porridge.'

Mr Clarke promptly put down his spoon and slit open the first envelope. He worked in the offices at Lime Street station but his family lived in Dublin and he corresponded regularly with a great many relations and friends. He was a widower, his wife having died half a dozen years previously, and though he was only in his mid-forties and a handsome fellow with a good deal of wavy dark hair and a pleasant way with him, he had told Emily that he did not think he would ever marry again.

'My Siobhan was the sweetest t'ing in nature,' he had told her, his eyes moistening. 'We've three kids, all fully growed now, but none of 'em came up to my Siobhan, either for looks or – well, I suppose you could call it sweetness. So though I love me family, especially me grandchilder, I'm better off workin' hard and enjoyin' meself from time to time, and savin' me pennies. I'll not be t'inkin' of trying to replace someone who just ain't replaceable.'

Emily, remembering her own happy marriage, had said she understood, and when Mr Payne showed what was probably no more than a friendly interest in her doings made it plain that she, too, had no intention of remarrying. Mr Payne, a quiet, grey-haired man whose chief interest in life seemed to be either playing bowls with his cronies out at Bootle or, rather surprisingly, growing vegetables and fruit on his allotment at Seaforth, had never actually so much as asked Emily out for a walk, so he probably had no interest in her save as his landlady. But sometimes she thought he looked rather wistful when Mr Clarke was talking about his family, and judged it safest to make it clear that a lodger was just that and should not get ideas.

Emily put a bowl of porridge down in front of Mr Payne and went over to the stove to brew the tea. Then she took three large mugs over to the table and sat down, though she did not start her porridge at once. First, she would read her letters. She opened Claudia's and was soon chuckling; the child had a gift, there was no doubt about it. As she read, she could see the cottage as clearly in her mind's eye as though Claudia had sent her a painting and not just a letter. The fowls scratching about in the back yard, the mean-tempered nanny goat with her kid at heel, waiting for poor Louisa to turn away unwarily so she could charge across the yard and butt her just as hard as she could in the behind; and if she knocked over the pail of milk which had just been wrested from her reluctant udder in the process, so much the better.

Smiling to herself, Emily read on. Because it was the school holidays, both girls were able to do a deal of work on the croft, but Louisa saw to it that they had plenty of fun as well. Jenny collected eggs, fed the hens and took Pickles the donkey to and from the moor, where she attached a long length of rope to her bridle

30

and hammered a wooden peg into the ground so that she could not wander away. One of the children would walk back to the moor every two or three hours to change the position of the peg and give the donkey a fresh spot to graze. Claudia told her grandmother how Jenny always rode the donkey to and from the moor, described also how Pickles would occasionally object to this and buck the small rider off. But Jenny never cried or complained, she simply scolded the animal and clambered back aboard.

In addition, Claudia had described the deep little lane that was a favourite walk in spring, when the banks were brilliant with primroses, violets and celandines, of which the children would pick bunches both for school and for the cottage. In summer, pink dog-roses scented the air with their perfume, and the girls picked the wild strawberries which grew on the tall banks. In autumn they gathered hazelnuts from the trees that arched overhead, and even in winter they loved traversing the little boreen and collecting fallen acorns and beech mast, which they fed to the fat old sow and her twelve bonaveens.

Emily felt that if a magician should wave his wand and she should find herself outside the cottage, she would be able to make her way to almost every place that Claudia had mentioned in her letters. Even the peat bog, which was a good three miles from the croft, would not be strange to her. She knew all about the clouds of midges that descended there as soon as the sun grew hot, and thought she would revel in the chat between the diggers, which made cutting peat not only endurable but something to which the cottagers looked forward.

Emily reached the end of the letter, laughing to herself over Jenny's badly written lines and then sighing with pleasure. She glanced at her lodgers as they pushed their porridge bowls aside and began to spread homemade jam on slices of bread; how lucky she was to share her home with two such nice people, she thought contentedly. When she had first decided to take in lodgers she had advertised for young women, but speedily realised that this was a mistake. Young women in big cities were poorly paid and, she soon saw, caused landladies a great deal of extra work. Her first lady lodger had been a charge hand in a factory, and was both untidy and demanding. She had announced that she did not like washing in cold water and wanted hot, and when Emily had told her, rather sharply, that she only had to descend the stairs, jug in hand, to fetch hot water from the kitchen, she had replied that she did not have a navvy's strength and thought her landlady should be the one to carry the full jug upstairs. She also thought Emily should empty her slop bucket, make her bed and hang up the garments which she left strewn about the floor; in fact she had expected her landlady to behave as her mother had done, for Miss Carruthers, Emily's first lodger, had been a spoilt only child.

Fortunately, Emily had been advised to give her lodgers a month's trial before taking them on on a permanent basis, so at the end of the month the young woman had left and Emily had asked around amongst shopkeepers and neighbours for anyone quiet and respectable who was looking for lodgings. Mr Payne had arrived on her doorstep, agreed at once to the trial period, and was speedily perceived by Emily to be the perfect lodger. In his turn he had introduced Mr Clarke, and the three of them had now settled into a comfortable relationship. The men were neither of them what Emily thought of as drinkers, but once a week, on a Saturday, they went down to the Throstle's Nest together and spent the evening yarning with other customers and enjoying a pint of Guinness or porter, depending, Emily thought, on the state of their finances.

For her part, she either visited friends or watched a film at the cinema or a play at the theatre, or even enjoyed a rubber or two of whist at the church hall. During the week, friends came round to her house and sat with her in the kitchen, drinking tea and talking, whilst the lodgers wrote letters home in the parlour, and on summer evenings got out their pipes. Emily had told them tartly that she did not intend her home to smell like an alehouse and would only allow cigarettes or pipes to be enjoyed indoors when the weather was clement enough for the windows to stand wide.

Then there was Danny. Ever since the Muldoons' departure for Ireland, he had called in at Blodwen Street two or three times a week, offering to get her messages and to do any other small tasks which needed attention. Emily had not thought that this would last, but she had underestimated her young friend. It was Danny who kept the yard clean, chopped the logs she bought into manageable pieces, black-leaded the stove and even whitened her front doorstep. In return, she gave him what she knew he wanted most, which was Claudia's letters to read, and a few pence, which she guessed went straight into his mother's purse. He was always grateful for some of her homemade buns or a piece of pie, and was touchingly anxious to help in any way he could. In fact, he was a thoroughly nice boy, and though she had been sorry when the correspondence between him and her granddaughter had lapsed she thought that their friendship remained firm, for in her own letters to Claudia she always included news of Danny and Claudia's letters to herself contained titbits for her old pal and fervent congratulations when he secured a job as an office boy at Cammell Laird's.

'Everyone well, Mrs Dalton?'

Mr Clarke's voice brought her back to the present and she smiled at him, then picked up the second letter. 'Well, Claudia and Jenny seem to think so. They're good kids. They work as hard as their mam and dad, but they play hard as well and never have a grumble so far as I can make out. Of course Claudia, being older than the littl'un, does most of the chores, but Jenny's beginning to pull her weight.' She looked enquiringly at Mr Clarke as he laid down his own letters. 'And your family, Mr C? All well there, I trust?'

'All's very well. Me daughter Ennis has a job now, which will be a relief to them. She's the one wit' three childer but even so she's real smart an' tidy. They've took her on at Switzers – that's a big store in Dublin – and I've no doubt she'll do well there. She's ambitious, is Ennis, and will work like a slave to prove herself, so she will. Right now she's just a cleaner, but they can't fail to see she's a pretty piece, and determined to bring in a decent wage. Why, she's the sort that could sell ice creams to Eskimos, as the sayin' goes. And when they realise . . .'

He continued in this vein for some moments, but he had set a train of thought going in his landlady's head and though she made appropriate comments from time to time she was really thinking of Claudia's future. If the Muldoons had been living in Blodwen Street, she could have named a dozen places where her grand-daughter could have found employment, and good employment, too. But beautiful though the countryside might be, the croft was three miles from the tiny village and even further from any sort of town. Louisa had given her mother to understand that there was plenty of work for all of them on the land, but Emily wanted more for her granddaughter than this appeared to offer.

What about a husband, for instance? In Liverpool Claudia, with her glossy blackbird's-wing hair and her big eyes, so dark a blue that they could have been mistaken for deep brown, would be much sought after. Her skin was like milk and her slender figure . . . well, if she came back to her gran and looked about her for a husband she would have plenty of choice, Emily concluded. The place was a port; sailors came from all over the world and hung about the dance halls and cinemas, and the big offices and shops employed hopeful, intelligent young men determined to make their mark in the world, men of ambition whose way to the top would be greatly enhanced by a wife as beautiful and intelligent as her elder granddaughter. Danny was now one of them, with a good job, and studying to better himself at night school. But in rural Ireland . . . well, Claudia would be lucky to get a feller who could read and write, let alone a man worthy of her, Emily thought sadly, and then smiled at herself. It would be many years before Claudia would be thinking of marriage, and a great deal of water would have flowed under the bridge before then.

But Mr Clarke's words had made it plain that there were jobs, and good ones, too, for those with drive and ambition. Emily had no idea how near Connacht Cottage was to Dublin, but she thought it could not be a great distance. She must find out, and if necessary she would send the child money so that she could explore the possibilities of working in the city.

It was then that she remembered something else. Long, long ago, when she had been only a girl herself, a friend of hers, Lavinia Evans, had married a Mr Makepeace and gone to Dublin to live. For a while the two had corresponded, but as their families grew up, and they themselves aged, the letters had gradually ceased. But I've still got them in me hope chest, tied up with pink ribbon, along with the love letters my Albert sent me, Emily reminded herself excitedly. If Dublin's too far for Claudia to go in to work every day then I'm sure Lavinia would either give her a bed or see that she got decent lodgings with someone else. Just until she's either married or in a way to being so, and then . . . oh, and then mebbe she'll come back to Blodwen Street and her loving gran!

Mr Clarke's chair scraping on the linoleum brought

Emily, blinking, back to the present. She saw that both Mr Clarke and Mr Payne, having fetched their snap tins from the pantry and put on their coats and caps, were looking at her curiously, and felt foolish. Whatever was the matter with her, dreaming of her dearest Claudia when her lodgers were waiting for her attention?

'Sorry, Mr Clarke. I'm afraid you talking about your Ennis set me to wondering what sort of work there would be for my Claudia when she's old enough,' she said apologetically. 'Supper's at seven, same as usual, and I'll be settin' it on the table prompt so don't you be late, because it's beef stew and dumplings, wi' a side helping of mashed potato.'

Mr Clarke smacked his lips and Mr Payne gave an appreciative murmur, then stared down at the unopened letter beside his landlady's still untouched porridge dish. 'I've done our washing up, Mrs Dalton, but you've not so much as touched your own breakfast,' he said rather reproachfully. 'Let alone read your second letter. I hope you aren't expecting bad news?'

Horrified at the thought, Emily slit open the envelope and pulled out the sheet it contained. 'No, indeed. Why, the letter from the girls is full of their recent exploits. This one's from Louisa, my daughter . . .' She stopped, and stared first at the page before her and then at her lodgers, a smile beginning to spread across her face. 'Bad news? It's the best news there could be,' she said exultantly. 'Me daughter's in the family way! The baby's due in December . . . and she wants me there for her lying-in! She says it gives me plenty of time to arrange for someone to look after me lodgers and me house while I'm away . . . oh, ain't that just the best news ever? But Claudia couldn't have known, or her letter would have been full of it. Oh, I'm that pleased! I can't wait to write back and tell her how proud I am!'

When the girls told Louisa that they meant to walk into the village to post their letter, Claudia thought her mother looked a little self-conscious, but she only nodded and said that if they waited a moment she would give them a letter she had almost finished to post with their own.

'Why not save the stamp and put both letters in the same envelope?' the practical Jenny suggested, but their mother shook her head.

'Not this time, queen,' she said. 'This time my letter needs to go separately.' She looked speculatively at her daughters who were already at the back door, preparing to leave for the village with a dozen hens' eggs in the old brown basket and a loaf of brack wrapped in grease-proof paper; a little gift for the old lady who ran the village shop and would sell the eggs for them. Louisa sat herself down at the kitchen table and pulled her almost completed letter from her pocket, scrawled the last few lines and her signature, and then beckoned them to join her. As soon as they did so, she took hold of a hand of each and spoke seriously.

'Can you keep a secret?'

'Course we can,' Claudia said stoutly, answering for them both. 'Only don't say you've changed your mind about going down to the shore tomorrow and taking a carry-out with us! Jen and me are really looking forward to it, but of course if you aren't feeling well enough . . .'

38

Louisa looked startled. 'What makes you think I'm not feeling well enough?' she asked curiously. 'I'm not poorly; in fact . . . but what made you say that, darling?'

Claudia looked as embarrassed as she felt. 'I – well, I heard you being sick this morning, when I was getting the breakfast porridge,' she admitted. 'At least, I thought that was what I heard.'

Louisa sighed and pulled her daughters close. 'My loves, I hadn't meant to tell you quite so soon, but of course I realise that that was foolish. I've already written to your gran telling her my news, which is why I don't want to put my letter in your envelope, and your father is telling Grandpa Muldoon.'

'Oh, Mam, are you goin' to have a young wan, like Tommy's mam?' Jenny broke in before her mother had finished her sentence. 'I told Claudia that Tommy's mam had been sick, mornin's, so when we heared you t'rowin' up . . .'

Louisa leaned back in her chair and laughed, then pulled her youngest closer yet and kissed her soundly. 'You're a little wretch, so you are,' she said. 'Yes, you're right. You're going to have a little brother or sister in a few months. What d'you think of that, eh?'

'Will he be Irish, like Tommy?' Jenny asked rather doubtfully. 'I'd like a baby brother all right, but . . . can he be English, like us?'

'We're only half English, because Daddy's Irish through and through,' Claudia said, giving her mother a hug. 'We did wonder, when we heard you being poorly this morning, but trust Jenny to let the cat out of the bag before you had a chance to tell us your news yourself!'

'So long as she doesn't tell anyone else, though,' Louisa said, and Claudia thought that if her mother was anything like Tommy's, there would be no hiding the fact that she was in the family way in a few weeks. She began to say as much, but Louisa shook her head.

'No, no, my darlings, the baby isn't coming till around Christmas and . . . oh, well, things can go wrong, so it's best not to tell folk too early.'

'We won't tell a soul,' Claudia assured her. 'And now we'd best be getting down to the village or we'll miss the post.'

The two girls set out, so excited about their mother's news that for the first mile or two it was the only subject of conversation. Jenny thought it was a shame that they could not tell their pals and saw no reason why anything should go wrong. As she said to her sister, their cows had a calf every year, the old sow had produced a fine batch of healthy bonaveens and Tommy's mam, who seemed to have swollen to at least twice her normal size, had produced all of her seven children without a hitch.

Claudia, however, said in a world-weary way that everyone was different. 'Mam's rather shy about what happens when the cat has kittens, or the sow has piglets,' she reminded her sister. 'Besides, once she starts to get bigger, like Tommy's mam, everyone will know and we'll be able to tell all our pals then. Not that they'll care much, because most of them have got lots of brothers and sisters and I'm not sure that they don't envy us. I mean look at Tommy. He gets put in charge of the younger ones when he'd much rather be playing football, or getting up to mischief. Oh, and you should say piglets, not bonaveens; you know Mam gets upset when we use Irish words instead of English ones.'

Jenny jutted a mutinous lip. 'Dad likes it when I say bonaveens instead of piglets, and when I hand him his caubeen instead of his hat,' she observed. 'And Grandpa Muldoon pretends not to know what I mean when I use all English words. Oh, I do love Grandpa Muldoon; he's me best friend, so he is! He tells the nicest stories in the world, and he'll be so pleased about the baby because it'll be someone else to listen to his fairy tales. Besides, he's always around the cottage, so he'll be able to give an eye to the little chap when we're in school and Mammy's milking the cows or feeding the pigs, or doing other jobs on the croft.'

'I love Grandpa Muldoon as well; nearly as much as I love Grandma Dalton,' Claudia said dreamily. 'Won't it be nice when they meet? They're bound to like each other, don't you think?'

'Ye-es; but why should they meet?' Jenny asked doubtfully. 'Gran's a million miles away across the water, and when Mam asked her over for a little holiday she said she couldn't leave her lodgers.'

'Oh, she'll come to meet the new baby,' Claudia said with complete confidence. 'You know what grandparents are like.'

Jenny frowned over this for a moment, then beamed. 'If you're right, and I 'spect you are, then that's the best t'ing of all – thing, I mean,' she said apologetically. 'When we first came to Connacht Cottage I could remember Gran clear as clear, but as time goes on she gets fuzzy and I can't see her face so plain. It'll be grand to have her with us so that when she goes back to Blodwen Street me picture of her will be unfuzzy again.'

Claudia laughed. 'I know what you're saying,' she admitted. 'But that isn't the reason I want Gran to come and stay with us. I've tried and tried to describe the cottage and the animals, and Grandpa Muldoon, but she really needs to see it all for herself. Grandpa Muldoon's stories sound very flat and ordinary when you write them down, but when he tells them to us . . . oh, it's *so* different, Jenny!'

'I know,' Jenny said happily, skipping along beside her sister. 'I say, here comes Tommy with two of his little sisters; how I wish we could tell 'em we're goin' to have a baby of our own at Christmas. Oh, Claudia, won't it be the best Christmas present in the whole world!'

It was the end of October and Jenny and Claudia were washing up the supper things. When Claudia washed and Jenny wiped the task was soon over, but today it was Jenny's turn to wash, which meant it would take them a good fifteen or twenty minutes longer. The reason was, as Jenny knew full well, that she played games with the water and the utensils, swishing them around to make bubbles and taking a very long time indeed to scrub the pans. There was a jar of silver sand on the draining board especially for this purpose, but Jenny waited until Claudia was busy, perhaps putting away plates on the big old dresser, or dividing knives, forks and spoons into their correct compartments, and then used the sand to make tiny sand pies, or sloshed it around until it formed a beach at the bottom of the sink.

Today, however, Claudia was keeping an eye on her sister and put a stop to Jenny's games by reminding her that she had already played dinosaurs in the swamp at the table, with the fish stew and mashed potatoes on her plate, and should not waste any more time. 'Because we have to take Mam's latest letter in to the village – she writes to Gran almost every day now with the baby coming – and we don't want to miss the post. Then when we get home Grandpa will tell us the story of Finn McCool, and how he made the beautiful lakes and mountains in Ireland.'

Jenny chuckled. 'He may start off with Finn McCool, but as soon as he gets talking he'll be on about the baby,' she said. However, she ran her hands through the washing-up water to capture any cutlery remaining within its depths and then, using a cup, began to bale it out into the enamel bucket that stood alongside the low stone sink. She then dried her water-wrinkled hands on a rough towel and turned back to her sister. 'Do you know, I thought it would be grand to tell all me pals an' me teacher that we would be getting a new baby come Christmas, but no one was a bit thrilled.'

Claudia smiled, but gave her sister an affectionate hug as they set off down the lane in the direction of the village. The girls had been given permission the previous day to broadcast their mother's news, for Louisa was definitely beginning to show. Claudia had taken it for granted that most of her class would not be particularly

43

surprised to learn that there was a new baby on the way, but Jenny had clearly expected exclamations and had been disappointed by the lack of interest shown by her classmates. Indeed, some of them were sorry for her, assuring her that a good deal of the attention she now received as the youngest of her family would go to the new baby.

'Especially if it's a boy,' her friend Nev had said wisely. 'I reckon your daddy must be desperate to get him another feller, 'cos who else will take on the croft when your da's too old to do the work?'

'Why, me and Claudia of course,' Jenny had said, ruffling up. 'Girls are as good as boys any day. We work very hard, and when we're full grown we could manage the croft same as our dad does.'

Nev had given a crow of derisive laughter. 'Is dat so?' he asked rudely. 'And when Grandpa Muldoon were took bad, who did he send for, eh? Were it one of his sisters? Or the widow McVeigh? She were hanging out for work around that time and would have been right glad to give your granda a helpin' hand, in return for a mention in his will. Well? Well? Did the ould feller get a neighbour to have a word wit' the widow woman, or did your granda get his son back from England wit' promises of givin' him the croft for his own self?'

Naturally, Jenny had flounced away without answering him and now she told Claudia of Nev's reaction, expecting her sister to be as furious as she was herself, but Claudia only laughed. 'You may not like to admit it, chuck, but your pal Nev was right,' she assured her

44

sister. 'Working the land is really hard and makes a woman old before her time, so the last thing I want is to be landed with the croft. I'll have to earn money when I'm old enough, and there's no work round here. I'll probably go to Dublin, or back to Liverpool, and so will you, queen, so we might as well get used to the idea.'

Jenny stared at her, round-eyed. 'But – but I thought you loved the croft, and the beautiful countryside,' she faltered. 'You've said, over and over, how much nicer it is than Blodwen Street. You've never said you'd go back to living in a big city . . . I thought you were like meself and loved Connacht Cottage and the animals.' Suddenly, the frown left her brow and a big smile broke out. 'Oh, you're kiddin' me, aren't you, Claudia?' She blew out her cheeks in a long whistle. 'Pheeew, worra fright you gave me! You wouldn't go back to Blodwen Street, norrif it were ever so!'

Claudia shook her head sadly and took Jenny's arm, for both children had stopped walking whilst they talked. 'Come on, or we'll miss the post. And you're right in a way, and wrong in another. I *do* love the croft and our lives here, I even enjoy the work – well, most of it – but I was talking about the future, stupid. When I'm really old, and Mam and Dad can manage without me, I'll have to go back to civilisation, and probably you will, too. So I'll be happy for this baby boy – if it is a boy – to take over the croft. You and I will make our own way, see if we don't.'

Jenny scowled and pulled her arm out of her sister's grasp. 'You speak for yourself,' she said with quite unaccustomed brusqueness. 'I shan't go back to the city ever. I mean to stay here and help Mam and Dad on the land until they're too old to work, and then me and the baby will work it for them. Oh, Claudia, I've always thought it was what we both wanted!'

'Well, don't get in a state,' Claudia said calmly. 'It's only what might happen to me, not what will . . . if you understand me. Now let's put our best foot forward and no more arguing. Right?'

'We never argue,' Jenny said, and tucked her hand into Claudia's arm once more. 'I'm sorry I was cross, but the thought of the croft without you frightened me. And now will you listen to me whiles I say me nine times table? It's the one I always get wrong, and me teacher will be so pleased wi' me on Monday if I know it as well as I know me ten times.'

Louisa was preparing for bed. She had washed and smoothed Pond's cold cream on to her face and was now brushing her hair. When she had worked at Miss Timpson's she had taken good care of herself, always creaming her skin before going to bed and brushing out her hair before confining it to its bedtime plait, because a good appearance was essential when you worked behind the counter in a dress shop. When they moved to Ireland she had been determined to continue with her nightly beauty routine no matter how tired she was, and now, having given her hair its nightly brushing, she began to plait it. This was not a particularly easy task since her dark hair curled naturally, but Louisa plaited doggedly on, ending the long braid with a neat little ribbon bow.

Only then did she abandon the stool which stood before the dressing table and climb into the large feather bed where Cormack already lay, watching her preparations with a dreamy smile on his face. Once it had worried him when he saw the care she took over her appearance, fearing, he told her, that she meant to return to Liverpool, but she had soon assured him that his worries were groundless. She missed many things about the life they had lived before coming to Ireland, but she had told him that now they were beginning to grow accustomed to the work – they were in fact doing really well – she had no desire to live anywhere but here. 'After all, if we went back to Blodwen Street there would be nothing for us to hand on to our children when we're too old to work,' she had said. 'At Connacht Cottage we're making provision for our old age and a future for our family. Isn't that what everyone wants?'

Cormack, mightily relieved, had admitted that she was right, and with her announcement that a new baby was on the way all his worries that she might long to return to what he thought of as her previous life had left him and the two of them had made plans for the future which completely excluded any suggestion of leaving Ireland.

Now, Louisa snuggled down into the softness of the bed, then turned to give Cormack a loving kiss. As she did so, the baby kicked vigorously, making Cormack grunt as the child's heel, or knee, or elbow, caught him a sharp blow. 'Can't you tell the little feller I'm his daddy and mean no harm in kissin' me wife?' he said plaintively. 'It's a footballer he'll be when he's growed

. . . or mebbe a boxer. But it's a boy, I'm tellin' you, acushla.'

'I hope you're right,' Louisa said sleepily. 'But whether it's a boy or a girl, hasn't it done your father a power of good? After he'd had that seizure, he couldn't so much as collect the eggs from the nesting boxes, let alone search the woods and fields for a hen that laid astray. But ever since we told him there was another baby on the way he's been marvellous. Not only does he collect the eggs, mix up the hen food and help the girls with the big potato patch, but his patience – and his story telling – seems endless.' She chuckled. 'He's even been choosing names, though he says it's just suggestions.'

Cormack chuckled too. 'I thought he'd go for something really Irish – Devlin or Séamus – but he says it wouldn't be right. He thinks Richard or Robert would be more in keeping, because the girls both have English names, after all.'

'Yes, I know he said that, but I heard him talking to Jenny the other day and she asked him why he was going for English names rather than Irish. You'll never guess what he said, Cormack; he said English this time but Irish next, and when Jenny asked what made him think there would be another baby to name, he said it was often the way that one baby opens the door for another, and that now we're living in Ireland and eating the good food we grow on the croft there'll likely be half a dozen or so in the next few years.'

'Well, I reckon he'll catch a cold with that one,' Cormack said sleepily. 'After all, there will be eight years between Jenny and the littl'un. Still, you never know, he could be right; time alone will tell. And now we'd best get some sleep because I mean to start the ploughing tomorrow.'

Chapter Three

Ever since his seizure, Grandpa Muldoon had grown used to not sleeping well but now that he was more active the ability to sleep soundly for at least six to eight hours had returned to him. For this reason, if no other, he was glad to work in any way he could, and no longer despised tasks that he had previously believed to be women's work. Of course collecting eggs, feeding stock and hoeing the potato patch could be done by any able-bodied person, and he had no hesitation in boasting of his ability when he took the donkey cart into the village so that he might enjoy a drink and a crack with his old friends of an evening. There was no public house, as such, in the village, but the grocer's shop contained a couple of rough wooden benches upon which the drinkers congregated, whiling away a few hours with a glass or two of beer.

On this particular morning, with Christmas only a few days away, he had awoken at dawn, determined to finish making a gift for the new baby. It was a string of woolly balls which he would loop across the hood of the cradle, so that the baby would have something to look at besides the newly whitewashed ceiling of the cottage. He had already made the cradle himself, from willow wands, and though he had pretended that it was something anyone could have done, he was really very proud of it. He had been secretly weaving it for many weeks, and though both Claudia and Jenny knew this their parents had been kept in ignorance, so their surprise and delight when he dragged it out of his bedroom was genuine.

When Fergal Muldoon had been a young man and newly married to his pretty, energetic wife, he had imagined that very soon they would have a large family who would, in the fullness of time, help him and Eithne with the work of the croft. And sure enough, after a year, Eithne had given birth to a fine healthy boy. They called him Cormack, and had waited for other children to follow, but eighteen months after Cormack's birth Eithne, who was pregnant again, became ill with a fever. She had lost the baby, and though she regained her full strength, she had never again conceived a child. They had tried everything, pilgrimages, prayer, even a visit to a well-known doctor in Dublin, but nothing had made any difference; Cormack had remained their only child.

So naturally, when Cormack had gone off to England, found himself a wife and announced that he would send his parents money but would not be returning to Kerry himself since he had a very good job with a local firm, they had been bitterly disappointed. But the money had helped them build up their holding to something worth having and both Fergal and his wife had hoped that Cormack might come home, if only for a holiday, and would realise that Connacht Cottage was no longer a burden, but a very real asset.

But this had not happened, and when Eithne died

Fergal had honestly ceased to care what happened to his holding. If his son had been interested . . . but this had not seemed to be the case; Cormack's main concerns had been all for Liverpool, his job at the factory and his wife and daughters. When Fergal's seizure had forced him, for the first time in his life, to beg Cormack for help, he had half expected a larger money order than usual, and a letter explaining that his son could not leave his well-paid job.

His delight when the lad had come over had been unbounded, and when Cormack's arrival had been followed a couple of years later by that of Louisa and the girls, he had thought his cup of happiness full to overflowing.

When Cormack had told him, shyly, that they were expecting another child, he had felt tears of joy rise in his eyes and trickle down his cheeks. It had been partly from delight of course, and partly from sorrow that Eithne would never see any of her grandchildren, for though she had met Louisa shortly after the marriage, it had never seemed possible for either party to abandon their busy lives, even temporarily.

After Eithne died, Fergal had done the bare minimum of work on the croft and expected never to know happiness again, yet now, he reflected, leaning forward to fasten the woolly balls on to the hood of the cradle, he thought himself the happiest fellow in Ireland, so he did. Louisa, Claudia and Jenny had taken to the farming life as though they had been born to it, and while the children did what they could Louisa worked with Cormack from dawn to dusk, so that very soon the croft became as productive as it had ever been. Because they had savings, Cormack had been able to insist that they bought the best seed potatoes available, the best grain, the finest milch cow to start their herd. He had built two more rooms on to the cottage so if the baby were a boy – and Fergal had no doubt that it would be – the little feller could, in the fullness of time, have his own room. Most families in the village simply divided a room by nailing a sheet across the ceiling and floor, but this would not do for Cormack and his father had heartily agreed with him. They must have the best for this boy, this grandchild of Fergal's old age . . .

A voice interrupted Fergal's thoughts. The walls of the cottage were thick, which meant that Cormack must have emerged from his bedroom. Hastily, Fergal threw back the blanket which he had wrapped around himself whilst he worked, for the weather was bitterly cold, and made for his bedroom door. He jerked it open just as Cormack drew level with it, and did not even have to voice the question that was on the tip of his tongue.

'I expect you've guessed the baby's started,' Cormack said. 'I'm off to boil water and make some tea, then I'll go down to the village. Louisa says there's plenty of time; it won't arrive for a while yet, but I mean to fetch the midwife and telegraph me mother-in-law to come over as soon as she can.' By the light of the candle Cormack held, Fergal saw a flash of white teeth in his son's tanned face as he grinned at his father: 'I can cope with sows and cows and that, but me strength goes out of me when I think of having to deliver a baby.'

Fergal chuckled and patted his son's shoulder. 'You

get off, lad; I'll boil water and make your good wife a nice strong cup of tay,' he said comfortably. 'You fetch the midwife – it's too early to send a telegram yet – and I'll wake Claudia 'cos, as I recall it, a woman waiting to give birth likes another female around.'

'Thanks, Dad,' Cormack said gratefully, leading the way down the narrow corridor and entering the kitchen. The fire looked dead but Fergal placed some kindling in the ashes and seized the bellows, and a couple of judicious wafts soon had the fire beginning to burn up brightly. He was pulling the kettle over the flame as Cormack shrugged himself into his coat and pushed his feet into his rubber boots. 'I'll take the donkey and cart since I'll be bringing the midwife back,' he announced, throwing open the back door and letting in a blast of icy air that caused his father to shudder expressively. 'Are you sure you'll be all right, Dad? You'd best get some clothes on, because a nightshirt isn't much protection against cold like this.' He peered into the dark farmyard. 'I'll be as quick as I can. Don't forget to wake Claudia. She's a grand girl, so she is.'

Fergal, having already hung the kettle on the hook over the fire, decided to take his son's advice and left the kitchen for the narrow corridor which Cormack had built so that it was no longer necessary to go through every bedroom in order to reach the one at the end. His hand was on the latch when the door next to his own opened cautiously and Claudia slipped out. 'Grandpa? I thought it were Daddy's voice I heard. Has our mam started with the baby? Shall I get dressed? I don't reckon

I ought to wake Jenny until it's light, but I will if you think she could be useful.'

'Yes, the baby's started and your da's on his way to the village to fetch the midwife, so you'd best get yourself dressed and then go along to your mammy's room,' the old man said. 'As for waking Jenny, that won't be necessary; you and meself will manage very well.'

'Right,' Claudia said briskly. She went back into her room and emerged with her arms full of clothing and her feet shoved, awkwardly, into a pair of ancient slippers. 'If you make some tea, Grandpa, I'll go in to Mam's room and get dressed in there. Then if she needs anything I'm on the spot, like.'

Fergal felt a wave of relief flood over him. He was no hand as a sick nurse and apart from making his daughter-in-law a cup of tea there was very little, he felt, that a mere male could do, particularly one of his age.

So he smiled benignly at his granddaughter, returned to his own room where he dressed as fast as he could, which was not, in truth, very fast, and then went back to the kitchen to find the kettle bubbling merrily and the fire beginning to blaze. Going over to the pantry, he fetched milk and made three mugs of steaming tea, placing his own upon the kitchen table. He tapped gently on Louisa's door and Claudia came at once, taking the tin mugs from his slightly shaking hands and assuring him, in a hissing whisper, that her mother had said the pains were not close together which meant, apparently, that it would be some time before the baby put in an appearance.

55

Fergal was glad to hear it, for sensible and efficient though Claudia undoubtedly was, she was only a child and no more experienced in birthing a baby than he was. So he returned happily to the kitchen to sit in the fireside chair, sip his tea and pray that all would go well with both his daughter-in-law and the new baby – and that nothing would happen before the midwife arrived.

Louisa lay in bed trying to make light conversation with the midwife, but this was proving more and more difficult because all she really wanted to talk about was how soon this wretched business would end. Indeed, her replies to the midwife's cheery questions – how were her Christmas preparations, had she made mince pies and a Christmas cake, when would they kill the large cockerel which she had seen strutting about the small enclosure – grew shorter and shorter as the pains grew closer, and when at last her body told her, unequivocally, that the time for idle chatter had passed and she must begin to bear down, she was glad to do so. And it wasn't so bad, after all, because no more than thirty minutes after she had begun her travail, the midwife announced that she could 'see the babby's head, so I can, and hasn't it got a fine crop of hair, the darlin''.

Louisa, panting between pushes, said breathlessly that she was glad to hear it and a bare five minutes later the midwife was holding up a wet and wriggling baby, slapping its small bottom and handing it to its mother. Louisa took one look at it and gave a squeak of joy. 'It *is* a boy,' she said happily. 'Oh, Grandpa Muldoon and Cormack will be tickled pink. Nurse, can you give my husband a shout? I'd like to tell him the good news myself.'

But to her surprise and slight consternation, the woman took the baby gently back from her, shaking her head. 'No, Mrs Muldoon, we can't have any men a-visiting for a while yet. If I'm not much mistaken, there's another babby to come. Did the doctor not tell you you were going to have twins?'

'Twins!' Louisa shrieked. 'It can't be twins! As for the doctor, once my pregnancy was confirmed I was too busy getting everything ready to bother seeing him again. Oh, how wonderful – two babies for the price of one!' She smiled seraphically at the older woman. 'Will it be another boy, nurse? Will they be identical, d'you think?' She laughed softly as something else occurred to her. 'Claudia and Jenny have all but fallen out over who should look after the baby, choose a name and take him or her into the village for the first time. Now they'll have a baby each; a living doll, so to speak.' She propped herself up on one elbow and reached for the cup of tea standing on the rough bedside cabinet. 'Is it all right if I have a swallow or two? Ah, something's happening!'

Something was indeed happening, for no more than ten minutes after the birth of her little son Louisa pro-duced a fine, healthy daughter.

As soon as the midwife had bathed the babies and dressed them in the little gowns which Louisa, no needle-woman, had lovingly, if painfully, stitched, she put the new mother into a clean nightdress, changed the bedding, unplaited her hair and brushed it out, and then bustled off to the kitchen to tell Cormack, Fergal and the two girls that they might come through now. Louisa heard Jenny asking eagerly whether she had a brother or a sister, but the nurse just smiled enigmatically as she ushered them into Louisa's bedroom.

For a moment, all four visitors simply lined up at the foot of the bed and stared. Louisa lay there against her lace-trimmed pillows looking, Claudia thought, like a cat that's got at the cream. Then she realised that there was a baby nestled in the crook of each of Louisa's arms. Jenny screamed and darted forward. 'Is they boys?' she asked excitedly. 'Oh, but I suppose they must be girls 'cos they're wearing dresses.'

Claudia gave her sister an impatient shove. 'They're nightdresses, you silly goose,' she explained. 'Don't you remember Mam making them? And me embroidering lazy daisies and love knots all over the waistbands?'

Jenny began to reply, rather indignantly, but stopped when Grandpa Muldoon hushed her and Cormack, who had been bending over to kiss his wife, announced that if Jenny was going to tire her mother out with pointless chatter, then she had best leave the room at once.

'Oh, but Da, we all want to know whether they's boys or girls,' Jenny pleaded. 'Well, Miss Clever? Is they boys or girls?'

Claudia opened her mouth, preparing to wither her sister for asking questions that only their mother could answer, but she had no sooner begun to speak than Louisa cut in, giving her a reproving look as she did so. 'We've got one of each,' she said proudly. 'This one is a little boy . . .' she took a minute hand in her own and waved it at the audience, 'and this one's a little girl.' She turned to her husband. 'Well, we thought of a lot of names for boys, but now we need a girl's name as well. Shall we let Claudia and Jenny pick?'

Cormack laughed and bent to kiss the babies on the tops of their bright ginger heads. 'No indeed; I think Grandpa chose pretty well when he said he'd like a boy to be called Benjamin, after an old pal.' He smoothed a hand lovingly across his wife's hair. 'As for letting the girls choose, that's an invitation to open warfare.' He looked lovingly down at his wife. 'What name would you like, alanna?'

'Bernadette Mary,' Louisa said at once, making it plain that she had been thinking about girls' names all along. 'I've always loved those names. And Benjamin Luke Muldoon sounds well, don't you think?'

'What do you think, Grandpa?' Cormack asked diplomatically. 'Does it sound well to you?'

Claudia smiled to herself as her grandfather pretended to consider, then nodded his white head and beamed at them all. 'Benjamin Luke Muldoon sounds just grand, so it does,' he said contentedly. 'And now we'd best go about the business of the day, or there'll be no dinner for anyone.'

Just as the girls were finishing their dinner the nurse called Cormack through to the bedroom, and presently the pair emerged carrying the cradle between them. Jenny and Claudia immediately jumped to their feet and bent over it. 'Would they like a nice drink of warm goat's milk?' Jenny asked excitedly.

The midwife laughed. 'Babies thrive best on their mother's milk. Think on, alanna, bonaveens suckle from the sow and calves from the cow. But these babies need sleep more than food right now. And I must go back and see to Mother.' She bustled out of the room.

Cormack stopped for a moment to smile fondly down into the cradle before returning to the farmyard. Grandpa Muldoon followed him, pausing in the doorway to remind the girls they were now in charge of the little ones. Then he closed the door quietly behind him and Jenny and Claudia returned to their contemplation of the babies, lying head to toe beneath the blankets their mother and Claudia had knitted.

Claudia saw Jenny looking carefully around as though to make sure they were alone before she spoke. 'Oh dear, aren't they're hideous! What's wrong with them? Their faces is all crumpled and red, almost purple. I thought babies were always beautiful, but these ain't.'

Claudia smothered a giggle and gave her sister a hug. Then, seeing the perturbation in Jenny's round, plain little face, she leaned over the cradle and touched the soft cheek of the child nearest her. 'Darling Jenny, just think what a hard time these littl'uns have just been through. Stroke the baby's cheek, like I'm doing. Go on, don't be afraid; I'm sure a touch won't wake them up. Their skin is soft as a rose petal, so of course it crumples easily, but by tomorrow or the next day it will begin to be smooth and beautiful. Their hair is wet because they've just been bathed, but that will dry out as well. Honestly, you'll be surprised the difference a day or two will make.'

Hesitantly, Jenny followed Claudia's example and stroked the baby's soft cheek. Then she reached over to the second baby. 'Which is which?' she asked, after a moment. 'You're quite right, Claudia, their skin is beautifully soft. I just wish they didn't have ginger hair.'

'Whatever's wrong with ginger hair?' Claudia said, puzzled. 'I think it's really pretty.' She began to explain that hair colour nearly always changed as babies grew older, but Jenny was shaking her head vehemently.

'No, you don't understand. The Irish kids in school say red hair is unlucky and I don't want bad luck for me little brother and sister.'

Claudia was about to refute this when she remembered hearing someone in her own class voicing the same thought. Quickly she said: 'Oh, that! That's just what we call an old wives' tale, Jen. Anyway, we're English, and it's only the Irish who don't care for red hair.'

'Oh, I see,' Jenny said, though Claudia thought her sister still sounded doubtful. 'But we're half Irish, Claudia, you know we are.'

Claudia heaved a sigh and turned away from the cradle. 'Now you listen to me, Jennifer Muldoon,' she said severely. 'All that talk about red hair is just superstitious nonsense, but it might upset Mam if she thought you believed it. So just you forget about it, do you understand? Your little brother and sister will be pretty as pictures in a few days and you'll be proud as a peacock when you show them to your school friends.'

She moved away from the cradle, but Jenny grabbed her arm. 'Awright. Me and Nev will punch the nose of any kid what says rude things about the twins. But you've not told me which is which.'

Claudia laughed and turned back to the cradle. 'The smaller one is the girl, Bernadette – she's in the foot of the cradle – and the bigger one of course is Benjamin. They look very alike now, but I expect they'll change quite a lot as they grow. Right?'

Jenny nodded, then returned to sit on one of the wheel-backed kitchen chairs, from which perch, Claudia realised, her sister could see into the cradle. 'I wish they'd wake up,' she said wistfully. 'If they did, we could hold one each. And thanks for 'splainin' why they aren't too pretty yet. I'm real glad they're goin' to improve before me pals set eyes on them!'

The doorbell rang when Emily Dalton had just put breakfast on the table and she sighed with exasperation as she set off down the hall in the direction of the front door. It could not be mail because the postman would have pushed it through the letter box, so it was probably someone selling something, or possibly a neighbour in search of a cup of sugar. Such demands, less than a week before Christmas, were more than she felt able to cope with at the moment.

Her daughter's baby was due any time now, so she had made her plans and thought that she had covered every eventuality. Further along Blodwen Street there lived a friend of hers – her whist partner, in fact – Maria Calvert. Like herself, Maria was a widow with one daughter, who had married around the same time as Louisa and Cormack. Young Millie Calvert had wed a

Scot and now lived in a tiny house up a narrow side street in Edinburgh, so Maria often had time on her hands. She was an excellent cook and housewife, and when Emily had asked her if she would be willing to take on the task of looking after the lodgers at No. 22 Blodwen Street whilst her friend went over to Ireland to help with her daughter's new baby, she had agreed at once.

A week previously, she had moved in for a couple of days for what both women referred to as 'a practice run' and proved herself to be perfect in every way. Mr Payne and Mr Clarke had praised her cooking and said the house was neat as a new pin. Emily had given her sheets and sheets of instructions, including menus and the names of the shops and stallholders who gave her a good price when she purchased foodstuffs from them. She had explained about Mr Payne's allotment, including the information that she always paid for the vegetables he provided.

As Emily hurried towards the front door, untying the strings of her apron as she went, it occurred to her that it might be her friend Maria, come to offer her services to do the messages, or give a hand with the extra cooking that Christmas was bound to entail. It was strange, though, because Maria had never called so early before, and Emily hoped devoutly that this visit did not mean that her friend was about to tell her she would not be able to take over No. 22 after all.

As she pulled open the heavy front door, she saw not Maria Calvert but a young boy in the uniform of the Post Office, holding out a piece of paper. 'Telegram, missus,' the boy said chirpily. 'And the sender paid an extra sixpence for a reply, so I'm to wait, and you can have up to five words.'

Emily fairly snatched the telegram from the boy's hand and read it rapidly, a smile breaking out over her face. She had opened her mouth to dictate her reply to the boy, who had fished a notebook and pencil out of his pocket, when a voice spoke from behind her. 'A telegram! Not bad news I hope, Mrs Dalton?'

It was Mr Payne, his expression honestly anxious. Emily patted his arm. 'No, no, not bad news; in fact it's very good news, Mr Payne.' She read the telegram aloud: 'Louisa had twins stop Boy and girl stop Please come stop Cormack.'

'Twins!' Mr Payne breathed reverently. 'And one of each; isn't that just wonderful? But I'm interrupting you; you were about to dictate your reply to the young gentleman.'

The 'young gentleman' smirked and licked the end of his pencil. 'Carry on, Ma,' he said cheekily. 'It ain't every day I delivers a telegram wi' such news as twins bein' born. I reckon I'll need a tip to help me on me way back to the telegraph office.'

'Cheek,' Emily said. 'As for me answer, just say I'm coming stop Mother stop.'

The boy scribbled away, then sniffed the air, tucking the notebook back in his pocket. 'I smell burning toast,' he said conversationally, and as she fled up the hallway Emily heard him thanking Mr Payne for his generosity and guessed that her lodger had stumped up, probably far more lavishly than she herself would have done.

Hurrying kitchenwards, she smiled to herself. Once, she would have tried to insist that he allowed her to reimburse him, but not any more. Mr Payne would say quietly that giving the boy a few pence for delivering such very good news was his pleasure and privilege, and would Mrs Dalton kindly not mention it again.

Emily entered the kitchen to find Mr Clarke scraping the burnt toast. He grinned at her as she began to explain that there had been a telegram, and to apologise for forgetting the toast.

'It don't matter, Mrs Dalton,' he said cheerfully. 'And I heard your news – you was reading it out as I come down the stairs. So you'll be off any minute, I dare say? Good thing you'd give your instructions to that Mrs Calvert. But don't you go leavin' before Mr Payne and meself have bought somethin' for the littl'uns.'

'I won't rush off today, tempting though it is,' Emily assured her lodgers, as Mr Payne took his place at the table and began to sugar his porridge. 'But tomorrow, first thing, I'll be on me way. Oh, I'm that excited!'

'You'll be in Ireland just in nice time for Christmas,' Mr Payne observed. 'A good thing your daughter contacted you so quickly, because I dare say the ferries will be full of folk returning to their homes for the festive season. The times of the ships may vary, and the prices as well, so if you'll take my advice, Mrs Dalton, you'll go down to the Pier Head this very day and get your ticket.' He smiled. 'Make sure you get a return passage,' he added, with unaccustomed roguishness. 'Mrs Calvert is a charming woman I'm sure, but there's only one Mrs Dalton.'

Emily said at once that she would take his advice, and as soon as she had washed the breakfast crocks she hurried along to tell Maria that the call had come. Then the two women went to the ticket office before returning to No. 22, so that Emily might pack.

'I know which train I need to catch when I reach Ireland, and which station I get down at,' she told her friend. 'Me son-in-law will meet me with the donkey cart, and mebbe Claudia will be there as well, if they feel they can leave the old feller and young Jenny in charge, that is. Oh, Maria, I can scarce believe I'll be with me family again in time for Christmas!' She pointed to a number of small parcels, wrapped in gaily coloured paper. 'Them's the little gifts I bought and should have posted two days ago, only Louisa said to bring 'em over when I came, to save postage. I'd have liked to buy Claudia a pretty blouse and Jenny a warm jumper, but I dursen't, 'cos of not knowing their sizes the way I once did. They'll have grown a good deal and I dare say they'll have changed an' all, but there's no fear I shan't recognise 'em when we meet. I'd know my little Claudia amongst a thousand others; and she'll know her old gran, I'll warrant!'

'Well, Mam, how do I look?'

Claudia, in her new winter coat and the scarlet tam o' shanter which set off her milky skin and night-black hair to perfection, came across the kitchen and pirouetted in front of Louisa, who was sitting in the largest of the fireside chairs feeding the twins, a shawl slung around her shoulders and pulled over her breasts for decency's sake, she said. She half closed her eyes and examined her daughter, and was about to speak when the kitchen door was pushed open and Jenny sidled into the room. She looked very self-conscious, and well she might, Claudia thought wrathfully. She herself had cleaned Jenny up after her sister had finished her chores for the day, and helped her into her nice woollen dress – which had until the previous year been Claudia's best – and long black stockings. Furthermore, she had brushed out her sister's lank, mousy locks, pinned a little brooch of her own on to the lapel of Jenny's coat and told her not to go messing herself up, but to remember they were meeting Gran and wanted to make a good impression. 'Mam doesn't want Gran to think we don't care what we look like now we live in the country,' she had told her sister. 'So if you must go out – and I don't see why you can't stay quietly in the kitchen, giving me a hand with preparing the supper – for the love of heaven don't go getting yourself as dirty as a pig in muck.'

Yet here was Jenny, hair in a wild tangle, mud to the eyebrows, and her stockings more ladder than wool, from what Claudia could make out. She sighed and closed her eyes for a pregnant moment, then pointed an accusing finger at her sister. 'What did I say to you when you wanted to play out? Oh, Jenny love, I could weep so I could! You know it's important that Gran sees we can work on the croft but still turn out nice and clean to meet her train.'

Jenny pouted. 'It weren't my fault, honest to God it weren't,' she protested. 'It were Nev; he dared me to climb on to the pigsty wall and I lost me footin'. I went splash into the mud – that's why me stockin's have got a teensy bit muddy – and when I climbed out I remembered I'd seen that dratted old hen sneakin' across the yard and into that thick prickly hedge, so of course . . .'

'You don't have to say any more,' Louisa cut in resignedly. 'Give yourself a good wash, because I can smell the pigsty from here, and then you'd better put on clean clothes. But I'm afraid you won't be able to go with Claudia to meet Gran, so you can give me a hand with the babies instead.'

'Oh, but Mam, if I hurry . . .' Jenny began, but stopped short as her father came in from the yard, well wrapped up in his winter coat, with a checked scarf wound round his neck and a blanket over one arm.

'I'm taking this to wrap round your mam's knees . . .' he was beginning, when Jenny tried to slip past him. 'Oh, alanna, what on God's good earth have you been doing? And the smell of you!'

'She fell into the pigsty,' Claudia said, beginning to giggle. 'Mam's just told her to wash and then go and change . . . don't you sneak off, Jenny! Washing comes first, remember, and you can do that over the sink in here. No point in carrying water through to our room.'

'Well, we can't wait for you, young woman,' Cormack said. 'To tell the truth, I'm not sorry that you aren't coming, because four in the donkey cart is a rare crush and I dare say your gran will have bags and packages and all sorts.'

'You're right, Da,' Claudia said. As she and her grandmother still exchanged letters every week, she was

68

well aware that Emily would be bringing a large Christmas cake. Such things took up space and must not be crushed, so Jenny's place in the donkey cart would be more than filled, even if Cormack chose to walk at the donkey's head.

Jenny, however, was not taking her dismissal well. 'It's not fair,' she whined, going with lagging footsteps over to the sink. She had shed her coat, letting it drop to the floor, and now she tugged her dress over her head so that her next remark was muffled by the navy wool. 'I couldn't help getting a bit mucky, and I found the old hen's nest, so I ought to be rewarded, not punished. It's horrible being the youngest, so it is, because you get blamed for everything. Oh, Da, if I hurry, won't you let me go to the station? If there isn't room in the cart, I'll walk; or I could ride Pickles so that there would be room for Gran's luggage.'

'Oh, alanna, poor Pickles will have enough to do pulling the cart without having you bouncing about on her back,' Cormack pointed out. 'You stay here and help your mam; you can give Grandpa a hand with the chores as well. So be a good girl and don't fret. I think your gran means to stay for a whole month, so you'll get plenty of chances to spend time with her.'

Claudia, however, knew how much Jenny had looked forward to the trip to the station, so she rushed across the kitchen, scooped up the heavy water pail, and poured some into the tin basin. She seized the bar of soap and began to wash her sister vigorously, so vigorously that Jenny squealed a protest, which Claudia silenced by shoving the bar of soap into her mouth. 'Shut up!' she

69

hissed, sloshing water. 'Dry yourself and then put your dress back on; I'll lend you a pair of my stockings, so don't you dare mess them up or make ladders, and I'll brush the hem of your coat, because that's the only other thing that got really dirty.' She turned to her father. 'You'll wait five minutes, won't you, Da?'

Cormack said, rather reluctantly, that he supposed five minutes wouldn't make any difference and Jenny, twisting round, gave her sister a wet, but loving, hug. 'You are kind to me, Claudia,' she said gratefully, as the older girl left the room. 'And you're kind too, Da, to wait for me. D'you know, I've never in my whole life met anyone off a train. I've told everyone in me class at school that I'm goin' to the station to meet me English gran, so if I'd not been able to go they'd have said, "Liar, liar, pants on fire," and even though it wouldn't have been true, you couldn't blame 'em, could you?'

Cormack laughed. 'You're a strange one, Jenny Muldoon,' he said. 'Ah, here comes Claudia wit' your clean stockings. If we hurry, we should still be at the station before the train.'

'Well, Mam? What do you think of my babies? Local folk have been quite rude about the colour of their hair, but we think it's attractive. Grandpa Muldoon says there's a superstition in Ireland that red hair is unlucky, but he says he's not a superstitious man . . .' Louisa chuckled, 'and besides, he thinks it will darken as they grow older.' The two women had just replaced the twins in the wicker cradle, one at each end, and now Louisa turned to her mother, raising her eyebrows. 'Well, Mam,

I bet you think they're horrible, don't you?'

Emily laughed, but shook her head, gazing dotingly at the small faces in the wicker cradle. 'They're perfect, and they're so good,' she exclaimed. 'I've been in the house now for two whole hours and neither of them has so much as raised a peep. I remember when Claudia was their age she cried for a few minutes whenever you laid her down, and Jenny was worse; she positively bawled if things weren't going her way.'

'You should hear these two if I'm late for a feed,' Louisa said ruefully. 'I don't know which howls the louder, but as you say, they're pretty good most of the time.' She went over to the fire, tested the kettle to make sure it still contained some water, and hung it over the flame. 'What do you think of the girls? I guess you must have noticed changes; Claudia is quite the young lady, and Jenny is beginning to be a grand help, both in the cottage and on the croft.'

'She writes a wonderful letter does Claudia and I like getting all your news. I know she's a great help to you, especially now the babies have arrived, but one of these days she'll be needing work – proper work. If you were still living in Blodwen Street . . .'

'But we aren't living in Blodwen Street, Mam, and there's work in plenty for her on the croft,' Louisa said gently. 'You've not met Grandpa Muldoon yet, but though he's a great deal more capable than he was when we first came to Ireland, we still need help if we are to buy more land and improve the croft. Of course I'm still feeding the babies every four hours or so, but Grandpa will soon be able to give an eye to them while I help

Cormack. The doctor said Grandpa must not be allowed to do heavy work, so Cormack and Dónal mostly tackle such things. I help when I'm able, and though Claudia looks slim and frail she's pretty strong too. You'll see for yourself when you've been here a few days.'

Emily nodded and was about to reply when the kettle lid began to hop and Louisa hurried over to make the tea. The women were settling down with their mugs in the saggy but comfortable fireside chairs when the back door opened and a man entered the kitchen. 'Ah, here's Cormack's dad!' Louisa exclaimed, as her mother got to her feet. 'It seems downright silly to introduce you because I feel you've known each other for years, but of course this is your first actual meeting.' She smiled from one face to the other. 'Grandpa, this is my mother, Mrs Emily Dalton. Mother, this is my father-in-law, Mr Fergal Muldoon.'

The two shook hands, murmuring greetings, and whilst Louisa poured a third mug of tea Emily took covert stock of the newcomer. He was a huge man with a magnificent head of white wavy hair, a very large white moustache and eyes of the same dark blue as Cormack's. He asked Emily what she thought of her new grandchildren, and despite his size his voice was low and gentle. Emily replied that the babies were beautiful, but all the time she was looking at Grandpa Muldoon and thinking him very different from her imaginings, gleaned from the description of this much loved grandparent in Claudia's letters. I got the impression that he was a little old man no longer in the best of health, yet now I've met him I'm reminded of those patriarchs in the Bible, she told herself. I had thought of him as being pretty useless, if I'm honest, and imagined an old feller who limped round the farmyard collecting eggs and maybe feeding the hens when everyone else was too busy. But I see now I was wrong; he may not be able to do much of the labouring work, but he's clearly by no means a burden to Cormack and Louisa; he's a great help.

Oddly enough, this did not please her. Instead, she felt the first stab of what she recognised as jealousy, which was plain stupid. Why should she, a successful landlady and a first-rate cook, well liked by everyone who knew her, be jealous of an old man who helped out on a small croft and probably found reading and writing a difficult chore? Then she remembered the letters that had arrived in Blodwen Street every couple of weeks, addressed in a neat and upright hand to her son-in-law, and could not help smiling to herself. What a fool she was being! Mr Muldoon had run a successful farming business for many years and would probably have been doing so still, had it not been for the seizure that had struck him down within eighteen months of his wife's death.

At this point in her musings Emily looked towards the old man and found him steadily regarding her, his expression a blend of gentle amusement and slight disappointment. He's read me perishin' thoughts, Emily told herself, dismayed. Oh, whatever must he think of me? I'm sure he's a grand chap really, and will look after me daughter and grandchildren when I've gone back to Liverpool . . . but the truth is, I hate the thought

73

that my little Claudia may end up loving him more than she loves me. Jenny's a dear child and the babies are lovely, but Claudia was my own girl and I still believe she'd be better off with me than stuck out in the middle of nowhere, labouring like a docker, when she could be queening it in one of the big departmental stores. Why, she could be a mannequin, drifting through the restaurant in beautiful clothes, and getting a commission on everything she sells!

However, the time to make such a suggestion was obviously not yet, with Claudia in love with the life at Connacht Cottage and apparently enjoying the hard work as well. She would bide her time, but plant the seed before she left here so that both Claudia's parents and the girl herself would realise that they did have a choice. Claudia could have a home with her and a good job whenever she chose to take up her grandmother's invitation.

The bursting open of the door that led from the yard brought Emily abruptly back to the present. The girls had met her at the station, Claudia looking immaculate in her navy coat, scarlet tammy and beautiful leather knee-boots, and Jenny trim in a blue dress which Emily recognised as having once belonged to Claudia. But they had rushed to their room to change as soon as they had reached the croft and had then gone out into the yard. Now they re-entered the kitchen breathlessly, Claudia with a basket of eggs on her arm and Jenny carrying a bucket half filled with potatoes.

Jenny went to the sink and emptied the potatoes into the basin, whilst Claudia put her basket down on the

74

table and crossed to the dresser to fetch a pretty blue bowl for the eggs.

'Look, Gran,' Jenny announced, turning from the sink and pointing to the bowl. 'Hens don't lay too well in winter – I don't know why – so Claudia only found two of those in the hen house. But I know where they goes when they wants to lay astray, which is into the ditch and then deep inside the prickly hedge, so I come up with half a dozen nice big 'uns.'

Grandpa Muldoon winked at Emily, who tried not to poker up; he meant well, she knew he did. 'And I dare say you had to hunt down them taties, young Jenny,' he said. 'Did they extend their little legs, like toytoyses do, and try to hide in the ditch or the prickly hedge with the hens?'

The girls and their mother laughed and Emily tried to smile as well, but even as she attempted to look amused Cormack came in, bearing a large cabbage in one hand. He grinned at his mother-in-law and flourished the cabbage. 'Look at the size of this 'un,' he said. 'You've said in your letters how one of your lodgers provides you wit' vegetables, but I bet you never saw anything half the size of this.'

Emily smiled. It was true, and she had no hesitation in saying so. 'But Mr Payne does very well, considering,' she assured him. She got up and went over to the sink. 'And now I'll show you that I've not come over to be waited on. I'll scrub them spuds and clean the cabbage and do anything else I can to help. Come along, girls, tell me what needs doing!'

*

'Isn't it a pity that Gran and Grandpa don't get on?' Jenny said thoughtfully. She had been worried when she first realised that there was an atmosphere whenever the two were together and had hoped for an opportunity to share her anxiety with her sister, for in Jenny's eyes Claudia seemed wise beyond her years. Jenny picked up a fat fir cone, examined it, then pushed it into the pocket of her jacket. 'I'll paint this the way Grandpa showed us, wi' the silver paint left over from last year.' She turned wide, enquiring eyes on her sister. 'They're the two nicest people in the world, after Mam and Dad, so I were sure they'd love one another, but they don't, not really, though they pretend like anything.'

Claudia and Jenny were in the wood and already carrying several short, well-berried branches of holly. It was Christmas Eve, and although it seemed that the Irish celebrated 'little Christmas', which took place on 6 January, rather than the actual day of Christ's birth, Louisa and Cormack liked the house to be decorated with holly and ivy on Christmas Day. That day itself was, of course, a religious festival, so the whole family would go to church morning and evening. Presents would be exchanged, a grand dinner served and games played on 6 January.

Now, Claudia reached up and broke a small piece of holly off one of the tall trees nearby before turning to answer her sister. 'It *is* odd,' she agreed. 'But the truth is, they don't know one another, not yet. When Gran's been here for a few more days and sees how good Grandpa is, I'm sure she'll start being more – more natural with him; I hope so, at any rate.'

'I hope so too,' Jenny said fervently. 'They're awful polite to one another, which makes it worse . . . but Mam's so busy with the babies she doesn't seem to have noticed and of course Dad's got far too much work on to worry his head over politeness.'

'I think they have noticed, they just know there isn't anything they can do about it,' Claudia said. 'It's the way Gran keeps saying "If we were in Liverpool now we could be buying tickets for the panto at the Empire", or "Paddy's market will have such-and-such piled up on the stalls, I shouldn't wonder" . . . or "On Christmas Eve they all but give stuff away, and there's such a lovely atmosphere" . . .'

'And then Grandpa says, ever so politely, that he'll accompany her into the town and she can have her fill of the street stalls which set up there on a Saturday. Or he reminds her that she missed the school nativity play by a couple of days and tells her that I were the sweetest Mary in me blue robe made out of a curtain, and Nev the finest Joseph, wearing a nice white sheet and a striped tea-towel . . .'

'And then Gran says . . .' Claudia deepened her voice and imitated her grandmother's scouse accent: ' "I hesitates to contradict you, Mr Muldoon, but my Claudia took the part a few years back and never was there such a pretty Mary . . . and she didn't have to make do wi' a curtain, but had a proper blue dress which were made by her mother".' She giggled, then returned to her own voice. 'I wonder if there's anything we could do to make them friendlier towards each other?'

Jenny looked doubtful. Claudia was the best and

cleverest sister any child could have, she knew that, but she could not imagine that there was anything they could do which would make Gran and Grandpa like one another. Presently, however, after a great deal of thought, an idea popped in to her head. 'Gran's always in the house, looking after Mam and the babies and helping with the housework,' she said. 'And now that he isn't needed indoors, Grandpa spends most of his time outside in the barn, helping Dad or seeing to the stock. They only meet at mealtimes; they don't even see much of each other in the evenings because Grandpa goes early to bed. But suppose there was a job they could share? They'd get to talking to one another and perhaps they'd have a laugh together. Because if we aren't careful, they'll spoil little Christmas when it comes.'

Claudia looked at her sister with dawning respect. 'You're right,' she said slowly, 'and I know just the thing to get them having to talk pleasantly to one another. Gran mentioned, the other day, that she didn't know what on earth she was going to get our dad for a Christmas gift, and I know Grandpa means to go into town in a couple of days to try to buy something for our mam. He'll take the donkey cart into the village, leave it in the grocer's backyard and then catch the bus. If we can persuade them to go together, it would be a start, anyway.'

Jenny dropped her bundle of holly in order to give her sister a hug. 'Oh, Claudia, you're the cleverest girl in the whole of Ireland,' she said exuberantly. 'Men always need a bit of help when they're choosin' a present for a woman, and women need help when they're gettin' a gift for a feller. Why, I wouldn't be surprised if they come back from their shopping trip firm friends.'

'It was your idea to start with,' Claudia said, but Jenny noted the blush of pleasure which rose in her sister's cheeks. 'And I do think it might work; it's worth a try, anyway.'

'When Grandpa first suggested a trip to town, I said we'd like to go too, and he said he'd buy us Italian ice cream from that wonderful shop in the High Street,' Jenny said. 'What excuse will we give for staying at home?' She heard the wistfulness in her own voice, but it disappeared as her sister gave her an approving smile.

'You are a good little girl to give up your treat. We'll have to pretend that the Byrne boys have asked us to go round to their cottage to look after Mrs Byrne's new baby whilst they do their messages. Grandpa will know it's just a made-up excuse, but he won't ask awkward questions. Gran, of course, if she agrees to go, will expect us to accompany them, but if we don't tell her till the last minute we'll say we can't possibly change our plans. And come to think of it, Gran may well believe that Grandpa means to buy for us as well, so won't want us along.'

'Claudia, you're bleedin' brilliant,' Jenny said, awestruck by her sister's quick grasp of the situation. She began to pick up the holly she had dropped on the ground. 'Let's get home at once so we can show Mam how much we've collected.'

'Yes, we'd best be getting back, because Mam wants to go to early service tomorrow,' Claudia said. 'We're having a cold dinner, and a late supper after Benediction.

Grandpa thinks we should walk to church, only if we do we'll barely be home before we have to set out again, so we're taking Pickles and the cart.'

Christmas Day passed uneventfully. Louisa saw to it that despite a cold midday meal, supper was a bacon joint boiled with a good variety of vegetables, rounded off with an apple pudding and thick cream, a rare treat.

Jenny thought her grandmother's attitude to Grandpa Muldoon was already beginning to soften a little, but perhaps it was just the constant attendance at church. However, on the following day, Gran snapped at Grandpa when he suggested that she might like to come out to the woodshed where the old tabby cat had just given birth to three lusty kittens. 'I should have thought there were enough perishin' animals on this farm without adding more,' she said disagreeably. 'But I s'pose you'd rather the fox got them dratted kittens and left that bleedin' noisy rooster alone.'

Claudia was helping her mother to change the babies and tidy the bedrooms, so did not hear this embittered remark, but Jenny was dismayed by it and looked anxiously at her grandfather, surprised to see him smiling. 'Now, now, Mrs Dalton,' he said peaceably. 'You must have got out of the wrong side of the bed this morning 'cos you know you doesn't mean a word of it. You'd be upset as anyone if you went into the woodshed and found blood and fur all over the place. As for the rooster, he won't be troublin' you after next week, 'cos he's our little Christmas dinner. Now come along and you can see the kittens. You might like to take one home wi' you when you go. One's ginger an' white, one's tabby, like his ma, and one's tortoiseshell.'

Gran began to say that she would do no such thing, then caught Jenny's reproachful eye upon her and got reluctantly to her feet. 'Awright, awright, I'm comin',' she said irritably. She glanced again at Jenny, who was hemming a large handkerchief as a present for her father. 'Sorry, chuck. I scarce slept a wink all night an' I reckon it's made me tetchy.'

Jenny waited, not unhopefully, for the two to return, and when they did they actually entered the room discussing the kittens in quite a friendly manner. Grandpa winked at Jenny as he began to pull on his old oilskins, telling her that it had begun to rain just as they emerged from the woodshed. 'I'm going to give your father a hand now wi' fencing off the piece of land he's bought for grazing,' he informed his granddaughter. 'I might as well do it today, because tomorrer me and Mrs Dalton is goin' to take a bus into town. We've a few things to buy which we won't be able to get in the village, so we're having ourselves a day's holiday, ain't that right, Mrs D?'

Jenny's grandmother nodded, rather bleakly her granddaughter thought. 'Yes, your grandpa's offered to take me shopping in town. Why don't you come along with us, Jenny? You and my little Claudia, of course?'

My little Claudia indeed! Jenny thought. She had to swallow a feeling of annoyance before she answered. Gran was downright possessive with her sister and it made Jenny feel unwanted. Gran said nice things about the twins, and thanked Jenny for any small service, but it was clear to Jenny, and probably to every other member of the family, that so far as Gran was concerned the only grandchild who mattered was Claudia. She was forever suggesting that Claudia should go home to England with her for a little holiday, and had started to hint that when she was old enough to take a proper job she might return to Liverpool, move into Grandma's house in Blodwen Street and send money home to the family. Claudia never said she did not intend to return to Liverpool – she was too kind and too tactful to say any such thing – but Jenny knew that even her gentle mother was upset by such suggestions.

'Well, queen? I dare say you girls would like a trip to town. If you come, I'll buy you a dinner at the best restaurant in town – Mr Muldoon as well, of course. How does that sound?'

Jenny sighed regretfully, but shook her head. 'You're going tomorrow, you said? Sorry, Gran. We shall be at the Byrnes', to babysit and give a hand generally, because Mr Byrne is off to a cattle market. He's sellin' two fatteners – them's pigs, Gran – and buyin' a cow with calf at heel, so he'll need his sons to help him with the stock, and says he'll be right glad if we'd spend a day with his wife.'

Emily pulled a face. 'Wharrabout your own mam?' she asked. 'How's she to manage if your grandpa and meself go off on this trip to town?'

'Oh, Mam'll manage fine; don't you worry, Gran. Dad's going to work on fencin' and such, so won't be far from the cottage all day,' Jenny said glibly. 'You go off and enjoy yourselves. You didn't see the town when

82

you arrived, 'cos it were growing dusk, and anyway we were all so busy talking that we never even pointed out the big shops or the main street. Now's your chance to have a good look round.'

Grandpa, clad in his old oilskins, stood by the back door, his hand on the latch. It was pretty plain he was waiting to put in his own twopenn'orth if Mrs Dalton decided to change her mind, but after a moment's indecision Emily sighed deeply and turned to him. 'Well, I dare say I oughtn't to leave me daughter in the lurch and go off for a whole day, but there's no disguising the fact that there's things I need which I can't buy in that village, if you can call it a village. Seems it's more like a hamlet to me; just a grocer's, a blacksmith's and a cobbler's shop strung out along a dirty little street,' she finished rather bitterly.

Jenny, much relieved, laughed as her grandfather slipped out into the yard. 'Oh, Gran, you really are cross, but it won't do no good, you know. Grandpa doesn't care if you say rude things about the village – he says rude things himself – nor if you pretend he's makin' you desert our mam, because he knows it's not true. Now come on, give us a smile! You'll enjoy a day in town, honest to God you will. It ain't huge, like Liverpool, but there's plenty to buy if you've a mind to part with your money. And folk are friendly. Everyone loves Grandpa Muldoon, so when he gets to bargaining for something they'll always take a few pennies off, and because you'll be with him they'll do the same for you.'

She peered out of the little window as she spoke and saw for herself the slanting rain, guessing that it might easily turn to snow before the morrow, for it was nose-nippingly cold. She turned back to her grandmother, who had got flour, fat and sugar out of the pantry and was beginning to put ingredients into a large yellow mixing bowl. 'D'you have any oilskins, Gran? I know you've got a real big umbrella, but if the wind gets up, or if it starts to snow, you'd best wear waterproofs tomorrow.'

'I haven't gorrany oilskins, nor I didn't bring me brolly,' her grandmother said, perking up. 'If it snows, I aren't goin', an' that's flat.'

'You can borrow Mam's; they're only a couple of years old and will keep you dry as dry,' Jenny said swiftly. 'Grandpa Muldoon always says that if it isn't raining in Ireland, it's snowin' or hailin' or foggy, so no use puttin' your plans off because of the weather. Make up your mind you're going to enjoy yourself and you will; see if I'm not right!'

Jenny expected either a flat refusal or a long grumble and was pleasantly surprised when her grandmother gave a reluctant laugh and pinched Jenny's chin with a floury thumb and forefinger. 'Awright, awright, I know what you're sayin',' she said. 'You're goin' to think me a miserable old woman, but the truth is I don't know nothin' about farms, or animals, or the countryside. To me, every cow is a mad bull, every pig looks as if it would like to eat me along with its pigswill, and when the hens flutter up to try and get a beakful more of the hot mash than the others, I'm sure they'll knock me to the ground and trample on me . . . don't you laugh, young lady, it's no joke to be frightened all the time.

Now I like a nice friendly cat what purrs by the fire and kills nasty, creeping little mice, but that wild creature what lives in the woodshed and never comes within doors ain't my idea of a cat. When I went in to fetch kindling for your mam a couple of days ago, that cat growled like a dog and then hissed like a snake; I didn't see her at first, 'cos it's dark in that woodshed, but she scared me half out o' me wits.'

Jenny smothered another laugh, but patted her grandmother's hand consolingly. 'You needn't be afraid of Tibby. She'd never hiss at you in the ordinary way, but right now she's protecting her kittens. And when we first came to the croft, I were afraid of all sorts. But you get used to 'em, honest to God. Why, Dad sends me up to fetch the cows in with only Shep for company, and if the old bull tries to come as well I only have to smack him on the nose and he falls back. But Gran, we ain't talkin' about the farm, or the animals. We're talkin' about a day in town.'

'That's right,' her grandmother said absently. She went over to the sink and dipped some water out of the bucket, poured it into a jug and returned to the table, beginning to mix her pastry. 'You're sure your mam can manage without me?'

'Course she can,' Jenny said robustly. 'Of course, when the twins are older and start crawlin' she'll need more help, but now all she has to do is put them to the breast every four hours and change their nappies reg'lar. So I'll wake you early tomorrow wi' a nice cup o' tea to get you going.'

'I reckon I'll be awake before you,' Gran said rather

grimly. 'Now is there anything you or Claudia might be needing that I could buy in the town? I know you've made gifts for your mam and dad, but there may be something I could get for you.'

'I'll ask Claudia when she comes in,' Jenny said, 'but I'm spent up. Thanks for askin', though.'

Chapter Four

Having agreed to the plans for the morrow, Emily sought her bed earlier than usual, though she did not expect to be able to sleep. She had so looked forward to being with her family again, looked forward to country living as well. She had imagined days spent helping Louisa, making herself so useful that they would beg her not to leave, but this had not happened.

For a start, as she had confessed to Jenny, she was afraid of the farm animals, but worse than this were the night noises that she had been too ashamed to mention. The sheepdog would bark if he heard a vixen scream from the nearby woods, waking her in a sweat of fright, and the hoots of a barn owl sounded sinister to one reared in a city. She now knew, because Louisa had told her, that the shrieks as of a lost soul which reverberated around the cottage were actually only tawny owls calling to one another, but despite knowing that the owls never came near the cottage and would not hurt anyone if they did, she was often unable to sleep for the sounds from outside.

Even worse than her fears was her disappointment over the way her daughter managed her home. The truth was that, though delighted to have her mother spending time under her roof, Louisa did not actually need help.

Oh, she thanked Emily profusely when her mother rolled up her sleeves and cooked large batches of soda bread, or scones, or delicious pies and puddings, but even Jenny could make pastry and was becoming a good little cook. Emily mopped and polished but had soon realised that, in anticipation of the birth, her daughter had spring cleaned the entire cottage and her son-in-law had done the same outside, so there really was very little for her to do. If she could have collected eggs, fed the pigs and the poultry, milked the cows . . . but she could not do any of these things successfully, whilst Grandpa Muldoon . . . oh, drat the man! Not only did he undertake such tasks without a second thought but she had been told proudly, by Claudia, that he could bake and make and was becoming quite a dab hand at cooking a meal, for had he not lived here alone before his seizure?

So Emily, far from being the help she had hoped, was, she sometimes thought, simply another mouth to feed. She knew of course that later on Louisa would be so busy with the babies that any assistance would be welcomed, but right now, with the twins being so good and almost never crying, she felt herself useless indeed.

So it was with little expectation of a good night's sleep that she climbed into her bed that evening. But perhaps because she had insisted on accompanying Claudia as the girl did her chores around the farmyard and had then prepared, served and cleared away the evening meal, she slept as soon as her head touched the pillow and was only awoken when Jenny stole into the room, a candle in one hand and a tin mug of tea in the other, to tell her that it was time to get up. 'But you've plenty of time to drink your tea,' she said in a hissing whisper, for Emily was sharing the girls' bedroom and Jenny obviously did not wish to wake her sister. 'Come along to the kitchen to wash and dress; Mam and Dad won't be up for an hour yet, but Grandpa Muldoon said as how I were to give a knock to his door when you were dressed and ready for your breakfast.'

Emily drank her tea, then followed her granddaughter along the icy corridor and into the kitchen. The room was warm for the fire was kept in all night, and Jenny had already added a block of fresh peat, so that it burned brightly enough to have the kettle already humming. Emily unhooked the kettle, took it to the sink and poured water into the basin. She added a judicious amount of cold, washed quickly and dressed with rather less than her usual care, for she had no wish to be discovered at her ablutions by old Mr Muldoon. As soon as she was ready, she began to cut bread and Jenny shot out of the room, saying over her shoulder as she went that Grandpa would be up and dressed by now and no doubt would enjoy a round of toast before going out to the stable to tack up the donkey. Emily refilled the kettle and replaced it on its hook. When it had boiled once more, she made fresh tea and was pouring the brew into three mugs when the door opened and Grandpa and Jenny came in to the room.

'Mornin', missus,' Grandpa Muldoon said cheerfully. 'No, I won't have another drink, thankee.' He chuckled. 'I can't rightly ask the bus driver to stop if I get took short.'

Emily saw the sense of this and pushed her own mug

aside, beginning instead to toast a couple of rounds of bread. She spread butter on both slices, handed one to the old man, and gave the second to Jenny, who shook her head. 'No thanks, Gran, you eat that one. I'll make breakfast for everyone when you're gone.'

After that, it was all go. Emily peeped into the yard and saw that the sky was clear, though every twig, every surface in fact, was rimed with frost and it was bitterly cold. Jenny, very grown-up and housewifely all of a sudden, helped her into the donkey cart which Grandpa Muldoon had driven round to the back door, and spread a rug over her knees, telling her in a motherly fashion to fold it and push it under the seat when she got down in the grocer's yard. Grandpa Muldoon chuckled at this, but was careful to check that his passenger was wearing her warmest garments and had a thick woollen scarf wound round her neck, and that her felt hat was pulled down over her ears, before he clicked to the donkey and they set off.

After they had travelled about a mile, neither of them saying much, Emily realised with some surprise that she was actually enjoying herself. Wrapped in the blanket, she was warm as toast and it was impossible not to be aware of the beauty of the dark sky above, with its twinkling stars and silver sliver of moon which lit up fields, woods and copses as they passed. She noticed a pond that was a solid sheet of ice, and Grandpa broke the silence to tell his companion that this was where he, and his son after him, had learned to skate. 'Last winter Claudia and Jenny were too timid to risk stepping on the frozen pond, and so far as I recall the ice never grew thick enough to bear 'em,' he said. 'But this year I believe they've both had a go, taking turns with the old wooden skates my father made for me when I were nine or ten. Tomorrow, if the frost holds, you and meself might tek a walk down here with the girls, so they can show us what they can do.'

'I used to be a dab hand on a frozen pond,' Emily said reminiscently. The sight of the big stretch of ice, silver in the moonlight, had brought back vividly to her mind the time when she and her pals had trekked out to Prince's Park late at night, after the keepers had gone home. They had climbed over the park railings, strapped boards to the soles of their shoes and taken off, swooping across the frozen surface and thinking themselves the luckiest kids in all Liverpool. Now, looking at the expanse of ice, she realised that she was itching to have a go on it herself, and turned to her companion. 'Do you know, Mr Muldoon, for two pins I'd jump down right now and have a slide meself!'

'You ain't the only one, Mrs Dalton,' the old man replied promptly. 'What say we have a go ourselves tomorrow? When the girls is tired of it,' he added hastily, 'since I don't fancy fallin' on me bum and makin' a fool of meself in front of me grandchildren.'

Emily chuckled, but shook her head regretfully. 'I reckon me bones are so brittle they'd snap, no matter how careful I were,' she said. 'Old age is horrible, ain't it, Mr Muldoon? You've got the knowledge and the desire to show the young 'uns how it's done, but your body kind o' lets you down. I reckon my skating days is over, but no one can take away the memories.'

Her companion nodded. 'Aye, you're right there, missus,' he said quietly. 'Seein' you in the kitchen yesterday, rolling out the pastry and fittin' it to the pie dish, I were reminded of my Eithne and how often I've seen her doing just that, an' glancin' up as I came into the room to give me her sweet smile, an' me laughin' 'cos she'd got flour on the tip of her nose . . .' He heaved a sigh. 'Oh aye, when you're our age, memories is both precious and painful, if you know what I mean.'

'I do know what you mean,' Emily said quietly. 'My Albert were a grand bloke and died far too young. I've a photograph of him looking straight at the camera, very grave, very serious. But when me mind gets to going back in time, I see him holding Louisa above his head an' laughin'. He were always laughin'. He were a happy bloke were Albert.'

Mr Muldoon nodded and for some while they drove on in silence, each busy with their own thoughts. When they reached the village, Mr Muldoon turned the donkey cart into the grocer's yard and helped Emily to alight. By now, morning had arrived and the sun was peeping over the distant hills, turning the frost to a tracery of silver and gilding the thatch of the cottages on either side of the street. In the early morning hush, the voices of two children, shouting to one another, had a clear, bell-like quality, and as they waited for the bus to arrive Emily felt ashamed of the way she had described the little village the previous day. In her softened mood she saw only the beauty of it, and was wishing her harsh words unsaid when the bus came round the corner and drew to a halt beside them. Mr Muldoon gave her a hand to climb aboard and insisted on paying her fare, though she protested. Then they sat side by side on one of the slatted wooden seats and Mr Muldoon began to describe his plan for the day ahead, suggesting that they visit the large shops first to get an idea of goods and prices and then investigate the market stalls before deciding where to make their purchases. Emily agreed, and as soon as the bus stopped in a wide and pleasant market square where stallholders were even now setting out their wares, she and Mr Muldoon headed for their first destination.

By the time they climbed back on the bus that would take them homewards once more, Emily, though so tired that she feared she might fall asleep, was happier than she had been for a long time. They settled themselves in their seat, well content with their purchases, and Emily realised that she had seldom enjoyed a shopping expedition more.

Despite only visiting the town half a dozen times a year, Mr Muldoon had known exactly where to go for everything they wanted. By twelve they had decided what they were going to buy, but they had put off the actual purchases until the afternoon since the stallholders, anxious not to be left with unsold goods on their hands just before little Christmas, would be reducing their prices as the day progressed. Meanwhile, they had agreed that Mr Muldoon should buy their midday meal and Emily should pay for high tea. They had gone to a pleasant tea room with a wide window overlooking a pond, and had watched with some apprehension as children tested the ice, daring each other to venture further.

They had had a good but simple meal during the course of which Mr Muldoon had begged Emily to call him Fergal, being, he said, as they were more or less related by marriage. Emily had thanked him and had felt it only polite to suggest that he should use her first name too, and they had left the tea room far easier in one another's company than they had been earlier in the day.

When they had completed their shopping they had returned to the little café, and though Emily had declared she was no longer hungry after the excellent meal they had enjoyed earlier, the sight of the food that was presently brought to the table had caused the water to rise to her mouth. Scallop and mushroom pie topped with creamy mashed potato had been followed by richly buttered brack and porter cake accompanied of course by several cups of tea, served by a cheerful little waitress who had informed Emily that her family had iced the porter cake.

Emily, having said that she could not eat a thing after the pie, had found the smell of the porter cake irresistible but had warned Mr Muldoon, as they had made their way to the bus stop, that she would probably wedge in the doorway of that vehicle, so full of food was she. However, when the bus arrived, they had managed to get aboard clutching their purchases and had collapsed on to the nearest seat, giggling like a couple of kids and pleased as punch with the gifts they had bought.

Now, Emily turned to her companion. 'You were right

about prices falling as the daylight faded,' she said. 'That beautiful blue scarf I bought for Claudia were priced at five bob this morning, but I gorrit for half a crown just now. It's the colour of her eyes, you know; Claudia suits blue.'

'Aye, 'tis always the way,' Fergal said with satisfaction. 'The mittens I bought for Cormack were a deal cheaper once it began to grow dusky.' He leaned back in his seat with a gusty sigh. 'But I reckon the most popular present for the girls will be this.' He tapped the box on his knee with a work-roughened finger. 'Young 'uns like livin' things, so havin' their own little flock of poultry will give 'em a lot of pleasure, I'm sure of it.'

Grandpa Muldoon had bought both girls half a dozen day-old chicks, which were imprisoned in the cardboard box he held so carefully. He chuckled. 'They'll be in lay by the time summer comes, so the girls will be able to sell the eggs; make themselves a bit of pocket money.'

'Unless they're cockerels of course,' Emily said, proud of the fact that she could make such a remark, but then sorry she had done so when she saw a look of dismay cross Fergal's face.

'Well, Emily, ain't you the knowin' one,' he said, marvelling. 'You're right an' all; they could be little cockerels, for they's too young to tell as yet. And if they are cockerels, the girls won't never let Cormack fatten them up for the dinner table. Why didn't I think of that?'

Emily laughed. 'Oh well, it 'ud be hard indeed if you'd picked out twelve little fellers,' she said consolingly. 'I were real envious when you showed me the chicks, 'cos

95

I'd not thought of buyin' livestock meself. And I'll wager Louisa will be more thrilled wi' your present than wi' mine . . .' she indicated the large parcel at their feet, 'but there you are, I knew she needed a smart blouse to wear for church, so that's what I bought her.'

Fergal had purchased a canary in a cage for his daughter-in-law, and though at the time Emily had thought this would merely mean Louisa would have to shell out for bird seed, she now realised that the little creature, with its shrill piping song, would be a welcome addition to the family rather than an added expense. She did wonder, though, how Fergal would manage to hide the canary from its recipient, but when she posed the question he tapped the side of his nose and gave her a knowing grin. 'I've arranged for young Sean Byrne to give an eye to it tonight,' he said. 'He's going to meet us at the grocer's yard when we get off the bus and we'll tek him up in the donkey cart, drive to the Byrnes' cottage and then go on home. He'll bring the little feller round as soon as it gets light, which is when me daughter-in-law will have her present.'

Everything went according to plan. Young Sean darted out as soon as the bus drew up to help them carry their parcels to the donkey cart. He had already tacked up the donkey and received a sixpenny piece from Fergal and another from Emily. The boy chattered like a magpie all the way to his cottage and when he dismounted there, with both the day-old chicks and the canary in his arms, he promised fervently to be at the croft before the cock had so much as opened his eyes.

Fergal Muldoon waited until the boy had disappeared,

then turned the donkey cart round and headed for home. It was bitterly cold but Emily, wrapped in her rug and still glowing with the pleasure of money well spent and a day enjoyed, was content with the donkey's ambling pace and the comfortable silence.

After about half a mile, however, Fergal slowed the donkey and turned to his companion. 'I've a feeling, Emily, that you've been a bit disappointed over Connacht Cottage and the life we live,' he said slowly, clearly choosing his words with care. 'You feel you ain't as useful as you expected to be because Louisa and Cormack have got things so well organised that not even the arrival of two babies when they expected one has put them out. You're a woman who likes to be doing and it were a shock to you to discover that though Louisa sent for you, there weren't a lot for you to do. Believe me, Emily, I know that feeling well. I'm a deal better now, but at one time I thought I were going to be just a useless old hulk, sittin' in the chimney corner and doin' women's work around the house. But when the family arrived, I pulled myself together and began to help out whenever I could. Now I do my share and never feel guilty when summat comes up what I can't manage. I love my life at the croft and I want you to love it too.'

Moved by his understanding and obvious sympathy, Emily felt tears form in her eyes. She fished out a handkerchief and blew her nose, then cleared her throat before she spoke. 'I wish I weren't so useless, of course,' she admitted. 'But it ain't just that. I'm afeared of the animals and I can't sleep because of the noises. Oh, I

97

know it's only foxes and owls, stuff like that, but it scares me, makes me realise I'm more of a burden than a help, though everyone tries to tell me it ain't so. But in my heart I reckon Lou will give a great gasp of relief when I goes back to Blodwen Street.'

Fergal gave a snort and pulled the donkey to a halt. 'That's nonsense, so it is. Oh, I don't deny the girls is useful, but neither of 'em can cook like you can, nor Louisa for that matter. It takes Claudia all mornin' to make a batch of soda bread that will last us a day; you make a week's supply in half an hour! As for bein' afraid of the noises and the animals, what d'you think I'd be like if the good Lord picked me up and dumped me down in Liverpool? I'd not sleep a wink for the noise of the traffic, the ships' sirens and the shouts of all the folk in the streets. I'd be scared o' the trams – I ain't never seen a tram but they sound fearsome things – and the motor traffic: buses, lorries and the like. While as for that underground train you talk about, you wouldn't get me going down into the bowels of the earth!' He patted Emily's shoulder. 'So don't think you're alone in being afraid of strange places and stranger noises. To my way of thinkin' you're doin' awful well, and remember, it's early days yet. Tomorrer's the sixth of January and you arrived just before Christmas. By the time you go home, you'll be collecting eggs, feeding the pigs and doing all sorts.' He loosened the reins, clicking to the donkey, and the equipage began to move forward once more. 'Would you like me to teach you to milk, m'dear? I'm sure you'd be as good a milker as you are a cook by the time you go home.'

Emily repressed a shudder. She had stood in the doorway of the cowshed at milking time and was sure she would never willingly touch those nasty pink dangly things, far less squeeze them between her fingers until milk hissed into the pail. However, it would not do to say this, so she temporised. 'There's other things I reckon I'll tackle first,' she said. 'Jenny says Buttercup can kick sideways and it 'ud be just my luck if she did that and knocked the pail flying. As for feedin' the pigs, they all but jump up and help themselves to the swill. I ain't denyin' they've got fine healthy teeth, but the last thing I want is for a pig to take a chunk out o' me arm or knock me flyin'.'

Fergal chuckled again. 'You don't have to go in to the pigsty to feed 'em, you just pour the swill into their trough,' he told her. 'I know we all go in to Belinda's pen at the moment, because she's just given birth to bonaveens, but no one would expect you to feed her.'

The cart rounded a bend in the lane and Emily saw the warm lights streaming from the cottage ahead of her. Seeing it thus, looking so cosy whilst she and Fergal were very conscious of the icy cold, made her long to be within doors. It evidently did the same for Pickles, who broke in to a donkey trot, swerved around the peat pile and would have headed straight for her stable had Fergal not pulled her to a halt outside the back door. He helped Emily to alight, handed her her parcels and then bent and whispered in her ear. 'Don't forget that you're the most welcome visitor ever to cross our threshold. Don't undervalue yourself, m'dear, for we all regard you highly. Now you go in and put the kettle over the fire, because a hot drink is all we need now for a good night's sleep.'

It was the evening of the day before Emily's departure and she was in her bedroom, packing her belongings into the small suitcase she had brought with her and the slightly larger bag that she had bought on her visit to the town. Until her shopping trip with Fergal Muldoon, Emily had quite made up her mind to leave her daughter after a fortnight, convinced that she was not necessary to either Louisa's happiness or the smooth running of the croft. After listening to Fergal, however, she had begun to pay more attention to life at the cottage and had realised that she could be a great help in many ways, particularly when the girls returned to school. Besides, her new-found friendship with Fergal had made all the difference. To be with someone of her own generation, who understood both her difficulties and fears, was a real treat.

As Fergal had anticipated, the girls had been delighted with all their presents, but spent more time over the chicks than with anything else they received. The canary, too, had been accepted with rapture and its cage hung beside the dresser where the little yellow bird could look across to the old mirror, situated by the back door. 'He'll sing to the bird he sees in the mirror, thinking he's met a mate,' Fergal had told Emily. 'Oddly enough, if you bought another canary and put it in the same cage neither of them would sing, or not often at any rate, but this way he'll sing his little heart out, hoping to attract the bird in the mirror to come to him.'

Jenny and Claudia had thought this was awfully sad, and so had Emily. But the bird's constant trilling song was so pleasant that Louisa had refused to agree to the purchase of another bird, though she did concede that it might be a kindness to let the canary – whose name was now Perky – fly free for an hour or so each day. 'Then he'll see for himself that there ain't another bird in the room, only his reflection,' Emily had said tactfully. 'If he goes on singing after that, you'll know he don't believe he's singing to a mate, just to a mirror.' Louisa had been afraid Perky might be impossible to catch after a taste of freedom, but Grandpa Muldoon had lured him back into his cage with the aid of a sunflower head which had gone to seed, so that had been all right.

Emily's thoughts were interrupted by the bedroom door shooting open to reveal Jenny's round and smiling face. 'All done, Gran?' she asked cheerfully. 'Oh, I wish you wasn't going. We'll miss you ever so; not just me and Claudia, but Mam and Dad and Grandpa as well.' She beamed engagingly at her grandparent. 'Claudia told me yesterday that you'd not been too happy when you first arrived. She said you was afeared of the night noises and even of the animals, and meant to go home early. But you've stayed your full month, haven't you? So I reckon you ain't scared any more and that means you'll come again, Claudia says.'

Emily smiled at her. 'Of course I'll come again; wild horses wouldn't stop me,' she said robustly. 'I can't say I'm not scared of the cows and the pigs, even though I know they wouldn't harm me, but never fear, I'll come back to Kerry, you see if I don't.'

Jenny blew out her cheeks in a long whistle. 'I just wish you could stay for a few more weeks now, because the countryside is beautiful when spring comes. But Grandpa Muldoon is real clever about the weather, and he says there's snow coming, lots of it, so I suppose it's sensible to go while you can.' She came fully into the room and picked up the suitcase. 'I should be in school tomorrow, but Mam says I can take a bit of a holiday. Grandpa's going to drive the donkey cart and Claudia and meself are coming as well, to see you off. Mam can't because of the twins, and Dad says he'd be one too many for poor old Pickles. Oh, and I quite forgot, Mam sent me through to tell you supper's on the table. It's an extra special one, because you're going away tomorrow, so if you've finished your packing we'd best hurry.'

Next day, the family assembled in the kitchen for a breakfast of porridge, eggs and bacon and toast, since Emily's journey was a long one and she might have no opportunity to get a hot meal until she reached Blodwen Street once more. Cormack gave her a smacking kiss before making his way to the milking shed and Louisa clung, and even cried a little, but was soon forced to hurry out of the room when the twins began to announce that they were awake and wanted their early feed.

Grandpa Muldoon saw that Emily had been affected by the parting with her daughter, and squeezed her hand as he helped her into the donkey cart. 'Think on, you'll be missing the snow, which won't be long coming now,' he whispered. 'The children love it, but it ain't too good for us older ones.' He eyed her anxiously. 'You will come back when the weather eases, won't you? You'll not want to miss seeing the twins, because one day they're babies and the next toddlers, if you understand me.'

'I will if I can manage it,' Emily said rather guardedly. 'But I can't promise nothing; I've got my lodgers to consider and though Mrs Calvert has stood in for me this time, I can't expect her to do so whenever I feel like it.'

Fergal started to say that he was sure she would arrange something, but at that moment the girls came tumbling out into the yard and scrambled up into the donkey cart, and conversation became general.

In due course they reached the station, and there were tears as Emily climbed aboard the train and waved farewell to the Muldoons. Then she settled back in her seat. Soon be home, she told herself, and soon be back again, provided Mrs Calvert will oblige.

As Emily had anticipated, the journey was long, and before it was half over it had started to snow. By the time she reached the ferry the flakes were whirling thickly, and when she disembarked at the Pier Head she glanced around her rather helplessly, for she could scarcely see across the street for snow, and did not intend to walk all the way to Blodwen Street in such weather. But where would she get a taxi? If she could only see a queue of people waiting . . . she had just bent to pick up her luggage when a hand reached out and took her case, and a voice hailed her.

'Grand to see you again, Mrs Dalton. Now don't you touch that suitcase; I can manage it easily. But you'd best tuck your hand in my arm, or we'll get separated, 'cos the snow's that thick, you can't tell friend from foe.'

'Oh, Mr Payne!' Emily exclaimed. 'How good of you to meet me. I was just wondering how I could get home in this frightful weather.' She was surprised and very touched that he should have gone to the trouble of meeting her, for though she had written to Maria Calvert saying that she hoped to be home in time for the evening meal, it had not occurred to her to tell her friend upon which ship she would arrive. Mr Payne must have met the ferry on the off chance that she was aboard and she appreciated his thoughtfulness, especially when she discovered that he had arranged for a taxi cab to wait for her arrival, with its meter ticking over no doubt.

Climbing into the back of the cab, she watched Mr Payne put her luggage aboard before joining her on the long leather seat. They smiled at each other as the taxi began to move.

'Well, Mrs Dalton? How did you leave your family? I trust they're all well.'

'They're fine, thank you, Mr Payne. The twins are so good, you'd scarce believe. Mind you, the moment they begin to cry either Claudia or Jenny rushes to the cradle and picks 'em up. I keep telling the girls their little brother and sister will be spoiled rotten, but of course they take no notice. Louisa says they're livin' dolls to her girls and I dare say she's right, though my Claudia is real motherly; getting to be a beauty as well. And Jenny's quite a help around the place. But how have you got on in my absence, Mr Payne? I know Mrs Calvert has took good care of you, but I've not seen a newspaper for a month; any news what might affect us?'

'Nothing of much interest, except the Depression has meant I've lost two junior clerks. The boss sacked 'em and expected me and Mr Clitheroe to do their work, as well as our own, and take a cut in wages. Only we stood out against him, knowing that he'd got no desire to do the work himself, and he backed down, so we're still getting our rightful salary.'

For the rest of the short journey Emily told of her own stay in Ireland, and when they reached 22 Blodwen Street she was surprised at the rush of pleasure, the real sense of homecoming, that overcame her as she pushed open the front door and walked into the neat hall and smelt the welcoming odour of a beef casserole. She was just saying as much to Mr Payne, who had followed her in, carrying her luggage, when the kitchen door shot open and Maria Calvert came hurrying to meet her, a big smile on her face and her arms held out.

'Oh, Em, me love, it's a treat to see you again after so long,' she exclaimed, giving Emily a big hug. 'I've done me best to tek your place, but your lodgers talk of nothin' but your grand cookin', and the way you have wi' a roast, and your lemon chiffon pie . . . but I'm holding you up. Come into the kitchen and we'll put your wet coat on the airer. I've got the kettle on the stove, so you can have a nice hot cup of tea before I start dishin' up the supper.'

Shortly after Emily's arrival, Mr Clarke came in, grumbling loudly that he was soaked to the skin and surprising Emily by giving her a hug; something which the more correct Mr Payne would never have dreamed of doing. 'Grand to see you, Mrs D,' he said boisterously. 'But what damn awful weather you've brung with you! I've a good mind to send you back to Ireland wi' a message that we'd rather have sunshine, 'cos they turn off the heating early in my office now. But I dare say Mr Payne's told you things have changed. I'm still in the booking office, thank the Lord, but I've had to take a cut in me wages. It's only a few bob, but it's the principle of the t'ing. Still an' all, I'm lucky to have a job, what wi' the Depression. I don't suppose you noticed how it's affecting them in Dublin?'

Emily was unable to give her lodger any news of Dublin since she had merely passed through it on her way to catch the ferry. But when she had thanked Mrs Calvert and begged her to join them for the evening meal – her friend refused, saying that she had prepared tea for herself at home – Emily and her lodgers sat down at the kitchen table and began to talk and eat.

'I dare say I know more about Dublin than you do, because me family tell me what goes on,' Mr Clarke said, pausing to help himself to another round of bread and butter. 'Folk are tightenin' their belts over there, same as here, but I've heard nothing about job losses. Me daughter works in one of the big departmental stores, as you know, and I gather her job's safe enough. Which reminds me, wasn't there some talk of you bringin' your granddaughter Claudia back here for a bit of a holiday? I were lookin' forward to meeting her.'

Emily felt a betraying flush steal into her cheeks. Now that Mr Clarke mentioned it, she remembered boasting – yes, it had been boasting – that she meant to bring

Claudia back with her, in the hope that the girl would so enjoy city life that she would take favourably to the idea of obtaining work here when the time was ripe. She was trying to think of a good reason for Claudia's non-appearance when it suddenly struck her that telling the truth would be the most sensible thing. Accordingly, she took a deep breath and began to speak. 'Well, I admit it were my intention, but Mr Fergal Muldoon had a bit of a chat with me and pointed out that Liverpool in winter ain't the nicest spot on earth. It's a grand city, of course, but Christmas is over and spring hasn't arrived, so the shops will be betwixt and between, if you understand me. Of course the picture palaces and the theatres and dance halls will still be open for business, but there ain't a deal of fun goin' dancin' all muffled up in your winter toggery. Mr Muldoon said I'd best wait until summer, for it would be a sad shame to let a kid of Claudia's age get the impression that a city were all wet pavements, overcrowded shops and bad-tempered people.'

Mr Clarke nodded sagely. 'Aye, the old feller were right. In summer there's all sorts, but at this time of year we lives our lives within doors, so to speak. So I tek it you'll be going back to Ireland, come the summer?'

'Well, I hope so,' Emily said cautiously.

Mr Payne, who had taken no part in the conversation until now, picked up the tureen and raised his brows at Emily. 'Another potato, Mrs Dalton? And there's more stew, if you're still hungry after your long journey.'

'Thank you, Mr Payne, I won't say no,' Emily said graciously, helping herself to a large floury potato and then adding some beef and gravy from the cast iron casserole dish. 'I must tell Mrs Calvert tomorrow that we ate every scrap of her good food, because she's an excellent cook; the only person I felt I could leave in charge with a clear conscience.'

Mr Clarke laughed. 'She's a fair cook, I'll grant you that,' he said. 'But there's no one your equal, Mrs D, so don't you go off again *too* soon!'

Chapter Five

August 1936

Emily was tidying her pantry so that when Maria Calvert arrived she would be able to see at a glance where everything was, for in less than an hour Emily would be on her way to the Pier Head to board the Irish ferry. She had visited the cottage once a year since the birth of the twins, but had missed the previous year as the twins had had measles. Now, getting ready for her journey, she was looking forward to her holiday. Excited at the thought of seeing her family again after so long, she had packed days before it was necessary, so now she had little to do but await the arrival of Mr Payne, who had taken the morning off work to fetch a taxi cab in which he would accompany her to the Pier Head.

Emily was glancing at the clock above the mantel when the back door opened and Mr Payne came quickly into the room. It was August and already beginning to be a warm day, but Mr Payne was very correct in his dark suit, light Burberry and tweed cap. He smiled at her and picked up a neat, navy suitcase, then stood it down again in order to get Emily's mackintosh off the hook by the back door. He helped her into it, then picked up the suitcase again as Emily seized her little felt hat with the bunch of cherries on the brim and placed it carefully on her head. She was pleased with the effect, for though she was greying at the temples most of her hair was still almost as dark as her daughter's.

Mr Payne headed for the front door, now carrying not only her suitcase but also her large umbrella. When she protested that this, surely, would not be necessary in August, he gave a prim little smile. 'They call Ireland the Emerald Isle because it's so green, and it's so green because it never stops raining,' he reminded her.

Emily laughed, but acknowledged the truth of his words. 'I reckon I told you that Mr Fergal Muldoon's favourite saying about the weather is that if you can't see the mountains it's because it's raining, and if you can see them clear as clear it means it's going to rain.'

Mr Payne smiled again. 'Then you're bound to want your umbrella,' he observed. 'No need to hurry, Mrs Dalton, we've plenty of time. But I mean to carry your cases aboard and see you comfortably settled before I return to Exchange Flags. As you see, I've found a cab without difficulty.'

He opened the back door of the taxi, which was standing by the kerb, and in a very short time they were aboard the Irish ferry and Mr Payne was finding her a comfortable seat and scolding her for not reserving a cabin. 'You would have been able to sleep,' he chided her. 'As it is, you'll arrive in Dublin tired and hungry, with still another day's travel ahead of you.'

'Ah, but I'm spendin' the night with me old friend Mrs Makepeace, as I did last time I were in Dublin, and won't set out on me journey again until tomorrow mornin',' Emily told him. 'There ain't a train tonight, so you see there's no point in hirin' a cabin for a daytime voyage.'

Mr Payne acknowledged that she was in the right and left as the ship's siren began to sound, indicating that they would be soon be off. Emily waved until he was out of sight and then settled down, hoping that the weather would remain pleasant, for she was not a good sailor.

'Bernie! Benny! Will you kindly remember that you promised your father you'd be a help and not a hindrance, and have you forgotten your gran is coming today for her summer holiday?'

Louisa's words caught the twins' attention and they stopped racing up and down the kitchen, climbing on and off chairs and generally misbehaving. They skidded to a halt close to where Louisa sat in the comfortable fireside chair, which today she had pulled into the back doorway to get what breeze she could. The twins had been placid enough as infants, but all too soon they had become energetic, noisy and wilful.

'What do you want, Mam?' Bernie said breathlessly. She turned and gave her brother a shove. 'Don't you crowd up on me or there'll be trouble.'

'I want some peace and quiet,' Louisa informed her children. 'Why are you playing indoors on such a hot day? Why don't you go and help Jenny to weed the potato patch? Or you could go to the dairy. Dónal is milking the cows and Claudia's putting the milk through the cooler, and then I expect she'll be making the butter.'

Bernie heaved an enormous sigh and poked her twin in the ribs. 'Well? You heard what Mam said; which would we rather do? Weed the perishin' spuds or work the butter churn for Claudia?'

Benny stuck out his lower lip and scowled at his sister. 'I don't want to do either,' he said crossly. 'Daddy said if we were good we could go to the station in the donkey cart to pick up the old woman.'

'Don't you dare speak so rudely of your grand-mother . . .' Louisa began wrathfully, but was interrupted.

'Sorry, Mammy, I couldn't 'member what we called her,' Benny said rather perfunctorily. 'But we'd sooner go wit' Daddy, so we would. We like to see the trains. I wish *we* were going on the train like we did when Claudia and Jenny took us to Dublin to see the pantomime last Christmas.' He grinned at his mother. 'We had a huge dinner and ices in the interval . . . oh, it were grand, so it were.'

Louisa sighed. She and Cormack had been happy to let the girls take the twins to Dublin, though it had cost rather more than they had anticipated. All four children had thoroughly enjoyed the occasion and had talked about it constantly. They had spent two nights with Emily's old friend, Lavinia Makepeace, and Louisa knew that she and Cormack had enjoyed the little break from the twins almost as much as the twins had enjoyed their visit to the capital city.

However, both Louisa and Cormack had suffered from pangs of guilt, and when the Muldoon young had returned they had been careful to say how lonely they had been, though this had caused Grandpa Muldoon to smother a laugh behind his hand. Franker than his son and daughter-in-law, he had told the twins that though he had missed them and was glad to see them back, he had enjoyed the peace they had left behind them. And he had listened to their stories of everything that had happened to them during their stay in the city.

'Well, if Daddy said he'd take you to the station, I suppose you'd best fetch your Sunday best through here so I can help you to change,' Louisa said. 'What were you playing just now, anyway? It seemed to involve an awful lot of running up and down and cheering.'

'We was playing 'lympics,' Bernie said proudly. 'Whoever went six times up and down the kitchen fastest got to stand on the podi . . . podithingy, and the other one had to cheer. Benny had just won and I were going to pin a medal on his chest 'cos he was Jesse Owens, when you stopped us.'

'Right; I understand,' Louisa said resignedly, well versed in the vivid imaginations of her offspring. 'And I suppose any minute now you would have picked up your grandfather's walking stick, hurled it across the kitchen and announced that you were Tilly Fleischer, winning the javelin event.'

Bernie's eyes opened wide and Benny's jaw dropped. 'How did you know?' they chorused.

Louisa laughed. 'I've known you two long enough to realise that you would both have to win a medal or there would be mayhem. What were you going to use as medals, by the way?'

There was a moment's uncomfortable silence, then Bernie plunged a hand into her skirt pocket and produced the brooch which Cormack had given Louisa last Christmas, together with one which Emily had presented to Claudia on her birthday some years ago.

Louisa sighed and took the brooches from her daughter's hot and dirty little paw. 'You've been in my room rifling through my trinket box, which you know very well you aren't allowed to do,' she said. 'I've a good mind to say you can't go to the station . . .' she saw both twins' mouths take on the square shape which meant they were about to howl and continued hastily: 'but just this once, I'll forgive you. Now go and get your Sunday clothes before I change my mind.'

In the dairy, Claudia had finished churning the butter, had tidied round and was walking past the cowshed on her way back to the kitchen when Dónal erupted into the yard and caught her arm. 'Hang on a minute, Claudia,' he said rather breathlessly. 'How would you like to come wit' me to see a fillum in town? It's starrin' that kid you like, Shirley Temple. I've bin savin' up me wages so's we can have a bite o' supper afterwards. Say you'll come!'

Claudia pulled herself free from his grip as tactfully as she was able. He was a fine-looking young man of twenty-one, good-natured and easy-going, but unfortunately his handsome looks were not matched by his mind. Claudia knew he had left school at fourteen, barely able to read or write, and though he was extremely useful about the croft, coping with as much of the heavy work as Cormack did himself, his infatuation for Claudia made her avoid him whenever she could.

Now, therefore, she patted Dónal's arm before turning once more towards the kitchen. 'I'm sorry, Dónal, but I can't expect my mother to get the evening meal and put the twins to bed without help, so I'm going to be pretty busy.'

Dónal scowled and caught hold of her sleeve. '*Why* won't you come out wit' me?' he demanded. 'I've saved up me money, bought meself a decent shirt and a new tweed cap. I've axed you to come to the fillums a dozen times and you've always got some excuse. What's wrong wit' me? I'm a good worker; your mam and dad seem to like me well enough, and six weeks ago I spent hours fillin' a basket wit' wild strawberries 'cos you told me you liked them. Even that weren't enough, though you took the strawberries . . .'

Claudia felt a warm blush invade her cheeks, and knew it was partly guilt and partly exasperation. She had done her very best to convince Dónal that she would never think of him as anything other than her family's employee, but it seemed that simply refusing invitations was not enough. She spun round to face him, beginning to say that she did not want to go out with any young man, but at that moment the twins erupted into the yard, dressed in their sailor suits, hair brushed and faces shining. They ignored Dónal, whose hand had dropped from their sister's arm, and began to drag Claudia towards the kitchen. 'Quick, quick!' Benny squeaked. 'Daddy's in the stable, harnessing the donkey to the cart, and Mam said if you'd kindly come indoors you could

115

get us a lickle somethin' before we goes off to meet the old wo— I mean our gran.'

Claudia felt a wave of relief at this timely intervention and turned politely to Dónal. 'I've got to go; can't let these kids travel all the way into town with nothing to line their stomachs . . .' she began, but Dónal was already speaking.

'It's any excuse for you to refuse me invitations,' he mumbled bitterly. 'If you'd just give me a chance . . .' He half turned towards her, his hand reaching out, but Claudia was having none of it.

'Come along, twins,' she said breezily, as though she had not heard Dónal's words. 'Mam made a couple of loaves of brack earlier and there's fresh butter in the dairy, so that should keep you from starving.'

'Oo, buttered brack; we loves it, so we does,' Bernie said. 'And there'll be milk to drink.'

As they entered the kitchen, both twins turned wide enquiring gazes on their sister, though only Bernie spoke. 'What's up wit' Dónal?' she asked bluntly. 'I t'ought Mammy said he'd stopped pesterin' you.'

Claudia stared at her little sister. The twins always seemed to be busy about their own affairs, yet they still managed to know everything that went on. 'I think Dónal's lonely,' she said after a moment. 'But I'll have another word with him, explain that if I go to the picture palace, I go with Jenny, or one of my old school friends. I'm sure he'll understand.'

'I don't think he will,' Bernie said bluntly. 'He's thick as two short planks, so he is.'

Claudia gasped. 'That's a nasty thing to say. You

116

should be ashamed, Bernadette Muldoon,' she said reproachfully. 'Now sit yourselves down at the table while I get your tea.' She turned to her mother, who was sitting in one of the fireside chairs, and lowered her voice. 'Did you hear that, Mam?' she whispered. 'I don't want to hurt Dónal, but it's getting beyond a joke. He's really persistent . . .'

Louisa put a finger to her lips. 'Hush, dear, walls have ears,' she said significantly, indicating the twins. 'I'll ask your father to have a word, or maybe it would come better from Grandpa. But we'll talk about it when little pitchers are in the land of nod.'

'Right, Mam,' Claudia agreed. Then she turned back to the table to cut and butter more of the fruit loaf and to pour tea for herself and her mother, Jenny and the two men, who would shortly be returning to the cottage.

Emily got down from the train with her suitcase in her hand, and headed across the platform to where she hoped her son-in-law would be awaiting her. But before she had taken more than half a dozen steps her suitcase was wrenched from her hands and Cormack was giving her a hearty kiss on the cheek, saying that he had tied Pickles outside with the children in charge, so they had best hurry before the twins took it into their heads to play some wild game or other and scared the donkey into galloping off, tethering post and all.

Accordingly, the two of them hurried across to where the cart, fortunately, was still parked against the kerb. Cormack stood Emily's suitcase in the well and then helped her aboard. The twins smiled shyly as she greeted them, telling them how much they had grown since her last visit and exclaiming how smart they looked, and as Cormack set the equipage in motion she took covert stock of her grandchildren. They were an attractive pair, she thought, with elfin faces, hazel eyes and wide grins that revealed tiny white teeth. They both had a great many freckles, which she thought a pity, but though Benny's hair was still undeniably red, Bernie's had lightened until it could have been described as sand-coloured. Both children were wearing sailor hats, but she could see that whilst Benny's hair was tightly curled, Bernie's was wavy and cut in what Emily thought of as a soft Dutch bob.

Presently, as they wended their way out of the town, Emily turned to Cormack. 'Where's Claudia?' she asked bluntly. 'I thought she would be sent to meet me, being as how we're such old friends. She still writes every week, you know. Oh, and how's Lou?'

'Claudia would have liked to come, but she's preparin' the meal,' Cormack explained. He looked curiously at his mother-in-law. 'You've not asked where our Jenny is.'

Emily felt a betraying flush warm her face. How could she have been so tactless? Jenny was a good-hearted child and of course she adored her elder sister. In Jenny's eyes Claudia could do no wrong, and since this was how Emily herself regarded her eldest granddaughter she had always applauded Jenny's preference. Now, however, she hastened to give the younger girl her due. 'Didn't I ask after Jenny . . .? How ridiculous, when I'm so fond of the child. How *is* she, Cormack? I expect she's quite the young lady now.'

Cormack grinned. 'I wouldn't say that. Louisa reckons Jenny's young for her age, but I think she only seems that way because Claudia is seventeen and the one who takes responsibility so that Jenny only has to follow her sister's example. But Jenny's just fine, so she is, as you'll see when we get home, because the whole family will be assembled to welcome your good self.'

'That will be grand,' Emily said sincerely. 'And how's your father, Cormack? He writes to me whenever he has a spare moment; a lovely clear hand he has. I'm looking forward to having a real old chinwag with him, just as soon as I'm settled in. I gather Louisa wants me to keep an eye on the twins so she can concentrate on giving the house a good clean throughout, which is only right and proper, and I hope Fergal means to help me whenever he has time.'

Cormack looked at the twins and pulled a face. They were playing Cat's Cradle with a length of string, but though this quiet occupation occasionally descended into a swift exchange of blows it seemed to Emily that they were behaving better than they had on her previous visit. She said as much to Cormack, who gave her a quizzical glance. 'They're behavin' like angels right now, because I reckon they're a bit shy of you,' he explained. 'But soon enough they'll begin to treat you like one of the family – which you are – and then it's look out for fireworks.'

'Oh dear,' Emily said, rather doubtfully. 'But I'm sure I can teach them to mind me.'

'Oh aye, because they ain't bad so much as – as ingenious,' Cormack explained. 'They think of t'ings what would never cross your mind, but, as you say, you'll have me dear old dad to help out until you can cope alone.'

'That's good,' Emily said, relieved. 'But how is Fergal? And the young man who works for you . . . what's his name? Dónal?'

Cormack was beginning to reply when Bernie cut across him. 'Dónal's been pesterin' our Claudia again,' she announced firmly. 'Mammy says Daddy must have a word. Or Grandpa Muldoon, 'cos it might come better from him.'

Cormack laughed – rather uneasily, Emily thought – but told his daughter not to repeat grown-ups' talk.

Bernie stared at him, her eyes rounding. 'Why ever not?' she asked indignantly. 'Grown-ups doesn't tell lies, does they?'

Cormack began to answer, then changed his mind. 'If I tells you not to do something, it's for a good reason,' he said seriously. 'Now get on wit' your playin', and no more argufying.'

Emily waited until the twins' attention seemed to be firmly fixed on their game, then she leaned forward and began to ask Cormack what was wrong with Dónal. 'I never really got to know him, seeing as how he was mostly out of doors,' she said. 'What's he like?'

'Very respectable, very hard-working, but he's not had much schooling,' Cormack said. He indicated the twins with a jerk of his chin. 'And now we'll talk about other t'ings, if you don't mind. Me dad's still a great help with tasks such as feedin' the hens and drivin' into the village a couple of times a week to fetch any post, but he has a rest most afternoons. He's a grand help wit' the twins, you'll find.'

Her initial misgivings that the twins might prove intractable were not realised, and Emily soon settled into the life at the croft as though she had never been away. Despite Mr Payne's fears the weather was good. In the two years since Emily had last visited them, the Muldoons had greatly increased the size and scope of their holding. Their nearest neighbour had been an old man whose son had long ago deserted his father's croft for a job at a cattle market in the nearby town. When the old man had become too infirm to manage even simple farming tasks, he had abandoned his holding and gone to live with his son. Cormack and Louisa had visited the place and been shocked by the deterioration of their neighbour's tumbledown cottage and wildly overgrown land, but when the father died and the son put it on the market, Cormack had told Louisa that the place would go for a song, including what was always known as dead stock, which meant farm equipment. He and Louisa had braved the bank manager in their nearest town, been granted a loan and had bought the property.

Now they were engaged in the cripplingly hard work of bringing their new acres back into productivity. They had doubled the size of their vegetable patch and Cormack had ploughed up a couple of acres of the scrub land which his neighbour's holding had become. It would have to be manured and fenced off, but when this was accomplished he meant to try his hand at growing barley, which thrived in this area and always commanded a good price. He also wanted to grow lucerne to enrich his hay crop, and talked of rebuilding the old man's cottage one day so that they might have two good properties to hand on to their children, though he suspected that his daughters, being pretty as pictures and clever to boot, would doubtless marry and move away from the family croft.

This was the only part of her son-in-law's plans with which Emily disagreed. Doubtless, there were many charming young men in the neighbourhood who would be delighted to marry one of the Muldoon sisters, but Emily thought that her granddaughters deserved better. She had seen for herself how extremely hard the women had to work on the land. Louisa was lucky; her man was doing well despite the Depression, because he and Louisa had had substantial savings, but even so Emily could see that the hard work was beginning to tell. Louisa's hair was streaked with white; her skin had lost its bloom and her hands were like those of any other labourer, with split and blackened nails and calloused palms. Emily could not bear to think of her beloved Claudia following in her mother's footsteps, for though the love between Cormack and his wife was there for all to see, Claudia might not be so lucky.

Now, Emily was baking the week's supply of farl in the cottage kitchen whilst she considered how best to persuade Claudia to return to Liverpool with her, when the back door shot open, interrupting her thoughts, and Fergal surged into the room, holding each twin by an ear. Bernie was bawling loudly and even Benny was shouting, though Emily saw that neither child had so much as one tear trickling down their red and indignant cheeks.

She tried not to smile. 'Well? What have you been up to this time?' she enquired resignedly. She had been at the cottage long enough to appreciate Cormack's remark regarding the twins' ingenuity. 'I know it's mischief or your good grandpa wouldn't be draggin' you indoors by your little lug'oles. Come on, say you're sorry and won't do it again or it'll be no supper for either of you.'

'We didn't know it were wrong,' Bernie shouted. 'Leggo me lug, Grandpa, or I'll bite you to the bone, so I will.'

'It weren't wrong . . . it weren't us,' Benny announced belligerently. 'It were a jay . . . them birds is mortal fond o' peas.'

Fergal, who had let go the twins' ears, made a grab for Benny, but the little boy ducked and rushed at Emily, clinging on to her skirt and dodging right and left as his grandfather attempted to catch him again. Emily sighed. 'Enough is enough. Sit down the pair of you and tell me just what you've been up to,' she said severely.

Fergal sniffed. 'You know last week their mammy set them to weeding between the rows of broad beans and to picking up stones from where the new potatoes have been planted?' he said. 'Well, I t'ought they'd done quite a good job and I know their mammy gave them a penny each to buy sweeties in the village.' He ground his teeth, trying to sound furious, but Emily could tell he was having difficulty in containing his amusement. 'Well,

Louisa asked me to fetch a feed of peas for supper tonight, so I went down to the vegetable patch and started picking. That's when I noticed that though the vines were fairly bursting with pods, a good many of 'em were empty. Something – or someone – had very carefully split the pods open along the seam, scooped out the contents and enjoyed a feast, leaving the empty pods on the vine!'

Emily's own lips were twitching, but she frowned at the small wrongdoers. 'Now come along the pair of you and own up,' she said. 'It's very wrong of you to try to blame the poor birds because no bird was ever born which could take peas out of the pod without tearing it from the vine. Bernie? Benny? What have you got to say for yourselves?'

'We told a tiny fib because Grandpa was so fierce and said he'd belt our little bottoms till they was red as radishes,' Bernie said. 'And that was before he'd even found out about the peas; it was when he'd pulled some radishes and found they was just tops. Only . . .' she glared at her twin, 'Benny said if we just ate the radish they would grow back, 'specially if we watered them, so no one would know. Then he said if we were real careful and took the peas without tearing the pods from the vine, them little knobbly things what hold the peas in place would probably swell up and be proper peas again before anyone wanted 'em.'

'Now Bernie, Benny, you've lived all your life in the country and you must know very well that Mam never cuts the green leaves off the radishes and sticks them back in the earth to grow more,' Emily said. 'She has to

124

start right at the beginning again, with fresh seed, ain't that so?'

Benny, looking ashamed, nodded his head but Bernie shook hers until her curls bounced. 'We thought that was so until Dad brought that stuff – what was it called? – oh yes, Swiss chard. He 'splained to us that it were everlastin' spinach, an' showed us how you could pick a grosh o' leaves and then come back a week later an' the leaves would all have growed back. So you see . . .'

'I see you're as cunning as a cartload of monkeys,' Emily said, and though Fergal agreed that Swiss chard could regrow he said he didn't believe a word of Bernie's explanation but would let them off this time, provided they went straight back to the vegetable patch to finish the weeding, swore on the holy book that they would steal no more and behave themselves better in future.

'We done the broad beans less'n a week gone,' Benny pointed out righteously. 'And we picked stones for a penny . . .'

But at this, Fergal moved so menacingly that both children bolted out of the kitchen door, shouting over their shoulders that they would be good and see that not a weed flourished in amongst the spuds.

The two adults settled down to have their laugh out and presently fell into a discussion about whether Claudia might find employment locally, since she had made it clear that she did not enjoy manual work and was in fact not good at it.

Emily pointed out that the money Claudia could earn would pay the wages for an extra pair of hands, but

Fergal shook his head. 'She wouldn't get a half decent job anywhere local. Times is hard, there's no money to spare, and if a job came up folk would give it to a relative or a close friend, not to an incomer, particularly one who speaks wit' an English accent. No, Claudia's best off here.'

'What about work in Liverpool?' Emily asked hopefully. 'She could earn good money there. She could live with me in Blodwen Street and come home for a holiday a couple of times a year – and send money home, I shouldn't wonder.'

Fergal raised one bushy white brow, his eyes twinkling. 'You don't want your precious grandchild marryin' an Irish farm labourer, and I can understand your reasons,' he said. 'You think there's little choice in these parts, and you're right, I know it. But have you thought of it from Claudia's point of view? If she had a fancy for Dónal, who's a good hard-working lad, or indeed for any other village boy, then she might prefer to stay in the countryside she's grown to love. For she does love it, Emily. Oh, I don't deny she'd enjoy life in a big city whilst she's young, but when it comes to settling down and rearing a brood of children, there's worse fates than a lovin' husband and a good little croft. This Depression can't last for ever and I reckon country folk are a deal better off than townspeople. We'll never go short of food, even if war comes . . . not that it will come, of course; it's just warmongering, as they call it. That Mr Churchill, he's always on about it, but that's a problem we don't have to face in Ireland.' He laughed. 'I can't see any country

126

declaring war on us; we're far too small and insignificant.'

Emily sighed. She had stopped forming her farl into rounds when Fergal and the twins had burst into the kitchen, but now she stood up and began to work once more. 'I suppose you're right. Maybe country life is healthier and better than that of a busy port,' she said. 'But try to understand, Fergal. I want Claudia to have a choice, a wide choice, before she commits herself to marrying anyone. When she lived in Blodwen Street, she was pally with a young fellow called Danny Callaghan. He was a poor kind o' kid, but he worked hard at school and he's doing real well for himself now. He attends night classes, did well in exams and has a good job in an insurance office. He also does the books for local tradesmen in his spare time. He was sweet on Claudia, even when they were a couple o' kids. I'm sure if he could see her now, he'd be fair dazzled. Ever since she left the city, he's popped in to see me at least once a week, offering to get my messages or to do various small tasks, and he always asks after Claudia. How about her visiting Liverpool for a little holiday, like? Then she could decide for herself which way of life she prefers. She's seventeen now and old enough to make up her own mind.'

Fergal grunted. 'Mebbe you're right and she should have a choice,' he said. 'You'd best have a word with Louisa, because it wouldn't surprise me if she'd agree with you. But time alone will tell, as they say . . .'

He stopped speaking just as the kitchen door opened and Louisa came in. She looked from one face to the other, a smile beginning. 'When I see you two talking so seriously I know Bernie and Benny have been up to something,' she said. 'Well, go on; what have they done this time?'

Chapter Six

Claudia was leaning on the stout wooden gate that her father had erected, gazing at the two new in-calf heifers that he had bought a week earlier at the local cattle market. They were fine beasts and Cormack had said that she and Jenny might have the naming of them. Jenny had vacillated between Bluebell and Poppy, but Claudia thought that Cowslip was a nicer name for the little heifer she had chosen.

When she had told Jenny of her choice, however, Jenny had said that Foxgloves was a nice name too, and now Claudia, leaning on the gate, still could not make up her mind which name she preferred. She wished she had not teased Jenny for not being able to choose, since she was equally unsure herself. Cowslip? Foxglove? She would call her Mignonette – Minnie for short – which would make a pleasant change from the conventional flower names with which the cows were usually christened.

Having decided, Claudia was about to turn towards the house when she was startled to hear herself addressed. 'Well, I've done for the day. Your da says I can go home early since there's a dance in the village hall this evenin'. Like to come? Your da said if I were to say "No strings", you just might come along o' me for once.'

'Good Lord, Dónal, how you startled me!' Claudia said, aware that she had jumped on first hearing his voice. 'Has it never occurred to you that it's daft to creep up behind someone? As for dancing with you, I don't want my feet crushed, so ta ever so, but I think not.' She tried to give Dónal a placatory smile to take the sting out of her words, but saw him flush scarlet and tighten his lips before he replied.

'That were real rude, Claudia, as well as being wrong. I'm a good dancer; ask any o' the village girls. Me and some o' me pals go into town every Saturday and have dancing lessons from Miss O'Hare and her sister. But you'd do anything rather than spend even half an hour in my company, wouldn't you?'

'Oh, Dónal, that's not true. You're my friend and I like you, but I don't want to start any of this courting nonsense, because I'm not on the catch for a young man, whatever you may think,' Claudia said. 'And you know what they're like in the village. If I go to the dance with you, they'll be nudging and winking and saying all sorts; believing it too. The fact is that because you work for my family there's already a deal of talk and I won't have it. Can you understand?'

Dónal heaved an enormous sigh. 'Aye, reckon I can,' he said gruffly. 'But won't you just come for a walk down as far as the river? We can chat as we go.'

'Oh, all right,' Claudia said, trying to keep the reluctance out of her voice. 'Tell you what, Dónal, if I do come with you, you might teach me how to tickle trout. Dad often talks about how he used to fetch out a fine fish for the family's dinner when he was a boy. But he's always too busy to show Jenny and me how it's done, and Grandpa Muldoon says he's too rheumaticky to go crouching on the river bank, and of course Mam wasn't brought up here, so she can't show us.' She smiled up at her companion. 'I'll just go and give Jenny a shout. I'm sure she'll come with us like a shot.'

Dónal started to protest, to say that it was she whose companionship he wanted, but Claudia ignored him, running all the way back to the cottage and bursting into the kitchen. Jenny was standing by the table, watching intently as their grandmother weighed ingredients on the elderly kitchen scales and poured them into the big yellow mixing bowl. Both looked up, startled by Claudia's abrupt arrival, and Jenny beamed at her sister. 'Gran's givin' me a cookery lesson, like she promised us,' she said happily. 'We're making a special fruit cake, and whilst it's in the oven we'll make a batch of scones. We made pastry earlier for a sausagemeat pie, but I'm afraid you missed that. Did you forget?'

'Oh glory, it went clean out of my head,' Claudia said remorsefully. 'But you don't really need a lesson, do you? You can make perfectly good scones and pastry already! And I need you to come with me.' She cast a quick glance at her grandmother. 'Dónal is going to teach us how to tickle trout. He's waiting by the paddock gate, so hurry out of your apron, because it's all floury. Besides, you don't want to get it muddy.' She turned to her grandmother with her most appealing smile. 'All right if I steal your little helper, Gran?'

She fully expected immediate agreement and was taken aback when her grandmother shook her head. 'No, queen. We're making me rich fruit cake, which is quite different from an ordinary fruit cake. It's me secret recipe, known only to a very few, so I want to pass it on to the next generation. If you can wait half an hour . . .'

'Oh, but I can't,' Claudia said, dismayed. 'And I don't much want to be alone with Dónal, even if he is teaching me to tickle trout. Gran, do I know the recipe for your rich fruit cake? If so, I'll teach Jenny myself, honest to God I will.'

She looked hopefully into her grandmother's face but though her smile was returned, Emily still shook her head. 'No, Jenny can't abandon me right now. She's going to zest the lemons for me and squeeze out the juice.' She chuckled. 'I never zest a lemon without I lose half me fingernails. But if it'll help, I'll send Jenny down to the river as soon as the cake is in the oven.'

Claudia stared at her sister. When she had made her request, Jenny's hands had flown to the back of her apron, but now she was looking uncertainly from one to the other. For a moment, Claudia was tempted to exert her influence on the younger girl, but then she realised she could not suggest that Jenny might obey her rather than their grandmother. So she smiled brilliantly and made the best of a bad job. 'Right you are,' she said, trying not to sound as annoyed as she felt, for surely no cake could be more important than her own desire not to be alone with Dónal. But it was no use expecting Gran to change her mind, so Claudia turned to her sister. 'You will come as soon as you can, won't you, Jen?' Jenny nodded and Claudia was about to leave the kitchen when another thought occurred to her. 'Where are the twins? I bet they'd love to learn how to tickle trout.'

'They've gone into the village with Daddy to fetch meal for the hens,' Jenny said. 'I'll be as quick as I can, Claudia. Think how thrilled Daddy will be if we catch a big brown trout, 'cos he loves 'em, you know he does.'

When Claudia arrived at the gate and told Dónal that Jenny would follow them when she had finished her cooking, she saw pleasure in his dark eyes. As they set out towards the wood she asked him, suspiciously, if he had no desire for her sister's company; a remark which made Dónal give a smothered chuckle before he replied that two were company, but three a crowd.

Claudia sniffed disapprovingly as they passed into the shelter of the wood. The path through the trees was narrow and winding and after a few moments Claudia realised that she was quite enjoying the walk and looking forward to finding out whether Dónal could really teach her to tickle trout. He was proving to be a better companion than she had imagined, pulling down a spray of honeysuckle for her when she remarked on its heady scent, pointing out a squirrel's drey high in a mighty beech tree and indicating a large hole in the roots of another such tree, which he told her was a badgers' sett.

When they reached the river, he explained carefully that they must not let their shadows fall upon the surface of the water in the pool, for this would alert the fish and it might be some time before they accepted – falsely of course – that there was no danger in the people on the bank. He instructed her to lie flat and to observe his movements closely. She watched as he edged his hand

and forearm into the water with infinite slowness and caution, watched as a trout approached his curled-up fingers, watched as the trout sidled close and saw the fingers begin their hypnotic stroking movements across the trout's silvery belly. Then there was a splash and a grunt of satisfaction from Dónal as a trout sailed through the air to land on the grassy bank, where it was speedily dispatched.

After that, it was Claudia's turn. Dónal took her hand and placed it beneath the water at a tempting angle, explaining that the trout would enjoy the movement of her fingers and would not notice when those same fingers hooked into its gills and flicked it out on to the bank. 'You'll mebbe not catch anything now because it's not as easy as it looks,' he said. 'It's practice which makes a good tickler, so it is. Now lie very still and keep your shadow out of sight and you never know, you might strike lucky.'

Half an hour later, Claudia was running through the wood, gasping and sobbing, her soaking skirt impeding her progress, brambles snatching at her clothing, nettles stinging her legs, for she had been forced to desert the path when she realised, by the sounds behind her, that she was being pursued. Now and again she heard her name called, the voice high and anxious, but she simply ran on, emerging from the wood with a hand clapped to a stitch in her side, but still making for the cottage.

She reached it ahead of the pursuit and burst into the kitchen, where her grandmother was placidly clearing up after her cooking.

Emily looked up and dropped the cloth she was holding, reached for her granddaughter and pushed her into a chair. 'Wharrever is the matter, chuck?' she asked, as Claudia began to hiccup that something dreadful had happened. 'Did you fall in the river? Your skirt's all wet and your hair's a right tangle. Now just calm down, young lady, and stop staring at the back door as though you expected a fire-breathing dragon or a mad bull to come charging in. I did as you asked and sent Jenny down to the river just as soon as me cake were in the oven. Do I take it she didn't find you? Not that that would be any reason for all this drama.'

'I – I – I never saw Jenny,' Claudia stammered. 'Oh, Gran, it was awful. I was so frightened . . .'

Louisa, entering the kitchen at this point, gave her daughter a hug, but just as her arm slid round Claudia's shoulders the back door shot open once more and Jenny came into the room. She eyed the assembled company anxiously, then turned to Claudia. 'What on earth were that all about?' she asked bluntly. 'I saw everything, you know. I came up a couple of minutes before you suddenly lit out but I didn't let on I were there because Dónal made hushing signs at me and I could see your arm were in the water and you were concentratin', so I . . .'

'Oh Jenny, it was awful. I thought – I thought . . . where is he now? Is he still followin' me? I could hear him crashin' through the trees behind me and shouting my name . . .'

Jenny sniffed. 'That was *me*, you eejit,' she said, and gave a muffled giggle. 'Dónal wanted to come after you

135

but I telled him to take the fish and go home and we'd sort it all out in the morning. He'd seen that I was there, you know, but he couldn't understand why you shrieked, fell half in the water and then belted off the way you did.'

Claudia stared at her, round-eyed and incredulous. 'He – he kissed my neck and pulled up my hair; he was going to – to . . . oh, I can't bear it! Daddy will have to get rid of him, employ someone else. He tried – he tried . . .'

Louisa had been staring at her eldest daughter, but now it seemed she had come to a decision. 'Sit down, Jenny. Your father and the twins haven't come back from the village yet, but Grandpa Muldoon's in the cowshed and he'll have finished the milking by now. I'll get him in and we'll have a family conference.' She turned to Claudia. 'Is that all right, love? Only you're not hurt, and Dónal is a very good worker and gets on well with us all, so we must talk this thing through before anyone does anything. Do you agree?'

'All right; but he'll have to go,' Claudia said. 'Dónal, I mean. Next time he might . . . he might . . .'

'Hush, my love,' her mother said. 'Go and wash and change, and then we must have the whole story.'

The family convened in the kitchen after Jenny had taken Claudia to their room and helped her to wash and change her soiled dress. Jenny, Claudia and Louisa sat side by side on the sofa, whilst Grandpa Muldoon and Emily took the saggy old fireside chairs.

Jenny, knowing herself to be the only unbiased

witness to what had happened down by the river, looked expectantly at her sister. She was puzzled by the whole affair, thought Claudia had been, to say the least, foolish to behave as she had and wondered what the explanation was going to be. Claudia had tried to explain whilst they were in their room, but Jenny had pointed out that it seemed daft to tell her story twice and had advised her sister, gently, to wait until they were with the family once more.

Grandpa Muldoon began by saying that in Cormack's absence he would, so to speak, chair the meeting. 'You first, Claudia me love,' he said. 'Best start when you reached the river bank, and tell us every detail mind, because in my opinion Dónal's a good young man and wouldn't overstep the mark deliberate like.'

Claudia sniffed, pushed her hair back from her face and began, hesitantly at first, to tell her story. She spoke calmly until she got to the point where she had been lying on the grassy bank, with one arm immersed in the water and a trout sidling up to her gently moving fingers. Then her voice began to shake, though Jenny could see that her sister was doing her very best to describe what had happened unemotionally.

'Dónal was kneeling next to me, telling me I was doing just fine and advising me how to move my fingers slowly, so as not to startle the fish. I – I was doing my best to follow his instructions, really concentrating. Then he said something, I couldn't catch what it was, and I felt his hand in my hair, pushing it away from my neck. Next thing I knew, he bent forward and – and kissed my neck. I twisted and tried to wriggle

137

away, shouting at him to stop, and before I knew what had happened I'd half fallen into the pool. The water felt shockingly cold and I gasped and shrieked and Dónal grabbed hold of me by my upper arms and began to pull me towards him. I got one knee on to the bank and then he put his arms right round me and heaved, but the minute my feet touched firm ground I screamed as loud as I could and gave him a hard push. I think the scream frightened him so much that he let me go and of course I just ran and ran, heading for the cottage. I – I thought he was following me, but Jenny says it was her, shouting and crashing through the undergrowth.' Claudia turned to her grandfather. 'Oh, Grandpa, I was too frightened to think straight, because Dónal is always pestering me and – and there's girls in the village what have had babies because a man grabbed them and kissed them and I don't, I really don't, want to have to marry Dónal. It's not as if I even like him, let alone love him!'

Jenny saw Grandpa Muldoon put a hand across his mouth, and decided that things had gone far enough. She had better speak out before blame was cast in the wrong direction. 'I think I'd best say what I saw when I reached the river,' she said bluntly. 'Claudia's got it right to a point, but what she doesn't know is that Dónal had a good reason for what he did. A wasp had landed in her hair and was actually on her neck when Dónal picked it off with his bare fingers. He was very gentle because he must have known that if he grabbed at it roughly, or tried to swat it, Claudia would get stung.' She turned towards her sister. 'I was standing within

138

two feet of you. I think Dónal was stung by the wasp, because I saw its horrible stripy body curl round his finger. He said: "Oh, you little bugger," but then you fell into the water and what could be more natural than that poor Dónal should grab your arms and pull you out? Honest to God, Claudia, he didn't so much as touch you, save with his fingertips when he was picking off the wasp.'

She looked across at her grandfather and saw him hastily wipe the grin off his face. 'So you see, Grandpa, Claudia ought to be thanking Dónal. If that wasp had got into her hair she might have had half a dozen stings; as it was, she didn't even get one, though I reckon poor Dónal will have a sore finger for a day or two.'

Jenny expected her sister to smile with relief and admit she had misjudged Dónal, but instead Claudia scrubbed at her wet eyes and when she spoke it was reluctantly. 'I truly thought he was kissing my neck,' she said unhappily. 'But, I know you wouldn't tell a lie, Jenny, so I suppose I really should be grateful to him for taking the wasp off me, and I guess I'll have to thank him, only – only I don't want him thinking I'm weakening, because I won't go out with him ever again, not even to tickle trout. To tell you the truth, I don't want to have to face him until the whole episode is forgotten.' She turned to her grandmother. 'We've often talked about my going back to Blodwen Street with you for a little holiday, Gran. When you go home, couldn't I come with you? Then I wouldn't have to face Dónal and apologise for being so stupid.'

Her grandmother began to say that this was a grand

idea, but before she could do so, Louisa cut in. 'I think you should go back to Blodwen Street, Claudia, because your gran is right. I hadn't realised, until this afternoon, how very solitary our life is here compared with the one we lived in Liverpool. I admit you help on the farm, but you have no girlfriends, no colleagues since you have no job, and no neighbours. I think it would be a very good thing for you to go to your grandmother's for a short while. You could stay for a few weeks, see how you like it, and then decide what is best for you to do. If you want to stay in Liverpool, we shall miss you of course, but a girl your age should have a job that she enjoys and a social life too. Why, here you won't even attend the village hops because you say there's no one you want to dance with, and that's about all the social life this area has to offer.'

Jenny stared at her mother. She remembered her friends from Liverpool, the crowded trams, the cinemas and theatres. She adored her Irish home, but now that she had left school she missed the companionship and even the lessons. It would be lovely to have a proper holiday and to meet her Liverpool pals once more. 'Couldn't I go too, Mam?' she asked. 'Of course if Claudia decided to stay, I wouldn't want to do that, but if Gran would see me aboard the ferry I could manage the journey home by myself, I'm sure.'

'I'll talk to your father about it,' Louisa said rather guardedly. Then she turned back to Claudia. 'But I'm afraid, young lady, that you cannot simply run away when something goes wrong. Before you go anywhere, you must explain to Dónal that you don't blame him because you fell in the river and apologise for screaming out and giving him such a fright. I know you don't care for him, but at least you should set his mind at rest, because I dare say he was as frightened as you when you screamed and ran.'

'I don't think he was that frightened, Mam, because he knew I'd seen what had happened,' Jenny said reassuringly. 'As I said earlier, he would have run after Claudia to find out what was wrong, but I told him to go home and said I'd make everything right. He wanted to apologise, saying it was his fault that Claudia had fallen in the water, so I think that was all he was worried about.'

Claudia looked up hopefully and Jenny saw that already her sister was regaining her composure. 'Then if that's all, need I apologise?' she asked. 'Oh, all right, all right, I'll tell him I'm sorry for scaring him.' She turned to her grandfather, giving him a wry smile as she did so. 'Perhaps this will teach me not to jump to conclusions,' she said ruefully. 'Oh dear, I have made a mountain out of a molehill, haven't I?'

Grandpa Muldoon chuckled, but shook his head. 'No, no, it was a mistake anyone could have made,' he said gravely. 'And though it may surprise you, alanna, I t'ink it's a rare good scheme that you go back to Blodwen Street wit' your gran. The truth is, you're too good to be wasted on a farmhand, for you've brains and beauty, to say nothing of sharp wits. What you're lacking is experience, and you'll get that if you go home with your gran.'

*

A week later, the matter had been talked over at length between the two women. Naturally, Emily was delighted with the suggestion that Claudia might accompany her, and quite willing to take Jenny as well, though she did wonder how Louisa would manage without either of her daughters to help out with the twins. But Louisa told her that she and Cormack had discussed the situation, and in addition to Dónal meant to employ his brother Sam to help with the work on the croft, so that Louisa herself might concentrate on the house and her family.

'The twins will be back in school, thank the Lord,' she said piously when her mother raised the question. The two women were enjoying a cup of tea and a slice of Emily's rich fruit cake, whilst the rest of the family were still finishing off their field work. 'And we're doing well enough now to pay the extra wages; the men can manage without me, and Fergal's a great help with the children.'

'Of course he is,' Emily agreed. 'And you needn't worry that I'll let either of the girls come to harm whilst they're with me, because if they want to go out and about when I'm busy, then I'll make sure they go together, or with Danny Callaghan, if he's not at work of course. Despite the Depression, he's doing awfully well and he worships Claudia – or did when she lived in Blodwen Street. What's more, he studies four nights a week at evening classes, and is always eager for a bit of extra money.' She chuckled. 'Claudia's in for a surprise when she sees him again, though, and so for that matter is he. Claudia was a pretty girl, but now she's a downright beautiful young woman, and I doubt whether either of them is prepared to meet the grown-up version, so to speak.'

'Has he got a young lady?' Louisa asked idly. 'I take it he's saving up so he can get married?'

Emily, however, knew better and shook her head. 'No; if you ask me, he's always been keen on Claudia, even when they were only children, and hasn't looked at anyone else since, to my knowledge. He told me he's saving up so one day he can have his own business. D'you remember his Uncle Matthew? Actually, he's his great uncle. He used to own a bicycle shop out at Edge Hill, though he sold it years back when he decided to retire. He's getting on now, must be over eighty, but he and Danny have always got on well. Danny goes up there a couple of times a week and it's my belief the old feller has encouraged Danny to think about going into business for hisself. Danny talks kind of wistfully about owning a bicycle shop too, but of course that's out of the question 'cos he couldn't save up the capital it 'ud need. He's keeping an eye out for something that will suit him, though. He doesn't plan to buy yet, but is looking for a place owned by elderly folk who'll be wanting to retire in three or four years, because by then he thinks his savings will match market prices.'

'A young man with vision,' Louisa said approvingly.

Both women laughed, but Emily agreed. 'Yes, Danny's very ambitious. His evening classes are in commerce, because he's not sure yet what sort of enterprise will suit him best.'

'How odd to think of grubby little Danny Callaghan

planning his future as a captain of industry,' Louisa said.

Emily frowned. 'It's a several years since you saw Danny last; don't be so quick to put him down,' she said reprovingly. 'He's been a good friend to me, has young Danny, and no doubt he'll be a good friend to Claudia as well, because she's bound to feel a bit like a fish out of water when she first returns to the city.'

'Don't forget she's just going back for a few weeks,' Louisa said quickly. Emily opened her mouth to speak, but Louisa continued before she could do so. 'I'm really sorry, Mam. That was a stupid thing to say, because I agree with you. If she can get a good job in the city and you don't mind having her to live with you, then she will be in line for a much better future. We can't offer her the sort of life she deserves, so I'm happy for her to go back to Liverpool. Why, when Cormack retires, we might easily end up back in the city ourselves.'

Emily smiled but shook her head. 'My dear Louisa, you would be mad to exchange what you have here for life in the city. Look at Fergal; he's as good as retired, yet he still does all sorts of little jobs around the farm and enjoys every moment. He'd be miserable in a city, with nothing to do but eke out existence on a small pension. Why, even if he chose to move into a little place of his own, he'd still keep hens and a pig, dig over his vegetable patch and harvest his crops. Oh, I know you'll say he couldn't do the rough digging himself, but I've seen how other old folk manage round here. They either pay a lad a few pence to dig over the ground, or they have a sort of barter system, using their produce instead of money. That way, nobody starves and the work gets done.'

Louisa nodded. 'You're right; neither Cormack nor myself would ever want to leave Connacht Cottage. And of course there's the twins; they'll inherit the croft . . .'

Emily bristled. 'What about Claudia and Jenny?' she asked sharply. 'Is there to be no inheritance for your daughters?'

'Oh, Mam, how you do take me up!' Louisa said, only half laughing. 'Of course the girls will get their share, but it will have to be in money because they won't have worked on the croft the way the younger two will, and the last thing we would want to do would be to divide the land. To tell you the truth, I've been putting money aside for a couple of years now. So please don't think the girls will ever go short.'

Emily got to her feet and patted her daughter's cheek, then crossed the room and peeped inside the teapot. 'Pass me your cup and we'll both have another drink,' she said. 'I'm a silly old woman to even think that you and Cormack wouldn't deal fairly with all your children.' She poured two more cups of tea, handed one to her daughter and carried the other back to her own seat. 'And now, my love, it's high time I was returning to my lodgers and Blodwen Street. Claudia has reassured Dónal that she did not mean to frighten him by running away, and she's said that she's going to Liverpool for a bit of a holiday. He told Jenny that he couldn't believe Claudia would be happy away from the croft, even for a week or two, and I'm glad to say Jenny didn't disillusion him. She's got a crush on him, I believe, though she's so young for her age, so I imagine she won't stay away for long.' Emily looked keenly at Louisa. 'What do you want for Jenny, queen? She's left school, but there's been no mention of a job here. Cormack doesn't need her on the croft and you don't really need her in the cottage, so if she does decide to stay with me it might be the best thing for everyone.'

Louisa sighed, but nodded. 'To tell you the truth, Mam, even if Dónal was interested in Jenny – which he is not – Cormack and I would not like the match. So if Jenny did find work in Liverpool and wanted to stay, I think it would be best for everyone. And now I know you want to plan your journey home. The girls can be ready to go in four or five days. Fergal will drive you to the station, and so long as you telegraph us to say you have reached Blodwen Street safely we'll continue to behave as though the trip to Liverpool is just a holiday, because we don't want scenes from either of the twins, or from Dónal.'

'Why not say a week from today?' Emily suggested. 'That will give me time to get in touch wi' . . . wi' Maria, who looks after number twenty-two . . .'

Louisa laughed. 'Mam, I can read you like a book, so I can! You want to get in touch with young Danny, so he can smarten himself up and meet you off the ferry! You've got a fancy to get Claudia and Danny back on their old footing, and what better way could there be than that he should carry your traps back to Blodwen Street?'

Emily felt her cheeks grow hot and smothered a laugh. 'Well, I did think I'd drop him a line,' she admitted. 'It's always nice to be met after a long journey. Mr Payne's done it a few times, as I'm sure I've told you, and of course he may come down again, but he's not a young man and whilst he can carry my suitcase easily enough, I dare say he'd find three lots of luggage more than he could manage.'

'You're probably right, so you'd best get a letter off in the post tomorrow; several letters,' Louisa agreed peaceably.

Danny thundered down the stairs. As he swung out of the front door, he almost collided with the postman, who gave a startled exclamation and stepped hastily to one side.

'Hey up, young feller! The Post Office always telled us to beware of big dogs, but I reckon I'm in more danger from young men rushin'. And don't you go off 'cos there's a letter for you.'

The postman riffled through the bundle of letters in his hand and gave him an envelope. 'Aha, it's from an old friend of mine,' Danny said. 'She's been visiting her daughter in Ireland; if she's coming home soon, then she'll likely need a hand with her luggage.'

'That's nice,' the postman said vaguely. He grinned up at Danny, for he was a small man, and cocked one eyebrow. 'There's a couple of letters for your mam's lodgers an' all. Stick 'em on the hall table, there's a good feller.'

Danny laughed. 'OK, but I want to get to the office early today,' he said. He and his mother still lived in Albemarle Court but now they rented the whole house and not just the three rooms. Mrs Callaghan had four lodgers and still did a couple of cleaning jobs, though with Danny's wages it was no longer essential that she should work. Danny put the letters down on the hall table and headed for Exchange Flags, where he stopped to open his letter. He knew Mrs Dalton's writing well, since she frequently gave him a list of messages, and tore open the envelope, expecting that it would contain details of her return. She had been away for six weeks and he had missed her, for ever since the Muldoons' departure for Ireland he had visited her regularly, enjoying her company, he told himself, as much as her cooking. Mrs Calvert was always pleasant to him and appreciated his help, but they were not old friends as he and Mrs Dalton were.

Having taken the letter out of its envelope, a horrid thought struck Danny. Suppose Mrs Dalton had decided to stay with her daughter? He began to read, and as he did so he knew that a foolish smile was spreading across his face. She was coming home, and bringing Claudia with her! He had always hoped that this would happen, but had almost ceased to believe it was even possible.

Mrs Dalton had told him that Claudia and Jenny loved the life in Ireland and were happily settled, would not even return to Blodwen Street for a little holiday, yet now she was calmly stating that both girls would be accompanying her, and without a word of explanation. But what did it matter? Claudia had been his best pal . . . no, that wasn't quite right. She was younger than him and boys did not have girls for their bezzies. He had always seen himself as her protector, but now he realised their relationship was bound to be different. She would be seventeen – he was twenty-three – and they had not met for eight long years. But she was still the person he most wanted to meet up with again; he just hoped it was the same for her.

All that day, whenever he was not actually working on long columns of figures, Danny wondered about Claudia. His mental picture of her was as he had last seen her, a child of nine, with a tear-blubbered face, touting an old bag which contained possessions she could not bear to leave behind. He had carried the Gladstone bag holding her clothing and shoes, and he had been fighting tears himself, for it is always hard to see a friend departing for a new life.

Right from the start, he had suspected that despite her hopes of a speedy return, she would not come back to the city. And now he realised, with a mixture of grief and pleasure, that he had been right. Young Claudia had not returned, could not return, for she no longer existed. The Claudia he would meet off the ferry in four days' time would not be the one to whom he had waved farewell. This Claudia would be a young woman, and just how she would feel about himself, he had no idea. He wished, fervently, that he had not allowed their correspondence to lapse, but he had done so, and though Mrs Dalton had shown him her letters in the early years, a great many details of Claudia's present life in Ireland were known to him only by report, which was not the same as hearing them in Claudia's own words.

But, as his mother was fond of remarking, there's nothing so useless as crying over spilt milk. After all, letter writing was a two-way thing. To be sure, Claudia had written four or five times to his once but she, too, had gradually stopped, knowing that if he was still interested in her news he could apply to Mrs Dalton. He had been sixteen at the time and working as an office boy in Cammell Laird's, starting at seven in the morning and finishing late, which left him little time for either writing letters or doing anything to write about.

'Danny! For Gawd's sake, get your coat! It's time to go home.'

'Sorry, Fred; me mind has been taken up with a bit of good news,' Danny said. 'D'you remember, years gone, I was friendly with young Claudia Muldoon? Well, she's coming back to Liverpool and her gran has written to tell me which ferry they'll be on, so I can meet it. I'm made up, I can tell you; in fact I've thought of nothing else all day.'

'Is she pretty?' Fred asked. 'No, don't bother to answer that; she must be a real looker 'cos you never asked me for a share of me butties and you'd not brought any of your own.'

Danny dived a hand into his raincoat pocket and drew out a packet of sandwiches, wrapped in greaseproof paper. 'My God, I even forgot to eat; I thought I was bloody hungry,' he said, unwrapping the packet. He took a large bite out of the first sandwich, grinning guiltily at his friend. 'It's cheese and pickle, my favourite, which just goes to show I've had my mind on other things.'

*

Claudia, Jenny and their grandmother got up very early on departure day, getting dressed as quietly as possible in order not to wake Bernie and Benny, for they did not want the twins to start creating when they discovered they were not to accompany the travellers to the station. Cormack was always an early riser and both he and Louisa were in the kitchen when the girls and their grandmother entered.

Claudia saw that there were already bowls of porridge set out on the table, whilst Louisa was pouring tea into six large mugs. As they settled themselves, the kitchen door opened and Grandpa came into the room. He beamed at them all, then sat down and pulled a bowl of porridge towards him. 'All set, ladies?' he said, reaching for the sugar. 'We want to get away as soon as we can in case those dratted kids wake up and demand a place in the donkey cart . . .'

'Hush, Grandpa,' Louisa hissed. 'If you wake the twins, they'll very likely run behind the cart until you're forced to stop and pick them up. You know what they are.'

'Sorry, sorry, I didn't think,' Grandpa Muldoon said, lowering his voice. 'Have you made their packed lunches? Oh dear, what a stupid question; of course you have. And what about a drink?'

'Oh, Grandpa, even *I* remember you can buy drinks when the train stops at a station,' Jenny said. 'And we're spending a night in Dublin, so we shan't need anything but our butties until we get to Liverpool.' She indicated a covered basket in the middle of the table. 'Mam's packed us no end of lovely things, buttered brack, ham

151

sandwiches, mutton pasties, cake and apples, so Gran won't have to cook when we reach Blodwen Street.' She scraped her spoon around her porridge dish, then leaned over and helped herself to a round of bread and butter. 'Pass the jam, Dad.'

'Oh, Jenny, d'you think you ought to eat so much?' Claudia said, for her sister was as round as Claudia herself was slim.

'It's time you were off,' Louisa said, and Claudia saw that her mother's eyes were swimming with tears. 'Oh, I'm going to miss you girls – and Mam of course – but I shall tell myself it's all for the best and look forward to your coming home.' She got up from her chair and hugged Claudia convulsively, gave Jenny a squeeze and a kiss, and then flung her arms around Emily. Claudia heard her murmur: 'Take care of my chicks, Mam, and take care of yourself, of course. Now let me help you on with your coat.'

Cormack stood up, kissed his mother-in-law and Jenny, and then gave Claudia a hug. 'Everyone has to leave home some time, alanna,' he murmured. 'I know that you're going to try and get work, so mebbe it'll be a year or two before you come back home, but it's for the best. There's nothing for you here, but England is a land of opportunity, even during a Depression. Only – only we shall miss you sore, for there never was a girl wit' a sweeter and more loving nature than yourself.'

Claudia, who had looked forward to this trip with eager anticipation, felt tears begin to form in her own eyes. She loved her father and mother, her little brother and sister, and of course her grandfather and Connacht

Cottage, so much at that moment that leaving them, even for a couple of weeks, seemed impossibly painful. So when Cormack tilted her chin and kissed her on the forehead, she wiped the tears away with the back of her hand and reached up to return the kiss. 'I do love you, Daddy, and my mam and Grandpa and the kids,' she said huskily. 'I couldn't possibly be unhappy with Gran, but if I miss you terribly badly and can't settle, I'll come home, honest to God I will.'

Chapter Seven

Claudia had been looking forward to seeing Liverpool again, ever since it had been agreed that she and Jenny should accompany their grandmother when she left the croft, but now that the longed-for day had arrived she was beginning to have doubts. The journey across Ireland by train was lengthy and tiring, and she was glad to spend the night at Mrs Makepeace's little house. When they boarded the ferry next day she felt much refreshed, but like her grandmother she was a poor sailor and was glad the sea was calm. Jenny was pretty good, helping as much as she could with luggage, tickets and so on, and of course their grandmother, who had done the journey many times, did her best, but still found it hard to understand the rich Irish brogue of such persons as porters, ticket collectors and the purveyors of snacks and drinks for travellers, and grew confused and uncertain. Claudia took over whenever her grandmother looked wildly round for help, and the responsibility, which she had never dreamed would land on her shoulders, did nothing to ease her worries that she might have made the wrong decision in leaving her home.

At last, the ferry set off from the port and began to wallow a little as it met the waves. Claudia settled her grandmother on a bench, with all their luggage around her, and went below to purchase hot drinks. Jenny accompanied her and insisted on carrying two cups of coffee, but though she eyed the doughnuts on display wistfully Claudia flatly refused to buy any food. 'Mam has given us enough to feed an army and you've already eaten more than your share,' she said, a trifle reproachfully. 'The last thing I want is to have you ill on my hands.'

Jenny stared at her, indignation writ large on her small round face. 'Ill? I'm never ill,' she protested. 'Well, not because of eating a doughnut, at any rate. In fact, doughnuts are one of my favourite things and there weren't any in the basket of grub our mam packed up for us.'

Claudia sighed. 'Look Jenny, you know I don't want to throw my weight about, or remind you that I'm in charge whilst Gran isn't feeling too good, but I'll do so if you keep bothering me to buy even more food. You're being downright greedy if you want the truth.'

'I'm awful sorry, Claudia; I didn't mean to be greedy,' Jenny muttered, pink-faced. 'It's just that Gran says we're on this perishin' ship for seven whole hours, so I thought a little snack . . .'

'Oh, darling Jenny, I'm a mean pig. I know you're not greedy, not really; you've just got a healthy appetite, which is natural at your age. Tell you what, we'll go up on deck and drink our coffee with Gran, and eat some more of the food Mam packed, and then if you're still hungry I promise I'll buy you the jammiest doughnut on board the ship. There! Will that do?'

As she spoke, Claudia put her arm round Jenny's

shoulder and gave her a squeeze, and Jenny responded by reaching up and kissing her sister's cheek. 'You're the nicest sister anyone ever had and there ain't a mean bone in your body. And you never said I were getting fat, which you could easily have done, because it would be true, and I know it.' Jenny sighed. 'I hadn't realised what a long train ride it would be just to reach Dublin, and now we've got an even longer journey aboard this perishin' ferry.'

The two girls returned to the deck and settled them-selves alongside Emily. Jenny handed her grandmother the cup of coffee, and as soon as Emily had drunk it she put an arm round each girl and advised them to lean on her and go to sleep. Much to Claudia's astonishment, she slept almost at once and did not wake until the clamour of arrival brought her up with a start. For a moment, she could not imagine where she was or what was happening, but Jenny patted her shoulder in a motherly fashion, having clearly noticed her sister's bewilderment.

'It's all right, Claudia. We've reached the Pier Head and folk are queuing to go ashore,' she told her sister. 'You slept like a baby, so you did, but I woke a good half-hour ago and asked Gran what were the best way to get ourselves and our luggage on to dry land. She told me that we needn't worry about our luggage, because before the sailors let the passengers start disembarking they signal porters to come aboard. They'll carry our luggage and either dump it on the quayside or take it out to the roadway. Gran says that she's asked Danny to meet us at the taxi rank – he'll already have bagged one of the cabs – so we shan't have to hang about or queue. I asked her how much the porters cost, but she said there's no fixed charge. She always gives the feller who takes her big case a bob, but the smaller bags she carries herself. So we'll do the same; I've got a florin out of me purse, ready to hand it over as soon as we reach the taxi.'

Claudia stared at her sister. She had always known Jenny to be practical, and now she realised that she had underestimated the younger girl; Jenny was competent as well. It had not occurred to Claudia to get help with their luggage, even though she had been dreading trying to struggle down the gangway with it, but Jenny had clearly considered what was best to be done and had questioned their grandmother as to ways and means.

She started to tell Jenny how grateful she was, but at that moment they heard the gangway crash down and almost before they knew it a large, red-faced man in uniform was offering to carry their luggage. 'Where d'you want it, missus?' he asked. 'You bein' met?'

Claudia opened her mouth to reply, but the man was looking at Emily, clearly regarding her as the person in charge, and Emily spoke up at once. 'We're being met out by the taxi rank,' she said crisply, and Claudia thought that all her grandmother's self-confidence had returned with their arrival at the port of Liverpool. 'There's three of us, but only two big cases. We can manage the bags, but do you want someone else to give a hand wi' the heavy stuff?'

The man picked up Emily's big case and swung it up on his shoulder, then took the smaller one and grinned at them. 'Don't you worry about me, missus,' he said jovially. 'I could carry twice this weight and scarce notice it. You all set? Got all your bits and pieces? Right, ladies, off we go.'

Claudia seized the straw basket that still contained quite a lot of food, her handbag and her umbrella, and turned to check that they had left nothing behind. Jenny, realising what she was doing, spoke quickly. 'It's all right, Claudia. We've not left anything, and all Gran's got to carry is her raincoat and the little parcel of farm butter which is her present for Mrs Calvert. Follow me!'

Claudia obediently followed in Jenny's wake, but made no attempt to catch her up. Instead, she descended the gangway demurely, but as soon as her feet touched dry land she began to hurry, for she had remembered that the meter on the taxi cab would start running as soon as it was hired, so the sooner they were aboard the cheaper the fare would be. She broke into a trot, her eyes scanning the throng ahead for either Jenny or her grandmother. She began to run towards the roadway and this was her undoing. She tried to change direction, and her straw basket, or maybe it was her umbrella, got between her legs somehow and she went flying, landing with sufficient force to knock all the breath out of her. Seldom, she thought, feeling dazed, had she felt more stupid.

Jenny realised that the young man standing by Gran at the taxi rank must be Danny as soon as she saw him, despite the fact that the last time she had set eyes on him he had been a scruffy lad of fifteen. Now he was a handsome young man. He was wearing a tweed sports jacket and grey flannels, and looked every inch the gentleman; a far cry indeed from the urchin who had taken care of Claudia and had been pathetically grateful for the cakes and buns which her grandmother had given their friends with so prodigal a hand.

Jenny bounced up to him, beginning to give him her friendliest smile, and then realised, rather ruefully, that though she might have recognised him he had no idea who she was. In most circumstances Jenny would have stuck out a hand and introduced herself, but she felt shy of this extremely good-looking young man who had changed so much. In the old days his mother had cut his hair herself, keeping it so short that one could see his scalp. Now his thatch was thick and curly, and cut to show the shape of his head. His eyes, she saw, were very dark brown, with laughter creases at the corners; he had a firmly cleft chin, and must be almost six feet tall. In fact, Jenny guessed that Claudia would be most impressed by the change in her old friend.

Right now, however, Danny Callaghan was frowning as his gaze met hers. 'Who are you staring at, queen?' he asked. 'Know me again, would you?' A look of horror suddenly crossed his face. 'You aren't Claudia . . . you can't be. You can't have changed that much!'

Jenny felt her cheeks grow hot with humiliation. All right, Claudia was beautiful and Jenny knew herself to be plain, but that was no reason for this gorgeous young man to look at her as though she had just crawled out from under a stone. 'Of course I'm not Claudia,' she said crossly and hoped he did not notice the little shake in her voice. 'I'm nothing like Claudia! Don't you remember me? I'm . . .'

'Oh, Danny, I'm so sorry, I should have introduced you,' Emily said quickly. 'This here's me granddaughter Jenny, Claudia's little sister. Don't you remember?'

'He didn't; it doesn't matter,' Jenny said wildly. 'It's eight years since we last met; mebbe Danny's forgotten what Claudia looks like an' all.' She turned to the taxi driver, who had just finished heaving their luggage into his vehicle. 'Something must have happened to hold my sister up. I'll just nip back to the quay and find her, so don't you go drivin' off without us.'

'I'll go . . .' Danny began eagerly, but Jenny cut him short.

'No you won't,' she said smartly. 'You'd likely not recognise her; in fact if you thought *I* might be her, you'd certainly not know her again. But I, of course, aren't likely to mistake me own sister for anyone else.'

Jenny would have set off to find Claudia at once, but Gran caught her arm, shaking her head disapprovingly. 'Let him go,' she murmured. 'I'll be bound he'll find your sister with no trouble. And you mustn't be upset because he didn't know you; after all, as you said, it's been eight years.'

'Oh, all right, you can go,' Jenny said sulkily to Danny's retreating back, but it was doubtful if he heard her, for he never so much as turned his head.

For a moment, Claudia simply lay where she had fallen, feeling the most awful fool, then she began to try to gather her possessions, for the apples and sandwiches had spilled out of her straw basket and were in danger of being trampled by the passengers crossing the quayside. She had just risen to her knees when she felt strong hands seize her beneath the armpits and lift her to her feet, and a deep young voice said: 'Were you saying your prayers, young lady? If so, you could have said one for me while you were down there, because the taxicab meter will be ticking away and we're none of us made of money!'

Claudia stared up at her rescuer, taking in his height, the dark curly hair falling across his forehead and the teasing smile on his lips. 'Danny?' she said incredulously. 'Oh, Danny, is it really you? And fancy you recognising me, because I'm sure I must have changed as much as you have!'

'Well, you have changed quite a bit,' Danny admitted, hooking her umbrella over his arm and beginning to pile the food back into the straw basket. 'But who says I *did* recognise you? I'm your modern St George, I am, ready to slay any number of dragons and rescue a score of beautiful maidens.' He finished packing the basket and took a firm hold of Claudia's arm. 'Now hang on to me, Miss Muldoon, and we'll go straight back to your gran.' He stopped suddenly, looking down at her in some consternation. 'What a fool I am. I never asked you if you'd hurt yourself! You went quite a purler, didn't you? Still, from the look of it your straw basket was the chief sufferer.'

'My palms are a bit sore and my stockings are ruined, or at least I expect they are,' Claudia said, but she spoke

161

cheerfully. She thought Danny quite the handsomest man and was looking forward to renewing their friendship.

As he led her back through the crowds towards the roadway, she decided that to be rescued from an embarrassing situation by Danny, a knight in shining armour, was very romantic. She stole a surreptitious look at her companion as they walked, taking in the strongly cleft chin, the square, capable hands and his air of self-confidence, as well as the crisp white shirt, tweed jacket and smartly creased grey flannels, and the shining brogues on his feet. Danny had indeed come up in the world and was a companion of whom to be proud.

Emily Dalton watched as Claudia and Danny came towards them, both smiling broadly. She was delighted to see that her granddaughter was clutching Danny's arm and that Danny was smiling down at Claudia as though he was proud to be her escort. All through the time Danny had been growing up – and growing better-looking and more self-confident with every day that passed – she had hoped that he and Claudia might renew their old friendship, might even marry one of these days. Now it looked as though her wish might actually come to fruition at last. So Emily smiled on them fondly, and ignored the fact that Jenny scarcely spoke, even though she saw that the younger girl could scarcely take her eyes from Danny. Schoolgirl crush, Emily told herself; she'll grow out of it as soon as she begins to meet lads her own age. It's a pity the child's so plain . . . but she'll change.

162

For the first couple of weeks, the two girls simply got to know the city again. They visited old friends and relatives, enjoyed the delights of having a choice of picture palaces and theatres, art galleries and museums, and spent some of their carefully hoarded money on such treats.

Claudia included Jenny in any trip which Danny suggested, not because she didn't like him – indeed, she liked him very much – but because she had promised her parents that she would not start getting serious with anyone until she had a much wider circle of friends than had been possible in Ireland. But it was difficult not to favour Danny, who was such a very good friend and had such delightful manners and of course was so handsome. Claudia had told him frankly that one of the reasons she had come to Liverpool was to get experience of the sort of life other girls her age took for granted, and Danny had said that he quite understood and would not press for a warmer relationship unless she suggested it.

However, despite knowing that she was supposed to be job hunting, Claudia kept putting off the evil hour. In fact had it not been for Danny she might never have started trying for work in earnest, for she felt herself unable to compete with girls who had already been working for months, even years.

Then one evening Danny arrived in the kitchen of No. 22 and, finding her alone for once, spoke sternly to her. 'If you don't pull your socks up and start applying for jobs, you're not the girl I thought you were,' he said severely. 'Think on, Claudia; you don't want to be an expense to your gran, always taking and never giving, do you?'

'Oh, but I *am* going to look for work,' Claudia said in a small voice. 'And anyway, you know very well that Gran offered to have us for a little holiday . . .'

'Claudia Muldoon, you've been here for two weeks, which is long enough for any holiday, and you've not tried for a single job yet,' Danny said and then, plainly seeing Claudia's embarrassment, chucked her under the chin and grinned. 'Look, queen, this morning I had a bit of luck. I met an old school pal who's working in Lewis's. Do you remember Johnny Franklin? Well, he remembered you. Anyway, I mentioned you were looking for work and he said Lewis's were interviewing tomorrow for a sales lady in Gowns. He's a clerk in their offices and said he'd slip your name in amongst the other applicants, so if you go round to Lewis's in the morning you'll get an interview. It may come to nothing, of course, but it'll give you an idea of how interviews are conducted. Will you do it? I can't make any promises but you never know, you might strike lucky. What do you say?'

The two of them were still alone in the kitchen and Claudia flung her arms round Danny's neck and gave him a hug. 'Of course I'll do it, and I do think you're the nicest fellow in the world,' she said excitedly. 'I don't suppose for one moment that I'll get the job, because this will be my first interview, but I'm sure that once I've got over my fear of doing or saying the wrong thing I'll try for other jobs.'

'You're a good girl; I knew it was just nerves that stopped you from trying for work . . .' Danny was beginning, when the kitchen door shot open and Jenny entered the room.

'Gran's sent me to make a cup of tea,' she said, hurrying over to the stove. 'Oh Danny, I didn't know you were here! Everyone's in the parlour, listening to the wireless . . . the programme's ever so funny; why don't you come through?' She was lighting the gas under the kettle when she suddenly turned to them, her brows rising almost comically. 'What's up? Have you been canoodling? You're standin' awful close!'

Claudia laughed but saw a faint colour rise in Danny's cheeks, and hastened to explain. 'Danny's got me a job interview at Lewis's, so I was giving him a hug to say thank you,' she said. 'It's tomorrow – the interview I mean – so I won't come into the parlour because I need to iron my dark skirt and white blouse. Oh, Jenny, wouldn't it be wonderful if I got the job!'

'Yes it would, because I've been feeling bad about us not paying Gran for our keep,' Jenny said, with all her usual frankness. 'Heat up the iron, Claudia; I'll run upstairs and fetch your clothes down. And if you get the job, which I'm sure you will, then *I'm* going to see if *I* can find work as well.'

'Good for you, Jenny,' Danny said, but Claudia thought his tone was indulgent rather than serious. 'If I hear of anything going which would suit you, I'll let you know.'

'Thanks, but I've an idea or two of my own,' Jenny said firmly. 'Gosh, wouldn't it be grand if we both got work! We'd have oodles of cash; I'd go to the cinema every night and the theatre at weekends!'

She left the kitchen and ran up the stairs, her heart thumping. She liked Danny so much, indulged in secret dreams just before she fell asleep that he would notice her, begin to realise that it was herself he loved and not the beautiful and charming Claudia. When she had seen them virtually in one another's arms, she had felt a pain in her heart and had had to pretend at first that she had noticed nothing. Then, when challenged, Claudia had made it pretty plain that she had only been thanking Danny for getting her a job interview. So that was all right. Except, of course, that in her heart she knew that her sister and Danny would marry one day because they were in love with one another, even if Claudia did not, as yet, know it. But she would realise, and then, Jenny told herself, when all her own hopes had quite gone, she herself might meet someone else, someone who would mean as much to her as Danny did now.

She had galloped up the flight of stairs which led to the lodgers' rooms and now took the second flight slightly more sedately. What she felt for Danny was probably only what they called a crush, or puppy love; perhaps she only felt the way she did because she had always followed Claudia's lead in everything, even falling in love.

She reached the attic rooms and went briskly over to her sister's wardrobe to extract her dark skirt and white blouse. Then she hurried downstairs, humming a tune to herself as she did so. She decided to put in a plea for

166

Claudia to get the job in Lewis's when she said her prayers that night. Every little helps, as the mermaid said when she weed in the sea, she thought, remembering the old saying.

And now there was her own future to consider. She had meant to come to Liverpool just for a holiday, but now she knew she would not willingly move away from Danny Callaghan. Therefore it behoved her to find work so that she could be independent, and then no one would be surprised when she did not return to Ireland.

Claudia walked briskly along Ranelagh Street, heading for the big department store. Her chief worry had been that her right to attend might be questioned, but Danny had assured her that the selection of applicants, according to his friend, had been pretty arbitrary. More than a hundred girls had applied for the job and interviews would be held over the course of two days, with the chief buyer for Gowns making the final choice after the applicants had been whittled down to half a dozen or so.

'There'll be a lot of hanging around,' Danny had warned her. 'But you won't mind that. I believe in such situations girls talk pretty freely to one another. One of my sisters attended an interview at the dairy on Brownlow Hill and whilst she was waiting to be seen, she heard a group of girls behind her discussing another job in a shop the other side of the city. She didn't wait for her own interview at the dairy but slid out of the place, jumped on a tram and got the job before the other girls had even applied.'

On entering the store, Claudia asked the uniformed commissionaire where she should go for a job interview. The man grinned down at her, then waved a large pink hand towards the backs of half a dozen girls who were heading for the stairs. 'Follow them girls, queen,' he said affably. 'They applies for every job what comes up in Lewis's – probably in the other big stores as well – so they'll be heading in the right direction.'

Claudia thanked him and followed the girls. If only she had known one of them, she told herself, she would not have felt so nervous, but as it was she could feel her knees shaking as she began to ascend the flight. However, since this was her first interview, she must simply tell herself that she was doing it for experience.

The girls ascended a great many stairs before they reached their destination and entered a sizeable room, already occupied by a large, white-haired woman who introduced herself as Miss Platt. She told them to sit down and asked them their names, writing them on postcards which she numbered one to ten. She looked a little surprised when she realised that there were eleven young ladies instead of the ten she had prepared for, and asked the room in general whether one of them might have mistaken the day or the time of the interview.

Claudia raised her hand, then hastily lowered it again. She was no longer a schoolgirl and had heard her neighbour give a stifled giggle. 'I'm sorry, Miss Platt, it might be me,' she said apologetically, remembering what Danny had told her to say if she was questioned. 'I had a letter telling me to attend for interview, but it gave no time.'

The white-haired one tutted. 'Well, well, never mind,' she said. 'You may go in when I signal you to do so.'

As Danny had foretold, waiting for the interview took a great deal longer than the interview itself, which was conducted by Miss Platt and two other women. At first, they asked simple questions, obviously designed to put applicants at their ease, but despite her best intentions Claudia fell at the first fence. Once she had given her name and address and produced her school certificates, she was asked to describe her previous employment. 'Whilst I lived in Ireland with my parents, I worked on the croft,' Claudia said. 'I've only been back in Liverpool a fortnight and this is my first interview, so . . .'

One of the ladies behind the big desk raised beautifully shaped eyebrows. 'You've never worked in a shop? Had no experience in retail?' she asked incredulously. 'Then how on earth were you picked for interview, Miss – er – Muldoon?' She frowned at Claudia. 'Are you aware that we had over a hundred applicants for this position? But I suppose someone looked at your pretty face and figure and remembered that whoever attains the position would act as a mannequin besides working in Gowns.' She saw Claudia's puzzlement and explained. 'Two or three times, morning and afternoon, the successful applicant will leave the counter and change into a tea gown or a smart tweed. She will then stroll around the store, and if as a result she sells some of the clothing she is modelling she will be paid a commission.' She looked at her companions, arching her brows. 'If only this young lady had had retail experience, she would have been ideal, but since that isn't the case . . .' She turned back to Claudia. 'Thank you, Miss . . .' once again she consulted the card which Claudia had handed her as she entered the room, 'Miss Muldoon. Please send in the next applicant.'

Claudia made her way out of the store, shaking her head ruefully when the commissionaire raised a questioning eyebrow. She would have liked to wander round the store but thought it wiser not to do so and instead made her way out to Ranelagh Street. Naturally, she was disappointed that she had not even been considered for the job because she was inexperienced, but how on earth would she get experience if no one would employ her? But then she realised that the only job she had applied for was not only at the biggest and best store in Liverpool, but it had been for a very exclusive and well-paid position. If she had known that Lewis's wanted not simply a sales person, but also a mannequin, she would not have expected to get the job for one moment.

In the waiting room she had looked consideringly at the young women around her and had decided that she stood a better chance than most. One or two of the girls were heavily made up, a few were gaudily dressed, and several wore high-heeled court shoes which would soon become uncomfortable, for shop work, Claudia had heard others say, was hard on the feet.

Now, of course, she realised that all the girls in the waiting room must have worked in some shop or other, and had to admit that even the awkward high heels might have been a better idea than her own flat shoes, since mannequins would scarcely be able to show off either tea gowns or smart tweed suits in heelless, though comfortable, footwear.

Claudia turned into Elliot Street and decided to treat herself to a cup of coffee; there was a nice little café quite close by, which she and Jenny had frequented when in the town centre. She would pop in there whilst she decided how best to break her bad news to the family, and Danny of course. She knew they would all be disappointed, but would understand at once that it had been lack of experience that had put her out of the running, and nothing more.

She was about to enter the café when she heard her name called and turned to find Jenny panting up behind her. 'I won't ask you how you got on, 'cos I can tell by the way your shoulders droop that you didn't get it,' Jenny said breathlessly. 'Poor old Claudia. I bet you would have, only Mrs Calvert said sometimes shops won't employ the Irish, because of the brogue, you know.'

'I don't have a brogue; it was lack of retail experience, which means I've never worked in a shop,' Claudia said gloomily, ushering her sister into the café and sitting down at a vacant window table. 'And how I'm to get experience if no one will give me a job . . .'

'But they will!' Jenny squeaked, just as the waitress approached and asked for their order. As soon as this had been given, the girl left them and Jenny continued. 'Look, Claudia, I don't want to blame Danny, 'cos what he did, he did for the best, but if you ask me, queen, you were aimin' at the moon.' She chuckled. 'Set your sights a whole lot lower, as Grandpa Muldoon would say, and in a year or two, when you've got that experience you talked of, you'll be able to try for any job in Liverpool. And get it.'

'That's all very well . . .' Claudia began gloomily, but was swiftly interrupted.

'Just you listen to me, Claudia Muldoon! Remember what I said yesterday, about having some ideas of me own? Well the truth is, I've been doing a bit of scouting for myself, when you and Gran were shopping or working in the house. The little shops – the ones on Byrom and the Scottie – don't advertise in the paper like the posh places do. They stick a postcard in the window saying *Staff Wanted*. There's all sorts of shops needin' assistants. Of course, they may only want someone one or two days a week, or mornin's only. Grocers want shelf-fillers and delivery boys, cinemas want usherettes for evening shows, or matinées of course; stallholders want someone who'll stop kids from priggin' their goods. Oh aye, there's all sorts of work if you look around you.'

'Oh, Jenny, it's sweet of you to look for part-time work, but that wouldn't do for me. I can't go on letting Gran feed me and so on, and unless I get full-time work I shan't be able to pay her even half what a real lodger would,' Claudia explained. 'It's all right for you, because you're just a kid and you can go home to Connacht Cottage whenever you want. Mam and Dad said right from the start that this trip to Liverpool would be a holiday for you, but it's different for me.'

'I'm sure they would say it could be a holiday for you as well, if you found you didn't like it here,' Jenny pointed out. 'Only you do like it, don't you, Claudia?

And you like Danny. So I guess you'd rather stay than go; am I right?'

At this point the waitress arrived at their table with buttered scones and a pot of tea for two. Claudia waited until she had gone and then began to pour the tea into dainty china cups, thinking hard as she did so. She thought of Kerry and the beautiful countryside, of Connacht Cottage and the hard, sometimes back-breaking, work of the croft. She thought of the loneliness, the long journey into town, the only picture palace in the area, which sometimes showed the same film for a whole month. She looked at her hand holding the teapot, with its smooth white skin and delicately varnished filbert nails, and she remembered how different that same hand had looked when she waved goodbye to Grandpa Muldoon as the train had drawn out of the station.

Then there was Dónal, greatly admired by the village girls and considered a good catch, despite the fact that he was known to be a slow thinker. She thought of Danny and his friends, all of them quick-witted, intelligent and ambitious.

But Jenny was growing impatient for a reply. 'C'mon, Claudia,' she said. 'Honest to God, girl, you've had long enough to think it over. Which do you like best, Liverpool or Ireland?'

Claudia laughed and wagged a reproachful finger at her sister. 'Don't try and back me into a corner, because the honest answer is, whilst I was in Kerry I loved that life, and now I'm in Liverpool I love this life. But you're right about one thing; if I went home it would be with my tail between my legs because I'd rather be here, so I mean to stay if I possibly can.'

'Right,' Jenny said thickly, through a mouthful of buttered scone. 'Then you and meself will spend the rest of the day scouring the little shops and trying for work; me as well as you, Claudia. There's a job in Woolworth's for what they call a school leaver, which is what I am, I reckon. I'll try for that first.'

The girls had agreed to meet in Dolly's canny house, so that they could discuss their attempts at getting work over a cup of tea and a bun. They were both so dispirited by their lack of success, however, that when they met they agreed to go straight home. 'I never knew Liverpool pavements were so hard,' Jenny moaned, tucking her hand into the crook of her sister's elbow. 'Folk were real nice, but I were either too young or they wanted someone who'd done shop work before, or they said they were already suited when I knew very well they weren't, 'cos they left their notice in the window, mean pigs! Oh, and I would have loved the job in Woolies, but they don't take on staff what's aged under sixteen. What about you, alanna? Any luck?'

Claudia shook her head gloomily. 'Not so's you'd notice. If I could have settled for part-time work, mind, I'm pretty sure I could have got something, but all the folk offering full-time jobs expect you to have had experience. I did think about lying, but what would have been the point? They'd have found out soon enough when I couldn't work the till, or add up a long column of figures in my head.'

'Never mind, eh,' Jenny said consolingly, as they turned into Blodwen Street. 'We've not even tried the Scottie yet and we've only done one side of Byrom. Tomorrow is another day; we'll ask Gran if she's got any suggestions.'

Emily greeted them cheerfully, saying that she was not surprised to hear that Claudia had not obtained the job in Lewis's. 'I met an old pal while I was doin' me marketin',' Gran told them. 'She told me it weren't just a sales lady they wanted, but someone to show off the clothes on a commission basis. Them jobs is rare as hen's teeth, so I'll be bound half of Lewis's own staff would have applied, as well as anyone with sales experience. Still an' all, you know what an interview's like now, so you won't feel awkward when you apply for other jobs. But where have you been all day?' She laughed and poked Claudia in the ribs. 'Took yourselves off to the cinema, did you, to make up for the disappointment? But I did think you'd come in around noon for a bite to eat.'

Claudia slumped into a chair, kicked off her sensible shoes and began to massage her feet. 'No, nothing like that, I promise you,' she protested. 'Jenny and I have been trying the little shops, mostly in Byrom Street, but we had no luck.' She looked hopefully at her grandmother, who was pouring three large mugs of tea. 'I think I could have been taken on part time, but I wanted a proper wage, so whenever someone said "afternoons", or "five hours a day", I just thanked them politely and came away. I don't know what we did wrong, Gran; Jen tried all the school leaver jobs and I

175

tried the rest, but we had no luck at all. Can you explain why?'

Her grandmother chuckled, handing each girl a mug of tea and then sinking on to a chair. 'Course I can.' She pointed at Claudia. 'You're dressed up fine as fivepence, which would suit Lewis's, but could put off a smaller shop. Then there's your voice, chuck. Your mam didn't want you to develop an Irish brogue, so she made sure you spoke nice, but what with that and your smart appearance I dare say small shopkeepers felt you wouldn't fit in. And you mustn't despise part-time work if that's all that's on offer, because, as you must have guessed, it's experience you lack and you'll gain that in a part-time job, same as you would in a full-time one.' She turned to Jenny. 'As for you, me love, it sounds as though you've decided to stay this side of the water, because you wouldn't be job hunting otherwise, and right glad I am to know it. I expect the reason you've not got work is because shopkeepers might think you were saggin' off school, since to tell the truth, pet, you don't look your age. But all these things can be remedied. Tomorrer, I'll take the pair of you in hand; I might even come with you, point you in the right direction. Have you got your leavin' certificate here, Jenny?'

Jenny took a long draught of tea, wiped her mouth with the back of her hand and nodded. 'Yes. I brought it with me just in case. Oh, Gran, there were a job goin' in a pet shop on Great Homer Street; they said no, but do you suppose they might change their minds if I took in my leaving certificate?'

'I reckon they mostly want boys for pet shops,'

Claudia cut in quickly, anxious not to raise vain hopes in her sister's breast. 'Now why didn't we think of age, Jenny? I'm so used to you being little that I never thought people might think you were only twelve or thirteen.' She finished her tea and stood up. 'Do come up to our room, Gran, and pick out what clothes we're to wear tomorrow,' she said coaxingly. 'I'm sure you're right and we'll both get work of some sort. Yes, I think tomorrow is going to be our lucky day!'

In fact it was not until October that both girls got jobs and were able to write home to their parents with the good news: . . . *I'm working full time at first, though I may have to go to part time after Christmas,* Claudia wrote exuberantly in her weekly letter home.

And Mam, you'll never guess where I'm working, or for whom! I don't know why I didn't think to apply right at the start for a job with Miss Timpson, because you were very happy there, but she didn't have a card in her window or anything like that. Then the other day, as I was passing, I thought I'd just pop in and remind her that I was your daughter, tell her how happy you are in Ireland, and after we'd had a nice little chat I asked her if she knew of anyone needing a shop hand who was keen and hard-working but had no retail experience . . . and the rest was simple. She said she'd had an old employee lined up to work over Christmas, but something had gone wrong, so she was free to offer me a job. Wasn't that wonderful, Mam? The money's pretty good but what is even better will be the experience.

So very soon now, when they ask me where I worked before, I can say, "in a ladies' dress shop".

Miss Timpson says if she can't employ me during January and February, which are her worst months, she will give me a glowing reference and ask around amongst her friends for any work that's going, and will recommend me. Everyone's thrilled for me. Danny is taking me to the flicks and out for supper afterwards. Gran bought me a lovely new blouse to wear with my dark skirt at work, and Mr Payne and Mr Clarke clubbed together and bought me a very smart propelling pencil with indelible leads, so that I can make out bills of sale for the customers.

There is more good news, but you'll know all about that soon enough . . .

Jenny wrote too, though her letter was a good deal shorter: *Dear Mam, Dad, Grandpa and twins,* she wrote.

Claudia isn't the only one with a job!! I am a washer-upper in a huge place on Heyworth Street; it's called Tuttle's Restaurant and Gran used to work there! She tells me it used to be really posh when Mrs Tuttle ran it herself, but it's not posh at all now, quite the opposite. The kitchens smell horrible and there are black beetles under the sink. I get to clear tables, throw away half-eaten grub and stuff that's gone bad, and go round to St John's Market if the cook runs out of something. I start eight in the morning and finish eight at night. I asked if the job was just for Christmas and the woman what interviewed me laughed and said she doubted I'd

stick it 'cos none of their dogsbodies does. Gran says to
keep me eyes open for something better, but at least I'll
be earning.

Take care of yourselves,
Your loving Jenny

Chapter Eight

Despite Claudia's fears that her job might come to an abrupt end in early January, this had not proved to be the case, and Miss Timpson had been heard telling friends that she had been as lucky with Louisa's daughter as she had been with the mother. 'It's downright remarkable the way you've picked up the business,' she had told Claudia when they had been working together for a couple of months. 'I believe you know the price of every garment in this shop, as well as being able to calculate how much we can reduce an item at sale times without harming our profit. And you're popular with the customers, too, which is a real bonus for me because it means we get a lot of repeat business. So you needn't worry that you're going to find yourself out of a job, because you aren't. Why, even Miss Rogers, who came to me when your mam left, wasn't able to take over so I could have a bit of a holiday, which meant that if I were poorly, or needed time off for some reason, the shop had to close. But now I'm confident you could cope without me . . .' she chuckled, 'and not bring my business to ruin!'

'You've fallen on your feet,' Gran remarked, when Claudia repeated the gist of Miss Timpson's remarks. 'There ain't many employers who would tell an employee that they were worth their weight in gold, but that's what your Miss Timpson means, no matter how she may put it. And you enjoy the work, don't you? Not like poor little Jenny, slavin' away in that dirty, overcrowded place, wi' never a word of thanks, no matter how hard she works. But I reckon she'll get somethin' better when things begin to look up; she certainly deserves to do so.'

Jenny herself, however, was not grumbling. It would not be true to say she enjoyed the work, but management was extremely lax and Jenny had chummed up with the other dogsbody, Betty Bright, and usually managed to escape from the restaurant for a couple of hours during the day whilst shopping for anything the cook required.

Betty was a short, square girl with a round, rosy face and a good deal of untidy light brown hair. In fact, she and Jenny were not dissimilar in looks and were often taken for sisters. The Brights lived in Cranbourne Court, off Hilbre Street, which was, as Betty said, only a step from Tuttle's, so they often popped in to visit Mrs Bright on their shopping expeditions, and share a cup of tea and a bun with the older woman. She was a fat and friendly soul, always delighted to entertain them, for there was nothing, she assured them, she liked better than a jangle over the teacups.

Sometimes the girls had to work late, and since they were never paid the overtime they earned they thought it fair to help themselves to either a bag of scones or several slices of fruit cake, which bounty they carried round to Cranbourne Court.

At first, when the manager, Mr Rolf, was asked if the

girls might take home a few of yesterday's scones, he had refused indignantly, but Jenny, who knew how valuable she and Betty were to Tuttle's – for normally washer-uppers seldom stayed for more than a couple of weeks – had argued that it could be thought of as overtime payment in kind. The manager had started to say that this was not on, but had changed his mind when Jenny pointed out that Tuttle's was not the only restaurant needing staff, and grinned instead. 'Well, don't take more than you're due,' he said. 'I dare say them scones would only get chucked away at the end of the week.'

'By the end of the week, the black beetles would have ate 'em, except they'd be too hard for even them to penetrate,' Jenny had said, but she had kept her voice low so that Betty was the only one who had heard.

It was a cold and frosty January evening as Claudia stepped out of Miss Timpson's Emporium on to the crowded pavement of the Scotland Road. Normally, she would have left the premises at six o'clock, but today she and her employer had been pricing sales goods, since both Miss Timpson and Claudia thought that a well advertised sale would clear the shelves for the spring stock which would soon begin to arrive.

A glance at her watch showed her that it was past eight o'clock which meant, she thought ruefully, that she would have missed the meal her grandmother and the lodgers would have enjoyed. She knew Gran would have saved her portion had she been able to tell her that she would be working late, but because of the increasingly warm friendship between herself and Danny they often went out together after work without warning, on which occasions Gran would simply offer her lodgers second helpings. Lately, Danny had been talking wistfully of starting a business of his own when he had saved up sufficient capital. He had taken the sisters up to Edge Hill, to see the cycle shop his old uncle had once owned, and Jenny had said excitedly that she was saving up too, and would put her savings into Danny's venture when he started his business.

Now Claudia smiled, remembering the way Jenny had beamed at them both. She is a dear, and I do believe she's almost as fond of Danny as she is of me, Claudia thought. I'm sure she thinks of him as the older brother she's never had, because I remember her saying, wistfully, when we lived in Kerry that it would have been nice to have had Dónal for a brother. Oh, and that horrible place she works in! She was saying the other day that the customers are beginning to grumble, but Mr Rolf simply tells them that they won't find a cheaper meal in Liverpool. He says that if they want unchipped plates at Tuttle's he'll have to buy new ones and they'll have to pay a bit more for their food. Gran had been outraged, but Jenny had only laughed. 'If it were just chipped plates it wouldn't matter all that much,' she had observed. 'But they're gettin' tired of stale cake and milk which ain't as fresh as it should be in the tea. It's too bad of Mr Rolf, because he's paid a good wage I believe, but poor old Mrs Tuttle has to live on the profits, and I bet she's feelin' the pinch.'

'I thought she'd passed on,' Gran had said, but Jenny had shaken her head.

'No, she's still alive all right. One of the waitresses – she's been there a hundred years and she's got huge bunions or corns or something, so she's very slow – told me that the old gal were took ill and decided to retire, but then she recovered, though she'll never work again. If Mr Rolf don't pull his socks up, though, she'll likely have a heart attack if she comes back to take a look at the place. Why, I've only worked there a couple of months, but it's gone down a lot since I started.'

Smiling at the memory of her sister's frank words, Claudia glanced once more at her watch. By rights, Tuttle's should have closed half an hour ago, and anyway she had heard enough about their kitchens and standards of cleanliness from Jenny to have decided long since never to eat there. She knew the staff were offered leftovers at meal times, knew also that her sister admitted she usually made do with bread and jam or a piece of apple pie, which was Cook's speciality and made fresh each day. However, if she called for Jenny now, they might go somewhere like Fuller's or Lyons Corner House, where they could be sure of freshly cooked food and unchipped crockery.

Accordingly, Claudia began to hurry. She had eaten nothing since lunchtime, when Miss Timpson had sent her to a nearby café for a couple of buns to go with the tea she brewed on a gas ring in the stockroom. The thought of travelling all the way home on an empty stomach was not appealing, so Claudia continued on her way and presently arrived at her destination. As she had expected, the *Closed* sign was up, though there were still people, staff presumably, moving about inside, and when she tried the door it opened and she stepped in.

She realised at once that something was going on. A number of waitresses, still in their rather grubby caps and aprons, were clustered round the man she recognised as Mr Rolf. Others were also present – she presumed they were kitchen workers – and everyone was talking at the top of his or her voice. As she drew nearer the group, Claudia could see Jenny, very pink in the face, with her friend Betty beside her.

Claudia was about to push her way through to where Jenny stood and demand to know what was going on when Mr Rolf banged both his fists down on the nearest table. 'Silence!' he bellowed. 'How am I supposed to know what you're complaining about when you all talk at once?' He turned to an elderly waitress. 'Mabel, what's been happening whilst I was out?'

Mabel was a big fat woman, with untidy grey hair. She wore a pair of old-fashioned spectacles on her button nose, and kept easing her weight from one foot to the other. She's the one with bunions who's been here a hundred years, Claudia thought. I wonder why Mr Rolf chose her to be their spokesperson?

'Oh, Mr Rolf, sir, it were awful,' Mabel quavered. 'I reckons we all knows they come in of a night time, but this 'un were a big old ginger feller, and when young Betty there tried to give 'im a kick he went for her. I see'd it wi' me own eyes, and they say rats' bites is poisonous.'

'A rat! And did it bite you?' Mr Rolf asked Betty,

looking quite unperturbed by the waitress's words. 'I don't believe I can see blood.'

Betty bridled. 'It bit me bleedin' boot,' she said, eyeing Mr Rolf defiantly. 'It hung on like a perishin' terrier, evil little bugger. I never knew they come indoors, though a course we all know they're in the back yard, a-scavengin' for just about anythin' to eat what they can lay their gobs to. I looked around for a hole in the skirtin' board, but there weren't any that I could see, so I reckon someone left the back door open and it just walked in.'

'I see,' Mr Rolf said thoughtfully. 'I could get the council ratcatcher in, or I could put poison down, whichever you prefer, but you must all promise me you'll not say a word about this outside these walls . . .' His roving eye suddenly alighted on Claudia and his face stiffened with shock. He addressed her angrily. 'This restaurant is closed. What do you mean by entering it when the *Closed* sign is displayed? Just who do you think you are, marching in here when I'm trying to have a staff conference?'

Claudia opened her mouth to reply but Jenny, clearly seeing her for the first time, spoke for her. 'It's all right, Mr Rolf, it's only me sister, come to call for me,' she said placatingly. 'She hasn't heard a word, have you, Claudia?'

'Well, I won't have heard a word, provided you really do get rid of the rats,' Claudia said, addressing the manager. 'They carry all sorts of diseases and I wouldn't fancy my sister working in a place where rats march in and out at will.' She gave Mr Rolf her sweetest smile.

186

'But I'm sure you're as eager as I am myself to see that the problem is tackled promptly.'

Mr Rolf heaved a deep sigh. 'I'll contact the authorities first thing tomorrow morning,' he promised. 'And now, ladies and gentlemen, let's get this place cleared up so we can all go home.' He turned to Jenny. 'You may go at once, my dear, and so may you, Betty. I'm sorry for your fright, but the problem shall be dealt with immediately! We can't afford to lose our staff!'

'Gran, you'll never guess what's just happened – well, not *just* exactly, because I've not come straight home, but what happened at Tuttle's this afternoon!' Jenny bounced into the kitchen, talking as she came, then clapped her hands to her hot cheeks and sank down into the nearest chair, gazing at her grandmother with sparkling eyes. 'Go on, guess!'

Gran was sitting by the fire, her knitting in her lap, her eyes fixed on her granddaughter's face. 'Well, since it's four in the afternoon and you don't usually finish until six at the earliest, I'd say you'd lost your job,' she said placidly. 'Though why that should make you all lit up like a Christmas candle I can't imagine.'

Jenny giggled and then did her best to look like a neglected orphan. 'Oh, Gran, you're so clever, really you are! But I've had nothing to eat since breakfast and I'm starving hungry so I am . . . any chance of a snack?'

'There's some cold boiled bacon and a loaf in the crock. Help yourself,' Gran said. 'And then tell me why you're as red as a poppy and grinning like – like as if

187

you'd won the pools. I don't suppose it's that really, but . . .'

'No, it's not that. But Gran, you'll never guess . . .'

'So you'd better sit down and tell me the whole story,' Gran said, as Jenny emerged from the pantry with both bacon and loaf and proceeded to make herself an immense sandwich. 'Start at the beginning as they say, and go on until you come to the end. Was it the rat?'

'You could say so,' Jenny mumbled through a mouthful of bread and bacon. 'The fact is, that old beggar Rolf said he'd get in the exterminators, only next day, when Mabel asked him what he'd done, he tried to put her off and then said he'd bought poison himself, because he knew the old lady – he meant Mrs Tuttle – would have a dicky-fit if she knew what they would have charged him. Mabel's ever so placid, but she told him to his face that he shouldn't have used poison on premises where food was sold and he told her to mind her own bloody business . . .'

'Language,' Gran said automatically. 'Then what happened?'

'Mabel tried to argue and then Mr Rolf lost his temper and sacked her and Mabel stormed out – well, actually she limped out, because of her bunions – and we didn't know where she'd gone; but we know now. She went straight off to the village on the Wirral where Mrs Tuttle lives and told her all about it. Apparently Mrs T knows Mabel very well and didn't doubt her word for one moment. Mabel said she's warned Mrs T before that things weren't right, but the old lady didn't want to interfere whilst the money kept coming in. Only apparently it's been getting less and less – the money, I mean – and what with the rats and the poison she decided it was time to put her oar in. So in she came, without a word of warning, mind, and Mr Rolf didn't even recognise her at first.' Jenny giggled. 'She looks a bit like a witch; very old and bent, with a hooky nose and chin, and wispy grey hair.'

Gran sighed. 'She used to be a handsome woman,' she observed. 'What was she wearing?'

'She was wearing a black fur coat and a big fur hat, and she came in leaning on a stick and went and sat at a table near the back of the room. Oh, I forgot to say she had a feller with her. Apparently he had driven her over – the car was parked by the jigger – so I suppose he's some sort of chauffeur, only he didn't sit with her but at another table, so we didn't take much notice of him until later. He ordered a pot of tea and sat there, meek as you please, drinking it slow, like. Mrs Tuttle ordered tea and toast and just sat there, not even attempting to sip the tea, but staring around her. Then she suddenly got to her feet, banged with her stick on the floor, and told the waitress to fetch Mr Rolf. She said she had a complaint. Mr Rolf was in the office, but he came out and started to apologise in a very smarmy way. He thought the tea must be too weak, or the toast burnt, but old Mrs Tuttle stared at him – she has very bright, piercing eyes – and said: "Rats!"' Jenny giggled again. 'By then the staff knew who the old lady was, because one of the waitresses recognised her, so we were all gathered in the doorway. We saw Mr Rolf's jaw drop and his eyes bulge, and then Mrs Tuttle pointed her stick at the floor. "This place is filthy; the linoleum can't have been scrubbed for a week, the tables are covered with crumbs, you can scarce see through the windows for dust and finger marks and the bread for my toast is stale," she said. Then she pushed through into the kitchen and oh, Gran, it couldn't have looked worse. A couple of the waitresses hadn't turned in – I reckon they'd spoken to Mabel and knew there was trouble brewing – so Betty and meself were trying to do all the kitchen work as well as waiting on when it were necessary.'

Gran tutted, but Jenny saw that her eyes were gleaming. 'Go on,' she said.

'There were dirty crockery and cutlery piled up on the draining board and the sink were full of greasy water. The floor was covered in peelings and grease and the smell was pretty awful. She turned to Mr Rolf and said: "Get your things; you're sacked. I'll pay you to the end of the week and that's more than you deserve. My God, if a health inspector came in here you'd be up in court, and lucky to get away without a prison sentence." Then she turned to the rest of us. "This place is closed," she barked. Yes, Gran, she really did bark and I can tell you, no one argued. One of the waitresses said wharrabout the customers who were already at the tables with their pots of tea and so on, and Mrs Tuttle agreed that they could finish their orders, but then they must leave at once and she would not charge them. Only no one else was to be admitted. Then she turned to us – the staff I mean – and said we'd be paid a week's money in lieu of notice and could go as soon as the last customer had left.'

Gran stared at Jenny. 'But what'll she do with the place?' she asked. 'She's too old to take it on again and I doubt she'll appoint another manager after the way Mr Rolf has behaved. Yet from what I've heard, she's financially dependent on the restaurant so she can't just shut it.'

'Well, she has,' Jenny said. 'My, she's a fierce old lady, ain't she, Gran? She stomped up the stairs to Mr Rolf's flat with the chauffeur and one of the waitresses to give her a hand, and next thing we knew, the chauffeur were chuckin' stuff down the stairs and Mr Rolf, very red in the face, was coming down wi' a couple of suitcases filled to bursting, shouting that someone was to fetch him a taxi. Then the last customer left, the staff were paid off, Mrs Tuttle sort of collapsed on to one of the chairs, and though we asked what were to happen to the place she didn't answer, just glared.'

Gran chuckled. 'And I bet no one tried to insist on a reply,' she observed. 'I wonder what she will do with the place?'

'Maybe she'll sell it,' Jenny said brightly. 'Only if she does, she's got a big task ahead of her because no one would buy it as it stands. Not during the Depression, at any rate. But anyway, I thought I'd best go round to Exchange Flags and tell Danny. Tuttle's is miles too big for a cycle shop, but if Mrs Tuttle means to lease it and isn't going to charge a huge sum – because of the state it's in, you know – then I thought Danny might be interested.'

Gran shook her head doubtfully. 'No harm in telling him, I suppose, but so far as I know he's never even thought of taking on premises that size,' she said. 'What did he say when you told him?'

Jenny pulled a face. 'He said he'd never even considered a tiny café, lerralone a damn great restaurant,' she said ruefully. 'And he said it's far too big for a cycle shop. As for catering, he said he knows nothing about it and was sure Mrs Tuttle would want more money than he could possibly afford. This is his evening for visiting his Uncle Matthew though, so he did say he'd discuss it with the old feller. I remembered Danny talking about his uncle getting a bank loan all them years back, when he started the cycle shop, so I reminded Danny but he just shook his head and said he'd need collateral, or colloteral – some long word anyway – before a bank would even consider lending him money.'

'Oh well, it's a pity in a way, but at least you're pretty experienced yourself in the catering trade,' Gran said. 'Waitresses and kitchen staff are always wanted, so I've no doubt you'll soon be in work again, and at somewhere a lot cleaner and nicer than Tuttle's.'

Danny had heard Jenny's news and had been unable to entirely suppress a sense of excitement, though he guessed that this was probably misplaced. Jenny was a sweet kid to rush straight round to the Winchcombe Assurance Company to tell him of premises which might shortly come on the market, for Danny had made no secret of his desire for his own business. He supposed, somewhat doubtfully, that it might be possible to convert Tuttle's into a cycle shop, but it would be an immense undertaking. What would one do with the large kitchen premises, for example? And then there was its position, halfway up a hill. No, it was good of Jenny to have thought of him, but next time he saw her he would tell her to forget it. Even if the bank agreed to a hefty loan, he would run his head into a noose of debt and find himself completely unable to stock such huge premises with sufficient machines to make it look like a proper cycle shop.

Having made up his mind, he left the office at his usual time and went straight to the nearest confectioner's shop. He had done his uncle's messages earlier in the week, but usually took a bag of buns or a fancy cake when visiting Uncle Matthew, since the old man had a sweet tooth. As he queued for the tram which would take him out to Edge Hill, Danny thought wistfully that it would have been nice to fetch Claudia from Miss Timpson's, for his uncle thoroughly approved of her and enjoyed hearing her chatter of her work in the dress shop. But Claudia was working late, pricing sale goods, so would not be available until later.

Old Matthew Callaghan lived in a neat house on Breck Road and welcomed Danny as he always did, with a fresh brew of tea and a plateful of cheese sandwiches, which they shared. Then Danny, knowing how his uncle would enjoy the story of Mrs Tuttle's descent on her restaurant, told him that Claudia's little sister was now out of a job and explained the reason why. As he had guessed, Uncle Matthew chuckled away to himself, though he had shuddered expressively at the mention of rats, but then he stared long and hard at his nephew. 'Flexibility,' he murmured. 'What you need in business, my lad, is imagination, determination, and a good helping of flexibility. But let me explain . . .'

Danny returned to Blodwen Street in a ferment of excitement, bursting into the kitchen without his usual preliminary knock. He had expected to find Claudia already home, but only Jenny and her grandmother huddled close to the fire, for it was an extremely cold night. They were both knitting, Mrs Dalton with brisk expertise and Jenny with more determination than skill, but they both looked up as Danny entered and Mrs Dalton smiled but shuddered, requesting him to shut the door at once since the draught was cutting her feet off at the ankles.

Danny complied, then burst into speech. 'Where's Claudia?' he demanded. 'I've got such news, Mrs Dalton . . . you'll never believe it! Only . . . well, I wanted to tell all of you, naturally, but Claudia . . .'

'She's working late; she'll be home in an hour or so, though,' Jenny said encouragingly. She put her knitting down with a sigh of relief. 'Want a cuppa, Danny? I could do wi' one – knitting's thirsty work.'

'No thanks . . . well, if you're making one . . .' Danny said as Jenny got to her feet and went to pull the kettle over the flame. 'I've just been visiting Uncle Matthew and I told him your news, Jenny. About Tuttle's, I mean. Uncle Matthew explained a lot of things about starting up a business which I'd not understood before. As you know, Jen, I've really only considered selling bicycles, but Uncle Matthew told me that when he started up he'd not exactly chosen to sell bicycles, it was what the old man who owned the premises had sold. He asked me lots of questions about my savings and whether I knew anybody who could help with such things as buying stock and so on. I told him that I supposed you and Claudia would know quite a lot about such things . . .' He turned to Mrs Dalton, giving her his most engaging grin. 'And I did mention you, Mrs D, because you used to work at Tuttle's, didn't you, when it was one of the finest eating places in the area? I still wasn't sure what he was driving at, because he knows my savings are nowhere near what any landlord would want, even for a tiny place. But then Uncle Matthew gave me a wicked old grin and said, if it would help, I could have the money he'd left me in his will right now, instead of waiting until he fell off his perch. Then he told me how much money I'd be getting! And it's an awful lot!'

Jenny and her grandmother had been staring at him, round-eyed, but now Mrs Dalton broke into excited speech. 'Danny, it's no more than you deserve,' she breathed. 'Forget cycles; it 'ud be far cheaper to stock it as a restaurant. I expect you'd probably still need a bank loan, because there's key money to consider as well as the fact that whilst you were cleaning the place up and making good you wouldn't be earning. But once you got started . . . well, that place was a gold mine when Mrs Tuttle ran it herself and it could be again.'

'I know it,' Danny said excitedly. 'But that isn't all. Back in the old days, Mrs Tuttle and Uncle Matthew were both in the Chamber of Trade and became very friendly. Indeed, when Uncle Matthew's wife was alive, she and Mrs Tuttle were firm friends. So he says he'll arrange an interview between the three of us, Mrs Tuttle, Uncle Matthew and myself, and come to the bank as well when I apply for the loan. He says he'll act as guarantor, if it's necessary. So it really looks as though I might get my own business at last, even though it won't be selling bicycles.'

At this point Jenny, who had poured three cups of tea, handed one to her grandmother and the second to Danny. 'That's the best news in the world, Danny,' she said exuberantly. 'I know I haven't been at Tuttle's all that long, but I've learned an awful lot about the catering trade. Remember, Betty and I were often sent out to buy stuff Cook needed, and Gran taught me how to bake when I were living at Connacht Cottage. As for cleaning, I'm sure Claudia and meself have been doing that ever since we were born, just about. I'm out of work, so I'll do everything I can to help you get straight; Claudia will too, though she'll have to keep her job or we shan't be able to pay Gran our rent.'

'I'll forgo my rent . . .' Gran was beginning when Danny interrupted.

'You're putting the cart before the horse,' he said. 'Mrs Tuttle hasn't said what she means to do about the restaurant, I haven't applied for a bank loan and we've not gone into such details as costs.'

Oh, I can't wait to see Claudia's face when she hears about the money Uncle Matthew means to give me, Danny thought. She had listened patiently, many times, to his plans for selling bicycles, but he realised suddenly, with a pang of dismay, that such a shop would not really have involved anyone but himself. It would have meant that Claudia could stay with Miss Timpson, doing the work she loved, until such time as Danny's cycle shop was up and running successfully. The restaurant – if he managed to get it – would involve them all, and would be very hard work.

Claudia had still not arrived home when Danny finished his tea and took his leave of Jenny and her grandmother, so he decided to go round to Miss Timpson's shop to tell her his good news. To his delight, she was over the moon. Miss Timpson pulled a face, saying that she could not afford to lose her most successful salesgirl, but Danny assured her that Claudia would not be giving up her job at Timpson's Emporium for some considerable while. 'And you must have realised that when Claudia and I get married she'll probably leave you anyway,' he added, highly daring, for though he and Claudia were acknowledged to be "going steady", he had not actually popped the question, knowing full well that Claudia's parents would say she was too young for such a commitment.

Miss Timpson laughed, but Claudia blushed rosily and her big blue eyes met Danny's for a fleeting moment before she turned her head away. She began to tidy up a selection of clothing that had been laid on the counter, and spoke without looking directly at Danny again. 'What's your next move, Danny? Have you given up even thinking about selling bicycles? I say, suppose Mrs Tuttle won't let you have the place? What will happen to Uncle Matthew's money then?' She shot a look at him through her lashes, a look brimful of mischief. 'We could buy a great big diamond engagement ring, I suppose!'

Danny laughed with her, but shook his head. 'No, an engagement ring will have to come later, I'm afraid, queen, but Uncle Matt did say that if the restaurant fell through, then he'd hold the money for me until some other suitable premises became vacant.'

Claudia dimpled at him, then turned a wide gaze upon her employer. 'How about you letting us buy this place, Miss Timpson? You could retire to a cottage in the country; you know, the one with roses round the door, that Danny means to have when he's rich as King Midas, the feller whose touch turned everything to gold.'

Miss Timpson laughed with her but shook her head, patting her neat helmet of dark hair and saying that she did not mean to retire just yet. 'But it's time you young people were off,' she said briskly, as Claudia finished tidying the counter top. 'I expect you have a great deal to discuss.' She smiled at Danny, then went over to the door and held it open for them to pass into the street. 'Congratulations, Mr Callaghan, on your good fortune. I'm sure it's well deserved.'

Little more than a week later, Danny came out of the bank manager's office and joined his uncle on the pavement. 'He seemed pretty keen until he realised that you and I weren't going into business together,' he observed. 'Then I think it was clear he thought I was too young and inexperienced to take on a place like Tuttle's. Even when you explained that Mrs Tuttle only meant to sell us a two-year lease and said that when the lease ran out we could have the option to buy, he didn't seem over keen to give us a loan.'

Uncle Matthew chuckled and patted Danny's arm consolingly. 'Didn't you notice how he cheered up when I explained I would act as guarantor?' he said as they began to walk. 'Of course it would be a good deal better if you didn't need to take out a bank loan and it may mean you find yourself running the place on a shoestring because servicing such a loan doesn't come cheap. But you'll manage it. For a start, you'll have to do all your own repairs, decorating and cleaning up, which is annoying because you won't be able to open as early as we would like, but once you get started . . .'

'Danny! Hey, Danny!'

The voice hailing him was strange to Danny, but he turned anyway and saw a tall blond man approaching, a hand held out and a broad grin on his face. For a moment Danny frowned unrecognisingly; then his brow cleared and the two shook hands and clapped each other on the back. 'Well I'm damned, if it isn't my old friend Rob Dingle!' Danny exclaimed. He turned to his uncle. 'Uncle Matthew, this is Rob Dingle. Rob, my uncle, Mr Matthew Callaghan.' The two shook hands and Danny continued, 'Mr Dingle's the feller who taught me all I know about the insurance business, and got me my very first job at the Winchcombe. We met at the Institute – he was teaching the evening class I was taking – and we got on fine, began to go around together. Only then he did the dirty on me, took a job as purser aboard a liner, jumped ship in America and never, so far as I know, came back.'

'Not until now,' Rob Dingle said. 'But all of a sudden I decided to have another look at the old country. I've done some travelling on the Continent, met people from a score of different countries, and I've come to believe that war will come, though maybe not for the next four or five years; and when it does, I want to be in my own country, with my money safely invested, which is why I'm here.'

'So you've money to invest, young feller?' Uncle Matthew said. 'That means you're in a similar position to my great-nephew here. He's looking for someone to take up a partnership in a restaurant business. Would you be interested?'

'A restaurant?' Rob said, his eyes lighting up. 'I've been in catering, though mainly on the administrative side, publicity and so on. Yes, I'm definitely interested, because there's one rule in a Depression, so far as I'm concerned: folk have to eat.' He looked round him, then jerked a thumb at a nearby café. 'Let's go and get ourselves a pot of coffee and talk this over, no holds barred. The truth is, I made myself a tidy sum whilst I was in the States, and if it simply lies in the bank it won't grow any bigger.' He grinned encouragingly at the two Callaghans. 'I guess this is our lucky day, guys!'

By the end of the month, it was all settled. Rob's money was not sufficient to make him a full partner financially, but the fact that he was twenty-eight and had had considerable experience both in advertising and catering made it advisable to put his name alongside Danny's on the leasing agreement, and Danny was only too happy to agree.

The money that Rob was putting up could have meant that a bank loan was not necessary, but the partners talked it over with Uncle Matthew and decided that it would be more sensible to take out a small loan. This would enable them to hire professional builders and decorators, which would allow them to open very much earlier, and would also mean that Danny could carry on working for Winchcombe Assurance until the restaurant was up and running.

Jenny had got a job quite easily in Dorothy's Tea Rooms and insisted on giving Danny her savings. 'Every little helps,' she said when he told her she should keep her money safe in case their venture failed, 'though I can't see your friend Rob halfway up a stepladder with a bucket of whitewash, or clambering over the roof to fix wobbly tiles, and unless he agrees to help the builders he's not going to be much use to anyone.'

'Don't you like him?' Danny asked, considerably astonished. Everyone to whom he had introduced his new partner had thoroughly approved, Claudia even going as far as saying that she thought the mere sight of someone so handsome and charming would bring customers flocking to the restaurant and thus ensure its success.

Jenny shrugged. 'How can I tell? I hardly know him,' she said flatly. 'Oh, I don't deny he's very handsome, but handsome men worry me.'

'I don't see why they should; worry you, I mean,' Danny said. 'But I do know what you mean when you say you don't really know him, because none of you met him until recently.'

Jenny sniffed. 'All right, I'm sorry; it's wrong to judge by appearances,' she said. 'Does he mean to help the builders, Danny? I heard him saying the other day that he'd been a lumberjack at one time, so he can't be afraid of hard work.'

'He's not,' Danny said quickly. He was fond of Jenny and knew that, but for her quickness in informing him of the trouble at Tuttle's, he would never have thought of mentioning to Uncle Matthew that the place might be coming on the market. 'But of course he won't go for a labouring job. In fact he will be pricing the goods that we'll need when we open, choosing the cheapest and best suppliers, and getting contracts and so on.' He smiled at his small companion, thinking that she looked even younger than her fifteen years. 'Rob may be handsome, but he's no shirker, I promise you. He'll work as hard as any of us.'

'Good,' Jenny said rather absently. The two of them were sitting on a bench, waiting for Claudia to emerge from Miss Timpson's, for they were presently going up to Tuttle's where they would take a look at the flat which had been Mr Rolf's and discuss what they would call themselves when they started in business. 'Are we meeting Rob at Tuttle's, or is he coming here?'

'Outside Tuttle's,' Danny said. 'He's seen the restaurant, of course, but like us, he's not seen the flat. The old devil – Rolf, I mean – took the key with him, and if there was a second one either he had lost it or he took that as well. But I went to the locksmith and got him to cut another, so we'll be able to have a good look round . . . ah, here's Claudia!'

Claudia smiled at them as she came hurriedly across the pavement. 'When do the cleaners start?' she demanded as soon as she reached them. 'Oh, I can't wait to see Tuttle's all smart and beautiful, the way it was years ago, when Gran worked there.'

Danny and Jenny got to their feet and the three of them headed for the nearest tram stop. 'They start tomorrow,' Danny told her. 'Rob will let them in and tell them where to start and so on. But they're a well-known and reliable firm and can be trusted to get on with the work without supervision. And as soon as the cleaners leave, the contractors move in. They reckon a fortnight will see the work finished, unless they come across unexpected snags, that is.' The three of them jumped aboard the tram as it drew up beside them, and Danny, taking a seat between the two girls, patted Jenny's plump shoulder. 'Don't worry, girl! Rob is arranging all sorts of events for our opening, which he reckons may be as early as the end of March!'

Jenny said, rather indignantly, that she was not worrying but simply wondering, which was quite a different thing, and when they arrived at the restaurant and found Rob awaiting them, she said this was a good sign. 'He's as keen as we are,' she whispered to her sister as Danny and Rob went ahead of them into the restaurant.

Although the firm of cleaners would do a proper job, Danny knew that Jenny and her grandmother had borrowed his keys and come in a couple of times, just to clear away the dirt which littered the kitchen. Also, he imagined, to dispose of dead rats and beetles, for they had used the period whilst the premises were not in use to get rid of what Jenny had termed, dismissively, 'unwanted livestock'.

He had said nothing to Rob about the rats, fearing that if his friend knew the reason for the restaurant's closure he might decide to put his money – and his undoubted expertise – into some other venture. He need not have worried, however. Rob had been asked round to Blodwen Street to share their evening meal and Jenny, with her customary brusqueness, had mentioned the rats, saying that when they moved in they would give a home to the largest and nastiest tomcat in the district. Danny had seen Claudia shoot an apprehensive glance at Rob – he was doing so himself – but the older man had merely grinned and said, placidly, that rats were always a problem on food premises and a cat was an excellent idea.

Now, however, the four of them mounted the stairs and Danny fitted his key into the lock. It turned easily and they trooped into a small, square hallway. Surprisingly, Danny thought, it was relatively clean; it was even nicely decorated, with white and gold striped wallpaper, white paintwork on the doors and patterned brown and gold linoleum on the floor.

'This isn't too bad,' Jenny said and Danny smiled to himself at her evident surprise. He knew she had not liked Mr Rolf and had probably expected the flat to be as filthy as the restaurant. However, he pushed open the first door and found a pleasant living room, which was empty save for a square of blue carpet nailed to the floor. He walked over to the window and peered out. The view was not particularly impressive since it overlooked a small jigger and the roofs and backs of a great many buildings, but Danny was pleased to realise that the room was clean and fresh.

'I like this room,' Rob said approvingly. 'Let's have a look at the rest of the place.'

The room next door was a kitchen and here, to their surprise, they found a perfectly respectable gas stove and a very large Welsh dresser. Jenny marvelled aloud how such a greedy man as Mr Rolf had come to leave two such useful items behind, but Rob told her this was easily explained. 'I imagine the gas cooker is on the mains supply, along with the equipment down below,' he said. 'And the Welsh dresser probably belongs to Tuttle's anyway, besides being too big to get down the stairs.'

Next was the bedroom, this time overlooking Tuttle's rear yard, as did the kitchen, and the only remaining door opened to reveal a bath, hand basin and lavatory, once more very clean and new-looking. 'Nice,' Claudia said. She turned to Danny. 'Who's going to live here, Dan? I expect we could get quite a good rent for it.'

Danny was shaking his head. 'Yes, I know what you mean, love, but unfortunately it can't be done since the only access is through the restaurant. And that means it's really got to be either Rob and myself, or you two girls. Of course, we could leave it empty until . . .' he glanced at Claudia, giving her his crooked smile, 'one of us gets married.'

Claudia returned the smile, then looked across at Rob. 'Unless you and Jenny decide to make a match of it, Danny and I are the only ones planning to buy that thin gold band,' she said, dimpling. 'But until we tie the knot, I reckon you two lads had better take on the flat.'

'Why?' Jenny said in an aggrieved tone. 'I'd love to live here, so I would. Why can't *we* have it, Claudia? Someone on the spot, to take responsibility if something goes wrong, would be really useful.'

Claudia stared at her little sister, thinking, not for the first time, how easy it was to underestimate Jenny. She was barely five feet tall, with a dumpy figure and rain-straight hair. She was not pretty, never would be, and she was not really clever, not in a bookish way, but she had a good deal of common sense and the sort of courage to take on a challenge which, Claudia thought ruefully, she herself lacked. When she and Danny married, she would follow his lead in whatever project he undertook, but she would not dream of starting an enterprise off her own bat, far less work in an unpleasant establishment in order to gain experience as Jenny had done.

When she had first heard Jenny outlining her plans for the restaurant that they might run, she had felt a good deal of dismay. Fond though she was of her sister she did not want to share her life with her. She wanted a place of her own with Danny always on call and, eventually, three or four children. In her mind's eye, she saw the cottage with roses round the door, the beautiful flower garden in front and the orchard at the rear. She saw herself serving up delicious meals to her doting husband and adorable children. She even saw Jenny and

Gran coming to visit, praising her husband's aptitude for business and her own abilities as wife and mother. Until today, she had never really envisaged how this beautiful picture tied in with the business which was to make them rich. Yet Jenny, two years younger than herself, had created a realistic picture and one which, if she were not careful, might easily become her own reality as well as her sister's.

Danny broke into her thoughts. 'Well, girls, what's it to be?' He turned to Claudia. 'You're the older of the two, so you'd best make the decision.'

Claudia cast an apologetic look at her sister. 'Look, Jenny, if we take on the flat we'll never be free of the restaurant. I know this because Miss Timpson has warned me about it. She says if you live over the shop then if there is trouble of any description, even another shopkeeper with a lost key or a stray dog accidentally shut into a yard, then it's the person on the spot who gets knocked up by the local scuffers. Oh, I know you think you could cope, but I'm not so sure.'

Jenny chuckled. 'And you've never been keen on cooking or housework,' she said, with a perspicacity her sister found unnerving. 'If we stay in Blodwen Street, Gran will do all that.' She turned to Danny and Rob. 'So now you know, fellers. You're going to have a flat all of your own!'

Both men laughed and Danny said at once that having a place of their own would suit him fine. 'To tell you the truth, I'm dying to try my hand at some fairly simple baking,' he said. He addressed himself to Claudia. 'As you know, my mam don't cook much apart from egg and chips on a Saturday night, so I'm a complete beginner. But if the three of us . . .' he looked apologetically at Jenny, 'the four of us, I mean . . . are going to run this restaurant we should know as much as possible about the catering trade.'

'I know a fair bit,' Rob said, beginning to usher them out of the flat. 'But remember, we're supposed to be discussing what to call our new property. If it had had a good reputation I would have recommended sticking to the old name, but as it is I think we'll have to go for something different. But not too different, so I suggest we sit ourselves down right now . . .' he produced a pad of paper from his pocket, 'and everyone writes a selection of possible names, and then we'll vote on the likeliest.'

Chapter Nine

An hour later, the four of them emerged on to the pavement and waited whilst Danny carefully locked up. A name had been finally agreed upon, though there had been a good deal of heated discussion and much laughter before they made their choice. Jenny had suggested Callaghan's and had not taken kindly to relinquishing her idea. Claudia had wanted something flowery, Rose's, Lily's or Lilac's, and Rob wanted Tootsie's, because he had worked for a short while in a sandwich bar of that name in New York. The final selection, however, had been Danny's own suggestion. He had said, laughingly, that they ought to call it the Mulberry Tree, because there was such a tree, small and feeble but nevertheless occasionally fruiting, in one corner of the restaurant's courtyard. To his surprise, the name had won unanimous approval, even Jenny admitting that it was different.

As they began to make their way along Heyworth Street, Danny put his arm round Claudia, gave her a squeeze and then kissed her cheek and Jenny, following on their heels, felt the stab of pain which always accompanied the witnessing of any show of affection between Danny and her sister. She knew it was silly, knew that Danny would never look at her the way he looked at Claudia, but nevertheless, any overt sign of the affection between them always caused her pain. She cast a quick glance at Rob, hands in pockets, whistling a popular melody beneath his breath, and envied him his indifference. It was all very well to tell herself that Danny was Claudia's and always would be; that did not stop the pain she felt when she was forced to recognise that the man she loved, loved another.

Presently, the couple ahead came level with Percy Crabbe's jeweller's shop and stopped, just as Jenny knew they would, so that Claudia might peer into the window, checking that a small sapphire ring which she particularly admired had not yet been sold. Jenny knew that Danny had offered to put a deposit on the ring, which he had promised to buy for Claudia as soon as he could afford to do so, but her sister had said this was not necessary. Jenny had applauded her decision because it put off the painful moment when the couple would become officially engaged. But when she had told her friend Betty, expecting the other girl to praise Claudia's courage – for the ring might disappear from the window any day – Betty had scoffed at the idea. 'Likely she thinks Danny will get rich when the restaurant opens and buy her an even bigger sapphire,' she had said mockingly. 'He's nice that Danny; bet he kisses lovely.'

The two girls had been washing up in Dorothy's Tea Rooms, for as soon as she had obtained a position in that delightful café Jenny had told the proprietor, Miss Entwistle, that Betty was also looking for work. Miss Entwistle had given her a week's trial and at the end of the week had offered her full-time work. Of course

Miss Entwistle must suspect that both her new kitchen workers would leave her when the new restaurant opened up, but washer-uppers seldom stayed long in any particular establishment and with unemployment levels in Liverpool some of the highest in the country, she would have no difficulty in filling the vacant posts.

Now, however, Rob pulled Jenny to a halt outside the jeweller's shop, and gave her a nudge. 'Look at those two!' he whispered. 'Good job you and meself aren't mooning around, gazing into each other's eyes, because talking to Danny when Claudia's around is wasted effort.' He gave Jenny's arm a little squeeze and grinned down at her, and Jenny reflected that it was impossible not to like him, if only for his enthusiasm. 'I reckon you and meself will be doing all the arranging for our grand opening, so we'll have a meeting just as soon as the decorators finish and we can see our way clear for beginning our plans. As you know, I was in advertising for a couple of years in New York, and I can tell you, if we do the job right we'll have customers queuing up to come in.'

'That sounds wonderful, but what'll it cost?' Jenny asked. 'Even quite a little advertisement in the *Echo* is expensive. I know because one of their sales people who's doing a full page spread over Easter for local businesses came round to the tea rooms to ask Miss Entwistle to take part, and she wouldn't. She said she had better things to spend her money on and anyway it was too pricey by half.'

'Good,' Rob said approvingly. He grinned. 'Less competition, you see. In the States there's a saying which

I'll bet your Miss Entwistle has never heard: "speculate to accumulate". You and I, Jenny, will have to bear it in mind, because the lovebirds . . .' he jerked his head at Claudia and Danny, still gazing into the jeweller's window, 'won't want to bother with anything as mundane as advertising.'

Jenny was flattered to be treated as a person of sense by someone as experienced as her companion. She still thought him too good-looking to be entirely trustworthy, but he was rapidly gaining ground in her mind as being a practical person, similar to herself. However, she was not at all sure what his words had meant, and was sensible enough to say so. 'Speculate to . . . what? And what the devil does it mean?' she asked, trying to keep a peevish note out of her voice and not quite succeeding. 'It must be an American expression . . . well, that was what you said, wasn't it?'

'It means you have to spend money to get more,' Rob said, but at that moment the couple before them turned away from the window and began to walk again, only now Danny's arm was round Claudia's shoulders and her head leaned close to his. *Pang*, went the little pain in Jenny's heart and she hastily started to talk about the restaurant, to wonder how long it would be before they could begin to stock the two big pantries and to make good the furniture.

'Not long really,' Rob said reassuringly. 'In fact when the decorators begin work, I'll tell them to start on the pantries first. Once the shelving has been finished and the refrigerators installed, we can start getting stock in.'

'I suppose that will be our biggest expense,' Jenny

said thoughtfully, remembering how Gran always advised her to try several shops when doing her messages, in order to get the best bargains.

Rob began to acknowledge the truth of this, then seemed to change his mind and shook his head. 'No, no, don't let me down by falling into a popular misconception,' he said, and Jenny wished he would not use such long words. 'What's the use of producing wonderful food if no one's there to eat it? Advertising, my dear child, is essential if a new business is to succeed. Remember, Liverpool is full of dining rooms, cafés, tea rooms and canny houses. We'll be in competition with all of them, so unless we advertise successfully we could go under without a trace.'

Jenny stared at him, round-eyed with horror. 'I thought if we provided really good food, the place was clean and pleasant and the service was quick, we couldn't fail,' she quavered. 'What'll we do if Danny and Claudia think advertising is a waste of our capital?'

Rob laughed. 'What would you have thought about advertising before this conversation?' he asked.

'Before this . . . oh, I see what you mean. I'd have thought it a waste of money,' Jenny admitted frankly.

Rob gave her his glinting smile and Jenny returned it, realising what the question – and her answer – implied. 'I'll tell them just what I've told you,' Rob said. 'Claudia knows the importance of a first-rate window display and an advertisement in the *Echo* when her boss is going to have a sale. As for Danny, he admires the know-how I picked up in the States and will go along with my ideas, once I've explained them to him. And now tell me about this cook who knows your gran, and is looking for work.'

Claudia and Danny had dropped back to walk with the other couple and Claudia answered the question for her sister. 'Oh, Mrs Bland, you mean. She's plays whist with Gran and used to work at Dorothy's Tea Rooms, but of course they don't do proper meals, only teas, coffees and light snacks, so she left. She's over fifty, just, which isn't a good age to look for work, but she's an excellent cook, can turn her hand to anything, and has already agreed to come to Tuttle's – I mean the Mulberry Tree – for an interview, as soon as we begin taking on staff.'

'If she's so good, why on earth did she leave the tea rooms?' Rob asked suspiciously. 'Oh, I appreciate that baking scones and that isn't the sort of work she's trained for, but surely any job is better than none?'

This time it was Danny who answered him. 'Mrs Bland has an older sister who has a canny house down by the docks. She's been helping out there and probably earning as much as Miss Entwistle could pay, though nowhere near the sort of money she'll get from us.'

'Right,' Rob said, apparently satisfied. 'What about waitresses, though? I gather from Jenny here that getting kitchen workers will be no problem, but our waitresses must be quick and smart, just like the nippies at Lyons Corner House.' He turned to Claudia. 'What about uniforms? You're the dress expert, so don't go suggesting black dresses, white collars and cuffs and frilly aprons. We want something striking and original . . .'

Claudia laughed. 'And cheap as chips,' she cut in.

'The good thing about little black dresses is that they are cheap, made in all sizes and worn by most waitresses, so proprietors expect them to provide their own uniform. If they move to another restaurant, they simply take it with them.'

Rob pulled a face. 'Mundane, boring,' he muttered. 'I fancied buttercup yellow.'

This remark was met with howls of derision from the other three. 'How like a man,' Claudia remarked, giggling. 'Imagine a splash of tomato soup or raspberry jam on a bright yellow dress! Honestly, Rob, you're mad as a March hare.'

Danny agreed but said thoughtfully that Rob had a point. 'We must be practical, but we'll want the girls to look different, too,' he said. 'How about maroon dresses, or navy blue, come to that?'

'You're as daft as your pal,' Claudia said at once. 'They'd be expensive, and the restaurant would have to buy them; we couldn't expect waitresses to use their own money on dresses which they couldn't take with them when – if – they left. Tell you what, though, if we have black dresses, I dare say we might find someone who could supply pink frilly aprons, and though I doubt any one sells pink collars and cuffs we could dye them to match the aprons ourselves, I suppose.'

Jenny snorted. 'Thank God I'm not going to be waiting on,' she said devoutly. 'All a kitchen worker needs is a huge canvas apron; we can wear whatever we like underneath.'

Danny shook his head at her. 'No way, Miss Clever-Clever Muldoon,' he said. 'You'll have to wear waiting on uniform so that you can take over a few tables if we get really busy.'

Jenny began to protest just as they reached Blodwen Street. The four of them burst into the kitchen all talking at once and Gran, zealously knitting, wagged a reproving finger at them, and got rather stiffly to her feet. 'I'll make a brew, because I reckon the walk will have given you a thirst,' she said. 'Jenny, my dear, there's a batch of shortbread in the pantry; fetch it out and hand it round and then one of you – just one – can tell me what you've decided to call poor old Tuttle's.'

Jenny had been worried right from the start of the partnership that Rob might not pull his weight, but it soon became obvious that, good-looking or not, he was a worker, not a shirker. Once the cleaners and contractors had moved out and the decorators had moved in, Rob requested that either she or Claudia might give up what he called their "day job" in order to help him stock the shelves and arrange the new kitchen equipment. 'If I do it, you'll find yourselves scaling ladders twenty times a day to fetch sugar or flour off the highest shelves, whilst something that you'll hardly ever use – tins of black treacle or boracic powder – will be handy and within easy reach.'

Both Jenny and Claudia realised that this made sense and told Rob that they would talk it over and decide which of them would give up work, though Jenny guessed that it would be herself. Claudia earned almost twice as much as Jenny and loved the dress shop, and she acknowledged freely that, never having worked in catering, she could not possibly be as useful an assistant to Rob as the younger girl.

The girls discussed the whole matter thoroughly, and Jenny was amazed when Claudia admitted that she hoped to keep her job on, even when the restaurant was open. They were in their bedroom in Blodwen Street and keeping their voices low, since Gran occupied the attic room next to their own and might not yet be asleep.

'But Claudia, surely you know that Danny and Rob need you to sit in the cash booth, taking the money, giving change and so on?' Jenny said. 'Surely you don't mean to let them down?'

'It won't be letting them down, silly, because I mean to give them some of my salary, then they can employ someone else,' Claudia said rather stiffly. 'I love my job, you know I do, and it's a really good one. If I give it up and the Mulberry Tree fails, I'd be out of work and utterly miserable. It's not fair to expect me to risk everything . . .'

'But we're all risking everything,' Jenny said, hotly, forgetting to speak quietly in her indignation. 'I'm going to leave Dorothy's, Danny's already handed in his notice at the Winchy, and Rob's been living on what's left of his savings whilst he sorts out our suppliers. Why should you be any different?'

'Oh, Jenny, do keep your voice down,' Claudia hissed. 'I've already explained. Can't you try to understand how important it is that at least one of us has a regular wage coming in? And besides, from what Rob says, we'll know within three or four days, or maybe a week, whether the restaurant will sink or swim. If it swims, then of course I'll give up my job and come in on the cash desk, but if it sinks . . .'

'It won't,' Jenny said vehemently. 'Have you told Danny that you don't mean to leave Miss Timpson's? Because if you haven't, you'd better do so at once. Oh, Claudia, do think again! You can't have Rob or Danny on the cash desk; it would look bad. They own the business, after all. Who else is there that they can trust? I'm an awful poor hand at arithmetic meself, I'd make all sorts of mistakes, and if you're thinking Gran could do it for a week or so, then you're out there.' Belatedly, she lowered her voice. 'She's too perishin' old,' she whispered. 'There'd be a queue a mile long just to pay for teas!'

The two girls stared at one another across the lamplit room, then began to undress without exchanging another word. It was only when they were both between the sheets that Claudia spoke again. 'Oh, all right, Jenny, you've made your point. I suppose I was being a bit selfish, though I didn't mean . . .'

Jenny leaned up on her elbow and smiled lovingly at her sister. 'You aren't selfish, you just hadn't thought,' she murmured. 'Only think what a lot this venture means to Danny. He's put all his money into it and all his hopes, and he's doing it for you, Claudia, as much as for himself. It's his way of giving you them roses round the door that you used to talk about.'

Claudia smiled sleepily across at her sister. 'You've got a head on your shoulders, Jenny Muldoon,' she said. 'You're only a kid and you may say you aren't clever, not in a bookish way, but you've got your head screwed on right. I'll give in my notice to Miss Timpson as soon as I get to work tomorrow, and I'll start sorting out what I'll wear, because I don't mean to look like a waitress. After all, I'm going to marry the proprietor. I rather fancy a neat little two-piece costume . . .'

Jenny giggled. 'In buttercup yellow of course,' she said. 'Night, night, Claudia; sweet dreams!'

'Well, Miss Jenny, I reckon we've done a grand job betwixt the pair of us.' Mrs Bland smiled, first at Jenny and then at the pantry, neatly stocked with everything she would need for the great cooking marathon which was about to start.

Jenny smiled back. 'I guess you've hit the nail on the head, Mrs Bland,' she said, imitating Rob's slight American accent. 'Gee whizz, wait until my gran sees the place. We've not let her come down whilst work was still being done so her reaction will be extremely interesting.' She had been staring into the pantry but now she turned to the cook. 'It's a good thing Rob agreed when I said we ought to involve you in the early stages, though. Left to myself I'd have got things all wrong, I know I would.'

'Ah well, I've been in catering nigh on forty years,' Mrs Bland said placidly. 'Have you heard Mr Dingle's latest idea? He wants me to make gingerbread men for the kids . . . I ask you! I telled him kids round here don't have the money for fancy bakin', but he says they'll be give away at the opening. Oh, not just to any kid, only to those that come in with their mams and grans.'

'I suppose it's fair enough,' Jenny said, having given

the matter some thought. 'Their parents will be getting a free morning bun for the first couple of days. I thought the free buns would be just for the opening, but Rob says that won't do. He's a great believer in what he calls "word of mouth", and he says folk will tell their pals they were given a free bun; then the pals will come in the following day and he doesn't want them disappointed.'

Mrs Bland nodded slowly. 'He's right there,' she observed as the two of them turned back into the spotless kitchen. 'To tell you the truth, Miss Jenny, I'm that excited over Saturday and eager to see how it works out that you'd think I had money in the venture meself. And now, if you'll fetch me all the stuff I'll need for gingerbread men, I'd best get started.'

'Right you are,' Jenny said, returning to the pantry and beginning to select various ingredients which she carried thoughtfully back to the cook. She looked at the older woman, hesitated, then plunged into speech once more. 'Only I know when Mr Dingle suggested that you might start baking scones and morning buns today, you wouldn't do it; you said they should be made fresh each morning. What's different about gingerbread?'

Mrs Bland laughed. She was a fat, comfortable woman with grey hair worn in a bun on top of her head, shrewd little eyes and a mouth which smiled most of the time. Now, pouring treacle and brown sugar into a large pan, and adding margarine from the wooden tub, she shook her head reprovingly at Jenny. 'Fancy me old pal Emily's granddaughter sayin' such a thing,' she marvelled. 'Gingerbread men is really gingerbread biscuit, and biscuits don't go stale the ways scones and buns would. So I can make them well in advance, see?'

Jenny giggled. 'Gran would have known,' she said remorsefully. 'I don't think she's ever made gingerbread men, but she'd have known. Now what else can I do for you, Mrs Bland? Oh, I can't wait for the grand opening!'

Gran, Claudia and Jenny met at seven o'clock in the kitchen of No. 22 Blodwen Street, for opening day had come at last and they were all both excited and apprehensive. Gran had been shown over the now completely refurbished restaurant the previous day, and had been satisfyingly impressed. She had admired everything, even the flat, and had actually offered to come in a couple of times a week to clean it, since in Gran's opinion the man wasn't born who could do housework.

Danny had demurred, saying that he was sure he and Rob could manage, but Gran had been firm. 'I looked in your cupboards under the sink and you've got no cleaning materials, norreven some Vim or a duster,' she had said accusingly. 'Besides, the pair of you will be that busy with the Mulberry Tree that you'll scarcely have time to make yourselves a meal, lerralone tidy up.'

They had been standing in the flat's small kitchen at the time and Danny had given her a hug. 'It's real good of you, Mrs Dalton, and we'd be glad of your help,' he said. 'Only we shan't be doing much cooking because I reckon we'll have most of our meals in the restaurant ...'

'Not breakfast,' Rob had cut in quickly. 'We'll be making our own breakfast.' He had rubbed his hands together gleefully. 'I fancy big piles of scrambled eggs and lots of crispy bacon, followed by toast and marmalade and coffee.'

'You greedy pig . . .' Jenny had been beginning when she saw Claudia shaking her head and stopped abruptly. 'Sorry, Rob; I were treating you like one of the family.'

Rob had grinned at her. 'It's all right, queen, I only said it to get a rise out of Danny. He's a tea and toast man and I guess if I'm to make it myself, then tea and toast will suit me too.'

As they had descended the stairs, Danny had leaned forward and tapped Gran's shoulder. 'My mam made a similar offer to yours. Maybe you could work out a sort of rota, because to be honest, neither Rob nor myself know much about housework, so we'd be really grateful for any help.'

Now, Gran took her coat off the back of the door, put it on and looked around the kitchen. 'Mr Payne and Mr Clarke have agreed to make themselves tea and toast this morning,' she said, ushering the two girls out into the greyness of early morning. They meant to walk to the restaurant, for at this hour the trams would be crowded with people going to work and anyway to get from Blodwen Street to the Mulberry Tree meant a change of trams, whereas if they cut through the back streets they could be there in good time.

Danny and Rob had taken up residence in the flat the evening before, so it would be they who opened up. Mrs Bland, Jenny's friend Betty, and two other kitchen workers would turn in by half past seven to prepare for the grand opening. The trio emerged into Heyworth

Street and paused, looking critically at the Mulberry Tree. 'The fellers are up already,' Claudia murmured. 'The lights in the kitchen are on and they've put the tubs of daffodils and early tulips out – don't they look nice!'

Jenny, who knew that the tubs of spring flowers had been Danny's idea, agreed fervently. She liked Rob well enough now that she knew him better, but he still came a long way behind Danny in her estimation. To be sure, all the ideas for advertising the Mulberry Tree had come from Rob, but she told herself defiantly that this was a small contribution compared to Danny's, for the younger man had done a good deal of what Jenny thought of as 'the donkey work' which Rob's bright ideas generated. It was Danny who had slogged round the residential streets, pushing leaflets through letter boxes, informing everyone within three miles of the restaurant that there was to be a grand opening, that a jazz band would play and a well-known group of Morris dancers would give a display. Furthermore, Danny had got Gran to give him cookery lessons, but when it had been suggested to Rob that he, too, might benefit from Gran's help, he had said it was not his scene. 'I've always been more on the admin side,' he had said, 'and if either Danny or myself have to start cooking it will be a sign of failure, because proprietors of restaurants do not cook.' He had grinned at Jenny and Claudia, who had made the suggestion. 'And my vocabulary does not include the word "failure",' he had ended.

Jenny had tried to explain that Danny was only learning to cook so that he might be useful if an emergency occurred, but Rob had waved this aside. 'That's what you are employed to do, my little pumpkin,' he had said, pinching Jenny's round, pink cheek. 'I know you class yourself as washer-upper and general dogs-body, but we think of you as our deputy chef.'

This had caused Claudia to go off into a hoot of laughter and Jenny's own lips had twitched as she imagined herself in the checked trousers, smart white jacket and huge hat of the true chef. She had not explained this to Rob, however, merely remarking: 'If I'm a pumpkin, wack, then you're a perishin' cucumber.'

Now, however, Gran pushed open the restaurant door and wended her way through the tables towards the kitchen whilst Jenny, who had entered last, held the door open for Betty and the other two kitchen workers, who were hurrying along the pavement and gesturing wildly. Together, they joined the others in the kitchen. Mrs Bland was already hard at work, weighing, measuring, stirring and spooning the result on to baking trays. Her cheeks were glowing and she smiled round at them before beginning to issue orders so fast that Jenny could scarcely take them in. She heard enough, however, to realise that Mrs Bland was taking it for granted that everyone present had come in early to help with the cooking.

She, Gran, Betty and the other two girls enveloped themselves in the big calico aprons hanging on hooks to one side of the kitchen. But Claudia wandered back into the restaurant itself, saying over her shoulder: 'Where are the lads? I made sure they'd be working hard by the time we arrived.'

Mrs Bland looked up. 'Mr Callaghan's gone to buy balloons; Mr Dingle suddenly remembered he'd meant to get some but had forgotten,' she said rapidly. 'And Mr Dingle's gone upstairs for something; he won't be a moment.'

Almost as though he had heard, Rob appeared at this point. He was grinning from ear to ear and looking very pleased with himself. He was also carrying a very large handbell and a pile of the menus which he and Danny had had duplicated earlier. Claudia looked across at him, her brow wrinkling. 'What have you thought of now?' she asked resignedly.

'Wait and see,' Rob told her. 'It's to be a surprise.'

Chapter Ten

March 1937

By the time they closed the restaurant after the grand opening, Jenny and Claudia were exhausted and longing for their beds. Gran had stayed the course manfully until two in the afternoon, when Danny had thanked her with true gratitude for all she had done and bundled her into a taxi. 'You've got your lodgers to think of, to say nothing of your poor feet,' he had said. 'I only hope you're not so tired that you won't be able to sleep tonight.'

Gran had laughed. 'I'm not such a poor thing,' she had assured him, 'and I wouldn't have missed it for the world.'

But of course, no matter how tired they might have been, Jenny and Claudia, along with most of the rest of the staff, had to stay until the bitter end. Not, Jenny thought now, as they entered their grandmother's kitchen, that there had been anything bitter, about either the end or the beginning. It had been a positive triumph. Right from the moment that they had opened the doors to the public, things had gone just as Rob had predicted. People had seen the jazz players in their brightly striped trousers, little red jackets and crisp white shirts playing their instruments on the broad pavement outside the

Mulberry Tree, and had come over for a closer look. Once nearer, the lure of a free morning bun with every cup of coffee purchased had persuaded shoppers to enter the gleaming new premises, and those with children much appreciated the gingerbread men. Jenny, having to wait on when every table was full and there was a short queue of people waiting for a seat, had heard two of the customers talking and had smiled to herself.

'No expense spared,' the first woman had said to her friend, in an awed voice. 'Did you get a look at the menu? I thought it 'ud be pricey but I were wrong. Every Monday, me and Sissy meets in Lyons for a chat over beans on toast and a pot o' tea, but next Monday we'll come here; why not? For threepence more than we pay at Lyons we can have steak pie and chips here.'

Jenny repeated this conversation now to Claudia and was pleased when her sister gave a little jump, squeaked with excitement, then hugged her. 'Oh, Jenny, love, I do believe it's going to work,' she breathed. 'I can almost feel that sapphire ring sliding on to my finger.'

'Yes, I'm sure you're right,' Jenny said, trying to ignore the usual little pang. 'And I suppose that means you and Danny will be getting married quite soon, and moving into the flat . . .'

'Oh, I wouldn't say that,' Claudia said quickly. 'Of course I don't mind living in the flat with Danny at first. Then one day, when we've made lots of money, Danny and myself can have that cottage with roses round the door . . . only I guess we'll have to save up really hard before then.'

Jenny nodded. 'And anyway, you're awful young to

get married,' she said, trying to hide her feeling of relief. I am so stupid, she told herself, because Danny and Claudia *are* going to get married one of these days and even if they weren't, Danny would never look at me twice. But at least now that the restaurant is open I'll be seeing him every day.

The two girls had taken off their coats and Claudia had gone to the cupboard under the sink to fetch out a couple of hot water bottles, for though the kitchen was warm enough both girls knew their attic bedroom would be freezing. Claudia paused, looking back at the kettle standing on the hob. 'Do you want a hot drink?'

Jenny shook her head. 'No thanks. I've been drinking tea and coffee all day. But what about you? Stuck behind the cash desk, you probably didn't have my opportunities.'

'Did I not? That's what you think,' Claudia said derisively. 'Rob and Danny were so worried I might not enjoy my work that they plied me with all sorts; even offered to take over so I could have a proper meal at a proper table. So you see, I fared just as well as the rest of you.'

Once in their bedroom, the girls bundled out of their clothes and into their night things, shuddering at the cold, then collapsed between the sheets, Jenny reflecting that it was the first time she had had a chance to think, coolly and objectively, about their wonderful day.

Snuggling down, she let her mind travel back. Yes, it had been a success far beyond her wildest dreams – beyond those of Danny and Claudia, too, though she suspected that Rob, who had planned the day so carefully, was not as astonished as his fellow partners. Jenny paused in her thoughts to savour the word, for to Danny's relief and on the advice of the solicitor who had drawn up the contract, both Claudia and Jenny, despite neither's having reached her majority, had been included on the papers as 'sleeping partners', whatever that might mean.

The day had started almost quietly, Jenny thought now, if you could call it quietly with the jazz band closely followed by the Morris dancers, both making enough noise to wake the dead. But it had been Rob's 'surprise' which had made the biggest impression on customers and staff alike. Rob had arranged for one of the actors from the Empire Theatre on Lime Street to 'borrow' the Humpty Dumpty outfit from the theatre's vast store of pantomime costumes and to appear outside the restaurant, then further afield, ringing the big handbell, shouting the news that the Mulberry Tree had opened, and thrusting, upon anyone who held out a hand, a copy of their menu for the next few days.

Now Jenny considered that it had been a masterstroke. The actor had a magnificent voice and equally magnificent legs clad in scarlet tights, and he danced along quoting bits of Shakespeare, only all muddled up, bits of their current play and lots of old pantomime jokes which had his audience in fits, and encouraged them to join in the fun.

Jenny had quite fallen for the actor, a middle-aged man with a wide, ingenuous smile and an ability, it seemed, to remember every catchphrase coined by every comedian who had ever appeared at the Empire. When

Rob said he had hired the man to do his act every Saturday morning for a month she was delighted, and suggested to Danny that they might supply him with sweeties of some description so that he could hand them round to the children who followed him up and down Heyworth Street, collapsing with mirth whenever he cracked a joke.

'Toffee would be best, because that can be homemade, can't it?' Danny had said, not merely telling her that her idea would be too expensive, which had been a possibility, she had thought. 'Do you know how to make toffee, Jen?'

Jenny replied that she did and now, thinking it over, she decided that she would involve Claudia in the making of the sweets. It would not hurt her big sister to help, for by and large Claudia had stuck to her cash desk, though it would not have been fair to say she had shirked doing her share. She had simply not done more than she felt was her duty. If she helped to make toffee, however, they could work either first thing in the morning, before the customers began to arrive at the Mulberry Tree, or in the evening, when their clients had left. She knew her sister was less than enthusiastic over kitchen work, but planned to tell Claudia that Danny and Rob would be most impressed if she, too, gave a hand. She knew her sister well enough to realise that Claudia would not wish the two young men to think she was not wholehearted in her enthusiasm for their new venture.

Having made up her mind on this score, Jenny was just at the delicious stage between waking and sleeping when one's body is warm and comfortable and one's mind floats towards dreamland when a voice spoke, startling her almost out of her wits and causing her to give an enormous jump. 'Sorry, Jenny, I didn't realise you were asleep,' Claudia said, low-voiced. 'But I've been lying here thinking about today and – well, and worrying. Today's Saturday, tomorrow we shan't do anything, even open, thank the Lord, but what about Monday? Rob was quite certain, when I asked him, that customers would come in on Monday just because they'd heard about what he calls the razzmatazz as well as the free buns and gingerbread men and so on, but I'm not so sure. Memories are short – I remember Miss Timpson telling me so – so suppose folk just don't turn up? It's not as though we'll have the jazz band, or the Morris dancers, or even the Humpty Dumpty man from the theatre to attract notice; it'll just be a restaurant, like Lyons, and Fuller's, and Dorothy's Tea Rooms.'

Jenny leaned up on her elbow and smiled across at Claudia, though she knew the other girl could not possibly see her expression in the darkened room. 'It's good that you were worrying, because it's proof that you're as involved as the rest of us,' she said. 'But you needn't have doubts, honest to God you needn't. It isn't just any restaurant, it's brand new – new menus, new furniture and fittings, new décor even. And the people who came in today, only it's yesterday now, congratulated the waiting on staff, said the food was first rate and the prices very reasonable. So go to sleep, big sister; we're on the road to success!'

Claudia, who had also propped herself up on her

elbow, lay down again with a contented sigh. 'You may be only a kid, but you've relieved my mind,' she said sleepily. 'Ta, little sister. Sweet dreams.'

Chapter Eleven

December 1938

It was cold outside, but warm in the kitchen, where Jenny and her grandmother were finishing off an early breakfast. Jenny peeped out through the window and pulled a face. There were frozen puddles in the small yard and she could see two or three icicles hanging from the woodshed roof. She turned to the older woman. 'I'm afraid you're in for a really cold journey, Gran, but you'll wrap up warm, I know. And you're taking a Thermos of coffee and some sandwiches, so you won't starve.'

Gran smiled at Jenny and poured herself another cup of tea. 'I'll be fine, queen. Danny will see me on to the ferry and of course Cormack will meet me the other end, so you can just stop worrying.'

Jenny laughed. 'Oh, well then, you're ready to leave, I take it. Only Danny will be here in ten minutes or so, and you know what men are like; he'll be terrified that something might occur to make you miss your sailing.'

Emily Dalton smiled lovingly at her granddaughter. A couple of weeks ago they had had a desperate letter from Cormack, telling them that Louisa had been 'rather poorly' and did not know how to cope with the children. He knew the restaurant was running smoothly and making quite a name for itself, and had suggested that Emily might come over to Kerry just to give a hand for a week or so. After the briefest of consultations, it had been agreed that she should go.

Then a letter from Louisa herself had arrived, saying that she was very much better and though she would welcome a visit from her mother, she thought she could cope without help. *I don't think Cormack told you, but I wasn't ill, exactly. I had a miscarriage*, her letter had explained. *Naturally, it weakened me – such things do – but I'm very much better now and will completely understand, dear Mam, if you decide not to join us at Connacht Cottage. I know how busy the restaurant is and guess you must be pretty well indispensable. Then there are the lodgers . . .*

But by then Emily's arrangements had all been made. She had organised Maria Calvert to look after the lodgers, baked a cake and bought her tickets for the journey. She had consulted Claudia and Danny, of course, and they had said that they could manage without her.

'So you've got your carry-out and your coffee, your big blue suitcase and your canvas marketing bag, with the presents packed away in it,' Jenny said, eyeing her grandmother's preparations with approval.

Emily was beginning to speak when there was a hasty knock on the back door and Danny came into the room, accompanied by a blast of cold air.

'Shut the door!' Jenny squeaked, whilst Emily lifted the lid of the teapot and informed the visitor that he was welcome to a cup if he felt they had time.

Danny glanced briefly at the clock on the mantel, then

rubbed his hands and said he had a taxi waiting, but he would be grateful for a hot drink. 'I can see you're all set and raring to go,' he said. 'We'll miss you, but to be honest, Mrs Dalton, we're going to be so busy that the time will simply fly.'

He broke off as the kitchen door opened quietly and Claudia, in a blue woollen dressing gown, came into the room. She drifted across the kitchen to give Danny a warm kiss, then flung her arms round Emily and kissed her cheek. 'Oh, Gran, you promised to wake me,' she said reproachfully. 'If I hadn't heard Mr Payne getting up, I'd probably still be asleep, and I should have felt awful because I'd not said a proper goodbye.'

'You said a very nice goodbye last night,' Emily said reprovingly. She turned to Danny as a car horn sounded. 'Heavens, that'll be the taxi, Danny. We'd best get a move on; I don't mean to miss the ferry.' She smiled at her granddaughters as Danny helped her into her winter coat. 'Oh dear, I thought Maria would have been here by now; she certainly said I wasn't to worry about breakfast because . . .'

'. . . because *I* am going to make the porridge and toast the bread this morning,' Jenny said firmly. She smiled at her elder sister. 'And the beautiful Miss Muldoon can jolly well brew the tea and wash the dishes afterwards!'

Emily chuckled, realising that fond though she was of Claudia, she had grown to appreciate Jenny's many good qualities since both girls had been working at the restaurant. Claudia was her darling, but Emily knew that Jenny was the stronger character of the two.

But Claudia was turning to her sister, looking guilty. 'Oh, Jenny, of course I'll brew the tea and wash up,' she said. 'You know I don't mean to let you do all the work . . . but you are much better at making porridge than I am!'

They were still laughing when Danny ushered Emily out of the door and into the waiting taxi, and Emily guessed that by the time the lodgers came down the porridge would be on the table and the toast in the rack. And soon after that, Maria Calvert would be arriving, and the girls would be off to work, for it was essential that either Jenny or Claudia should be there to supervise the staff as they arrived at the restaurant. Of course, if Rob came down he would take the responsibility, but he was not an early riser.

'I'll take your luggage aboard . . .' Danny was beginning as they got out of the cab at the landing stage, but Emily shook her head.

'There's porters what'll do that,' she said briskly. 'Ah, here comes one now!' She seized Danny's hand and shook it, then reached up to kiss his cheek. 'You're a good lad, so you are! Look after my girls.'

When the train drew into the small station it was Fergal who directed the porter to carry Emily's cases and who shook her hand hard, an expression of delight on his weather-beaten features. 'It's grand to see you, so it is, alanna,' he said. 'And thank the good Lord that the rain's stopped, though I've a big umbrella and I see you've got one as well.'

As he spoke, they emerged from the station and to

Emily's surprise when they reached the roadway he led her to a large piebald cob harnessed to a smart trap. She began to ask Fergal where Pickles was tethered, but he laughed delightedly and pointed to the smart equipage before them. 'Didn't Louisa tell you? We've gone up in the world, so we have. Cormack travelled all the way to Limerick to buy this little lot, and rare pleased we are with it, I'm telling you. We still use Pickles and the donkey cart for the farm work, but when we take goods into market, or drive the children to school, 'tis the horse – he's called Guinness – what does the work.'

'He's lovely,' Emily said appreciatively, as Fergal helped her into the smart little vehicle and spread a blanket across her knees.

'There you are; snug as a bug in a rug,' he said cheerfully. He looked at the sky overhead. 'By the look of it, we've had our quota of rain for the day, which is a good t'ing, since I want a word wit' you. Louisa has been poorly, as you know, but she won't ask you to stay longer than usual. She would say it wasn't fair because she believes you work at the restaurant, but I don't think you does. Am I right? She tried to put you off coming at first. Oh, not because she was so much better, but because she felt guilty taking you away from Liverpool when she felt you were needed there. It were a lucky thing that you'd already made your arrangements because I'm telling you, Emily, if Louisa goes on working every hour God sends, whilst she's still weak from losing the babby, I won't be answerable for the consequences.'

'Thanks for telling me, Fergal. I'll stay as long as Louisa needs me, because you're quite right,' Emily said.

'To be sure, when they first set up in business, I did help out from time to time. But that came to an end . . . oh, ages ago. The place runs like clockwork now. They've good, reliable staff, and the four of them know exactly what they want done. Even little Jenny can manage the place, knows at a glance when they're running short of something. Why, they bought a second-hand van six months ago and either Danny or Rob goes off in it to various farms in North Wales or the Wirral for supplies. They buy cracked eggs, meat straight from the slaughter house . . . anything they need and can pick up cheap . . .'

'They've got sense,' Fergal said, patting her knee approvingly. 'So you ain't essential to the business, then? And that means you won't be hurrying back to Liverpool until Louisa's recovered her strength, which relieves my mind, I'm tellin' you.' He slapped the reins on the cob's neck and the horse moved forward. 'Well, we'll make your Christmas summat to remember, I promise you.'

They arrived at Connacht Cottage after a pleasant – and dry – ride, to the warmest of welcomes. Cormack ushered them indoors and went to stable the horse and do all the other things that were necessary. But first he gave his mother-in-law a hearty kiss and muttered into her ear that he was grateful she had arrived, so he was, and she must tell him if she needed anything which was not already to hand in the cottage.

Emily was rather puzzled, for Cormack was a man who did not wear his heart on his sleeve, but as soon as she got within doors and saw her daughter, she understood the reason for his words. Louisa had never been plump, but she had had a beautiful figure and a rosy, smiling face. Now she was pale as milk, and though she greeted Emily with real enthusiasm she could not stop tears from forming in her eyes and trickling down her cheeks. And when the twins, who were over-excited, began to boast and shout, she collapsed into a chair with her hands over her face, whilst Fergal ordered the children to go to their room and to stay there until they had remembered their manners.

Emily went quickly to her daughter, knelt on the floor beside her chair and took Louisa's hands in hers. 'It's all right, love; Mam's here and you'll soon begin to feel more like your old self,' she crooned. 'I know Cormack's got help with the work on the croft, but why have you not got a girl from the village to give a hand until you recover your strength?

Louisa returned the grip of her mother's hands, then let go in order to knuckle her eyes. 'Oh, Mam, it's like a miracle having you here,' she said. 'And I did have some help from the girl whose father runs the hardware shop in town. Fergal picked her up each morning in the trap after he'd left the twins at school, and took her home each evening. But oh, Mam, the twins were real little devils and played her up so bad that she gave in her notice.' Louisa sniffed dolefully, then gave a watery chuckle. 'You've no idea the tricks they played on the poor girl.'

'I can guess,' Emily said grimly. 'But I think you'll find I can cope with the twins. They know me and know also that I won't stand none of their nonsense. Why, at their age, they ought to be a real help and not a burden.'

Fergal, who had followed the children into their room,

returned to the kitchen at this point. Louisa, who had pulled the kettle over the fire as soon as her mother and father-in-law arrived, tried to get to her feet, saying that she would brew the tea, but Fergal shook his head at her. 'No you don't, young woman,' he said reprovingly. 'From now on, you will sit in a chair by the fire and supervise the work which needs to be done. You'll go for walks when the weather's kind, to work up an appetite, and if you're very good your mam and meself might let you drive into town with us on market day, but otherwise you'll just rest and grow strong.' He turned to Emily and struck an attitude. 'That's the decision of Dr Muldoon and Nurse Dalton here; ain't that right, Emily?'

Louisa gave a watery laugh at her mother's enthusiastic agreement. 'But I can't let the two of you do all the work and cope with the kids as well,' she said weakly. She turned to her mother. 'Fergal can manage them but he's doing all my yard and dairy work, and I'm afraid I just give in because I'm too tired to deal with them as I once did. So they've got out of hand . . .'

'I noticed. But don't worry, queen; the twins are good-hearted and will do as they're told once they realise Fergal and meself are in charge,' Emily said. She had been kneeling by her daughter's side, but now she got rather stiffly to her feet and turned to Fergal. 'And now, where's that tea you promised me?'

Gran was settling the twins down for the night and had told them a bedtime story, then made them promise not to get out of bed again before morning. 'But suppose we want to widdle?' Bernie said plaintively. 'Even Grandpa lets us get out to use our potties and he's ever so strict, and our mam will be furious if we wet the beds.'

Emily sighed. 'Of course you may get out of bed for that sort of thing,' she said. 'You're not a baby, Bernie, you know quite well what I mean, but your daddy is going to roast chestnuts on the living room fire and I know what you two are like. I'll save you some which you can have tomorrow, but only if you don't put in an appearance this evening; do you understand me?'

Bernie opened her mouth, but Emily cut in. 'If you say one word, I'll have your guts for garters,' she said, leaving no room for argument. 'And it will be no roasted nuts and very probably no dinner either. So stay where you are, or else.'

She waited a moment for either twin to object, then left the room, closing the door quietly behind her and rejoining the rest of the family in the living room. Cormack was just withdrawing a shovel, packed with chestnuts, from beneath the glowing fire; he looked up and grinned as Emily entered the room. 'I take it they's in bed?' he asked. 'Just wait till the smell of roasted chestnuts reaches 'em, though. They'll be back in here like a dose of salts.'

Emily returned his smile. 'No they won't,' she said triumphantly. 'I told 'em they'd get no nuts nor no dinner tomorrow if they so much as poked their noses round the door.' She fixed her daughter with an admonitory glare. 'And the children, by now, know that what I threaten I'll perform, unlike some, Louise Muldoon.'

Louisa gave a shamefaced giggle and Emily noted with pleasure how much better her daughter was looking. When I arrived, Emily told herself, she was tired to death, and she was letting the twins get away with murder because she was too weary to make them mind her. Now she's rosy and smiling, almost her old self once more. I reckon if I stay another couple of weeks she'll be in command again and will wave me off without a qualm. On the thought, she sank into a chair and took some of the chestnuts her son-in-law was holding out to her, hissing in her breath sharply, for they were still extremely hot.

They ate the chestnuts without any interruption from the twins, chatting amiably, and presently Fergal got to his feet. 'Time for a brew of tay and a slice of buttered brack,' he said. 'Will you come wit' me, Emily, so these two lovebirds can have some time to themselves before midnight? If we're to sit up to see in the New Year, like you want, we'll need a bite and a sup, for there's another half-hour to go.'

Emily followed him into the kitchen, aware that he probably wanted a quiet word in her ear, so was not altogether surprised when, after he had made tea in the big brown pot whilst she sliced and buttered the delicious, moist brack, he turned to her, his cheeks flushing. 'Well, Emily? I know you usually come in the summer, but what do you think of us in winter, eh? To tell you the truth, alanna, I've been hoping you'd give some t'ought to stayin' here in – in a more permanent sort of way. I didn't like to ask you when you'd not suffered a winter here, but now you know the worst. The twins get bored wit' bein' shut in, the rain falls twenty-three hours out of the twenty-four, the cold gets into old joints . . .'

Emily laughed. 'The hens don't lay as many eggs, the cows hold back their milk and the piglets don't fatten so well,' she finished for him. 'I knew all that before this visit, my old friend. I was here when the twins were born, don't forget, which was around Christmas time. So what makes you think that another winter visit might make me feel differently about Connacht Cottage?'

Fergal slammed down the teapot and put a detaining hand on Emily's, preventing her from cutting another slice of brack. 'Emily Dalton, I'm trying to ask you if you'd consider . . . if you'd not take it unkind of me . . . oh, hell and damnation, I'm no good at dis sort of t'ing. Well, when I asked my Eithne to wed, I were younger, wit' more to offer. This time there's only the cottage, the one the old feller let go to ruin. Cormack and meself, wit' help from Dónal and his brother Sam, have rebuilt it, and only last week Cormack said if I ever got sick of livin' wit' me family, I could have the old cottage and welcome. He were jokin', of course, but I'm not. Emily, would you . . . could you . . .'

Emily stared at her companion. 'Well, Fergal, you could knock me down with a feather,' she breathed. 'But what's brought this up all of a sudden? I'm rare fond of you – we've been good friends for many a year – but marriage? At our age? And then there's me little house in Blodwen Street, me lodgers and of course Claudia

243

and Jenny. They still live with me, you know. Not that they'll be doing so for much longer, or at least Claudia won't. She and Danny plan to marry . . . but you know all that.'

Fergal sighed deeply. 'I wish I could come courtin', persuade you that what I feel for you is as real as what I felt for Eithne, though different,' he said. 'If I were to talk about love, you'd t'ink I'd gone mad.' He gripped her hands tightly and Emily saw that his blue eyes blazed with sincerity. 'Will you t'ink about it, my dear? Will you give me a chance?'

'Yes, of course I will, 'cos I'm rare fond of you, Fergal, but marriage is a serious business,' Emily warned him. 'And now we'd best get back to Cormack and Louisa, or they'll wonder what the devil has been holding us up.'

Back in the living room an hour later, the four of them had toasted the New Year in Louisa's homemade blackberry wine, exchanged friendly kisses and finished off the brack which Fergal had carried in earlier. Now they looked at one another, aware of a feeling of anticlimax as they settled once more by the fire. 'I wonder what 1939 will bring,' Louisa said idly, staring at the flames. 'The world's in a mess. If you ask me, anything could happen.'

'War will happen; bound to,' Cormack said decidedly. 'Last year I'm told they dug trenches in Hyde Park; this year I can't see any alternative to war. And when it comes I'll join the navy . . . or the army . . . or maybe even the air force.'

'You won't, because it won't be our war,' Louisa said sharply. 'And anyway, it may not happen.' She jumped up and went over to Cormack, giving him a hug and a kiss on his broad, tanned forehead. 'Please don't let's talk about it! And as for you joining up, what nonsense! You're far too old.'

'Thank you,' Cormack said dryly. 'But I won't talk about it if you'd rather I didn't.' He turned politely to Emily. 'What do you think 1939 holds for you, Mother-in-law? And for this restaurant the young 'uns are running?'

'Oh, all sorts of good things,' Emily said at once, though she could see from the expression on Fergal's face that he had hoped she might give quite a different answer; indeed, had she wished to do so it would have been the ideal opportunity. 'For a start, the lease of the Mulberry Tree comes up for renewal in March, and Danny means to ask Mrs Tuttle to sell them the place outright. Fortunately, it was her idea to start with and she had it valued then, so that will be the price they'll have to pay, rather than what it is worth now, though Rob thinks Mrs Tuttle would be entitled to add a bit more. And then there's the wedding . . .'

'Oh, I'm looking forward to the wedding,' Louisa said at once, her eyes brightening. 'My eldest daughter is going to get married and I'm missing all the fun! Have they fixed a date yet? I know Claudia insists on making her own dress, and probably she's right to do so because she's a clever little needlewoman and will make a good job of it. In fact she's actually designing the dress herself, or so she said in her last letter. I've offered to make the bridesmaids' dresses, but I'll need Jenny's measurements, though of course I know Bernie's size off by heart.' She turned to Emily. 'Or do you think Jenny would prefer to choose her own dress and accessories? I shan't be offended if she'd rather buy something off the peg.'

Her mother chuckled. 'Jenny hasn't really changed at all, you know,' she said. 'She never even thinks about clothes and would probably be perfectly happy to traipse up the aisle behind her sister in a calico apron and wellington boots! What is worse, she'd probably tread on Claudia's train, which I understand is to be twelve feet long, and jerk the proceedings to a halt. But quite honestly, my dear, Claudia won't even consider letting anyone else make the dresses. You may say she shouldn't have to work so hard, but Claudia scarcely looks on sewing as work, and she'll talk Jenny into wearing whatever she makes, which is more than you could do from here!'

Both her male listeners laughed, but Louisa shook her head sadly. 'When will that child grow up?' she asked plaintively. 'Claudia writes every week, no matter how busy she is, but Jenny scrawls half a page about once a month and seldom mentions any sort of social life, though I understand from Claudia that the four of them go around together quite a bit. She says when they go to the Grafton, or the Daulby Hall . . .' she smiled at Fergal, 'they're two of the biggest dance halls in Liverpool, Dad . . . she prefers sitting out and watching the action, rather than taking part herself, though Rob keeps asking her to dance with him. And that's odd, because from what Claudia tells me, this Rob Dingle is very attractive.'

Fergal made a derisive noise in the back of his throat. 'Handsome is as handsome does,' he said sententiously. 'Are you trying to say, Lou, that he likes our little Jenny?'

Louisa shrugged helplessly. 'I don't know; I shouldn't think so. Unless Jenny has changed a great deal she's still young for her age, and when girls aren't interested in men then men aren't interested in girls; isn't that so, Mam?' She looked at her mother for confirmation and Emily nodded slowly.

'I know what you mean, queen. What interests Jenny at the moment is making a success of the restaurant. She and Rob get on pretty well, I believe, and she gets on even better with Danny, because she's known him longer, I suppose. But I don't believe either man thinks of Jenny as a young woman; she's just a fellow worker, and a very good one at that. Mind you, she's got an old school friend, Tommy Woo, she goes to the flicks with sometimes, but he's just a friend, like Danny and Rob.'

Cormack, who had been listening in silence and apparently dreaming as the fire began to sink in the grate, suddenly brightened. 'Tommy Woo? I remember him! Fat little Chinese chap in Jenny's class at school. But I read her letters too, you know, and I reckon she's just too busy at the restaurant to go gadding like her sister does.'

Louisa began an indignant rebuttal of this remark, but Emily shook her head. 'No, no, it's fair enough, and why shouldn't Claudia enjoy herself when she's not actually working? I assure you Jenny does; enjoy herself I mean. She actually likes going into other restaurants to see what they're charging and how they present their food. Why, it's her idea to expand the Mulberry Tree into the upstairs flat, though Danny won't make any move of that nature until they've actually bought the place. You see, on Thursdays and Saturdays folk have to queue for a table and once or twice Jenny has seen customers leave the queue and go off to another restaurant. That was when she thought it might be an idea to convert the flat, because if they tore out all the dividing walls they could seat at least another forty people up there, if not more.'

'But what about Claudia and Danny?' Louisa asked rather anxiously. 'I know the boys are living in the flat at the moment, but I thought Claudia and Danny would move in when they came back from their honeymoon. You surely don't want them living with you, Mam?'

'No room,' Emily said succinctly. 'But Claudia has never been keen on what she calls "living over the shop". They've already started looking at smallish houses on the fringe of the city. They'll rent at first, of course, but the way money is mounting up it won't be long before they can buy.' She smiled at her listeners, her eyes sparkling. 'I can't wait for you to come over and see what those children have achieved,' she said. 'I believe Claudia is thinking about the middle of March for the wedding, before the lease runs out at the end of the month.'

'Yes, I could get the bridesmaid's dresses done in time,' Louisa breathed. 'Oh, and we'll make a proper little holiday of it, won't we, Cormack? Dónal and Sam will do all the croft work whilst we're away.'

'Hey, don't go making plans too soon,' Emily said,

laughing. 'Nothing's settled yet, so far as I know. But the wedding will be some time in the coming year, that's for sure.'

'Oh, Gran, we loves you. Don't go, don't go!' That was Bernie, grimly clinging to Emily's right hand.

'Oh, Gran, Bernie's right; stay wit' us and we'll be good as gold, honest to God we will. We wishes we hadn't been so bad; we wishes we'd not told you the eggs were hard boiled when they was raw, we wishes . . .' That was Benny, attached to Emily's left hand.

Emily laughed and began to free herself from the twins' octopus-like embrace. The three of them were in the kitchen, Emily already packed and wearing her coat and hat all ready to leave. 'I'm flattered that you think so highly of me,' she said drily. 'Now can it be because there are two bags of sweets on the mantelpiece, designed to keep you quiet and happy whilst your grandpa drives me to the station?'

The cheeks of both twins glowed pink even as they shook their ginger heads. 'No, it ain't that, honest to God it ain't,' Bernie said, speaking for them both as she so often did. 'We want you to live here with us for always. We want you to marry Grandpa.'

'Why?' Emily said bluntly. She knew her grand-children of old and was not surprised when Benny said promptly: 'Because if Grandpa moves out, we can have a bedroom each.' This earned him a ferocious glare from his sister and an admonitory kick on the ankle. 'Oh, I shouldn't have said that. Only Mammy said . . .'

'Never mind what your mammy said; one thing is

certain, that you were meant to neither hear nor repeat it,' Emily said, though her lips twitched. 'As for marrying, what makes you think people of our age go around marrying one another?'

Both twins looked crestfallen. 'I dunno. Only old people do marry sometimes and we thought – we thought . . .' The door opening behind them put a stop to Benny's mumbling and Fergal's cheerful voice, plainly oblivious of the conversation going on, saved Emily from having to make any sort of reply.

'Ready, alanna? Then we'll be off.'

The drive to the station might have been both difficult and embarrassing, Emily thought, but Fergal eased matters by saying at once that he had decided not to press her for an answer to his proposal. 'You're going to have a lot on your mind for the next few months,' he said seriously. 'There's the wedding for a start; any mention of you and meself following suit might take the shine out of Danny and Claudia's big day. Then as you say, you've responsibilities both to your lodgers and to young Jenny. So I'll wait for me answer until you visit in the summer.' He smiled down at her with the lively affection and understanding she realised now that she had come to expect from him. 'So don't worry that I'll pester you or reveal me hopes in that direction, because I shan't.' He chuckled. 'A feller my age has learned patience if nothing else.'

Emily felt tears rise to her eyes and reached across to squeeze his hand. 'You're a grand feller so you are, Fergal,' she said sincerely. 'And I'm hoping me answer in the summer will be one we both want to hear . . .'

Fergal gave a subdued whoop and the cob, which had been trotting sedately, flicked back its ears and broke into a canter. 'And you're a grand woman, so you are, Mrs Dalton,' he said jubilantly. 'I can wait for me answer until then.'

Chapter Twelve

When Jenny stepped out of the front door it was into a wild and windy day; a typical March day in fact, she told herself, wrapping her scarf more firmly around her neck and doing up the top button of her coat before battling her way along the pavement. Usually she and Claudia walked to work together, chatting as they went, for this was the time of day when the sisters were able to discuss plans and was, Jenny thought, valued by both of them. Once they reached the Mulberry Tree intimate conversation was impossible, for the restaurant was always busy.

Today, however, Claudia was having a lie-in because she had arranged to see the florist who was supplying the wedding bouquets and the flowers for the reception. This was to be held at the Mulberry Tree, which made things easier in some ways and more difficult in others, Jenny told herself, slogging along the pavement, head down against the wind's attack. Naturally there was great excitement amongst the staff, who entered whole-heartedly into all the arrangements, which was just as well, Jenny thought, since Claudia could talk of nothing but her glorious wedding dress, veil and headdress and tended to dismiss details such as what food would be supplied to the eighty wedding guests.

Since Rob was to be best man and Jenny the chief bridesmaid, she came in for quite a lot of ribbing, both from her friends and from members of the staff. With one voice, everyone assured her that the best man and the chief bridesmaid always 'made a go of it', and since Bernie was still very much a child Jenny had no choice but to pair off with Rob at the reception at least, for after the meal, Claudia insisted, there would be dancing. She had hired a band and even planned a light supper, to be served just before midnight, when the guests would begin departing.

Danny confided in Jenny that the wedding was going to cost them a great deal of money, for both Danny and Claudia realised that it would be unfair to expect the Muldoons to shell out when the restaurant was doing so well. However, he also said that, since it was the most important day in a girl's life, he did not grudge a penny, and Claudia, being the artistic member of the family, had made the wedding invitations herself as well as the name cards which would be put round the tables. He told everyone who would listen that he was just grateful that she had found time for such mundane tasks. She had also insisted upon making the bridesmaids' dresses despite her mother's offer to do so and even Jenny, largely indifferent to what she wore, thought that her sister had created the most beautiful dress for her that she had ever seen; certainly she had never worn anything so wonderful. Indeed, when Danny told her, a trifle tongue in cheek, that she and Rob would have to follow himself and Claudia when the dancing began, she took it very well. However, she started practising her steps whenever no one was looking, for though not particularly fond of Rob despite what everyone thought, she did not mean to let him down on the dance floor.

Long and hard had been the arguments over the menu. Claudia had said gaily that they might as well do what everyone else did, which meant ham salad and tinned peaches, but Jenny had said firmly that they must remember they were in a very competitive business. Folk would see what sort of reception they put on, and might book their own weddings at the Mulberry Tree as a result.

The wedding had been fixed for the last weekend in March, which meant they had less than a month in which to prepare, but at least everyone now agreed on the food to be served. Roast chicken and all the trimmings would be followed by the Mulberry Tree's famous trifle, and of course everyone would either take home with them, or devour on the spot, a slice of the wedding cake which Mrs Fleming, an experienced confectioner, would ice and decorate just a few days before the wedding itself.

Jenny turned into Heyworth Street, glancing at the clock over the chemist's as she passed it. Good: despite having to battle against the wind, she would still arrive at her usual time. Although Mrs Tuttle, Danny and Rob had agreed that the partners should buy the restaurant, Danny had refused to start work on the conversion of the flat until everything was signed and sealed and the entire premises were theirs to do with as they wished. However, in anticipation of his marriage, he was spending a good deal of time at the house he and Claudia had rented in Sydenham Avenue and this meant that the early supervision of the staff was often left to Rob, provided he was awake in time, or to Jenny herself, for Claudia was always either at the cash desk or in the office getting the books up to date and was not directly involved in the restaurant itself.

When Jenny reached the Mulberry Tree, she could see from the light streaming out of the kitchen that some member of staff – or indeed Rob himself – had already arrived, so there was no need for her to produce her key. She was stretching out her hand towards the door when another hand, large and capable, descended on her shoulder and a voice in her ear said: 'Morning, Jenny wren! Where's Claudia?'

Jenny turned and smiled up into Danny's familiar face. She still thought him the handsomest man she knew, thought his dark good looks made the blond and blue-eyed Rob seem pallid, almost insignificant by comparison. But Danny was looking at her, his dark eyes enquiring, so she hastened to explain. 'She's gone to the florist to talk about her bouquet.' Jenny chuckled. 'I'm sure my sister has no thought in her head for anything not connected with her wedding. But fancy you forgetting about the flowers! And just where have you been at such an early hour of the morning?'

Danny pushed open the restaurant door and ushered her inside. 'I've been at our house again; mine and Claudia's,' he explained. 'I'm redecorating the whole place from attics to cellar, and if I don't finish until really late I just kip down there for the night. I'm hoping to have finished the redecoration by the time we're married.'

'Oh, Danny, what a grand idea,' Jenny said enthusiastically. 'I could come along after work if it would help. In fact if you've not finished by the time you go off on your honeymoon I could work on it then. When's the furniture coming? Have you chosen it yet? Honest, Danny, I'd be happy to help in any way I could.'

She was looking at Danny as she spoke and thought he looked rather hunted, though he tried to give her his usual friendly smile. 'It's all right, queen, I'm getting along pretty well and should be able to finish before the wedding,' he said awkwardly. 'I keep asking Claudia to come with me to choose furniture, but she always seems to be too busy. Of course I'm not allowed to see her dress, but I gather it's taking even more work than she envisaged at first. Then there's all the little details which a man never thinks about: headdresses, shoes, the menu . . . and of course the wedding ring itself. I keep telling her we must go down to Crabbe's and choose one, or she'll be the only bride in the world without a wedding ring, but she says, "Plenty of time," and goes on about a wreath of white roses to support the veil, or patent leather pumps . . .'

'Patent leather pumps?' Jenny said scornfully. 'She'll be wearing elegant court shoes in white leather which will cost the earth, if I know my sister. But I'll have a nag at her about the wedding ring, tell her I'll lend you a tuppenny curtain ring from Woolies if she doesn't get a move on.'

Danny smiled at her but shook his head. 'It's all right, queen; I'll buy the ring myself if she's too busy,' he said. 'Sometimes I wonder if she really wants to get married.

Oh, I know she's very keen on the actual wedding itself, but I honestly don't believe she's thought much about the rest. For instance, I wanted her to come to Sydenham Avenue to see what I was doing on the house and she looked at me as if I were mad and then said, quite crossly, that she'd have the rest of her life to look at it. It quite took me aback, I can tell you.'

Jenny chuckled. 'That's typical of my sister,' she said, following Danny across the restaurant and into the kitchen. 'Don't worry, Danny, she's snapped at me more than once this past week when I've tried to get her to talk about the wedding, and Gran says brides are always like that and get worse and worse as the wedding gets nearer. Once it's all over and you're off on your honeymoon, she'll relax and become her old self.'

'Well, I'm glad of that . . .' Danny was beginning rather ruefully, when the door which led to the flat opened and Rob lurched into the room. 'Whazza time?' he said thickly. 'Had a heavy night of it with a couple of pals. Oh, God, my head!'

Danny grinned. 'Mrs Bland will have the kettle on and Jenny here will make you a really strong black coffee,' he said as the three of them pushed through the door to the kitchen. 'I won't ask you if you've had breakfast because I know you haven't, so I'll put some bread on to toast. You'll feel a lot better with black coffee and some grub inside you, old feller.'

Jenny was as good as her word and she and Gran both gave Claudia a proper talking to, which had the effect of sending Claudia hotfoot to Percy Crabbe's the very next day. Danny accompanied her, of course, and they chose a wide gold band with the words *I love you* engraved upon it.

When Jenny had told her Danny was worrying, Claudia had not been very sympathetic at first, saying that no one could be more anxious than she. 'I want everything perfect,' she told her sister. 'I want it to be the very best wedding Liverpool has ever known. And it will be, provided I'm allowed to get on with it.'

'I know what you mean,' Jenny admitted. 'But I expect Danny feels just the same, only he's afraid he'll mess things up because . . . well, you have rather pushed him into the background these past few weeks, haven't you?'

After some thought, Claudia admitted, though reluctantly, that maybe Jenny was right. 'I'll try to get up to the new house and admire what he's done there,' she said. She thrust a hand up into her dark curls. 'Honest to God, Jenny, if I'd known what hard work a wedding was, I doubt if I'd have wanted to get married!'

Jenny was shocked, but when she told Gran what her sister had said that wise woman only laughed. 'I actually told my darling Bert that I'd changed my mind and didn't mean to marry anyone, three days before our wedding,' she said. 'And I was so nervous and bad-tempered that I'm surprised he didn't take me at my word and find himself someone less difficult. But then the day arrived and as I began to put on my dress I knew it was the beginning of the most important day in my life. I walked up the aisle, through all the guests, but all I could see was the back of Bert's dark head, and when he took my hand I knew I was the luckiest girl in the world. It will be the same for Claudia; just you see.'

Jenny was immensely comforted by this and relayed it to Danny, who admitted that Mrs Dalton's remarks had cheered him up no end. 'Because Claudia has always been sweet and gentle, and I wouldn't like to think marriage was going to change her into a shrew,' he told Jenny. 'Oh, shan't I be relieved when we're on the train heading for our honeymoon and Claudia smiles at me with her old sweet smile once more!'

Jenny had returned from the restaurant so tired that she expected to fall asleep the moment her head touched the pillow, but had remained downstairs with Gran and the lodgers until they sought their beds. Claudia – pleading exhaustion – had gone up some time before, so Jenny undressed in the dark, not wanting to disturb her sister, and crept into her bed as quietly as she possibly could.

Despite her expectations, however, sleep simply refused to be courted. Worries over things left undone and fears that all might not go well at the wedding reception chased themselves round and round in Jenny's head, forbidding sleep. Presently, sighing and turning over yet again, she wondered if she should begin counting sheep. She was actually trying to do so when she heard a slight sound, which seemed to be coming from the floor below. She whispered Claudia's name, but the dark shape in the other bed did not stir. Suddenly alert, Jenny stared across at the door and was horrified to hear a stealthy step on the stair leading to their attic room. Quickly, heart thumping, she got out of bed and leaned over her sister. 'Claudia, wake up!' she hissed. 'Can you hear footsteps on the . . .'

As she spoke, she seized the dark figure in the bed, meaning to shake Claudia awake, then drew back with a tiny squeak of alarm. Claudia's bed contained, not her sister, but a bolster!

For a moment Jenny was so surprised that she did not move a muscle, but then she heard the steps pause outside their door and, quick as a flash, she lay down on her own bed and waited, scarcely daring to breathe. She watched as the door slowly – and silently – opened and saw her sister slip into the room, closing the door carefully behind her. Only then did she say, in a low voice: 'Good night, Claudia! Or should it be good morning?'

Claudia jumped and gasped, then collapsed on to her bed, a hand pressed to her heart. 'Jenny! Oh my God, what a fright you gave me! But whatever are you doing, awake at this hour? D'you know what the time is? It's well past midnight, and if you don't get some sleep soon you'll be a nervous wreck by morning.'

'If I frightened you by speaking, how do you think I felt when I realised it wasn't you in the bed, but a pillow?' Jenny asked reasonably. 'Answer me that!'

The room was in darkness, but faint light was coming in through the window, for the girls always drew their curtains back as soon as they were in their nightclothes, and Jenny saw that the hands of the alarm clock actually pointed to half past one. There was no point in mentioning it, however. Instead she said, trying not to sound too critical: 'Where have you been, Claudia?'

'Oh, I went down to the privy,' Claudia said quickly. Too quickly, Jenny thought. 'Is there anything wrong in that?'

Her tone was belligerent and Jenny hesitated before shaking her head. 'Surely you can do better than that?' she said chidingly. 'You're fully dressed and you're wearing shoes, not slippers. Please tell me the truth, Claudia! I'm sure you must have had an important reason to go out at this hour. And before you start to tell me that you dressed and nipped downstairs for a quick look at your wedding gown, I might as well tell you that I know very well you've been gone quite a while. You came up to bed before me, but for some reason I simply couldn't sleep. Naturally, I kept glancing across at you, never guessing that it was a pillow in your bed and not you, so I know you've been gone for ages and I'd very much like to know just what you're playing at.'

Chapter Thirteen

For a moment Claudia said nothing, but merely continued to sit on the edge of her bed, staring down at her hands and twisting her little engagement ring round and round on her finger. Jenny was about to repeat her question when Claudia heaved a deep sigh and spoke. 'All right, I suppose I'll have to tell you. Oh, Jenny, if only you were a bit older, had a feller of your own, you'd find it much easier to understand. When you're on the very verge of the most important moment in your life, you want to make certain you're doing the right thing. Being in love the way I am changes the way you look at everything and you realise you want to be with your man by night as well as by day . . . oh, all the time.'

'But you are with him all the day and quite a lot of the evening as well,' Jenny pointed out, feeling her heart lurch sickeningly at a mental picture of Claudia in Danny's arms. 'I don't see . . . but I shouldn't interrupt; go on, Claudia.'

Claudia sighed. 'We're never alone, just the two of us,' she said. 'Married people spend their nights together, as well as their days, and I thought – I thought . . .'

'Claudia!' Jenny said, truly shocked. 'But you'll be married in a few days; surely you didn't . . .?'

'Oh, don't think I've been doing what bad girls do; we just had to be together, to be sure . . . it was just cuddles and a good deal of kissing. It didn't hurt anyone and it's made me feel a good deal better. You know they say brides always get pre-wedding nerves? Well, it's perfectly true; can you understand?'

'Yes of course I can, even though I don't have a feller of my own,' Jenny said rather huffily. 'And I expect Danny puts your mind at rest because he's so kind and so understanding.'

Claudia giggled, then leaned across the small space between their beds and took Jenny's hands in both of hers, wagging them gently from side to side. 'Idiot! I told you we didn't do anything wrong and I meant it. But getting married is a serious business – frightening in a way – and of course because we've been so busy with the restaurant and the house in Sydenham Avenue, we've scarcely been alone for two minutes. When I told him I was getting nervous, he suggested meeting when everyone else was asleep, so that's what we've been doing for the past four or five nights.' She leaned closer to her sister and even in the dimness Jenny could see the anxiety on her face. 'You won't tell anyone, will you, Jen? I'd feel such a fool if it got about that I was – was scared about getting married.'

Jenny licked her finger and drew it across her throat in the old childish gesture. 'See this wet, see this dry, cut my throat if I dare to lie,' she said promptly. 'Of course I won't say a word to anyone; what do you think I am? A tale clat?'

Claudia gave Jenny's hands a final squeeze then let

them go and began to undress, pushing her pillow back to the top of the bed and slipping her nightgown over her head before scrambling between the sheets. 'Thanks, darling; always remember I love you, Jenny,' she said sleepily as she cuddled down. 'And don't think badly of me, will you?'

Jenny's brows rose; why on earth should she think badly of her sister just because she sneaked out to have a kiss and a cuddle with her future husband? But she assured Claudia that she could never think badly of her, no matter what, and presently both girls slept.

The next day, at the Mulberry Tree, Danny was waiting on since most of the employees were engaged in preparations for the wedding reception. They were rushed off their feet between twelve and two and needed all the help they could get, but by three o'clock the restaurant was emptying and the staff took it in turns to repair to a table at the back for a meal. Danny and Jenny had finished theirs and were chatting when Claudia arrived at the table. 'Dearest Jen, do go and sit in the cash desk whilst I get myself something to eat,' she said rather breathlessly. 'You won't be troubled by many customers, and the ones that are in are all tea and scones or fancy cakes, so you won't have any big bills to add up.' She looked brightly from Jenny to Danny as her sister stood up. 'And what have you two been talking about so seriously? I'm dying to know!'

Danny smiled lovingly at her, then stood up and pulled out a chair. 'Sit down, darling,' he said. 'We were talking about arranging supplies for the kitchen; pretty boring stuff, but very important, of course. And now, what can I fetch you? You poor love, having to wait for your meal until pretty well the last. But there's plenty of grub left; how about bacon and egg flan, new potatoes and peas? Oh, and a big pot of tea?'

'That sounds wonderful,' Claudia said gratefully, sinking into the proffered chair. She looked around her. 'Where's Rob? Has he already eaten? I thought he said he'd wait until last.'

Jenny, on her way to the cash desk – with her fingers crossed that she would not be asked to add up a large bill or give change for a five pound note – addressed her sister over her shoulder. 'He's gone to see the man who sells us cracked eggs, to see if he can order extra for tomorrow, when we start the big bake for the wedding breakfast. He shouldn't be long.'

Even as she spoke, the big plate glass doors of the restaurant swung open and Rob appeared. It struck Jenny that he was looking very pleased with himself, so he had probably been successful in his errand, and she sighed with relief as she settled into the cash desk. Perhaps everything was going to be all right after all.

Today was Monday, and on Tuesday evening the family would arrive and take up residence in a boarding house a stone's throw from Blodwen Street. On Thursday, Gran and Mam would help Mrs Bland make the trifles and on Friday prepare the vegetables and, once the restaurant had closed for the day, get the room ready for the wedding on Saturday.

Late on the following evening Gran, Claudia and Jenny were down at the Pier Head watching the Irish ferry, with the Muldoon family aboard, beginning to draw up alongside the landing stage. Suddenly, Jenny clutched Claudia's arm. 'There they are, there they are!' she squeaked. 'Oh, Claudia, isn't it good to see them again?' She turned to her grandmother, who was standing on tiptoe, trying to see over the heads of the crowds on the quayside. 'Dad's wearing a blue shirt with a scarlet handkerchief tied round his neck. Grandpa Muldoon is next to him; he's wearing a white shirt and a blue handkerchief. I know Mam and the kids must be there somewhere, but I can't pick them out. I can only see Dad and Grandpa Muldoon because they're right up against the rail and they're both a lot taller than most of the other passengers. Have you found 'em yet, Gran?'

'Yes, I can see them; your dad's taken off his red handkerchief and he's waving it,' Gran said rather tremulously. 'I know I saw them at Christmas, but I've missed them so! I've missed the farm as well, and though the kids is terrors I've missed them too. Oh, I can't wait to see how your mam is gettin' on, though she tells me in every letter that she's just fine and scarce needs the new young girl what helps out when the twins aren't in school.'

'Well it won't be long before we find out because they're lowering the gangway right now,' Jenny said, hopping with excitement. She gave her sister's arm another tweak. 'Aren't you excited, Claudia? Or does the thought of your wedding put everything else out of your mind?'

'Yes it does, rather,' Claudia admitted. 'Oh, look, look! They're almost at the end of the gangway. Grab Gran's other hand so we don't lose one another and we'll go over and meet them!'

Half an hour later, the whole family were sitting round the table in Emily's kitchen whilst Emily, Claudia and Jenny bustled about making a large pot of tea, slicing cake and putting out plates of sandwiches and biscuits for the weary travellers.

Once the initial greetings were over, Cormack had hustled them all into two taxis, stopped off at the lodgings to leave their luggage, and then told the drivers to take the party to Blodwen Street. Once there, Jenny reflected, it had been all go, with everyone talking at the tops of their voices and more huggings, more exclamations of surprise at how the twins had grown, until the food was set out and everyone began to eat.

Claudia, Jenny noticed, said very little, though she smiled a lot and promised her mother that she and her husband meant to spend a couple of weeks in Ireland later in the summer. They were to have a week's honeymoon in Llandudno and, Claudia said, would have to say their goodbyes when the wedding was over, since the Muldoons would have to return to Connacht Cottage on the Monday after the wedding celebration.

'Dónal and Sam have moved into the croft and they've promised to give an eye to our beasts while we're gone, but it will stretch them to the fullest extent at this time of year,' Cormack told the girls. 'You've not been back home for more than two years, so you won't appreciate how enlarging the croft has also trebled the work, and we can't expect the lads to take on so much extra work

267

for more than a few days. Now, when are we going to see this restaurant, this Mulberry Tree, which we've heard so much about?' He turned to his elder daughter and smiled. 'You and Danny – we're looking forward to meeting him again after so long – are in business for yourselves, just like your mam and me, so how have you arranged things? You can't expect neighbours to run a business for you, and you won't want to lose even one customer through lack of staff.'

'Oh, but the other partner, Rob Dingle, will do all the things Danny does, and there's me, I'll do anything. Then Gran's going to come in whilst Claudia's away to take over the cash desk,' Jenny explained eagerly. 'Rob will see to all the business side of it because I'm not good at that sort of thing, and we've got a really marvellous cook, Mrs Bland, my pal Betty who cleans and washes up, and full time waitresses.' She beamed at her father. 'Don't worry, Dad, I do believe we've thought of everything and we should be able to manage fine whilst the bride and groom are honeymooning. You'll meet the staff tomorrow when we take you round the Mulberry Tree.'

Louisa, who had been cutting more bread and buttering it, looked quizzically across at her eldest daughter. 'You're very quiet, alanna,' she said gently. 'Are you worried that the business won't run as smoothly as Jenny hopes whilst you're not there?'

Claudia jumped. 'Sorry, Mam, I was miles away,' she said apologetically. 'No, I'm not worried; if I was, we'd have agreed to put off our trip to Llandudno. But I think the Mulberry Tree will be safe enough.'

'That's good,' Louisa said, beginning to hand round the bread and butter. She had already poured mugs of milk for the twins and watched as the children ate, Jenny having added a generous helping of strawberry jam to each plate. 'And as soon as we've had this lovely tea that Gran and the girls have prepared for us, I think we should make our way to our lodgings and get ourselves to bed, because we've had a long day and it's well past the twins' bedtime.'

Jenny had been eyeing the children covertly ever since they had reached Blodwen Street. She thought Bernie a most attractive child with her masses of long red-gold hair confined in two thick braids. She was no longer the spitting image of her brother but had neat elfin features, whilst Benny's hair had darkened until it was more brown than red, and exactly matched his round, inquisitive eyes. Neither of the twins had been talkative, in fact they had both behaved beautifully, but Jenny, who was a realist, put this down to tiredness and imagined that by next morning the ebullience that she remembered would have returned.

She said as much to Gran when they met in the pantry, bringing out more cake, and Gran laughed softly and nodded her head. 'You're right there, queen,' she whispered. 'I've never seen 'em so good and quiet before and doubt I ever will again. Fergal told me that Bernie made the voyage hideous by demanding to be told what her bridesmaid's dress was like and prancing around ordering her brother about. Yet here she is, actually under the same roof as the perishin' dress, and not one word has she said about it.'

Gran had spoken very quietly, but clearly not quietly enough, for Bernie suddenly jumped to her feet and came to life, reminding Jenny forcibly of a jack-in-the-box she had owned as a child. 'Mammy, Mammy, where's me bridesmaid's dress? You said I could try it on before the wedding, so what's wrong wit' now?' She turned to her eldest sister. 'I'm to have me plaits made into a coronet on top of me head, with lilies of the valley to hold it in place – or was it white roses, Mam? I disremember what we decided.'

'We didn't decide anything,' Louisa said firmly. 'We can't until we know what Jenny's wearing, because bridesmaids have to be the same, you know.'

Bernie began to argue at once, but Jenny stepped in. 'I'm not going to tell you, but the headdresses have already been bought, so tomorrow morning you can try on the whole outfit, apart from shoes, that is. We'll both have the same satin slippers, but mine will be rather large because I've got big feet and yours will be small and dainty, just like yourself. And now, if you've finished, Claudia and I will walk you round to your lodgings.' She patted Bernie's shoulder, then addressed her mother. 'Will you come round here straight after breakfast, Mam? Then we can have a grand trying on of our bridesmaid's gear.'

'Then I aren't perishin' well comin',' Benny shouted, as he was ushered out into the hallway. 'I'm sick to perishin' death of weddin's and weddin' clothes and Bernie's precious coronet of plaits, or whatever. I want to go down to the docks and have a ride on the dockers' umbrella. I want to skip a lecky like Daddy's pals did when they was boys. Grandpa, you don't want to see stupid dresses, do you? Oh please, please take me on the overhead railway! I'll be real good.'

Grandpa Muldoon said they would have to see, and then Jenny and Claudia seized a twin each, Louisa tucked her hand into the crook of Cormack's arm and Fergal fell into step beside them. 'I knew such good behaviour couldn't last,' she said ruefully, then addressed her eldest daughter. 'Never mind, love, I promise you they'll behave beautifully at your wedding because your father has sworn to cancel all their privileges if they say one word out of place. Now, are you sure you want the whole family to come round early? If you prefer it your father and grandfather will take the kids off somewhere. You've only got to say the word and we'll all leave you in peace until later in the day.'

Jenny half expected Claudia to jump at the idea but her sister shook her head firmly. 'I want you all at Gran's house as soon after breakfast as you can make it,' she said. 'After all, Bernie's got to try on her bridesmaid's dress, because if it doesn't fit – though I'm sure it will – we'll have to do some emergency stitching. And no matter how little Benny may want to see his sister in all her finery, I'm sure Dad and Grandpa won't want to miss it.'

'Right; then we'll all come round first thing, and then, after Bernie's tried on her dress, we can decide what to do next,' Louisa said as they neared their lodgings. 'We could go straight to the restaurant, I suppose. Who's holding the fort for the two of you tomorrow?'

'Danny, Rob and the rest of the staff,' Claudia said.

'Don't worry, Mam, everything has been planned like a military manoeuvre. It will all go like clockwork. And now Jenny and myself had best be getting back; we'll need our beauty sleep with all that we've got planned for the next few days.'

Having bidden the Irish party goodnight, Jenny and Claudia made their way back to Blodwen Street and up to their own room, and, once there, examined Bernie's dress for what felt like the umpteenth time. 'It's a good thing we allowed for growth, because though Bernie's slim, I'm sure she's taller than I was at nine,' Claudia commented. She had taken the dress out of the wardrobe to examine it more closely and now returned it to its place. 'I'm going to get up early tomorrow – really early – so I can get the breakfast on the go,' she said. 'Don't worry about setting the alarm; I'll give you a good shake and wake you up.'

As she spoke she was undressing, folding her garments neatly and placing them on the chair at the end of her bed, whilst Jenny took off her own clothes, slung them impatiently on the dressing table and rolled between the sheets with a deep sigh. 'I'm worn out already, so God knows what I'll be like by Saturday,' she mumbled. 'Good thing it's not me getting married, because if someone else's children wear me out, however would I cope with my own?'

Claudia, who had snuggled down, sat up again and peered across the room at her sister. 'Children?' she said blankly. 'You don't have to have children just because you're married, you know. Why, if I started having children the minute I got married, how could I possibly work at the Mulberry Tree? Oh no, having children is the last thing I shall do.'

Jenny giggled. 'I know what you mean; since Benny and Bernie are our brother and sister, I suppose that any child of ours might well turn out like them,' she observed. 'But married people usually have a baby within a year of their marriage. I've heard talk about what they call birth control, but I wouldn't know where to start. Have you and Danny actually discovered what birth control means?'

It was Claudia's turn to giggle. 'You're an unmarried girl and shouldn't be discussing such things,' she said reprovingly. 'It's not the sort of subject . . .'

'Oh, come off it; you're an unmarried girl yourself,' Jenny said promptly. 'I know you'll be a married lady in a couple of days, but for now you're single, just like me. So you might tell me if I'm going to become an aunt in the next twelve months.'

Claudia had been giggly and light-hearted, or so it had seemed to Jenny, but suddenly all that changed. 'I told you I don't mean to have children, and that's all I intend to say on the subject,' she snapped. 'And now for God's sake shut up and let me get some sleep.'

With that, she turned her back ostentatiously on her sister, lay down and heaved the covers up round her ears. Jenny stared; she did not think Claudia had ever snubbed her so totally before. She was about to reply sharply herself when it occurred to her that it had not really been her own dear sister speaking, but a nervous and hard-pressed bride-to-be. Though they had all done their best to prepare everything well in advance, there was still a great deal to do which could not be done until nearer the day itself, and in addition to the work, the restaurant and similar arrangements, they now had to cope with the young Muldoons. She must not blame Claudia if she grew a little impatient with her sister's questions.

Sighing to herself, she was about to snuggle down too when she realised she had not drawn back the curtains. She got out of bed to undertake this mundane task, and heard a muffled voice from the other bed. 'Sorry I snapped,' Claudia mumbled. 'But I feel like a cat on hot bricks. Oh, how I wish Saturday was over!'

Jenny stole over to the bed and kissed her sister's cheek. 'I'm sorry too,' she said. 'Just you forget all your worries and remember you're about to become the wife of the nicest man in Liverpool. Night night, queen, and God bless.'

Comforted by her own words, Jenny returned to bed, then realised that she had one question unanswered; she had meant to ask Claudia just where she had gone the other night to meet Danny, for she did not imagine that they had met in the street, or one of the local parks. She was still wondering when the answer occurred to her. Of course! Danny had been working on the couple's new house in Sydenham Avenue, and had told her he was sleeping there from time to time. She remembered his hunted look when she had offered to help him with his decorating, and smiled to herself. Poor Danny; the last thing he would have welcomed was her presence when, later in the night, Claudia was going to turn up on his doorstep!

Sleepily, Jenny wondered how Claudia had got to and from Sydenham Avenue, for it was a long way from the bedroom in which the two girls lay. Claudia would not have walked such a distance alone . . . but no doubt Danny had sent a taxi to pick her up at an arranged time.

I wonder how she got out of the house – and back in again – without anyone noticing, though, Jenny asked herself just before sleep claimed her. Then she remembered the little landing window on the first floor, through which they had once or twice sneaked out when they were kids. Claudia was slim; doubtless she had left by that route, though it would have been safe enough to return by the back door, using the key which Gran kept above the lintel.

Satisfied, Jenny heaved the blankets up over her ears, for it was a cold night, and slept at last.

Emily Dalton was always first down and this morning was no exception, though she was quite surprised to find that someone had made up the kitchen fire. She thought it might have been Mr Payne, or even Mr Clarke, for both men completely understood how far from usual the next few days were likely to be. They had arranged to have their breakfast at an extremely early hour and had agreed to go round to Mrs Calvert's place for their supper, thus leaving the house free for the Muldoon clan. Considering how helpful Mr Payne always was, it would have been in character for him to come down specially to put fresh fuel on the fire.

So Emily pulled back the curtains, set the kettle on to

boil and began to make the porridge. Whilst it was cooking she laid the table, and presently Mr Payne and Mr Clarke came down, greeting her with the cheery smiles of two people who intended to enjoy every minute of the wedding on Saturday without having any responsibility for its smooth running. Naturally enough, they were very interested in all that had gone on the previous evening, Mr Clarke expressing his disappointment that he was probably not to meet the Irish Muldoons until the wedding day itself.

'I shall be giving them all their meals except breakfast,' Emily had told her lodgers some days before. 'Which is why Mrs Calvert will be providing you with your suppers on Wednesday, Thursday and Friday. Then it'll be the wedding, so you won't want feeding after that because we're bound to over-cater; folk always does. Sunday you'll be having a midday meal and supper with Mrs Calvert, then Monday it's back to normal routine, because the Muldoons will be off to catch the ferry at the crack of dawn.'

So now the two men tucked into their breakfast and were about to depart when the kitchen door shot open to reveal Jenny, very flushed and wearing only her long white cotton nightgown. 'Jenny!' Emily said. The girls both knew that they should never leave their room without first donning a dressing gown and slippers whilst her lodgers were in the house. 'Whatever are you thinking of, child? What's happened?'

'Where's Claudia?' Jenny said hoarsely. 'Oh, Gran, she's gone and so is her going-away suit and her new shoes. There was a note on her pillow, too.' She flourished a crumpled sheet of paper. 'It just says: *Jenny, I'm real sorry. I thought I could go through with it, but I can't.* Oh, Gran, do you think she's – she's killed herself?'

Chapter Fourteen

Emily stared at her granddaughter, trying to take in what Jenny had said. But then she heard the panic in the girl's voice and pulled herself together. 'My dear child, of course she wouldn't dream of killing herself! I expect she's gone round to Danny's lodgings, full of doubts and fears, because that's how brides tend to feel. Remember, queen, that Claudia is about to take the biggest and most important step in a woman's life. Naturally a sensitive creature like your sister will be suffering with her nerves.'

'I hope to God you're right, Gran . . .' Jenny was beginning when Mr Payne interrupted.

'Of course she's right, Miss Jenny,' he said reprovingly. 'No one who's going to commit suicide does so in a brand new suit and matching shoes! But I'm told nine out of ten brides suffer from pre-wedding nerves.' He smiled reassuringly at Jenny. 'Now, you go upstairs and make yourself respectable and Mr Clarke and meself will go round to see if she's with her mam at their lodgings in Chaucer Place. If she isn't, then we'll visit Sydenham Avenue if that's where Danny's spent the night. I'm sure we'll find your sister at one or t'other.' He turned to Mr Clarke. 'Here am I, taking your name in vain, Don! But I reckon it'll be best if we go together, and since we're neither of us due at our places of employment for another hour we shan't even have to mention to our bosses that we're late because we've gone on a bride hunt!'

Mr Clarke grinned and nodded. 'Aye, I'll come with you,' he said. 'If we find her immediately, we'll come straight back here, but it occurs to me that she might have gone to the Mulberry Tree. I reckon Mr Cormack Muldoon may want to try there, so if Miss Jenny will lend us a key Mr Muldoon can let himself in and check the flat.'

'Thank you both ever so much, but if you'll wait five minutes I'll nip upstairs and get dressed so I can come with you,' Jenny said. 'I'm afraid Claudia may feel awful foolish when she realises I've read her letter to both you and Gran. It'll be easier, really, if you come with me but stay outside the house; don't you agree?'

Mr Payne, looking relieved, began to say he did when the back door burst open and Danny erupted into the room, white-faced and sweat-streaked. He stared around for a moment, then crossed the kitchen in a couple of long strides and seized Jenny by both arms. 'Where's Claudia?' he said urgently. 'When I got up I went round to the restaurant – I was staying in Sydenham Avenue last night – to have a word with Rob. When I got there I found the place hadn't been opened up, so I let myself in and went straight up to the flat. There was an envelope on the kitchen table addressed to me in wobbly capitals and the envelope was sort of scrumpled . . .'

'Danny, for God's sake get to the point!' said Emily. 'What did *your* letter say? Claudia wrote a note to Jenny, but it simply said she couldn't go through with it, meaning the wedding I imagine.'

Danny sighed and collapsed on to a chair. 'I'd better read it to you,' he said resignedly. 'There were two letters in the envelope. I'll read Claudia's first.' He cleared his throat and began to read, but had only got as far as *'dear old Danny,'* when to Emily's consternation he broke down and began to weep with hard, difficult sobs. Quickly she took the letters from Danny's hand.

'I'll read them; you won't mind Mr Payne and Mr Clarke listening, only they've offered to search for Claudia and they've already heard the note she left for the rest of us, so . . .'

Danny was slumped in his chair, his head buried in his hands, but on hearing these words he sat up and looked hopefully at Jenny, not appearing to notice she was barefoot and wearing her nightdress. 'Have you guessed where she's gone?' he asked eagerly. 'Oh, but of course that's impossible, because she says in her letter . . .' He rubbed at his eyes. 'Sorry, Mrs Dalton; yes, I'd be very grateful if you'd read them.'

Emily went over to the dresser, picked up her reading glasses and perched them on her nose, then returned to her chair and indicated that her lodgers and her granddaughter should also sit down. Only when they were settled, did she begin to read aloud.

'My dear old Danny,
'I feel so guilty when I realise what I am doing to you, yet so wildly, unbelievably happy when I think of my future. Oh, Danny, I've loved you ever since you

rescued me when I was just a little kid, and when I came back to Liverpool and you were so successful and grown up, all my old love for you came flooding back. When you asked me to marry you, I was over the moon; all my dreams had come true and I was sure we were made for each other.

'Only then you introduced me to Rob and very soon I knew, dear Danny, that I had never been in love with you, except in the way a sister loves a brother. The feeling I had for Rob was so different from anything I'd ever felt before that I thought at first it was just infatuation, but when he told me he felt the same about me I realised that if I married you I'd be doing you a great disservice.

'Oh, at first I truly meant to go through with the wedding, because I thought once we were married and sharing a home and a bed I'd start to feel for you the way I feel for Rob, but as time went on I knew this would never happen and that by marrying you I would be committing the worst act of my life. You see, whilst Rob was alive, I'd want him whether I was married to someone else or not, and that would be adultery, wouldn't it?

'Danny, he was very good, very patient. He felt bad, as I did, particularly as the wedding was so near. But a week ago we agreed that by marrying you I'd ruin three lives, so Rob bought a special licence and we're going away together. We'll come back, of course, because we shall need to talk about the Mulberry Tree and our future. But by the time we return, we'll be man and wife and arguments or reproaches will be pointless.

'Try to forgive me, Danny; I love you still, but only
as my old school friend, or an older brother,
'Claudia'

Gran laid down the letter, took off her reading glasses
and pinched the bridge of her nose, then glanced at the
faces around her. Claudia had always been her favourite
grandchild and she knew Louisa, too, had always
favoured the older girl, but now Emily wondered how
the two of them could have been so blind. By spoiling
Claudia, it seemed they had created a monster of
selfishness. How could the girl have penned such a letter
in cold blood, never once admitting that she had behaved
disgracefully, seeming to expect, if not Danny's
approval, at least his compliance and understanding?
And she was not surprised that the faces around her
reflected her feelings; they all knew what a bombshell
this would be to the entire family.

Emily replaced her glasses, picked up the second
letter, and then handed it to Jenny. 'You read this one,'
she began brokenly. 'I can't.'

Jenny took the letter and began to read, her voice not
quite steady.

'Dear Danny,
'You'll think I'm a rotter and a heel and I suppose I
am. I knew months ago that I loved Claudia but she took
some persuading. When I realised she felt the same as
me I was over the moon, couldn't believe my luck. I
wanted to tell you right away, but Claudia wouldn't let
me. Poor kid, I think she imagined something would

happen, like you falling in love with someone else, or another world war breaking out! Daft really, but women are like that.

'So she went ahead with her wedding plans, wouldn't listen at first when I said she was being unfair to everyone. Then a couple of weeks ago I played my trump card. I said if she wouldn't call the wedding off and marry me instead of you, I'd go back to America, or top myself; I said she could choose.

'No need to tell you, me old pal, which she chose. So we're off to get hitched. I got a special licence a while back, so we're taking a couple of weeks off and we'll discuss what to do about the Mulberry Tree when we're in Liverpool once more.

'I'm real sorry, old chap, but these things happen in the best regulated circles!

'Rob Dingle'

Jenny put the letter down. Emily leaned across to pat Danny's shoulder. 'I think we're all agreed that both Claudia and Rob have behaved disgracefully,' she said quietly. 'You could try to pursue them, Danny, but even if you caught up with them later this very day, I'm afraid you wouldn't change their minds. What we must do now, all of us, is to clear up the mess which these two very selfish people have left behind them. Fortunately, the only wedding guests who were coming from away are Rob's relatives. But we've got time to put them off before Saturday if we act at once.'

Jenny snorted inelegantly. 'I bet Rob has already told them,' she said calmly. 'He's very keen on money, is

Rob, and his relatives are probably the same. If they travelled all the way to Liverpool on a wild goose chase, first they'd be absolutely furious and then they'd demand their rail fares back; Rob knows that, so he'll have written already. And as for our family, they'll be a real help, won't they Gran? Dad and Mam will back us up, you know they will.'

Emily smiled at her granddaughter. What a good girl Jenny was; both sensible and practical! She had not argued that Claudia might be persuaded to change her mind, but was simply getting on with the task of cancelling all their arrangements with as little ado as possible. Emily gave her an approving nod, then turned to Danny. 'Danny dear, this is very hard on you and I'm sure we'll all do everything we can to spare you as much pain as possible, but you are the only person who can cancel the priest and the church.'

Danny looked desperately from one face to the other. 'But surely if I can find out where they've gone, it might still be possible to get Claudia to change her mind. I'd do anything, anything at all. Oh, dear God, I've spent so much time on the restaurant that I must have neglected her, made her think I didn't really care. If I could just find them . . .'

Mr Payne and Mr Clarke had been sitting very still in their chairs, glancing from face to face, but now Mr Clarke spoke. 'You've done nothing wrong, la',' he said, his voice rough with concern. 'Don't you go thinking any of this muddle was of your making, because it weren't. If you'll forgive me saying so, I never took to that there Rob. Too charmin' by half, he was.'

284

Mr Payne nodded grimly. 'Oh aye, a young fellow with charm can get away with all sorts, but I wouldn't be surprised if he had some swindle going in America which was about to come to the notice of his superiors. Come to that, I'd like to know why he and Miss Claudia waited until the restaurant was on the point of being sold to you, Danny, before making their move. If I were you I'd have a word with your bank manager and make sure Rob hasn't walked off with more than your young lady.'

Danny jumped to his feet. 'I'll do that just as soon as the bank opens,' he said, brokenly. 'But I must find Claudia before it's too late. She knows nothing of Rob except for what I've told her and of course I never said a word against him. Why should I? He put money into the Mulberry Tree, worked like a dog to set it up . . . I've simply got to find her!'

'Over here, miss!'

Jenny, in a black uniform dress and frilly apron, pushed a hand through her hair and turned towards the man who was calling her. It was almost six o'clock on the day Claudia and Rob had run off, and Danny had gone in pursuit of them, telling Jenny to take any decisions she saw fit. Jenny might have considered this a compliment had she not realised that Danny would have allowed a chimpanzee to take over at the Mulberry Tree in order that he might pursue his fiancée and her lover. Not that Danny knew Rob was her lover, Jenny reminded herself, for he knew nothing of Claudia's midnight wanderings, but Jenny had little doubt now that her sister and Rob had not merely met to exchange a few cuddles.

Now, however, she hurried over to the customer who had hailed her, and apologised for the delay in serving him. 'I'm afraid a couple of waitresses and a member of the kitchen staff failed to come in this morning,' she said, giving him her friendliest smile. 'My mam and dad, and my gran, are all helping out but they aren't as quick as the regular staff, as you can imagine.'

'Aye, I can that, and we've no complaints about service,' the man said jovially. 'In fact we've had a rare good meal, me and the missus, but we thought we'd round it off wi' a nice cup of tea. So if you'll be kind enough to bring our bill and a pot of tea for two, we'll be well satisfied.'

'You shall have the tea in a trice, and your bill of course,' Jenny said, pouncing on their empty plates and hurrying back to the kitchen. Betty and her mother were washing up and stacking dishes whilst Gran was making up the orders as they were brought through from the restaurant, though these, she thanked the Lord, were slowing from a stream to a trickle as closing time approached.

Now, putting together a tea tray for two, Jenny reflected that it had been the devil of a day. When Danny had told her that she was in charge, she and Gran had rushed round to the Muldoons' lodgings, since Jenny had decided immediately that they should open the restaurant as though no disaster had occurred. Fortunately she had not had to explain anything to her parents since Claudia had left them a similar letter to that addressed to Danny, and to do them justice, the Muldoons had not wasted time in repining, but had left the younger members of the family with Fergal and come straight to the Mulberry Tree.

Jenny poured hot water into the teapot, checked that she had filled the little milk jug and sugar basin, and looked round wildly for the waitress who had served that particular table. It was Freda, and she had just come in from the restaurant, so when Jenny gave her the table number she was able at once to make out their bill, which the customer would hand to Cormack, who had taken over the cash desk.

Jenny delivered her tea tray and the bill, and was returning to the kitchen when Freda caught her up. She was an excellent waitress, quick and efficient, despite being the wrong side of forty and weighing in at fourteen stone. She had worked like a slave all day, showing no signs of tiredness, and now she addressed Jenny in her usual calm fashion. 'Shall I go and turn the *Open* notice on the door to *Closed*, Miss Jenny?' she enquired. 'I know it ain't quite six o'clock, but if folk keep coming in we'll be here till midnight, so we will.'

'Oh, please, Freda; you're a brick, you think of everything,' Jenny said gratefully, knowing it was true. Both waitresses and kitchen staff turned to Freda when they had questions which Jenny couldn't answer, and though Mrs Bland was a first-rate cook, her working hours finished at four in the afternoon when she hurried home to take over responsibility for her three grandchildren so that her daughter, who was employed as a cinema usherette, might have a meal in peace before going off to work. Jenny watched through the swing doors that divided the kitchen from the restaurant as Freda turned the sign from *Open* to *Closed* and clicked the lock across. Then she glanced around the restaurant and was pleased to see that only three tables out of the thirty were still occupied. Earlier, she had voiced astonishment at the sudden influx of customers wanting an evening meal, but Jane, the younger waitress, had enlightened her. 'There's been a sale of fire-damaged goods at a warehouse near here,' she had said. 'I dunno who tells folks – perhaps there's a notice by Lime Street station – but they get to hear of it and come along, hopin' for bargains. It's awful stuffy in the saleroom, an' that makes 'em think to theirselves that a cuppa would be nice, then as they make their way back to the city centre they see the Mulberry Tree, all clean paint and shiny chairs with a board saying special offer on tea and scones, and they pops in. Next thing you know they're tellin' their pals as how it's grand grub and low prices and news like that spreads like . . .' she giggled, 'like wildfire. So it's bully for us, ain't it, Miss Jenny?'

'It certainly is,' Jenny had said and even now, tired out though she was, she rejoiced in the money they had taken for she knew they needed every penny to buy the place and make the changes they wanted. It would be grand news to pass on to Danny, when he reappeared from his fruitless search. That it would be fruitless she was sure. Claudia's mind was made up, and even if Danny did find them before they had actually married, Jenny was certain that her sister would not even consider returning to Danny. She had burned her boats too thoroughly to back down, and though Jenny could not begin to understand how anyone could prefer Rob to Danny, she was sure that her sister must be deeply in love to take such an enormous step – and one which must leave her open to the suggestion that she was a heartless jilt.

Despite the notice on the door it was seven o'clock before the family were able to leave the restaurant. Jenny offered to take her parents to Sydenham Avenue, but Cormack set his lips in a tight line and when he spoke it was with chilly formality. 'I'm not interested in Claudia's nest-making, if you can call it that,' he said grimly. 'I've not met the feller she ran off with, nor do I want to, but I do know Danny, who's a grand, hard-working chap and doesn't deserve what she's done to him. As for this house, does she intend to come back here and live in it with this – this Dingle feller? Because if so, I think Danny may have a thing or two to say.'

'Oh, Cormack, my love, don't be too hard on her,' Louisa pleaded and Emily saw, for the first time, how white and strained was her daughter's face and how tear-filled her big blue eyes. 'I'm her mother and a mother's love never dies, you know. I can't just wash my hands of my beautiful daughter because she's behaved so badly. She's in love, and love makes women do strange things.'

'Well I can't condone what she's done,' Cormack said, 'and I'll tell her to her face what I'm telling you now, that she'll never cross my threshold again, for she's forfeited the right to be treated as my daughter.'

Emily nodded sorrowfully; Claudia had always been her favourite but this time she had gone too far. What she had done was unforgivable and Emily felt betrayed by the dreadful, shaming way Claudia had behaved. She supposed, rather guiltily, that she had always known Claudia was selfish and went her own way; always known in fact that Jenny was the more sterling character of the two.

'Darling Cormack, you couldn't be so cruel!' Louisa said. 'Oh, I know she's done wrong and you're angry with her now, but you mustn't set your face against her and forbid her our home. Why, if Danny will have nothing to do with them when they return, whatever are they to do? They'll want to come to us, having nowhere else to go, and I couldn't . . .'

She tried to throw her arms round her husband's neck, but he held her off, his expression unyielding. 'No, Louisa,' he said, his voice colder than Emily had ever heard it. 'Claudia has made her bed and now she must lie on it. C'mon; God knows me poor father has had the kids for quite long enough. It's time we all took a turn.'

Danny left the house in Blodwen Street telling himself that he had done right to put Jenny in charge of the Mulberry Tree whilst he himself searched for Claudia and Rob. He knew Mrs Dalton thought he should cancel the wedding immediately, yet in his heart he thought it still possible that his marriage might go ahead, if he could find the runaways, that was. He was sure Claudia had been influenced, nay persuaded, by Rob, and if he could just talk to her, explain that this was simply a bad case of pre-wedding nerves, she might come to her senses.

He was halfway along the Scotland Road when it occurred to him that he had no idea where the runaways might go. They could be staying in any guest house or even in a hotel, and he could scarcely search every such establishment in the city. Yet he could not imagine either Rob or Claudia wanting to remain in the vicinity; they would be afraid to emerge on to the streets of Liverpool in case they were spotted, for he was pretty certain the last thing either of them wanted would be a confrontation. No, they would leave Liverpool as far behind them as they could. Then, when they reached their destination, he supposed they would marry, which made it even more important that he should catch up with them.

When he reached Lime Street station he went straight to the booking office, meaning to ask whether a young couple, the woman dressed in a leaf-green going-away suit, had booked tickets on a very early train that day, but before he was halfway up the queue he remembered that someone had mentioned a special licence. He had a vague feeling that a special licence had something to do with a flight to Scotland, so he decided to change his enquiry to ask about trains going in that direction.

When he reached the head of the queue, the booking clerk seemed amused by his question. He waved a hand around him at the crowded concourse. 'I seen a couple of hundred gals like what you describe, with a young feller in tow,' he said largely. 'D'you want a ticket or don't ya? I'm a booking clerk norra bleedin' enquiries office.'

'Sorry,' Danny muttered, turning away. Now that he looked the facts in the face he saw that his mission was impossible; searching at random for two young people was like looking for a needle in a haystack. The sensible thing to do, and perhaps in his heart he had always known it, was to give up all thought of finding his darling girl and get back to the restaurant, where he knew very well he was needed.

He was turning back towards Heyworth Street when another thought struck him, a thought so astonishing that it stopped him in his tracks. He had booked their honeymoon weeks ago and paid a sizeable deposit too. If he could get in touch with the Wavecrest Hotel in Llandudno, then it was just possible he would find Claudia and Rob already there. Yes! It would be the obvious thing to do, for surely with that special licence they would be able to marry in the seaside town as easily as they could have done in Scotland.

Danny turned on his heel, hurried back to the station, and re-joined the queue at the booking office. It was a pity the Wavecrest was not on the telephone, but in this instance a personal visit would be best.

It was two in the afternoon before Danny crossed the concourse again and hesitated on the pavement outside the station. All he had done, he reflected savagely, was to waste a perfectly good morning, for his trip had been fruitless. There had been no sign of the couple anywhere in Llandudno, and when he had asked at the Wavecrest the proprietress had told him that she had neither a Muldoon nor a Dingle from Liverpool staying in her establishment. Danny had thanked her and turned blindly away. Although he realised it was pointless, he had wandered round the town, thinking that if the runaways were here he might bump into them, but of course he had not done so and after a miserable hour he had returned to the station and caught the next train back to Liverpool.

Now, however, he began to head for Heyworth Street, thinking he might as well give a hand at the Mulberry Tree and talk over with Jenny what his next move should be, though this would be admitting failure, which he was still reluctant to do.

As he hesitated on the pavement he realised, suddenly, that he was both hungry and thirsty, and turned impulsively into a small café. He ordered tea and a ham sandwich and was beginning to eat when another, and nastier, thought reared its ugly head. Mr Payne had advised him to visit the bank; suppose Rob had seen fit to take out the money he had put in when they had bought the lease of the Mulberry Tree? In a way, Danny supposed such an action would be fair enough, because Rob and Claudia could scarcely survive on the small salaries which the partners took out of the business. But if Rob had taken his money, though he might still be able to buy the restaurant, it would mean giving up all idea of converting the flat, for the present at any rate.

Danny finished the sandwich, drained his cup of tea, paid the waitress and left the café, turning his steps towards his bank on Castle Street. As he hurried along, he glanced at the clock, remembering that the banks closed at three and realising that he would only just make it in time.

In fact he was within a few yards of the imposing doors when one of the bank clerks with whom he had become friendly ran lightly down the steps and greeted him cheerfully. 'How you doin', Danny? You're cuttin' it fine, aren't you? I take it you're payin' in?'

'How're you doin' yourself, Stu?' Danny said glibly. 'No, I'm not paying in; I want a word with the manager concerning our account.'

Stu pulled a face. 'You'll get short shrift from Mr Valentine if you ask for an interview when he's all geared up to go home,' he observed. 'He'll not look kindly on you this afternoon and he likes to see people by appointment, you know. Tell you what, I'll come back now and book you in for tomorrow mornin'. Eleven o'clock suit you?'

'I'd rather earlier; by eleven o'clock the Mulberry Tree's getting pretty busy and – and we've a bit of a staff shortage, so I'm needed at the restaurant,' Danny said. 'Why do you suggest eleven o'clock?'

The other man laughed and ushered Danny up the steps and into the bank ahead of him. 'Because the old feller has his cup o' tea and biscuit at a quarter to the hour an' it puts him in a good mood,' he explained. 'So I'll book you an appointment for eleven o'clock, right?'

Reflecting that he might need a bank loan if Rob had indeed withdrawn his money, Danny nodded.

'I'll be here,' he said. 'Thanks, Stu.'

Walking back down the steps, Danny felt it was only

fair that he should return to the restaurant and see how they were getting on, yet he was still reluctant to do so. He knew he must consult with Jenny, young though she was, because she was still his partner and anyway, she loved and admired Claudia and would, he was sure, do her best to understand just what had happened to make her sister behave the way she had. On the other hand, he had no wish to be forced to hear his love's behaviour discussed by the rest of her family, so he decided to kill time and meet Jenny when the restaurant closed.

Accordingly, he strolled aimlessly around the city centre until he guessed that the restaurant would be closing, when he made his way up Heyworth Street. He was lucky enough to arrive at the Mulberry Tree just as Jenny was emerging from it. He saw she was looking sad and preoccupied, but when she glanced up her eyes brightened and a smile of relief crossed her face.

'Danny! Oh, thank God you're back,' she said fervently. 'When you didn't come in for a bite of dinner, or some supper come to that, I got real worried. I mean Claudia and Rob could be anywhere, not just in Liverpool, but anywhere. I've read in books that people wanting to get married, when they're under age like Claudia is, run away to Scotland, and I was afraid you'd not got enough money for a ticket, because tomorrow's pay day and none of us carry much cash.' She took his hand and gripped it tightly for a moment, then turned back towards the restaurant, fishing her key from her coat pocket. 'Are you hungry? I can make you a meal in two ticks, or a drink come to that. But I knew the moment I saw you coming up the road that you'd not had any luck, so I do think we should have a serious talk, and it might as well be over a meal. You look as if you could do with one.'

Danny forced a laugh, though he knew it was a pretty poor effort. 'I've just had a sandwich and a cup of tea, so I don't need feeding,' he said somewhat untruthfully. 'I did think about Scotland, you were right there, but then I remembered Llandudno. We'd booked into the Wavecrest Hotel, from Saturday, and I thought . . . hoped . . .'

Jenny's eyes rounded and he saw that they were filled with tears. 'Oh, Danny, how awful for you! But not even Rob would be mean enough to take over your honeymoon booking.' As they turned away from the restaurant, she tucked a small hand into his arm. 'Look, dear Danny, I know you don't want to come back to Blodwen Street and my family, but we've got to be practical. Gran's getting all the Muldoons a meal, but she won't serve it until I turn up. She's making out lists of what must be done, and though I know it will be painful you're the only one, now, who can advise her. Will you come back with me?'

Danny heaved a great, trembling sigh, then nodded. 'Of course I will,' he said and noticed, almost with pride, that his voice was steady. 'I kept hoping that the wedding might still go ahead, but I can see it won't happen, and I'm very grateful to Mrs Dalton and you Muldoons for the help you're offering. Let's go!'

By the time Danny and Jenny returned to No. 22, Emily had fed the twins and hustled them off to bed in their lodgings, where the landlady had promised to keep an eye on them, though Emily thought, privately, that this would probably be unnecessary for their day had been a busy one. Fergal had been marvellous, as usual, somehow managing to keep the twins happy whilst helping her in every way he could.

Now, however, the family settled themselves round the kitchen table, Danny white-faced and grim-looking, Jenny pale and unhappy and even Louisa and Cormack showing signs of strain, which was scarcely surprising. They would have the double duty of telling their Liverpool friends and their Irish ones that the wedding had come to nothing. Emily, horribly aware that she had always favoured and spoiled Claudia, guessed that Louisa would feel the same. But right now was no time to dwell on the mistakes of the past; now they must plan for the future.

She dished up the stew which had been simmering for a couple of hours on the back of the stove, and left everyone to help themselves from a big tureen of boiled potatoes. Her lodgers were at Mrs Calvert's for their supper, and knowing the situation would come back and go straight up to their rooms so that the family – and Danny – might plan their next moves without interruption.

Emily waited until the meal was over, then piled the crockery and cutlery into the sink and got out the notebook in which she had been jotting down the many tasks to be performed. She put on her spectacles and began to read out loud, glancing up occasionally to make sure everyone understood. 'First, I've a list of all the wedding guests who live in the area, and whenever I wasn't too busy in the restaurant today I wrote postcards to all of them. We'll get one of the local kids to deliver 'em. I'll choose a reliable lad, so don't worry about that. One of the waitresses – Freda it were – has made a lovely notice for the window of the Mulberry Tree, saying the place will be open as usual come Saturday.' She looked kindly at Danny over the top of her spectacles. 'There's nowt we can do about the wedding cake, but Mrs Fleming says she can skim off the names and that, and the baker will put it in his window, which will be a saving when it sells. I'm sorry if I maybe jumped the gun a bit, Danny, but time is runnin' out.'

'It's all right, Mrs Dalton, honestly it is,' Danny said, his voice cracking. 'I suppose I knew from the moment I read Rob's letter that the wedding wasn't ever going to take place, so you did right to let folk know.'

Emily nodded. 'Yes, I thought you'd see it that way. But Danny, there are two things you've simply got to do for yourself. Only you can cancel the actual wedding ceremony; I think you ought to go round to the presbytery tonight and tell Father O'Donoghue what's happened, and the other thing of course is the honeymoon. That must be cancelled, and again that's something only you can do. I checked that the Wavecrest isn't on the telephone, so I'm afraid it will have to be a telegram, but of course there's absolutely no need for any explanation other than "unforeseen circumstances", which will do very well.'

Jenny looked across at her grandmother. 'Wharrabout the house in Sydenham Avenue?' she said. 'Danny won't want to live there all by himself, I'm sure. And there's the furniture; I don't think the shop will take it back, and it was awful expensive, Claudia told me so.'

'I'll go and see the landlord tomorrow morning, before I go to the bank,' Danny said wearily. 'The fact is, Mrs Dalton, if Rob has taken out the money he put into the business two years ago, we won't be able to convert the flat as we had planned, so I can live there. That's why I'm seeing the bank manager tomorrow. As for the furniture, we'll have to sell it second hand, at a loss, I suppose.'

No one had spoken whilst Emily had read out her list, but now Cormack cleared his throat and addressed Danny. 'I'm awful sorry me daughter's behaved like a right little trollop,' he muttered awkwardly. 'I guess it's natural for me to want to blame the feller, but if I'm honest I have to admit that Claudia's as much at fault as Dingle. She's been taught to know right from wrong and should have steered clear of a feller like Rob, seeing as she was engaged to you, Danny. I just wish we could help more than we've done so far.'

'It's all right, Mr Muldoon; no point in laying blame,' Danny said gruffly. 'What puzzles me is how the devil they managed to fall in love right under our eyes without any one of us so much as suspecting . . .'

His voice trailed off as Jenny waved an arm, as a school pupil might have done. 'It were when you moved into Sydenham Avenue,' she said sadly. 'I caught her coming back into our room at an ungodly hour one night. I asked her where she'd been and she let me think she were with you, but now I reckon she went to the flat to be with Rob.' Danny made a choking sound and Jenny hastened into speech once more. 'Oh, Danny, I'm so sorry; perhaps I shouldn't have said. But she swore she'd not done things bad girls do; she said it were just talking, getting to know each other. That's why I thought it were you. Oh, Danny, I shouldn't have said.'

Danny gave a harsh bark of laughter. 'Well, you've solved one mystery,' he said, getting to his feet. 'And now I'm off to the presbytery.' He turned to his hostess. 'Thanks for all you've done, Mrs D, and for a grand supper, but I'd best gerron my way.'

Jenny jumped to her feet as Danny began to put on his overcoat. 'I'll come with you,' she said eagerly. 'You don't want to go alone on such a horrid errand.'

Emily waited for him to refuse but was glad when he nodded his head, took Jenny's coat from its peg, and helped her to put it on. Then the two of them went out into the chilly March night, closing the door gently behind them.

Emily smiled round at the grave faces of her family. 'There's hope for him yet,' she said consolingly. 'He's thought the world of Claudia ever since they were a couple of mucky kids playing cherry wobs in the gutter, and you don't get rid of feelings like that overnight. But he'll meet another pretty girl, one who appreciates him, and realise that Claudia throwing him over was really a great piece of luck.' She went over to the stove, took the kettle from the hob and carried it over to the sink. 'And now let's get the washing up done and put away,' she said briskly. 'Tomorrow's another day, and until Danny can advertise for extra staff we shall have to be round there at the crack of dawn, giving a hand. So let's gerron with it, Muldoons.'

Jenny had accompanied Danny to the presbytery, as she had promised, and waited for Danny in the hall. He had been closeted with Father O'Donaghue for an hour and had emerged with a rather fixed smile saying, almost cheerfully, that once he had cancelled the honeymoon there would be nothing left to do save get on with their lives as though the wedding had never been planned.

'You've got to see the bank manager,' Jenny had reminded him. 'If you are right and Rob has withdrawn the money he put into the restaurant, then you'll need a bank loan, which may take some negotiating, I suppose. So I'll open the restaurant, put up the notice telling customers that the Mulberry Tree will be open as usual on Saturday since the private party has been cancelled, and get on with all the normal work. You'll come along to give a hand as soon as your interview with Mr Valentine is finished. Right?'

'Sounds fine,' Danny said, and Jenny thought that whatever the priest had said to him, it had helped him to accept the situation.

Danny had walked with her to the nearest tram stop, then turned away saying, rather apologetically, that he would spend the night at the house in Sydenham Avenue. 'To tell you the truth, I didn't sleep much last night and today's been pretty exhausting,' he said, giving Jenny a rueful grin just as the tram drew up alongside. 'See you tomorrow, queen.'

Next morning, Jenny woke early and was able, for

the first time since the drama had begun, to examine her own feelings. It was odd, she reflected, getting out of bed and beginning to prepare for the day ahead, that she had not secretly rejoiced upon realising that Claudia did not mean to marry Danny. After all, she had been dreading the moment when they became man and wife. Yet when it had actually happened and she had known that Danny was as free as he would ever be, she had entered into his feelings of loss and despair so thoroughly that it was only now she began to hope once more.

Oh, she didn't hope that Danny might transfer his affections from Claudia to herself, but merely that their old friendship might gradually ease his pain. One day Danny would fall in love with another pretty girl, but Jenny decided, washing her arms with a soapy flannel, that she would face up to that when, or if, it happened. For the present, she would simply support Danny in whatever course he decided to take. And right now, the best way of supporting him was to get down to the Mulberry Tree, open up and start the day's trading. She knew that the family would be at the restaurant before it opened, and having washed and dressed she hurried downstairs to get breakfast going, for she thought that Gran might have overslept since the previous day had been pretty hectic for all of them.

Upon entering the kitchen, however, she realised that she had misjudged the older woman. Emily was spooning porridge into four bowls and the lodgers were already seated at the table. It was early, but no doubt they had heard Gran descending the stairs and had realised that she would be needed at the Mulberry Tree, so had come down early themselves.

Nice fellers, Jenny thought gratefully, sliding into her place, greeting everyone with a cheerful 'good morning' and sprinkling brown sugar on her porridge. Nice fellers, who would do anything they could to help.

Emily poured tea and handed the mugs round, then settled down to eat her own breakfast so fast that when Jenny finished her tea and stood up, she followed suit. 'I'm coming with you this morning,' she said when Jenny raised her eyebrows upon seeing her reach her coat down from its peg. 'I know you'll say you can manage, but another pair of hands is always useful.'

Jenny smiled at her, put on her own coat and bade the lodgers a cheery farewell, and the two women set off. Another day had begun.

At eleven o'clock, Jenny thought of Danny talking to the bank manager, explaining as best he could what had happened and why it would now be necessary to apply for a loan. On the other hand, now that Danny had decided to relinquish the rented house in Sydenham Avenue and live in the flat above the restaurant himself, a bank loan might not be necessary; Jenny had always been useless at arithmetic. But when Danny had not reappeared by noon, she guessed that he must be applying for a loan.

The rush for dinners started at around twelve o'clock, as it always did, and this took Jenny's mind from the interview with Mr Valentine to the practicalities of the restaurant. Gran, bless her, was in the cash desk; she was not as quick as Claudia, having had far less experience, but a lot quicker than everyone else. Louisa was in the kitchen, helping Betty with the washing up, and Cormack and Fergal had taken the twins for the long promised ride on the overhead railway. Jenny herself waited on, sorted out orders and generally saw to it that everything went smoothly.

When the restaurant door shot open at almost one o'clock and Danny rushed into the restaurant, Jenny couldn't help smiling with relief until she saw how pale he was, saw the look on his face. What on earth could have happened to make him look so grim, she wondered, but was not left long in ignorance.

'Jenny! You'll never believe . . .' Danny began, then stopped short, seeming to realise for the first time that everyone was staring at him. He was breathing hard, clearly very distressed, but when Jenny pinched his arm, warningly, he pulled himself together. 'Come into the office, Miss Muldoon,' he said, and Jenny could hear the anxiety behind every word. 'I've got to speak to you.'

As soon as they were both inside the office, Danny shut the door and sank into the chair, staring up at Jenny, who was still standing, but saying nothing. He was still breathing hard.

Jenny sat down in the other chair and had opened her mouth to ask him what had gone wrong when he spoke. 'They've gone and taken all the money, every last penny piece,' he said bitterly. 'We're finished, Jenny, washed up, kaput. Even if Mrs Tuttle would agree to extending the lease – which she won't – I doubt we'd be able to continue trading.'

Jenny stared. 'But . . . how's that possible?' she stammered. 'Are you certain? What did Mr Valentine say?'

'He was very sorry but said he knew we were buying the business, so naturally thought when Rob cleared the accounts that the money would go to Mrs Tuttle, or perhaps I should say the majority of the money. He was very good; let me telephone the police from his office and a couple of the major shipping lines, because now we know they've taken the money he thinks, and I agree with him, that they'll have gone abroad, probably to America. We checked the shipping lines for the name Dingle or Muldoon, but no luck.'

Jenny jumped to her feet. 'They won't use their own names,' she said excitedly. 'I reckon Rob's been planning this for a while, ever since Mrs Tuttle offered to let us buy the Mulberry Tree in fact. And I think Mr Valentine was right: they'll go abroad, probably to America. There's a liner sailing to the States today; d'you think it's possible . . .?'

Danny jumped to his feet. 'Bless you, Jenny wren,' he said hoarsely. 'Why didn't it occur to me that they wouldn't use their own names? I must get down to the docks at once; I'll sail with the ship, if that's the only way to catch them and get our money back.'

He made for the door, but Jenny grabbed his jacket as he passed her. 'I'm coming with you,' she squeaked. 'She's my sister and I can't believe she can know that Rob's taken money that doesn't belong to him. He's a thief, Danny, and thieves, when they realise they've been found out, are like cornered rats. I know you'll want to do something desperate. I wonder, can the dock police stop them leaving?'

Danny ground his teeth. 'If I catch up with him, I'll stop him going anywhere, except to hospital,' he said grimly.

They left the restaurant and erupted on to the pavement where Danny hailed a passing taxi, which drew into the kerb at once. Distractedly, he patted Jenny's shoulder. 'You go back, queen,' he said hastily, as the driver came round and opened the passenger door. 'Someone's got to keep an eye on the Mulberry Tree . . . I may have to go aboard the ship . . .'

'Bugger the Mulberry Tree,' Jenny panted, piling behind him into the taxi. 'I'm coming too.'

'Oh, OK,' Danny said resignedly. 'Tell you what, Jenny, if we manage to find them, you hang on to Claudia whilst I deal with Rob. I don't want to have to use physical force if I can help it, but it may be the only way.'

A few minutes later, the taxi drew to a halt and they jumped out. Danny thrust a hand into his pocket, drew out some money and pushed it into the driver's hand, then turned to scan the quayside. A big liner was preparing to leave . . . and suddenly Danny gave a triumphant shout. 'There they are! See them? They're already aboard, but if I hurry . . .'

On the words, he ran recklessly towards the liner. Jenny shrieked a warning as two large lorries converged upon the running figure. Helplessly, knowing she could do nothing, but unable to prevent herself from trying, Jenny, too, ran into the road but stopped short as she saw Danny actually thrown into the air by the impact. Then he crashed to the ground and even from where she was standing, rooted to the spot with horror, Jenny saw the blood. She also saw the couple Danny had mistakenly believed were Rob and Claudia, turning away from the rail.

Jenny screamed and screamed, running towards the crumpled body in the roadway, whilst both lorry drivers tumbled from their cabs to assure passers-by, and each other, that the young man had run straight in front of them, that they had had no chance of avoiding him. Jenny fell on her knees beside Danny, then turned to glare up at the circle of faces surrounding her. 'Don't just stand there, get an ambulance,' she ordered, her voice breaking on a sob. 'And hurry, for God's sake!'

Chapter Fifteen

For several weary days Danny lay in the Stanley Hospital in a coma, his life in the balance, and for most of that time Jenny sat by his bedside, sharing the duty with his mother, though the older woman was so distressed by her son's appearance that she wept continually during her vigil, which Jenny privately thought could not possibly help Danny, but on the contrary might do harm. However, since he had not yet regained consciousness, she said nothing but consoled Mrs Callaghan as best she could.

At first Jenny could scarcely bear to look at his poor injured face, with the lines of stitches marching across cheek, brow and chin. Yet nothing would have made her leave him. He had a great many injuries beside the facial ones, most of them on his left side: a cracked collarbone, a left arm broken in two places, four broken ribs and a fractured tibia. The surgeon told Jenny that they had had to put a metal plate into the collarbone and another in a hip joint, but it was his head injury which worried the doctors most at first. However, the consultant said that Danny's youth and strength would stand him in good stead in the battle for recovery. Jenny had feared that what with his injuries and his despair, he might simply die and leave her for ever bereft, but the doctor's words reassured her. 'Sometimes a coma can actually assist recovery,' he had told her when he saw the worried look on her face. 'Of course, with so many broken bones it will be a while before he can work again, but I take it you are managing the restaurant in his absence?'

'I'm doing my best,' Jenny said gruffly. 'When Mrs Callaghan takes over here for a while, I go back to the restaurant to check on what's being done. Then I write out instructions for the next day and put them on Danny's desk in the office. But do you realise, Mr Todd, that when our lease runs out in a few days Mrs Tuttle will sell the Mulberry Tree to the highest bidder?'

The surgeon raised a quizzical eyebrow. 'Not to you? Or rather not to Mr Callaghan?'

Jenny sighed, but explained the situation as briefly as she could.

Mr Todd nodded. 'I understand. Then I take it money will be short?'

Jenny shrugged. 'I'll get a job as soon as Mr Callaghan's well enough to be left,' she said rather guardedly. 'It's quite likely that whoever buys The Mulberry Tree will need a manageress . . . but that's all for the future.'

Jenny knew that whilst Danny was so ill a bank loan to prolong the lease was out of the question, especially as she was still a minor and would not be considered even as a tenant. She still found it difficult to accept that anyone would deliberately steal from a friend, yet every time she went into the restaurant a wave of pain and rage engulfed her, for though she hated to admit it even to herself, she knew that Claudia must have connived with Rob over the theft. Her sister was bright and clever; she would not have been deceived by any story Rob had made up to account for his sudden wealth. She must have realised Rob was a thief, yet she had still run off with him, deserting both her fiancé and her little sister.

As they had planned, the Muldoons left Liverpool for Ireland on the Monday following Claudia's flight. Louisa had offered to stay on and so had Fergal, but Jenny had insisted that they leave. The restaurant was Mrs Tuttle's concern now, she had told them firmly; their responsibility was to their croft. Anyway, now that Danny's prognosis was better, she could cope very well, with the help of Gran and her lodgers.

Now, sitting by Danny's bed one quiet afternoon in early April, holding his hand and reading to him from a copy of *Treasure Island*, she raised her eyes from the page for a moment and saw, with a stab of excitement, that Danny's eyes were open and fixed on her face with an expression of painful intensity in their depths. She dropped the book and leaned over the bed. 'Danny? Oh, my— oh, Danny, you're awake! I'll fetch a nurse . . . the doctor . . . oh, Danny, I was beginning to think . . .'

'Did we catch them?' Danny's voice was slow and slurred, but it was clear that he was in full possession of his senses. 'I remember seeing them, then I ran into the road to try to catch up with them . . . then . . .'

'You were knocked down,' Jenny said briefly. 'And the people you thought were Rob and Claudia weren't anyone we knew at all.'

Danny heaved a very small, very defeated sigh. 'What

else have you done to try to find them?' he asked, rather hopelessly. 'And how long have I been here? What's happening to the Mulberry Tree? Have you arranged that loan?'

Poor Jenny was in a dilemma. She simply did not know how much it would be safe to tell Danny, so she said rather feebly: 'You've been here quite a long time, Danny; more than two weeks. But everyone's been very good. The bank manager can't do much, though, until you're able to sign things.'

There was a long pause whilst Danny stared into space, a frown creasing his brow, before he spoke. 'I'm tired,' he mumbled. 'Tired, tired, tired.' His heavy lids drooped over his dark eyes in their shadowed hollows and for a moment Jenny thought that he had gone to sleep. Then his lids lifted again and he looked straight at her. 'You're a good kid,' he murmured. 'Find them for me. I know if it's possible you'll do it.' Then he gave a little sigh, his head rolled on the pillow, and Jenny knew from his breathing that this time he really was asleep.

When she repeated the conversation she had had with Danny to the doctor, he was immensely cheered by it and assured her that Danny would make a full recovery. 'Of course it will be a long job,' he told her. 'I doubt he'll be out of here for a couple of months at least, but you never know, and if you manage to find his missing partner and sort out the financial problems it would do wonders for his morale.'

When Mrs Callaghan came to relieve her, Jenny was able to give her the good news. She said that Danny had come round and was in his right mind, seeming to remember everything that had happened until the moment he had been struck down.

Mrs Callaghan wept tears of joy and Jenny lent her a handkerchief, patted her shoulder, and watched her mop up. Then she set off for the restaurant, where she had agreed to meet Mrs Tuttle and that good lady's lawyer, and presently heard what was to happen to the Mulberry Tree. Their lease had run out some days previously and Mrs Tuttle had taken over paying the staff, including Jenny, but she needed the money the sale of the property would bring in.

Now Mrs Tuttle revealed that she had already found a buyer for the restaurant, a local tradesman, and the lawyer told her kindly that she need not think that Mr Callaghan would be a pauper, for he would be nothing of the sort. The new owner would have to pay for the fixtures and fittings, for these had been bought by the four partners when they had first opened the restaurant. And there was also the matter of something he called the 'goodwill'.

Jenny wondered aloud how something as ephemeral as goodwill could be bought and sold, but though Mrs Tuttle and the lawyer both laughed they assured her that this was so and the lawyer named a sum which had Jenny gasping with relief, for it would see them through until she and Danny were able to get good jobs once more.

'And then, there's the firm's van,' the lawyer said, as the three of them prepared to depart. 'I believe the restaurant does own such a vehicle? If so, Mr Pettifer, the man who's buying the restaurant, would like to purchase it from you. Will it be convenient for his clerk to see the van one evening this week and agree a price?'

Jenny had completely forgotten about the van but brightened at the thought of getting a sale. She decided to ask Mr Clarke, who was keenly interested in such things, to accompany her when she took the man to their lock-up garage. Don Clarke would know how much she should charge and, like Mr Payne, had said over and over that he would like to help in any way he could.

Satisfied that she would be acting in Danny's best interests by selling the van for the best sum she could get, she saw Mrs Tuttle and the lawyer off the premises, then returned to tell Gran and the staff that Mr Callaghan had regained consciousness and seemed in a fair way to recovering completely.

'The surgeon is very pleased with him,' she assured her audience, for she had gathered all the staff and helpers around her to save having to repeat the good news. 'He says Danny is young and strong and may only be in hospital for a couple of months, maybe even less. He also said that good news will help his recovery, so I mean to see he gets some this very day. Has anyone heard of a thing called "goodwill"?'

Most of the staff understood the term, and presently Jenny closed the restaurant for the day and walked home with Emily. Jenny told her grandmother about Mr Pettifer, and the possible sale of the van, skulking in the lock-up garage they had rented. She also said that she would appreciate it if Mr Clarke could accompany her any evening which suited him, when she took Mr Pettifer's representative to examine the van.

'I'm sure Mr Clarke will be honoured to advise you,' Emily said. 'As you know, he and Mr Payne feel you've been very badly treated by that wretched young man. And as for Mr Pettifer, I've known him for years; a real nice feller, honest as the day is long . . . and pretty comfortably situated, too. He owns at least three confectioner's shops and sells the nicest bread in Liverpool – apart from what we bake at the Mulberry Tree, of course,' she added hastily. 'He's a fair-minded employer, too, doesn't stint his staff, so I'm pretty sure he'll not dream of dismissing experienced kitchen workers and waitresses. He'll employ them all on the same terms they're on at the moment . . .' she glanced rather hesitantly at Jenny, her granddaughter thought, 'which will likely include yourself as manageress, for I tell you straight, love, that me lodgers were only saying the other evening that the restaurant would have foundered long since if it hadn't been for yourself. Oh aye, your mam – and others – thought Claudia and her pretty looks was responsible for the Mulberry Tree's success, but Mr Payne pointed out that Claudia just added up the bills, took the money and gave change, whereas you was responsible for feedin' the five thousand, as you might say, and makin' sure that everyone was served with their orders as quick as possible. And you saw to the stockin' of the shelves, the ingredients, the . . .'

'Oh, do stop, Gran,' Jenny mumbled, red to the ears. 'Danny managed the stock, paid the bills . . . my God, I wonder what we'll learn when we start work on the

314

books? Once a thief, always a thief; I'll be very surprised if we find that Rob hasn't spent his time creaming off money whenever no one was looking over his shoulder.'

'And it's no use me saying that Claudia knew nothing of it, because she must have done,' Emily said sadly. 'But we'll speak to Mr Clarke as soon as we reach Blodwen Street, because me lodgers is always home before me when I'm on the cash desk.'

Jenny explained the situation to Mr Clarke as soon as they reached home, and when he and Mr Payne had stopped congratulating her on Danny's return to consciousness they arranged that Jenny and Mr Clarke would go down to the garage the very next evening and examine the van, accompanied, if he could manage it, by Mr Pettifer's clerk. Jenny went to the nearest call box and rang the number Mrs Tuttle's lawyer had given her, and the man agreed at once to meet them outside the restaurant at four o'clock in the afternoon, for he wanted to see the van by daylight. Mr Clarke, when Jenny popped into his office on Lime Street station, said that he would arrange to leave work early next day.

The next afternoon, therefore, Jenny and her two companions were standing outside the garage whilst Jenny fumbled for the key, produced it, turned it in the lock and swung the doors apart.

'There it is, and . . .' she began, but the words died on her lips. The little garage was empty.

Jenny could not believe it at first. Where on earth had their precious white van gone, and who would have taken it? But Mr Clarke, less involved and more experienced in the ways of men, solved the problem at once.

'No wonder you didn't find their names on no passenger lists,' he said after a moment spent simply staring at an empty space. 'We should have guessed, Miss Jenny, honest to God we should have guessed! That Rob were as clever as a whole wagonload of monkeys; why hang about right near where you've committed a crime, eh? Oh sure, you want a port, but why should it be Liverpool, where you and your lady-friend – beg pardon, Miss Jenny, but facts is facts – where you and your lady-friend are well known? And you've a good little van stuck away in a lock-up on Jasmine Street; why not bundle your stuff aboard and make for . . . oh, any port where big ships set off for America just about every perishin' day?' He turned to the clerk. 'Don't you agree? Oh, I don't deny they'll be long gone, but they'll have left the van parked somewhere inconspicuous, for they can scarcely drive it all the way to the United States, or wherever they've decided to hide themselves.'

Jenny looked from one face to the other, then nodded her head slowly as the clerk said it would likely be Southampton, or perhaps Portsmouth. 'If you'd like to alert the police that the van's been stolen, maybe they'll manage to trace it,' he said. 'It's still your property though, Miss Muldoon, and my employer is still willing to buy it at a fair price.'

Entering the hospital that evening on her way to visit Danny, Jenny reflected that all their questioning of the Liverpool dock officials had been time wasted; she should have guessed that Rob was far too fly to have boarded a ship on the very doorstep of the man he was cheating. Instead, he had added to his crime by stealing the firm's neat van and used it to take himself and Claudia to either Southampton or Portsmouth, or even some very much smaller port where their presence would not be questioned. But it was no use repining; she must tell Danny that she had informed the police of the theft and just hope that the van would soon be traced.

'But you can't say they stole the van exactly, because they wouldn't be able to take it aboard the liner,' Gran had pointed out. 'You can put the police on to it, but it will take time to trace, and standing out on some cold dockside . . . well, it won't improve its value much. Still an' all, you've got to try. Yes, you've got to tell the police it's been took.'

Jenny had sighed. 'I don't know that there's much they can do, even if they take me seriously, which they probably won't,' she observed. 'You see, I'm not a proper partner, because I'm too young, but only what they call a sleeping partner. So although Danny trusted me to look after the restaurant when neither he nor Rob were around, I don't think a complaint of mine against the Dingles would carry much weight.' They were in the kitchen, the lodgers, Gran and herself, and now she looked straight at Mr Clarke's honest, worried face. 'You must have guessed that when Rob and Claudia left, they took all the money we'd saved up,' she said resignedly. 'Danny's solicitor advised us to tell as few people as possible – something about affecting confidence, I seem to remember – only by now I expect everyone has realised: the staff at the Mulberry Tree, even the

317

tradesmen who supply us. Normally we run accounts with our larger suppliers and pay at the end of the month, but since Rob and Claudia left we've been told politely but firmly that we must pay cash for everything we buy in. Mrs Tuttle was a brick, but of course it was in her interest to keep the place going. Once we'd got a week's takings in the till we managed to limp along, though it might not have been possible without you, Gran.'

Her grandmother pulled a face at her. 'It were the least I could do. Remember, one of the guilty parties was me eldest granddaughter.'

'I know. But as soon as I explained what had happened and why we were in such a pickle, Gran withdrew fifty pounds from her Post Office savings book and insisted that I should take it. It kept us afloat for the first few days and now, instead of paying the takings from the restaurant into our bank account, we've been using them for supplies, wages and so on. We'll pay Gran back as soon as we can, although she says it was a gift, not a loan. Why, she's been working in the restaurant for nothing!'

'Your gran's a wonderful woman,' Mr Payne observed, speaking for the first time. 'And you're a grand young woman yourself, Miss Jenny.'

Jenny turned her head away from him so that he should not see the tears forming in her eyes. 'You never know what good friends you have until bad things happen,' she said huskily. 'Why, the waitresses refused to take their wages at the end of the first week and the farmer who supplies us with cracked eggs sent us half a dozen trays over and above what we'd ordered, and wouldn't take a penny for them.' She chuckled suddenly. 'So we put omelettes on the menu at a special price and made ourselves a nice little bit of extra profit.'

As luck would have it, Jenny was in the Mulberry Tree, manning the cash desk, when the new owner of the restaurant arrived. He was accompanied by Mrs Tuttle's lawyer, so Jenny guessed at once that all the legal requirements had been met. She left the cash desk doing her best to look welcoming and friendly, though she felt nothing of the sort. In fact she found herself struggling to hide a distinct feeling of resentment.

As she approached him, Mr Pettifer smiled at her and held out a large hand. He was a big man, six feet tall and broad to match, with close-cropped curly grey hair, a large stomach and a pair of very tiny, very shrewd blue eyes. Jenny liked him on sight but all she could do was compare him with Danny and think how unfair it was that this man, who had done nothing to deserve it, should simply walk into the Mulberry Tree and take over.

But he was speaking, smiling at her. 'Good morning, Miss Muldoon. So we meet at last,' he said pleasantly. 'I hope you doesn't mind, but I've signed up to buy the Mulberry Tree this very day and I couldn't resist comin' round to look over me new property. Also, of course, I mean to buy as much of your equipment as you're willing to part with, so we'll need to discuss prices . . .'

Jenny beckoned Freda to take her place at the cash desk, then smiled at Mr Pettifer and held out a hand.

'How d'you do? I'm temporarily in charge of the restaurant whilst the boss is in hospital,' she said. 'I understand that you will employ all existing members of staff on a weekly basis. In fact your representative hinted that you might offer me the job of manageress – just for a few weeks – but I'm not at all sure . . .'

Mr Pettifer's face fell ludicrously. 'I'm offering a first rate salary . . .' he named a sum which made Jenny gasp, 'because I've been impressed by the way you've run things over the past couple of months, very impressed, and I can see you would be well worth it,' he said. 'Did my clerk tell you that I would also let you have the flat, for a peppercorn rent, if you'd stay at least until I'd got myself established? You must understand, of course, that this is a new venture for me, catering not being my trade. I've a big bakery on Everton Road and for some time I've wanted to expand, but there's no chance where I am now. I don't mean to run the Mulberry Tree myself, of course, but I shall employ an experienced man or woman to do so for me. If you would stay for a few weeks . . .'

He stopped speaking as Jenny shook her head firmly. She was tempted by the salary but hated the thought of the restaurant without Danny. 'I'm very sorry, Mr Pettifer, but I hope to have other plans quite soon. I've spoken to Mr Callaghan, however, and though it will be a long time before he can do much physical work I'm sure he'd run things from the office if you were willing to employ him.'

'I understand. I've heard all about Mr Callaghan's accident, but I won't be offering him a job, for how could

it suit him to take orders where he had once given them?'
Mr Pettifer said, going a little red about the gills. 'I dare
say he's had other offers, or mebbe he'll go for a complete
change, but you, Miss Muldoon, as I mentioned before,
would be paid an excellent wage and could have the
flat for almost nothing while you remained in my
employ. And I should hope to confirm you in a permanent appointment eventually. Can't I persuade you?'

Jenny sighed. Pointless to tell him that the restaurant,
without Danny, held no attraction for her. 'Oh, I don't
know, Mr Pettifer. It's very tempting but it needs a good
deal of thought; I've no idea what Mr Callaghan means
to do, you see. So perhaps it would be fairer if I said no
to your kind offer, though I'm sorry to have to do so.'

'So am I sorry,' Mr Pettifer admitted. 'And I won't
deny I'm disappointed; you might say bitterly disappointed, Miss Muldoon. My clerk told me you was
young, but he said you was up to every trick.' He turned
to Gran, hovering interestedly in the background. 'I
suppose there's no chance of you persuading her, Mrs
Dalton? My clerk told me you was helping out whilst
things are in such a parlous state. If you could change
Miss Muldoon's mind, I'd be that grateful. In fact I'm
willin' to wait a few days for an answer, if that's what
it takes.'

Jenny and her grandmother had not spoken about the
possibility of a job offer since the day Danny came round,
though Mr Pettifer's clerk had hinted that such an offer
might well be made. Jenny, however, had been secretly
convinced that when Mr Pettifer saw her he would think
her far too young for the post of manageress and would

not suggest it. Even so, she expected her gran to back her up and was surprised, and even a little dismayed, when the older woman said: 'Certainly I'll speak to her, Mr Pettifer. With so much unemployment in the city at present . . . but I'll say no more until I've consulted my granddaughter.'

Mr Pettifer thanked her and left the restaurant, saying he was well satisfied with his purchase and would be making an offer for the fixtures and fittings as soon as his man of business advised him what such an offer should be.

When he had gone Jenny turned on her grandmother, but before she had a chance to assure that good lady that she had no intention of accepting Mr Pettifer's offer, Gran told her abruptly that such matters were best discussed under their own roof.

Jenny felt the hot colour flood her cheeks and lowered her head, knowing that Gran was right; knowing in fact that she had been wrong to turn down the offer of work when she had nothing else in view. As Gran said, unemployment was rife, and though there might be temporary jobs it would be downright foolish to pretend that she could earn anything like the sum Mr Pettifer was offering. Regarding the tenancy of the flat, however, she felt she had no need of it whilst she was living with her grandmother.

Once back in Blodwen Street, Gran made a pot of tea, sat Jenny down at the kitchen table and addressed her sternly. 'Jennifer Muldoon, I know very well why you turned down Mr Pettifer's offer of work, and it's a foolish reason. You can't bear to see him succeed where you and Danny have failed, through no fault of your own. Well, madam, I'm afraid you've got to think again and this time use your intelligence. Don't just lash out blindly, because, me love, these days no one can afford to turn any job offer down.'

'No-o-o, but the job wouldn't be for ever, just until he finds someone else suitable . . .' Jenny began, but was overridden.

'How ridiculous you're being, you silly child! Where would Mr Pettifer find anyone to manage his business as well as you could yourself? I'm sure, after a few weeks in the job, he would offer you a permanent position and confirm you as tenant of the flat.'

'But I don't *want* the flat,' Jenny almost wailed. 'I want to stay with you, Gran. If he would offer it to Danny, that would be different; I'd be his manageress, no problem.'

'Oh Jenny, will you please let me finish,' Gran said, giving Jenny an angry glare. 'For a start, you've not consulted Danny. Financially, he must be in desperate straits since that wicked pair stripped the bank accounts before they left. Any money you earn can be added to whatever sum Mr Pettifer pays for the fixtures and fittings and maybe that will be enough to pay rent for a room for Danny when he comes out of hospital, because I can't see Mr Pettifer renting him the flat.' She reached across the table to pat Jenny's hot cheek. 'Where do you intend him to stay until he's found himself work and got himself together? Right now, he's very dependent on you and needs all the help and support he can get.'

'I hadn't given the matter any thought,' Jenny said miserably, then turned eager eyes on her grandmother's well-loved face. 'Are you saying that if I took the flat – and the job of course – you would let Danny have my old room for a – a – peppermint rent? Only if so . . .'

Gran chuckled. 'Peppercorn rent, queen, not peppermint. But no, that wasn't what I was thinking.' She sighed, and for the first time she did not attempt to hold Jenny's gaze but looked down at her own hands for a moment in complete silence. When she spoke, it was with some difficulty. 'Jenny, love, there's something I've been meaning to tell you when the right moment came, but somehow it never did. Whilst I was staying with the family in Ireland, Fergal asked me to marry him. To tell you the truth, love, I wasn't as surprised as you might think, because your granddad and meself have grown very close over the years. As you know, your dad employs someone to give an eye to the twins in the school holidays, and would continue to do so, and Fergal has assured me that he isn't asking me to marry him just to help Louisa out, because we both know that would never work. He waited, good kind man that he is, until he thought that the restaurant no longer needed me – not that it ever did – and I was happy to pass my lodgers over to Maria Calvert, confident that she would do right by them. Then he popped the question, knowing how I love Kerry and Connacht Cottage, to say nothing of your parents and the twins – and Fergal himself, of course.'

Jenny's heart had descended into her boots at her grandmother's words, but she knew better than to show

324

how she felt. Gran had every right to a life – and a love – of her own, and far be it from Jenny to make the older woman feel guilty. So she jumped to her feet, ran round the table and gave Emily a big hug and a kiss on the cheek. 'That's absolutely wonderful news,' she said and realised, with some surprise, that she meant it. 'Dear Gran, I've thought for a long while that you and Fergal were made for each other, but somehow I'd always assumed . . . oh, I don't know . . .'

Emily chuckled and returned the hug. 'Don't say it; you thought we were too old for that sort of thing,' she said merrily. 'And you'd be right, of course. We're too old to fall in love, only we've done it. I'd be the happiest woman on earth if I didn't feel I was letting you down – you and Danny.'

Jenny returned to her own chair, plonked her elbows on the table, cupped her chin on her linked hands and addressed her grandmother severely. 'Oh, Gran, how absurd you are! You aren't letting anyone down. Why, if Maria takes over here, then we can all go on as before; Maria could have my room for Danny . . .'

She stopped speaking as Gran began to shake her head. 'No, love, you've forgotten Mrs Callaghan. She'd be awful hurt if Danny came here. Why, she told me only the other day that she's let one of her lodgers go so Danny can go back when he's out of hospital. But of course you've not consulted Danny yet; he may have ideas of his own.'

Secretly, Jenny doubted it. Her grandmother had visited Danny several times and he always put on a good act for her, but Jenny knew that he would not want to make any decisions at this stage. Only the previous day, when she had thought to cheer him up by talking of his soon being able to leave the hospital, he had been so obviously worried and distressed that she had hastily changed the subject. However, if she were to accept the job and the flat, Danny would simply have to know, so she decided she should involve the hospital staff. If the almoner were to mention, casually, that Danny could be out of the ward quite shortly, then he would realise decisions must be taken. Once, he had been so brisk and determined, eager to plan ahead, but all that seemed to have disappeared with the Dingles' defection. However, she would talk to Sister, a woman she greatly admired, for she did not wish to delay Danny's recovery by forcing him to confront problems he was not yet well enough to tackle.

But Gran was looking at her enquiringly, so Jenny began to outline her thoughts. 'I don't know that I *can* consult Danny, Gran,' she said slowly. 'I honestly don't think he's well enough to make any big decisions just yet. But I'll talk to Sister, and if she's agreeable I'll tell Danny about the job offer. I won't mention the difficulties that will raise their ugly heads when he comes out of hospital, but I will tell him your good news, because I honestly think he'll be glad for you, and in a way for me. He knows I've been concerned that Mam's been doing too much and the twins might be getting out of hand, so if he knows you're going that'll be one worry off his mind. Gran, I think you've talked me round. Tomorrow morning, first thing, I'm going over to Mr Pettifer's shop on Everton Road to tell him that you've persuaded me to take the job and the flat. If he's willing to employ me for at least a couple of months, then he's got himself a manageress.'

Mr Pettifer greeted the news with delight and was only sorry that Jenny did not feel she could move into the flat at once, though she assured him she would do so when her grandmother left for Ireland.

'She's marrying an old childhood sweetheart,' Jenny told him, crossing her fingers behind her back and thinking guiltily that she was becoming rather too quick to discard the truth when it suited her. 'And her friend is taking over her house in Blodwen Street, so she knows her lodgers will be well looked after.'

'Good, good,' Mr Pettifer said, beaming at her. They were in his small office at the back of the bakery and now he held out a large hand. 'Let's shake on it, Miss Muldoon. I'll guarantee both your job and your tenancy of the flat from today until later in the year when we can talk again.'

Shaking his hand, Jenny thought that if only he had wanted to employ Danny as well as herself, she would have been happy to sign up for a lot longer than a couple of months. She had seen this morning how his employees at the bakery liked and trusted him and thought she could do the same. She even understood why he did not want to employ Danny. Had he done so, she realised, her own loyalties would have been divided and so would those of the restaurant staff. Everyone would have turned to Danny when in doubt whereas now she knew that Mr Pettifer would be in command, would take decisions, hire and fire, and generally captain the good ship Mulberry Tree.

'Let me see, is there anything else we should discuss?' he said, releasing her hand. 'I've still not met Mr Callaghan, but thought I'd leave visiting the hospital for a bit since both the bakery and the restaurant are likely to be busy. But in a week or so, if you – and the hospital staff – think it would be all right, I'd very much like to see him.'

'I'll ask Sister,' Jenny said rather evasively. She liked Mr Pettifer very much, but worried that the sight of the new owner might upset Danny. He was still far from his old self, did not seem interested in the restaurant and tacitly refused to discuss the future, though he had congratulated Gran on her engagement to Fergal with obvious sincerity.

'That's fine, just fine,' Mr Pettifer said, crossing the office and opening the door for her. 'And now I suppose it's time we both got back to work!'

As Mr Pettifer had hoped, the restaurant continued to thrive under Jenny's stewardship. She would have been rushed off her feet had not Mr Pettifer employed two additional and experienced waitresses, a kitchen worker and an assistant cook, telling them that their jobs were unlikely to be temporary as he had at first supposed since the restaurant was handy for a couple of factories which the government had set up, so trade might well continue to be brisk. Despite Mr Chamberlain's 'peace for our time', both factories were engaged in making equipment which would be needed should war come, and Jenny was happy to provide the workers with either carry-outs or hot meals.

Jenny emerged on to Heyworth Street just as it began to rain. Sighing, she erected her umbrella and glanced ruefully at the clock over the chemist's, beginning to walk towards the nearest tram stop. She had intended to go straight home to Blodwen Street, making the most of her remaining time with Gran, but now she hesitated. Last time she had visited the hospital, she and Danny had had a row – their very first – and Jenny had marched out of the ward, calling over her shoulder as she went that she would not return until he felt like apologising. The argument had come about because she had agreed with Mr Pettifer that she would move into the flat when Danny left hospital. She had tried to tell Danny this, except that he had said, bluntly, that he wasn't interested and had started to talk of the possibility of war, a subject she found frightening.

I really must have been tired to lose my temper the way I did, Jenny thought remorsefully, splashing through the puddles. But I've tried so hard to get Danny to talk about what he wants to do when he comes out of hospital and the nearer the day of his release comes, the more important it is that he should talk about the future. Simply refusing to think about it is just stupid, and I know full well that Danny is not a stupid man. The trouble is, at the moment, he's frightened and confused. Oh, if only he'd talk to me, or at least listen when I try to sort out his future! He's said he doesn't want to go back to his mam's house, so why not share with me? He simply says he'll find somewhere and ignores the difficulties. It's not everyone who'll take in a man straight from hospital who still needs a deal of attention. But if he would agree to move into the flat, with me to look after him and so on, then at least he'd have somewhere to stay until he made other arrangements. I know there's only one bedroom, but I could have a put-you-up in the living room, so that wouldn't be a problem.

She reached the Pier Head just as a No. 22 tram halted beside her and jumped aboard, knowing she would remain on the tram until the Stanley Hospital was reached. She would eat humble pie, tell Danny she was sorry she had shouted at him, and then try to persuade him to discuss his future. If he simply refused, as he had done in the past, she would have to leave it to the almoner to see what she could do.

By the time the tram arrived outside the hospital, Jenny was beginning to look forward to seeing Danny again. She had not visited for three whole days, hoping that Danny would miss her, but now she felt some trepidation. Danny had been taken off traction and had been encouraged to practise walking with crutches, lifting small objects and doing all the things he would have to do when he was released, so Jenny had no idea where she might find him.

But as luck would have it, as she made her way towards the ward she saw him approaching her, swinging along quite nimbly on his newly acquired crutches. The last time she had seen him his expression had been angry and antagonistic, but now he grinned, and as she reached him he dropped his crutches and gripped both her hands in his. She opened her mouth to apologise, but he forestalled her.

'Oh, Jenny, I'm so sorry I shouted at you, because you've been so good to me. I know you're right really and we must start talking about the future, especially since the doctor has said that as soon as I can manage with a couple of sticks instead of the crutches, I can go home.' He laughed a trifle bitterly. 'Home! That's a good one! Still, he meant it kindly . . .'

Jenny felt her cheeks grow hot with pleasure, but bent quickly to pick up his crutches in order to hide her burning face. She had always known instinctively that it would embarrass Danny if he ever realised that her feeling for him was not merely friendship, so now she burst into speech. 'That's grand, Danny. We'll have a good long talk and sort something out; just something temporary, you know.' As they returned to the ward, Jenny added: 'Mr Pettifer is going to visit you quite soon. I know you won't like it, but I didn't see how I could put him off . . .'

Danny laughed. 'Don't worry, I promise I won't be rude to your new boss,' he said lightly.

Jenny laughed too, but uneasily. 'I'm afraid I lost my temper,' she said apologetically. She longed to hear him say that he had missed her, but knew he would not do so. 'Is it all right if I arrange for Mr Pettifer to come a-visiting on, say, next Wednesday? You'll know him because he'll probably be taller, fatter and better dressed than any other visitor. I think you'll like him.'

By now they were seated side by side on the visitors' bench in the ward, but at these words, Danny clutched her arm. 'Not alone,' he said urgently. 'You must come too, Jenny.' He tried for a lighter note, but his voice was strained. 'I – I can't face strangers yet, not without some support. You will come, won't you?'

'Yes of course,' Jenny said, truly delighted to realise that Danny did value her company, even if he did not know it. 'And it will be a good opportunity to explain to Mr Pettifer that you will be moving into the flat for a short period, so that I can keep an eye on you.' She looked enquiringly at her companion. 'What d'you think, Danny?'

Danny's eyes rounded. 'The flat? Me, live in the flat?' he asked incredulously. 'How can I manage those stairs while I'm on two sticks? And I thought *you* were going to move into the Mulberry Tree. I can't imagine that Mr Pettifer would want someone not even vaguely connected with the business living over it.'

Jenny stared at him. He seemed to have got hold of the wrong end of the stick with a vengeance. She began to stammer that he had not quite understood her, then took a deep, steadying breath and started to explain. 'I'm going to live in the flat, Danny, of course I am, but that shouldn't stop you living there as well. You could have the bedroom and I'd sleep on a made-up bed in the living room. I can't see Mr Pettifer objecting to that, can you?'

'Yes I can,' Danny said frankly. 'I wouldn't have agreed to it when I was in charge of the Mulberry Tree had anyone suggested a similar idea. Remember, Jenny, Mr Pettifer doesn't know me. He might think that I would delight in undermining his authority. It'd be

different if we were married . . . or at least it might be
. . . but I'm afraid that is a horse which won't run. I'd
be horribly embarrassed, and miserable, living over the
restaurant, truly I would.'

'Right,' Jenny said briskly. 'Then I'll tell Mr Pettifer
that I can't accept the tenancy of the flat after all, and
I'll look around for someone wanting two lodgers. I'll
choose ground-floor rooms, as near the Mulberry Tree
as I can get them. Then I'll be able to keep an eye on
you, get your meals and so on.'

Danny heaved a sigh. 'Jenny, I'm not a child, you
know,' he said gently. 'I don't mean to upset you, or
make you feel I don't value you as I ought, but even
though it's the last thing I want I'm going to live at
home with Mam for a while at least. As soon as I'm fit
enough to work, I'm going to look for somewhere well
away from the city. Anywhere will do, so long as it's
cheap and the landlady will provide me with one hot
meal a day. Now will you kindly stop worrying about
me and get on with your own life!'

He had almost shouted the last sentence and Jenny
knew she should have been snubbed by his words, but
instead she felt a smile begin to spread across her face
and knew a lightening of the heart. This was the old
Danny speaking, the one she had begun to fear had gone
for ever; it seemed that, at long last, he was considering
his future. If he truly meant to find work in the countryside, then she imagined lodgings would not be difficult.
But what could he do while still only able to walk with
the aid of two sticks? She was about to voice her fears
when Danny spoke.

'Jenny?' he said tentatively. 'I didn't mean to hurt your feelings. You've been a tower of strength all this time but, as I'm sure you realise, I must begin to take control of my own life.' He poked her in the ribs. 'And now you can jolly well tell me why you're grinning! Have you spotted a flaw in my argument?'

Jenny gave a snort of amusement. 'No. If you'd be happy out in the country, you'll soon find lodgings, though a job may be hard to come across. If you'd wanted a room in the centre, that would have been a different matter. But you'll need to be within easy reach of the Stanley. They're bound to want to see you on a fairly regular basis for some time. As for me smiling, I'm just so glad to realise that you've been thinking about your future, even though you wouldn't talk about it. What sort of work do you intend to look for, once you're well enough to work, I mean? Something in catering? No, I suppose you wouldn't want to start that all over again. Insurance, then? Or a similar job in an office?'

'I want to be my own boss,' Danny said. 'I thought perhaps I might apply to be the tenant of a public house; not a big city one, but a country pub, perhaps in Wales, or the Lake District. Somewhere quiet, where I could get the sort of experience which would lead me, eventually, to being able to own my own place.'

'That's a grand idea,' Jenny said approvingly. 'With your experience in catering, I should think a brewery would snap you up. Only isn't there a lot of competition for country pubs?'

Danny shrugged. 'I don't know. If so, then I wouldn't mind a village shop and post office . . . something like

334

that, anyway. As soon as I'm fit enough, I'll start getting my solicitor to look into things for me. He'll point me in the right direction.'

'That's true; Mr Briggs has been awfully helpful,' Jenny agreed. Then a thought struck her. 'Danny, what about a little farm or a market garden? I remember when you and Clau . . .' she saw his expression change and hastily amended what she had been going to say '. . . when you and I were young, you used to talk about getting a place of your own in the country, keeping pigs and chickens and so on. How d'you feel about that?'

Danny laughed rather bitterly. 'Oh yes, I can just see myself stumbling about my acres on two sticks,' he said sarcastically. 'My dear girl, I probably shan't even be able to cope with a full week's work of the most sedentary kind for months. But I hope I'll be able to sit behind a counter by the time summer comes, depending on how I get on.'

'But if you went for a place in Ireland, somewhere near Connacht Cottage, you know my family would give you all the help they could,' Jenny said eagerly. 'And of course, if you went to Ireland, I'd come as well, because there's nothing to keep me . . .'

Danny interrupted her at once. 'No!' he said forcibly, almost shouting the word. 'The last thing I want is help from the Muldoons. Oh, I know you're going to say it wasn't your family's fault that I lost the Mulberry Tree, and I suppose you'd be right, but this time I truly mean to be independent, to go it alone, without a penny of Muldoon money, or their advice. Can you understand?'

There was a long silence whilst Jenny wrestled with

remarks she would have liked to make but could not, because she knew in her heart that Danny was right. If there had been no Claudia, he would have kept a much closer eye on Rob. But because he was so straightforward and honest himself, he had never even considered the possibility that the woman he had loved – still loved – would join with his friend and colleague to cheat him. And Jenny realised that she, too, had assumed the pair were honest; had never thought to question her beloved sister, for Claudia had been straight as a die until she met Rob.

'Jenny? I know it's a lot to accept . . .'

'I'm sorry, Danny, and of course I understand how you feel,' Jenny said at once. 'But – but I'm a Muldoon too, and you've let me help in any way I could. You're not saying you don't want my help either, are you?'

She had been staring down at her lap, but now she lifted her head and looked Danny in the eye, saw his embarrassment, but would not look away. If he included her in his desire to cast off any connection with the Muldoons, then she would have to back off, to stop seeing him, and even the thought gave her such pain that she felt her eyes sting with tears.

'Oh, Jenny, I'm so sorry, I didn't mean to hurt you,' Danny said earnestly. 'Whilst I'm in Liverpool and you're working at the Mulberry Tree I'll be very grateful for your help. But, my dear girl, whatever I end up doing, I'll do it a long way from here. As for you, jobs in the country won't pay nearly as well as being Mr Pettifer's manageress does. I can't expect you to throw away your career just so I have a shoulder to weep on

336

if things go wrong. When I get my place in the country – and it won't be for a while yet – then our ways must part. I hope we'll stay friends, but obviously we shan't see so much of one another.'

Jenny's heart plummeted at Danny's words; she could not imagine life without him, had taken it for granted that whatever they did when her job at the restaurant finished, they would do together. But she mastered herself with an effort, blew her nose and stood up. 'Well, that's all for the future, and since neither of us is psychic we don't know how things will turn out,' she said with artificial briskness. 'I know you want to be independent, Danny, and I'm sure you'll make a go of whatever you decide to do, but just remember, if you need me . . .'

Danny stood up too. 'I'll walk you back to reception,' he said. 'I'm practising on the crutches as much as I can, though I have to admit that I get quite a bit of pain from my broken shoulder if I use them – the crutches, I mean – for more than ten or fifteen minutes at any one time.'

Jenny was beginning to reply when the bell that announced the end of visiting rang out, and she turned towards the swing doors. 'I didn't bring you the cakes Gran made for you because I didn't mean to come tonight,' she said. 'I wish you could have come back to Blodwen Street at the weekend, if only for a couple of hours, but Sister said she didn't advise it. So I'll come tomorrow and bring the cakes, if that's all right.'

'I shall look forward to it,' Danny said politely, and set off so quickly that Jenny had to run to catch up.

'Do be careful, Danny,' she said breathlessly as they negotiated the swing doors at the end of the ward and turned into the corridor. 'Sister says if you go on as you have been doing you'll be home in a month, but if you fall and fracture another bone . . .'

Danny slowed, grinning appreciatively down at her. 'What would I do without my little Mother Muldoon?' he asked mockingly. He was smiling at her with a sort of wry understanding in his eyes. 'Sorry, Jenny. What a horrible thing to say – that our ways must part,' he said. 'After all you've done for me, all the help you've given me . . . forgive me, Jenny. I'm a bad-tempered bear.' And to Jenny's considerable surprise, when they reached the front hall, he tucked both crutches under one arm, pulled her towards him, and dropped a kiss on her cheek. 'You're a grand girl, so you are,' he said softly. 'You put up with all my crochets and bad temper without a word of complaint. And I'll get in touch with Briggs tomorrow morning; find out whether taking on a pub would be possible.'

With these words he turned and made his way back across the hall without once looking back. Jenny stood quite still for a moment, one hand on her hot cheek. She felt warm and full of happiness. Danny might not love her, but he liked and trusted her; it was enough, for now at any rate.

Chapter Sixteen

It was a fine morning in early July when Danny and Jenny set off for Norfolk, having arranged an interview with a brewery that had advertised two public houses, available for 'the right tenant'. Jenny had stared when Danny had named Norfolk as his preferred destination, but he had said that he wanted to get right away from Liverpool and that he had chosen Norfolk for a reason which he would not share with anyone until all was settled; and Jenny had to be content with that.

Danny had intended to go alone, for though Jenny had said firmly that she had warned Mr Pettifer that she meant to accompany him to whichever pub he settled for, he had resisted what he termed 'such a sacrifice'. However, Jenny had pointed out that he was still using two sticks for long walks, which might put would-be employers off, whereas if she were with him he could manage with one stick and her arm.

Danny had thanked her, rather grudgingly, and they set out for Norwich together. They reached the brewery in good time for their interview with Mr Brown, who greeted them with great geniality, thanked Danny for his 'full and frank' answers to the questions he had put to him and then, to Jenny's astonishment, turned to her and began to ask her a number of searching questions.

She was glad she was wearing the smart navy costume that Mr Pettifer had bought her so that no one could doubt who was his manageress, and thankful for the experience in employing staff that had been her lot when she was in charge at the Mulberry Tree. She knew which replies had pleased both herself and Mr Pettifer and saw the satisfaction grow in Mr Brown's face at her swift, decisive answers.

Presently he turned to Danny and proceeded to chat, drawing Danny out so that it seemed less like an interview than an informal discussion between friends. 'Well, Mr Callaghan, I have no hesitation in telling you that your good lady has tipped the scales in your favour,' he said at last. 'She is an ideal wife for a landlord and will speedily build up the reputation of any house with which she is involved.' He turned a beaming smile upon Jenny. 'I think you've made up my mind for me, Mrs Callaghan . . .'

In the stunned silence that followed, no one spoke, then Jenny heard a voice and realised with astonishment that it was her own. 'Oh, Mr Brown, I'm sorry; I didn't realise Mr Callaghan hadn't made it clear. Danny and I aren't married, but I've volunteered to work for him . . .'

To say that Mr Brown's face fell, Jenny thought, was the understatement of the year. In fact he looked stunned, as though he could not believe his ears. He looked accusingly first at Jenny and then at Danny himself. 'But surely, Mr Callaghan, the literature I sent you must have made it plain that the company policy is to employ only married couples in our public houses. We would not dream of offering such a position to a single man.'

340

Abruptly, his face cleared. 'Or are you and this good lady proposing to marry in the near future? If so, of course, that puts an entirely different complexion on the matter.'

There was a moment of startled silence before Jenny broke it. 'That's right, Mr Brown; we *are* planning to get married, but we wanted to be sure that we had a job and a roof over our heads before we took the plunge.'

Mr Brown beamed once more and Jenny had to stifle a giggle when she looked at Danny's face, for now it was he who looked stunned, though when he spoke he did so coolly enough. 'So will you offer me – and my good lady – one of the two pubs we've discussed?' he asked bluntly. 'You will appreciate that we must know where we stand before taking any further steps.'

Jenny hoped that Mr Brown would say yes at once, but he was shaking his head. 'I can't do a thing until I see your marriage certificate,' he said, and whether his reluctance was real or assumed Jenny could not tell. 'But I can promise you this . . .' he smiled at them both, 'as soon as you are married, you will be offered whichever house you prefer, at the agreed tenancy price, of course.' He got to his feet and held out his hand. 'I know they say there's a war coming, but that will not affect our decision. All being well, you will only have to send us a copy of your marriage certificate and the place will be yours. And now my colleague, Mr Herne, will drive you to the Feathers and to the Cat and Fiddle, and you can see which you think would suit you best.'

After they had left the office, the enormity of what she had done struck Jenny for the first time. She began a stumbling apology, said that Danny could contact Mr Brown any time, blame her for the deception, and tried to explain that the words had simply popped out of her mouth when it had seemed that Danny might lose the chance of a tenancy if they were not married.

Danny, however, now leaning heavily upon his stick and looking totally exhausted, shook his head at her. 'You did what you thought best,' he said wearily. 'And now you will bloody well stick to it, as I shall. After all, we don't have to live together, not in the accepted sense of the word. We'll be business partners, that's all.'

Jenny nodded and steered Danny towards the firm's car park where they were to meet Mr Herne, then cleared her throat and spoke. 'I didn't mean to say what I did, but if you really don't mind, I don't either. If it's the only sure way of getting a pub.'

Danny nodded bleakly. 'It seems like it, so we'll get wed as long as you know it can't possibly be a real marriage. I've never stopped loving Claudia, you see, and you've never loved anyone. So on the understanding that we don't have to pretend to each other, we'll go ahead.'

Murmuring agreement, Jenny felt a rush of pleasure so intense that she feared it might show on her face. However, when she spoke it was gruffly, with her head turned away. 'That's fine by me. I've always wanted a career and being your business partner will be a career, won't it?'

'Yes,' Danny agreed. He eyed her thoughtfully. 'It's a pity you look much younger than you really are, because you'll be working behind the bar and folk might think you're still at school and object to being served by a child.' He chuckled suddenly. 'We'll have to frame your birth certificate and hang it up in the bar, though I dare say folk will realise you're older than you look when they see how hard you work and how efficient you are.'

Jenny beamed at him. 'How kind of you to say so, partner,' she said teasingly.

'I think we should have a quiet wedding; no white dress, no top hat and tails, no reception,' Danny said. 'I'm sorry if I'm doing you out of all the things girls dream about, but if it's just ourselves and a couple of witnesses, is that all right by you?'

'Fine,' Jenny agreed. 'Only we'd better invite our parents . . . and Gran, of course, and probably the lodgers, otherwise there'll be talk.'

Danny began to say he could not imagine why anyone should talk and then, for the first time since the interview in Mr Brown's office, he grinned broadly, actually chuckled. 'Shotgun wedding, you'd think they'd say, eh? Never mind. Once we're married, we'll clear off and they can think what they bloody well please.'

At this point they reached Mr Herne's car and Danny ushered Jenny into the back seat, then climbed in beside the driver. Mr Herne was an elderly man, with a face like wrinkled leather and very bright blue eyes. He grinned at them, revealing startlingly white false teeth. 'All set, together?' he enquired in a broad Norfolk accent. 'Then orf we goo.'

Mr Herne took them first to the Feathers, a small but

pleasant pub on the main street of a sizeable village. It was half-timbered and had a tiny garden at the back, a large public bar, a cosy snug and a fair-sized kitchen, whilst the landlord's accommodation was reached by a flight of stairs and consisted of two small bedrooms and all the usual offices, including a bathroom and lavatory, which Jenny much admired.

'That's a popular place for the villagers, and folk come out from the city I believe,' Mr Herne told them. 'Mr and Mrs Grant do a fair trade. But he's gone for a soldier as they say, and Mrs Grant's goin' back to her ma, soon as the new landlord take over.' He looked from Jenny to Danny. 'You'll prefer this 'un to the Cat and Fiddle,' he said confidently. 'Still an' all, Mr Brown say you'd best see both.'

Danny and Mr Herne chatted as they drove along tiny narrow lanes and Jenny was almost asleep when Mr Herne announced that this here was the village of Cumber, and the pub would come into view at any moment, which caused Jenny to sit up abruptly and begin to take notice. The village seemed to consist of one main street, flanked on either side by an odd mixture of houses and cottages, some thatched cob, others built of brick and flint. She saw a general store, a blacksmith and a red telephone box, and then they were driving slowly between enormous alders and willows, through which she could see the glint of water.

She almost missed the Cat and Fiddle, surrounded as it was by mature trees. It was a big house, standing tiptoe on the edge of what looked like a large lake, though Mr Herne informed her, as he halted by the front door, that this was actually a broad – in fact it was Cumber Fen.

Jenny, following the two men into the house, cleared her throat. 'Does – does it flood in winter?' she quavered. 'It must make the house damp. And where's the landlord?'

'He retired near on six months ago, my woman,' Mr Herne told her. 'It were gettin' too much for him, which is why it look so neglected. As for damp, or floods, I never heard tell of any. No, it's the position what puts folk off. Kind o' remote, wouldn't you say? The big village, Cumber Magna, is across the water, so anyone takin' on the old Fiddle needs a boat as well as a car . . .' he chuckled, 'but that's reflected in the price o' the tenancy, which is the cheapest the brewery has ever offered, to my knowledge.'

'So long as it doesn't flood . . .' Jenny was beginning, but Mr Herne was ushering them into a large bar with wide windows overlooking the water, and rattling off what was clearly his spiel when touring one of the brewery's public houses. He took them into a vast, old-fashioned kitchen, quarry-tiled and chilly despite the bright sunshine, then through an enormous scullery into a cobbled yard, surrounded by farm buildings – a cow-shed, stables, a pigsty and a hen run – which Mr Herne said easily the previous tenant had used to supplement his income.

'Years ago this was a farm what sold ale, if you understand me, because there weren't enough customers to call it a pub. But the last landlord let most of the land and outbuildings to Mr Grigg, what run the farm past the orchard, the meadow beyond and the birch wood. I dare say whoever take the tenancy will do the same, since I doubt they'll be thinkin' of keepin' stock,' he said genially, shooting them a surprisingly shrewd glance. 'I reckon I'll leave you to look over the property and have a bit of a chat whiles I walk into the village to see a pal, for there's bound to be things you want to discuss.'

Danny and Jenny waited until Mr Herne had disappeared, then Danny limped purposefully up the stairs, saying over his shoulder to Jenny that they had already taken a good look at the ground floor, and should now examine the bedrooms.

Jenny began to say that there was no point, that the place would never pay and that the Feathers needed almost nothing doing. 'We could walk into it tomorrow and start trading at once,' she said. 'And this village isn't even a village really, it's more like a – a hamlet, so we shan't get many local customers. I think . . .'

They were now at the head of the stairs and Danny turned to her and put his finger across her lips. 'Hush now. We'll look round up here and then I'll tell you how I feel,' he said.

Presently, downstairs once more, Jenny would have reiterated her previous remarks, but Danny grabbed her wrist and pulled her down to the edge of the broad. 'See that sort of shed thing, over the water?' he said excitedly. 'It's a boathouse. Let's take a look. It's all part of the property.'

Jenny hung back, trying to say that boathouse or no boathouse it would be madness to take on the Cat and Fiddle when the Feathers was so clearly a better

346

proposition, but Danny told her to button her lip until they had inspected everything, and though Jenny laughed, she obeyed him.

The boathouse contained two sturdy-looking rowboats and a larger vessel, which had sunk below the water line, causing Jenny to give a contemptuous sniff. 'A fat lot of good that would be,' she observed as they returned to the pub. 'Oh, Danny, you can't be seriously considering taking on this place? Why, there isn't even a daily bus route, lerralone houses nearby. Do let's take the tenancy of the Feathers.'

Danny cast his eyes up to the sky and sighed deeply. 'This place has seven bedrooms,' he said impressively. 'Five doubles on the first floor and two little ones in the attic. And it's got a modern bathroom and lavatory, which is more than I expected, to be honest. You and I can have the attic rooms and we can let the rest.'

'Oh, yeah?' Jenny said sarcastically. 'To whom, may I ask?'

Danny sighed again. 'You've heard there's a war coming, haven't you? Oh, I know all about Mr Chamberlain's trip to Munich, but that was last year and I don't think even the old boy himself believes peace in our time is possible. They're not digging trenches in Hyde Park for fun, you know. Why, if it weren't for my injuries, I'd be in the RAF by now. War is coming, and I think everyone knows it.'

'I don't see what that's got to do with anything,' Jenny objected. 'Or do you imagine refugees will pour across the North Sea and hire rooms here? Because if so . . .'

Danny's eyes sparkled and he actually took hold of

347

Jenny's shoulders and gave her a shake. 'This pub has an airfield less than five miles away; in fact there must be at least half a dozen within striking distance. That's why I thought of coming to Norfolk. Do *think*, Jenny wren! Wives and girlfriends, or RAF personnel, will want to visit their chaps; they'll stay at the nearest inn, which will be us. Then the pilots and aircrew will want somewhere they can relax. Oh, they can go into the city for cinemas and dances, but if they want a quiet afternoon sculling a boat about on the broad . . .' He grinned at her, the flush on his cheeks proclaiming his excitement. 'Then there's the land and the outbuildings. I know nothing of farming or land management but you, my little country bumpkin, will know just what to do with that side of the business, having spent your early years on your dad's farm in Ireland. I'm telling you, Jenny, properly managed, the Cat and Fiddle could be a real goldmine. Remember, because we'll be buying the tenancy, all the profit we make will be ours. Are you game to give it a go? Will you trust me?'

For a moment, Jenny's picture of herself behind the cosy little bar of the Feathers glowed before her mind's eye. She turned to look back at the towering bulk of the Cat and Fiddle, then she smiled up into Danny's excited face. 'Of course I'm game and of course I trust you,' she said, with a gaiety she was far from feeling. 'It'll mean a great deal of hard work, and rather a lot of money spending too, but I'm sure we should take on the Cat and Fiddle. And you're quite right about my farming experience; when I was a little girl, I always told folk I meant to marry a farmer . . .' she grinned up at him, 'and it looks as though I'm going to do just that. And now let's go and winkle out Mr Herne, because we'll have a great deal to arrange before we can start doing all the things that are necessary to make this pub into the sort of place you want.'

Five weeks after that first meeting with the brewery representatives, Jenny sat hunched up in a corner seat on the train that was to carry them on the first leg of their journey to Norfolk. Danny, slumped in the seat opposite, had his eyes closed but Jenny thought crossly that he was only pretending to be asleep. He had been in a vile mood ever since the wedding, which had taken place the previous Saturday, and been ruined for her by his whole attitude. His temper had stemmed from the fact that all the Muldoons had come over from Ireland for the ceremony and Gran, having asked Maria Calvert to tell all the neighbours that her granddaughter and Danny Callaghan were getting wed, had secretly invited what felt like half Liverpool to a reception in the church hall, which was her wedding present to the young couple.

As soon as her mother had heard that Jenny was to marry, she had suggested that her daughter should wear the beautiful bridesmaid's dress which Claudia had made for her but Jenny, mindful of Danny's feelings, had said she would do no such thing. Determined, however, to ensure that her daughter did not march up the aisle in something thoroughly unsuitable, Louisa had set to and made Jenny the most beautiful pink silk dress, and Gran had bought a coronet of pink rosebuds and a pair of pink satin slippers to complete her grand-daughter's outfit.

Jenny had been delighted, both with the dress and with her family's presence, and had never thought that Danny would be so bitterly resentful, even though she knew he had wanted a quiet wedding. He had apparently been under the misapprehension that it was she who had invited everyone to the reception. He had arrived at the church in his one and only dark suit, but when he saw the congregation assembled he had been furious and to Jenny's horror had not believed her protestations that she had not said a word to anyone but her grandmother.

'Then why are they here?' Danny had hissed as they walked down the aisle when the ceremony was over. He had flicked the pink gown contemptuously. 'I *told* you not to dress up, so why this?'

Poor Jenny had felt tears sting her eyes, but she had been angry too. It might not have been a proper wedding, but it was the only one she was likely to have. 'I suppose Gran told everyone, because though I said it was to be a quiet wedding I never said it was a secret,' she had hissed back. 'As for the dress, my mother made it, so it's cost us nothing. I couldn't hurt her feelings by refusing to wear it, not even for you, Danny; and you only said not white, so what's wrong with pink?'

Danny had said nothing more. He had attended the reception, been polite in a stiff and formal manner to the guests, and had insisted that he and Jenny leave as soon as they decently could, saying that they had a train to catch. Naturally, everyone had assumed that the newly-weds were off on their honeymoon, and had let them go without too much fuss. Now they were on their way to Norwich, where they would show their wedding lines to the brewery before making their way to the Cat and Fiddle.

Jenny sighed to herself. She had said her goodbyes to her family the previous evening, and knew she should be looking forward to the new life that stretched ahead of her. Despite appearances, it seemed that the Cat and Fiddle, though in need of redecoration, was structurally sound. At Danny's insistence, the brewery had had a survey done and the result had pleased the Callaghans – I must remember I'm a Callaghan now, Jenny reminded herself – though they would still have to employ someone to perform the tasks which Danny could no longer tackle. If only Danny would cast aside his resentment over the wedding, how happy I would be, she thought miserably. If only he would accept that I couldn't turn my parents away . . . if only he would be reasonable . . .

Opposite her, Danny's eyes flickered open for a moment, then closed again, and abruptly Jenny felt a rush of anger. He was a grown man, years older than herself, but he was behaving like a spoilt child. She had never thought of Danny as being the type to bear a grudge, but he was bearing one now all right, and it was not good enough. He had said they were partners; well, if they were to have a proper partnership, then they needed to talk, to share worries and successes.

The carriage was crowded, with little chance of private conversation, but even as she leaned forward the train slowed to a halt and a porter came along the platform, announcing the name of the station and the fact that passengers for Norwich Thorpe – amongst other destinations – should change here. Jenny got to her feet and reached up to the rack, then realised that Danny had not moved. Glad of an excuse, she seized his shoulder and gave him a hard shake. 'Wake up, Danny!' she said loudly. 'We've got to change trains here, so you can just stop pretending to be asleep and give me a hand with our luggage.' She reached up as she spoke and jerked the smallest of the four suitcases down from the rack. It was heavier than she realised and she managed to clout Danny on the knee as she tried to stand it down whilst wrestling to get the carriage door open.

Danny exclaimed, his eyes shooting open in hurt surprise, and Jenny could not forbear an inward smile at the thought that she was giving him a well-deserved taste of the dictatorial and unpleasant manner he had used towards her since their wedding. He got to his feet. 'What did you do that for?' he asked in an injured tone. 'I was asleep.'

Jenny gave a contemptuous snort. 'No you were not; you were just pretending,' she said crossly. 'For good-ness' sake, start getting the cases off the rack or we'll get carried on to heaven knows where.'

Danny began to mutter that she should know he could not hurry, or carry heavy weights, but whilst Jenny was manhandling the smallest suitcase, other passengers, seeing Danny's sticks, heaved the rest of their luggage from the rack and stood the suitcases down on the platform for them, advising Jenny to find a porter, since 'your young feller can't possibly manage all four of 'em, even wi' your help, young lady'.

Jenny took this advice and presently, aboard another train, she sat herself down next to Danny and addressed him. 'It's no use being cross with me because you wanted a quiet wedding – so did I, for that matter,' she informed him. 'Remember we're partners . . .' she glanced uneasily round the carriage, but the large family who were their new travelling companions were wrapped up in their own affairs and taking no notice of the young couple who occupied the only other two seats, 'and when there are just two of you, you can't afford to fall out.' She smiled hopefully into Danny's strained and pallid face and stuck out a hand. 'Shall we shake and be friends? Only I hate to be at odds with you, Danny, especially since it really isn't my fault.'

Danny began to speak, then changed his mind. He took Jenny's hand in both of his, then leaned forward and lightly kissed her cheek. 'I'm sorry, truly I am,' he said. 'It was just the shock of seeing all those people at the wedding . . . but you're quite right and I have been behaving badly. I shan't do so again, because no one could have a better partner than I've got.' He grinned suddenly and put the backs of his fingers against her hot cheek. 'Little idiot; why should you blush when I'm only speaking the truth? Now, let's both get some rest; we'll have to hurry to the brewery as soon as we reach Norwich, so that they can see our marriage lines, and once we get to the Cat and Fiddle we'll have plenty to do before we can go to our beds.'

'Oh, Lor', I hope the auction rooms have delivered

the beds,' Jenny said, suddenly apprehensive. 'Getting them up the stairs will be hard work. But Mr and Mrs Harker said they'd come round and give a hand as soon as we need them, which will be an enormous help.'

'So it will,' Danny agreed. As soon as the wedding date had been confirmed, Danny had taken on Mr Harker as cellar man, and his wife to serve in the bar and give Jenny any help she might require. 'But we won't put the beds upstairs if the men from the auction room have left them in the bar. Remember, we shan't arrive at the Cat before dark, so if the beds have been delivered we'll set them up in the kitchen, just for a night or two.' He grinned at her. 'It'll be like camping out for a while, quite an adventure! Just until we can get our licence and can open up, I mean.'

It was a sunny day in mid-August; the sky was blue and a gentle breeze stirred the leaves on the tall trees that surrounded the Cat and Fiddle. The Callaghans were having breakfast and Jenny had just presented Danny with a plate containing two fried eggs, a pile of crispy bacon and a couple of large field mushrooms which she had discovered growing in the pasture at the back of the pub. Danny, no country boy, eyed the mushrooms suspiciously and was in the middle of demanding proof that they were not toadstools when the postman banged on the door, flung it open, came across the kitchen and slapped some letters down beside Danny's plate.

'That look good,' he observed. 'I see you're fond of mushrooms; I am myself. Cor, I'm that thirsty I reckon

I could drain Cumber Fen. Any chance of a cuppa, missus?'

'I'll pour you a cup as soon as I've dished up my own grub,' Jenny said readily. 'Fancy a bacon butty, Mr Askham?'

The postman laughed. 'If you mean a bacon sandwich, then I'm your man,' he said genially. He watched as Jenny put a fried egg, some bacon and the remaining mushroom on her own plate and raised his eyebrows. 'You goin' on a diet or suffin'? Now sit you down an' eat your grub. Seein' as how you're my last call this mornin', I'll make my own sandwich.'

Jenny poured the tea and began to eat as Mr Askham slid bacon on to a round of bread. Folding this over, he took a large bite and spoke through his mouthful. 'Hey up, Mr Callaghan!' he said as Danny opened the largest envelope. 'Good noos or bad?'

Danny gave a subdued whoop. 'Good,' he said exultantly. 'It's the licence for the old Cat and Fiddle. We can start trading from the first of September, which means we can open up for business! Thank the Lord, because we need to make some money before much longer.'

Mr Askham wiped bacon fat off his chin and looked approvingly about the room, at the clean whitewashed walls, the immaculate red quarry tiles and the Aga cooker, upon which, he knew, Mrs Harker had spent many busy hours. 'Congratulations. I must say you and your good lady deserve to succeed and I'm sure you'll do so. I guess you've wondered where your customers will come from and I dare say it'll be just us locals at

355

first, but once folk know you're here they'll come from all over, mark my words. And I'll be the first.' He walked over to a calendar hanging on the wall and examined it closely. 'Let's see, the first of September is a Friday, so that give you a fortnight to get ready; fifteen days if you open on the Sat'day. Do you think you can do it? I'll put the word about and a good foo will come over from Cumber Magna, so you won't be short of company.' He picked up his bag and slung it over one shoulder. 'Only will you have supplies in by then? It won't do to offer the fellers tea, you know.'

Danny laughed and flourished the letter. 'The brewery will bring the stock we've ordered by the end of August, and Jenny and Mrs Harker will do a big cook and make piles of sandwiches. The food will be free on opening night, but I'm afraid we'll have to charge for drinks.'

Mr Askham pulled open the door and stepped into the yard, then hesitated and glanced back. 'Why not get in touch with the fellers on Cumber airfield? If they know it's a party, with free grub, they'll likely come over in a couple of them lorries – gharries, they call them – what normally take them into the city. Worth a try, wouldn't you say?'

'You're right there,' Danny said. 'OK, we'll decide here and now: we'll have our opening do on the second of September – two weeks tomorrow.'

After Mr Askham had left, Danny and Jenny stared at one another. 'I've longed for this moment, but now that it's come I feel downright terrified,' Danny said, and Jenny knew he was only half laughing, for she felt pretty scared herself.

She said as much but then added reassuringly: 'I know there's still a lot to do, but the bar and the kitchen, and that nice little parlour which we're going to call the snug, are as near perfect as we can make them. Even the bedrooms are beautifully clean, though of course they're empty and will stay that way until we can afford to buy furniture. The indoor bathroom and lavatory are respectable, though there's no linoleum on the floor, or curtains at the window yet. But the outside privy in the yard is where most of the men will go, not realising we have indoor sanitation.' She nudged Danny. 'Wouldn't it be exciting if we really did get the boys in blue from the airfield! Oh, Danny, this is our big chance and we've got to grab it with both hands!'

Danny put down his knife and fork and went over to the dresser. He picked up a pad and pencil, then returned to the table. 'One thing that thieving swine Dingle taught me was the value of good advertising,' he said. 'He was always hiring a lad to hand out leaflets with our latest specials printed on 'em. I reckon since it worked for the Mulberry Tree, it'll work for the Cat and Fiddle as well.'

For a puzzled moment, Jenny envisaged a lad handing out leaflets in Cumber village. Even if he went as far afield as Cumber Magna, there wouldn't be many takers. And how were they to get such leaflets printed? She began to point this out, but Danny cut across her remarks impatiently. 'No, no,' he said. 'I just mentioned the leaflets as an example of how Dingle used advertising to get the Mulberry Tree well known. We'll make some posters up ourselves and send a lad on a bicycle all

357

round the district, pinning them to notice boards in church porches or on village greens.' He wrote busily in his notebook. 'We can make up some posters this evening, and we might as well do a few leaflets as well. Then I'll have to go to the newspaper office in Norwich. I'll pay for a nice big advertisement to appear in the *Eastern Evening News* every night for the week leading up to the opening.'

'I say, that's a marvellous idea,' Jenny said reverently. 'You *are* clever, Danny! But won't it cost an awful lot?'

'I don't know, but even if it is expensive, what was it that swine Dingle used to say? Speculate to accumulate, that was it. And honestly, Jen, you must admit it worked. And whilst I'm in Norwich, I'll ask some of the smaller shops if I can send them leaflets to hand out to customers, because it will be a day or two before we've made them – the leaflets, I mean. How long will it take us to make the posters and a few dozen leaflets? Oh, damn, I forgot. You'll be cooking the food with Mrs Harker, won't you?'

'We shan't start cooking until two or three days before the event,' Jenny said firmly. 'Whilst you're in Norwich, you'd best buy some big sheets of paper for the posters and a box of paints. Oh, and some coloured ink and fine pens for the leaflets.'

Danny had been scribbling as she spoke, but now he sighed. 'I wish to God I was fit enough to drive, then we could hire a van, but I'm afraid it's not possible yet,' he said regretfully. 'I know you wanted to learn, but we've been so busy . . .'

'I think I'd rather use the old bicycle, the one we

borrowed off Mrs Harker's daughter, rather than learn to drive,' she said apologetically. 'I ride it whenever I need to reach Cumber Magna in a hurry. I know she'd sell it to us for a quid, so maybe we ought to grit our teeth and hand over the money. Then I can cycle to every airfield within reach and ask the man on the gate to let me put up a poster in their canteen, or cookhouse, or whatever they call it.'

'It'd be a fair old cycle ride,' Danny said rather dubiously. 'I'd do it myself like a shot, only my bad leg won't bend and it would get in the way of the pedal. But perhaps it would be better if we hired a local lad . . .'

Jenny jumped up and ran round the table, snatching the pencil from Danny's hand. Then she bent over and read the list he had been writing:

1 Make posters and leaflets.
2 Pay young Bostock to put posters up in all surrounding villages.
3 Put advert in newspaper and get permission from city shops to hand out leaflets as well.

Jenny pointed an accusing finger at the second item. 'I suppose you're about to suggest that young Bostock should visit the RAF stations! Really, Danny, I thought you wanted the air force to take us seriously. Ernie Bostock is a nice little lad and we know he's honest because he's the Harkers' grandson, but he's only eleven. You're insulting me by suggesting that he could visit the airfields instead of me! But of course, if that's how you feel . . .' She watched as Danny's face slowly became scarlet, and gave him a friendly shove. 'All right, all right, you'd not thought of it like that . . .'

'I was trying to spare you a long bike ride, that's all,' Danny muttered, clearly horrified by Jenny's reaction. 'I feel so guilty. You do so much . . . climbing ladders, carting great bags of shopping back from the village, even digging and clearing the garden beds . . . and I do nothing.'

Jenny did not reply but added a further line to Danny's list:

4 Buy Lizzy Harker's bike and get Jenny to sweet talk the guards at the airfields to put up the posters.

'Right,' Danny said. 'As soon as the posters are finished, we'll start distributing them.'

'And now let's talk about the food we're going to offer,' Jenny said. 'I thought sausage rolls, Cornish pasties, stuff like that which is cheap but filling. Have you any other suggestions?'

For a moment they talked of sandwich fillings, soft drinks and vol au vents, but as soon as Danny had left the room Jenny picked up the envelope addressed to her, slit it open and began to read. It was from Gran, and even the sight of the address at the top of the first page – *Blackbird Cottage* – made her give a reminiscent smile. Gran and Grandpa were so happy! They had married in June and the wedding had been all the things which her own had not. Quiet and somehow beautiful, with only her parents, the twins, herself, Danny and Gran's lodgers present. 'You've only got to look at 'em to see they's happy as sandboys,' Maria had muttered to Jenny as they had clustered round the kitchen table in Blodwen Street, which was groaning under the weight of all the food which Gran and Mrs Calvert had prepared. Gran had anticipated that the neighbours would come to the church, invited or not, and so it proved. Fortunately, Mrs Calvert had not gone to the church, but had stayed behind to put on the kettle, heat the sausage rolls and do other such necessary things. She had said, humorously, that since she was taking on No. 22 and Gran's lodgers as soon as her old friend – and her old friend's brand new husband – quitted it for Ireland, she might as well keep her hand in by seeing to the grub.

Jenny smiled to herself now, remembering. Much to Louisa's amusement Cormack had been best man and had played his part to perfection, insisting that he would manage everything, and actually doing so. He had gone with Fergal to buy the ring, had checked the twins when they threatened to get out of hand, had even booked the honeymoon for the newly-weds, though both Emily and Fergal had insisted that they were too old for such shenanigans and had planned to spend a couple of days quietly in Blodwen Street before going home to Ireland, and their new abode, which they called Blackbird Cottage and Emily had never seen save as a tumbledown ruin some way from her son-in-law's neat and thriving croft.

Though Emily had steadfastly refused to wear anything resembling a wedding dress, she had put on a pale blue suit and matching hat whilst Fergal had, like

361

his son and indeed like Danny, worn his only dark suit. Much to Bernie's delight she had been allowed to wear the bridesmaid's gown her elder sister had made for the wedding which had not taken place, and Benny had donned his Sunday trousers and a new blazer. Jenny herself had put on the neat navy costume and white blouse which was her uniform as Mr Pettifer's manageress, for at that stage she was still working at the Mulberry Tree and living in the flat, whilst Danny was with his mother, and grumbling to Jenny that 'the old lady ought to take cooking lessons from your gran, else I'll be skinny as a rake before I find myself moving out just to line my stomach wi' some decent food.'

After the ceremony and their return to Blodwen Street Gran had thanked them all for coming to the church and had given her new husband a look so charged with affection that Jenny had felt tears rise to her eyes and knew she envied them their love. If only . . . but she knew Danny had attended the wedding to please her, and that meant he liked her, didn't it? He was beginning to grow stronger with every day that passed, talked, when they were alone, about his hopes of getting the tenancy of a country pub . . . She meant to work for him in one capacity or another and he had not yet repulsed her.

'You're rare quiet, Miss Jenny! Letter from an old flame, gal?'

Mrs Harker's homely Norfolk voice cut across Jenny's musings, and she jumped, then laughed. 'Oh, Mrs H, how you startled me! But you mustn't forget I'm a married woman, and we don't have old flames! Actually, it's from my gran, the one who got married to Mr Fergal Muldoon. But I mustn't sit here mooning over it, with so much still to do!'

Chapter Seventeen

Jenny awoke. The sun was streaming through her attic window and she thought, guiltily, that she must have overslept. She was about to swing her legs out of bed when she remembered that it was Sunday. For a moment she frowned, wondering why she had not woken earlier, and then, with a stab of delight, she remembered. The opening party! It had been a great success, far exceeding their expectations. It had started at six and gone on until midnight, by which time every scrap of food she and Mrs Harker had prepared had vanished. Jenny imagined that they would probably need to replenish most of the drinks the pub sold, though the bar had not been her primary concern. Danny, Mr Harker and a couple of sensible, middle-aged women from the village had coped remarkably well with the bar customers, whilst she and Mrs Harker had watched the food disappear, brought out fresh supplies and, when even those had gone, prepared another mound of sandwiches, sending young Bostock up to the village to beg, borrow or steal as many of the makings as folk could spare.

Jenny lay back against her pillows. Danny had told her not to set the alarm because even after all their guests had left there had been a great deal of clearing up to do, so neither she nor Danny had got to bed until past two o'clock. In fact Jenny could only just remember stumbling up the stairs, undressing with fumbling fingers and getting between the sheets.

No wonder she had overslept! A glance at the alarm clock told her that it was past eleven o'clock and guilt at her tardiness had her hurrying out of bed, for normally she was up by seven, if not earlier. She was about to go down to the bathroom when someone tapped on her door, and she got hastily back into bed as Danny entered the room. He was carrying a tray containing two cups of tea and what looked like two bacon butties. 'Morning, Jenny . . . just!' he said. 'It's half past eleven, but I didn't want to wake you because I know you and Mrs Harker were still clearing away downstairs when I finished in the bar and came up to bed.'

'I wasn't long after you; I think it was about half past three,' Jenny said, eyeing the tray and its contents with a watering mouth. 'My, that smells good! I thought the customers had eaten every crumb we had in the house . . . how come I missed the bacon?'

Danny put the tea down on Jenny's bedside table – which was actually a small tea chest – and handed her one of the bacon butties. 'You didn't. Mrs Ryder from the bakery in Alby sent us a couple of loaves, guessing that you wouldn't have kept any back, and Mrs Harker's next door neighbour provided the bacon. Everyone's pleased as punch that the opening went so well, because it means a lot for a village to have a popular and successful public house. But you've missed Mr Chamberlain's announcement . . . can you guess what he said?'

Jenny stopped with her sandwich halfway to her mouth. 'Oh my God,' she breathed. 'Everyone was talking about it last night, but we were so busy it went completely out of my head. What did he say? Has Hitler backed down?'

'No, of course he hasn't,' Danny said grimly. 'He said we're at war with Germany. I guess it was no surprise to anyone, because Hitler isn't the sort of man to let anyone push him around. Last night, the chaps from the airfields were talking of war as though it were already a fact.' He grinned at Jenny, sat down on the edge of her bed and reached out to pat her cheek. 'Good thing the old Cat is up and running. When I tell you how much money we took, you'll be flabbergasted. We'll be able to furnish a guest room now, which is a good thing since one of the air force chaps asked if his girlfriend could stay with us next time he gets leave. She's from Scotland, too far off for him to visit her when he's only free for a few days . . .' He beamed. 'Oh, Jenny, things are going right for us at last!'

Christmas was over and the Callaghans were settling into their new home and beginning to adjust to a very different way of life, Jenny thought, going over the last few hectic weeks in her mind as she faced the prospect of getting out of her warm bed. Autumn had brought an elm tree crashing down in the gales and though only one branch had reached the house, it had done a certain amount of damage to the roof. Jenny and Mr Harker had climbed a ladder and surveyed the damage, which looked dreadful to Jenny but not, she was thankful to see, to Mr Harker. He had said that one beam would have to be replaced, and possibly a dozen tiles, and though Jenny had offered to labour for him he had said that she had plenty to do without mending roofs. 'I know a young feller in Cumber Magna what's waitin' for his call-up papers. Him and me betwixt us will have it sound again before you've put your Christmas bird in the oven.'

Looking back now, Jenny realised that she had never worked so hard in her life. When they had been putting the Mulberry Tree to rights, they had actually done very little themselves. Building contractors had tackled such things as roofs, walls and floors, cleaners had been hired to take on the filth which had built up in the kitchen and decorators had dealt with plastering and painting.

How very different it had been at the Cat! She and Danny had had no money to spare, so apart from a good deal of help from the Harkers they had had to do everything themselves. Danny had done what he could, but the majority of the work had fallen to Jenny's lot and she remembered the surge of relief with which she had greeted Mr Harker's offer to deal with the damaged roof.

Sighing, Jenny got out of the bed, noting with a little shiver that the window was opaque with frost. Shrinkingly, she placed her warm palm on the glass and peered through the gap she had made. Frost spangled the trees, but the sun was shining, lighting up the fen and making getting up seem a lot more attractive than it had done earlier.

Jenny splashed water into the basin on her washstand,

having to break the ice first, and thought, not for the first time, that it would have been nice to wash in the bathroom. She seldom did so, for Danny needed hot water for shaving and she could manage perfectly well with cold, she reminded herself, rinsing briskly and then dressing with all speed.

Presently, she hurried downstairs. Having been warned by the government that in the event of war rationing would have to be imposed, Danny had taken Jenny's advice and bought a large sow and two baconers at Acle market. He had also purchased two dozen in-lay pullets and talked of keeping a couple of goats, though they had done nothing about that as yet.

Because she had had a good deal of experience, Jenny had taken it for granted that she would look after the stock, so Danny would come down presently and make the porridge whilst Jenny toiled back and forth, carting swill and poultry meal, and collecting any eggs which the hens had laid in the nesting boxes. Danny had proved to be perfectly capable of making breakfast and even of starting off their supper, and Jenny saw no reason why this arrangement should not continue until Danny was strong enough to help with outdoor work.

Because Cumber Magna was three times the size of Cumber, Jenny did a good deal of her shopping there, and even with the aid of Lizzie's bicycle she had often had to make two or three journeys simply to stock up with food they needed both for her and Danny and to sell over the bar. However, with her usual good sense, she had eyed their small row boats with a mixture of fascination and dread, summoned up all her courage and, one calm and sunny day in early December, persuaded Mrs Harker to give her a boating lesson. Mrs Harker was a patient teacher and after three afternoons during which Jenny had 'caught crabs', got tangled up in the reeds and rammed the bank so hard that she had nearly toppled off her seat, she got the knack and was now able to scull across the fen, load up her shopping and scull back, saving herself hours of time and a good deal of aggravation, for a heavily laden bicycle was hard to control on the deeply rutted lanes.

Danny could row already, but his injured shoulder hurt him when he tried to use it, so he talked of reclaiming the yacht which still lay on its side beneath the water in the boathouse. 'We could have some fun with that when summer comes,' he had said wistfully. 'Mr Harker says in June and July the fen fairly hums with pleasure craft; they come down the cut from the bigger broads and go out on the far side to join the river. By then we'll be more organised, have time to enjoy ourselves, and what could be nicer than taking to the water?'

Agreeing, Jenny had thought longingly of summer, for despite their best endeavours the Cat was still an extremely cold house. Thanks to the elm tree, the fire in the bar was kept going from mid-afternoon until closing time, and the Aga in the kitchen was not allowed to go out either, since it was their sole means of cooking and heating water. But the little attic bedrooms were icy, as were the scullery, the big pantry and the larder, though Jenny suspected that this last was meant to be cold since the shelves were slabs of marble and the hooks

369

on the ceiling spoke mutely of the days when previous landlords had hung great joints of beef and bacon from them.

Ever since the Cat had opened, Jenny had resumed weekly letters to her family; she had felt awkward about corresponding with them after the wedding, assuming that Danny had felt in some way belittled by his failure to bring Rob Dingle to book for both his stealing of Claudia and his theft of the money Danny had made. Now, however, Danny was running a successful business, with herself as his only partner, and the Muldoons knew, even if Danny did not actually acknowledge it, that she herself would never do anything to harm either Danny himself or the Cat and Fiddle.

Once, Jenny had offered to let Danny read the letters from her parents, Gran and even the twins, but though he had thanked her, he had said that he would feel like a spy, reading letters which were neither addressed to him nor meant for his eyes. Jenny had not tried to persuade him to change his mind, and as she lay in bed one morning in February, willing herself to brave the sub-zero temperatures outside her cosy little nest, she was glad she had not, for her mother had written triumphantly that at long last she was in touch with Claudia, actually knew her address.

'Tis the war which has persuaded my girl to get in touch, Jenny had read in the letter she had received the previous day. *She was so worried that we might all be killed and she'd never know that she posted off a card with her address, and we've been writing to each other ever since.*

Jenny had wondered whether to tell Danny that friendly relations had been resumed between her mother and Claudia, but had decided against it. She and Danny were absorbed in the Cat and Fiddle; Claudia – and indeed her former life at the Mulberry Tree – seemed a lifetime away and that, Jenny told herself, was how she liked it. Reading her mother's letter she had smiled to herself, noticing that Mam had not even pretended that her husband approved of her acceptance of Claudia's sudden desire to be in touch with her family. Indeed, Cormack might not even know about Claudia's letter, since as soon as war had been declared he had caught the ferry to England, lied about his age and been accepted. He had done his basic training and was at present aboard a troop ship, heading for a destination that he would not know for certain until his arrival. Jenny had written to him but had not mentioned Claudia.

Now, Jenny sighed, got out of bed and pulled back the curtains, then gasped. The window was completely covered with frost flowers and when she breathed on them and cleared a space she saw that snow lay thick on everything and flakes still fell from a leaden sky. Hastily, she donned her old dressing gown, pushed her feet into her scuffed slippers and headed for the stairs. She and Danny had worked out a routine and now took it in turns to use the bathroom, so that whoever got downstairs first would start breakfast.

Today, however, she decided she had best wake Danny first, because they would need to clear a path across the yard to the sheds and sties before the snow got any deeper. Accordingly, she rapped on his door, shouted the news that it was snowing, and snowing hard furthermore, and then descended the stairs and went into the bathroom.

Twenty minutes later she was in the kitchen, making porridge and reflecting, rather smugly, that when the Harkers arrived she would be able to tease them roundly, for only the previous evening Mr Harker had announced that 'it were too cold to snow'. As she stirred the porridge and felt the draught whistling under the door, she thought that the snow would be the perfect excuse to have a day indoors, working on the guest rooms, some of which still needed attention.

She was still congratulating herself on her plan when Danny came into the kitchen, fully dressed and in his thick winter coat, a scarf in one hand, gloves in the other. 'Morning, Jenny wren,' he said breezily. 'Thanks for waking me. I'll start on snow clearance at once; care to join me?'

'Yes, but not until we've both lined our stomachs with porridge and tea,' Jenny said severely. 'No point in trying to work on empty bellies.'

'Right. Brekker first, then we'll clear a path to the pigsty and the hen house,' Danny said. 'It's exciting to see so much snow, though . . . don't you think? Oh, I know snow happens most winters, but when you live in a city someone else does most of the clearing. This is our first taste of really bad weather in Cumber. I wonder if the fen will freeze?'

A couple of weeks after that first fall, the snow became a real menace to the Cat and its tenants. The fen had indeed frozen over and the Callaghans had kept a clear path across it, but as the drifts in the lanes grew higher and higher it became more difficult for their various suppliers to deliver. Farmers who had clamps full of potatoes, turnips and carrots could not reach the provender buried under great snow drifts; bakers had nothing to bake and the brewery lorries could not get through the tortuous little lanes, many of them filled up with snow and giving no hint of their existence.

Danny, Jenny and the Harkers had managed to keep the lane from Cumber to the pub more or less clear, but for a whole nerve-racking week the RAF personnel, who had made the Cat and Fiddle their favourite pub, were unable to leave the airfields. However, Danny had insisted that a roaring fire should welcome anyone brave enough to face the drifts, and this had in fact proved a real draw for the villagers of Cumber and also of Cumber Magna, who fought their way through many a blizzard, even after Danny had had to ration them to one pint of beer per evening. The men sat around the fire, warming themselves for the return trip to their villages and exchanging what Danny suspected were tall stories about other, even more terrible winters.

Feeding the stock was easier because of Jenny's fore-thought, Danny considered now as he crossed the yard with a steaming bucket of hen food in one hand and pigswill in the other. She had 'done a deal' with a feed merchant in North Walsham because, as she had said, they had plenty of storage space and prices always rose and never fell. Danny had been doubtful whether it was sensible to spend their hard won profit on sacks of meal and grain, but now he was heartily glad they had done so. His little partner might seem to be just a child, but she was as shrewd as they came and had clearly not wasted her time in Ireland. Mr Harker, looking approvingly at the vast sow and her fourteen piglets, had commented that Mrs Callaghan knew a thing or two, despite being a city gal, and Danny had explained that his wife had spent her girlhood on a farm in Ireland. Mr Harker had nodded sagely, giving it as his opinion that Mrs Callaghan would make a grand farmer if they ever decided to give up the Cat and take to the land, and Danny had passed the comment on, smiling when Jenny went pink with pleasure.

Now, he reached the pigsties, emptied the swill into the troughs, then made his way to the hen house. He slid open the pop-hole through which the hens could gain the outside world, cleared the snow off the ramp, and was not particularly surprised when a hen's head appeared and was hastily withdrawn. As soon as he cleared a patch of snow and began to scatter the steaming contents of the bucket, however, the hens came pouring out of their cosy retreat, attacking the food with as much enthusiasm as though they had not been fed for a week.

Danny opened the door and went into the warm but strong-smelling interior. He collected six eggs from the nesting boxes and emerged into the yard once more, just as the back door opened and Jenny, in wellingtons and an ancient, much patched duffel coat, came out. She had tied her hair into two bunches with a piece of binder twine and Danny, smiling affectionately, was just thinking that the hairstyle made her look younger than

374

ever when he was brought up short. Jenny's growing pretty, he thought with considerable surprise. Oh, she would never be beautiful like her sister, but he realised that her face was no longer simply round and pink. He did not know whether it was hard work or worry which had caused her countenance to fine down so that now he could see the shape of her cheekbones and the jut of her small, determined chin. Was it that which made him think her pretty, he wondered. Or was it the glow that brightened her eyes when they met his own?

Well, whatever it was, he suddenly realised that he was not the only person to notice how she had changed. A short, plumpish mechanic from Cumber airfield showed a distinct interest in Danny's young partner, and there was a stringy Australian tail gunner who spent a good deal of his time telling her all about his home country whenever he came into the bar.

But of course there's nothing in that, not really, Danny told himself as Jenny grinned at him and swerved aside to peer into his bucket. Both the Aussie and the mechanic knew Jenny was his wife, so their interest could only be friendly. 'Where are you off to, Jen?' he said lazily.

'I'm on my way to feed the goats,' she told him. 'Then I've got to bake some bread. Oh, good, six eggs! How do you fancy an omelette for your tea tonight?'

Danny, still mentally reeling from the sudden realisation that Jenny was not a child but a pretty young woman, said rather feebly that an omelette sounded fine and watched Jenny's back view disappearing into the cowshed, where they kept the two nanny goats which Danny had bought from a neighbour as a Christmas present for his wife. At the time, he had seen nothing wrong with such a gift, but had realised later that others thought it strangely unromantic when they considered that Jenny was still a bride. I suppose they were right, too, Danny told himself now, following Jenny into the cowshed. But he had known the goats were what Jenny wanted. In the shed, he saw that she was standing on tiptoe, trying to pull down a bundle of rather dusty hay from the loft overhead, and tutted. 'I'll do that,' he said peremptorily. 'You go back indoors and start breakfast.'

Jenny obeyed at once, but all through the meal Danny struggled with the thought that had occurred to him with such force that morning; Jenny was a young woman, not a child, and she had admirers. It had never struck him before that either of them might want to break the partnership, which was how he – and Jenny of course – had regarded their marriage. Indeed, it was what they had agreed. If he had considered it at all, it had been only from his own point of view. He had loved Claudia and could not even imagine falling in love with someone else. As for his partner, until very recently he had regarded Jenny as a child who was a stranger to more adult emotions. But now, having seen how she had grown up in the last few months, he realised that the boot might well be on the other foot. She, so much younger than he, might easily fall in love with any of the young men who came, on an almost daily basis, into the Cat and Fiddle. If she did so, then he had no right to keep her tied to a partnership which he now realised, belatedly, was very much more to his advantage than to hers. Immediately, he flinched away from losing her;

how would he manage alone? But he must be fair to her, must tell her that if she wished for her freedom he would agree to a divorce and would simply have to employ someone to take her place. He thought about the financial side of it, but knew Jenny too well to think she would expect money for her share in their business, which, after all, was still far from free of debt. There was the bank loan . . . but no point in meeting troubles more than halfway. First of all he must speak to Jenny.

The opportunity did not come, however, until one snowy afternoon when he and Jenny were clearing a path across the fen, which was still frozen solid, shovelling, brushing, and doing a good deal of slipping and sliding as well. They had wrapped themselves up in every available garment but were soon removing mufflers and gloves, for the work was hard and both of them were shortly red-faced and sweating. When a gharry full of the boys from the local airfield drew up before the Cat and Fiddle, both Jenny and Danny rested on their shovels and looked hopefully at the new arrivals.

'Hello, fellers,' Jenny shouted. 'Care to give a hand? If you do, it's free mugs of hot tea and newly baked scones as soon as we've cleared the path and got back to the Cat. Any takers?'

'Gawd, yes, but we'll need tools,' someone called back, and Danny recognised the mechanic they called Pudden, thanks to his habit of entering the cookhouse and shouting to the corporal doling out the food, 'What's for pudden, wack?'

He grinned at the younger man, knowing that Pudden had a weakness for Jenny, a fellow Liverpudlian. 'There's bass brooms and other stuff in the wooden shed near the back door,' he called back. 'Help yourselves.'

The men disappeared and presently came back to the fen clutching an assortment of tools: bass brooms, a shovel or two, a hoe and, in Pudden's case, an old dustbin lid which, rather to Danny's surprise, he wielded with great gusto and considerable success.

Everyone set to with a will and very soon the forerunners were climbing the bank on the far side of the fen and cheering on their companions and Danny, leaving Jenny sweeping the last few traces of snow from the path they had made, hurried down to the grocer, Mr Sewell, who had their order all packed up and ready. He returned to the newly cleared pathway across the fen and was calling out that he had the shopping and was making his way back when someone – he thought it was the Fred the Aussie tail gunner – shouted, 'Jenny!' He saw his wife turn an enquiring face towards the gunner, who drew back his arm and without apparently even taking aim hurled a snowball, scoring a direct hit on Jenny's face with such force that she staggered backwards.

Immediately, all hell broke loose. Pudden scooped snow, and whilst Jenny was still spitting snow out of her mouth and brushing it from her cheeks he took up the cudgels in her defence, hurling a snowball at Fred and shouting, as he did so: 'That's my favourite girl you're peltin' wi' snow, so take that!'

To his own astonishment, Danny felt a knot of anger form itself in his stomach, but before he could do anything about it a full-scale snowball fight was in progress. Missiles flew through the air and the combatants divided themselves into two armies, both of which were soon violently engaged. Danny saw one of his efforts land on Pudden's forehead, and shouted: 'Take that, you . . .' before he remembered that it had been Fred who had started the snowball fight – by aiming at Jenny, what was more. But it had been Pudden who had shouted something about Jenny being his girl, and without stopping to think he launched himself at Pudden to such effect that the younger man landed on his back. Whereupon Danny jumped on him, laughing wildly, and began to stuff snow into Pudden's surprised mouth.

He was thoroughly enjoying himself when someone seized his shoulder and a voice in his ear said: 'What the devil are you at, Danny? Throwing snowballs is one thing . . .'

It was Jenny, round-eyed and reproachful. Hastily, Danny got off his foe's recumbent body and helped the other man to his feet. 'Sorry, old feller,' he said. 'I thought I were a kid again, in Prince's Park, one of the Albermarle Court gang gettin' the better of a feller from round the corner. You all right?'

Pudden laughed, brushing snow off his face and spitting it out of his mouth. ''S awright, wack,' he said. 'Blimey, I could eat a perishin' horse.' He turned to Jenny. 'Lead me to them scones, queen!'

Everyone set off towards the pub, Danny only remembering that he had been carrying three paper carriers when one of the men brought them over. 'You dropped 'em when the fight started,' he said. 'I put 'em behind the piled-up snow on the side of the path to keep them out of the way of the fight.' He grinned at Danny, handing him the bags. 'I guessed the fellers would start a snow fight because we've been cooped up for so long, so I made a pile of ammo on the way to Cumber Magna and when we came back I saw your stuff near my cache and stowed it away where it wouldn't get trampled on. I don't know what's in the parcels, but I expect it's grub, and grub's going to be hard to find now that rationing is more or less in place.'

Danny thanked him. When they reached the Cat, he hurried out to the shed to fetch in more logs, then locked the bar, since that could not be used, even for dispensing tea and scones, until opening time. He thought no more about his attack on Pudden, but when the gharry returned and the men were beginning to climb aboard, he turned to Jenny to find her eyeing him rather thoughtfully.

'Wharrever gorrin to you, la'?' she said, employing a Scouse accent which he had not heard on her lips for years. 'Old Pudden meant no harm. If I'd not stopped you . . .'

'I got carried away,' Danny mumbled. 'We were all acting like kids and I suppose . . . when Fred's snowball got you right in the gob . . .'

'It don't matter,' Pudden interrupted, looking rather surprised but also a trifle sheepish. He was already aboard the gharry and now he grinned at them. 'I reckon we all forgot we wasn't kids, and it were all in fun. Wha's more, them scones was worth a gobful of snow; you're a grand little cook, Mrs Callaghan.'

'So she is,' Danny agreed, but when they were back

380

in the kitchen, preparing for the evening ahead, he broached the subject which had been on his mind now for some while. 'Jenny, I've been meaning to talk to you about . . . well, about . . . oh, hell and damnation! It's just that Pudden made me realise . . . Jenny, you know there's no chance of me ever f-falling in love with anyone other than Claudia, and she's married to someone else and living in another country. But you . . . well, it's different for you. When we wed and agreed that it would be more like a business partnership than a marriage you were still just a kid, but since taking on the Cat I've – I've realised that you aren't a kid any longer but – but a young woman. It's all right for me; our partnership suits me very well, but you . . . oh, Jenny, you could fall in love with any of the fellows who come into the bar of an evening, and if you did . . . divorce isn't much spoken of, but I reckon . . . if you wanted your freedom . . . oh, hell, I'm putting this very badly . . . the thing is, you've never been in love, but believe me, when it hits you . . . and I'd hate you to think you were tied to me and the Cat because of our – our partnership . . .'

'Then don't bother, because as it happens you're quite wrong,' Jenny said gruffly. They were sitting one each side of the kitchen table, sipping a last cup of tea before opening up, though since it had begun to snow again, the flakes whirling past the window in what speedily became a blizzard, it seemed unlikely that the evening would be a busy one. 'I know I'm not very old, but to tell you the truth, Danny, one reason for my agreeing to our – our partnership was that I had been fool enough to fall in love, and . . .'

'Oh, I don't mean a crush, what you might call puppy love,' Danny said quickly. He knew, or imagined he did, how few opportunities Jenny had had to meet young men whilst they were working in the restaurant, far less fall in love with any of them. 'I mean . . . oh, the sort of feeling that there's only one person in the entire world who matters, one with whom you would like to share your life . . .'

'Yes, that's what I mean, too,' Jenny said. She had been staring down at her mug of tea as though she were a fortune-teller gazing into a crystal ball, but now she lifted her gaze to meet Danny's eyes. 'I was in love, what you might call proper love, but he – the feller – was pretty involved with someone else; in fact, they're married now. So you see, I'm probably even less likely than you to want to go falling in love again, let alone involve myself in such things as divorce and remarriage. I'll never love anyone else either, I can promise you that. So do stop worrying!'

Danny was astonished at the wave of relief which washed over him. He beamed at Jenny, jumped to his feet, then took her hands, squeezed them, and pulled her out of her chair and gave her a big hug, almost squeezing the breath out of her. 'Right; that's a command. I shall stop worrying right away, because you're the best partner a feller could have,' he assured her. 'We're both in the same boat, then!'

Jenny returned his smile and the pressure of his hands in hers. 'And we're paddling pretty well, considering, so no fear of drowning in misery,' she told him, then glanced at the clock above the mantel. 'Aha, opening time! Back to business, partner!'

Later, when he lay in bed that night feeling drowsy and contented, a thought occurred to Danny which drove all the drowsiness and contentment out of his head. Of course, he should have guessed! Jenny, silly brainless little creature, had been in love with Rob Dingle! Oh, they had teased her, said she was bound to fall for him, working closely as they had been. But Danny had not, until this moment, realised that it had happened; that Jenny had been pining for the other man as he, Danny, had pined for Claudia. Well, he thought now, though he had not got over his love for Claudia, with Jenny it must be a different matter. He told himself firmly that at her age she had simply not recognised the difference between love and a crush; she had had a crush on the fellow, that was all, and she had made it pretty clear this very day that though the crush was over, the memory of it would prevent her from falling in love again.

Satisfied, Danny rolled over, heaved the blankets up over his ears, and told himself that he was a lucky dog to have a partner as sweet-tempered and efficient as young Jenny. She may have been silly and brainless once, as he had called her in his mind, but she was so no longer. She was steady, reliable, hard-working and . . . oh, dammit, she was sweet and as wholesome as one of the scones she baked every day, even if she could never be described as pretty. Soon, Danny slept, and his sleep was untroubled by dreams.

'Steady, steady! Here she comes! Of course there's bound to be damage, but I don't think any of it's too bad,'

Danny said, looking lovingly at the small sailing boat which he, Harker and Jenny had just carefully pulled to the surface. 'What do you think, Mr Harker?'

Mr Harker sniffed, for the sailing boat which they had just rescued from its watery grave in the boathouse looked somewhat battered, but admitted that there was 'Nothin' a bit of work wun't put right, allus provided we can foind a noo mast and a stretch o' canvas for a sail.'

Jenny grinned and poked Danny in the back. 'We'll have her fit for use in a couple of months,' she said reassuringly. 'Then you won't have to row across to fetch the shopping, though of course now we've got a van the boat isn't as necessary as it was in the winter.' She said nothing about the pain in Danny's shoulder which made rowing something to be avoided, knowing her partner was sensitive about his continued inability to use his left hand and arm. Ever since they had managed to buy a van from a local lad who had joined the navy and no longer needed it, things had become easier, though driving was a chore which Danny avoided whenever he could.

'Yes, a couple of months' work, whenever we've got the time, should sort it out,' Danny said now, looking proudly at the little boat. 'Thank God for better weather, though. A fat lot we'd have been able to do with it a few months ago. Still, we got through the worst and aren't likely to have to do so again . . . not for a good while, at any rate.'

He was referring, of course, to the previous winter, which had been the worst anyone could remember.

There had been times when Jenny and Danny, despite their brave words, feared that the Cat might not survive, that there would come a time when they could not pay money owed, but somehow it had never happened. They had always managed to scrape enough together, though it had meant a good deal of going without. Danny had insisted that they should be fed, but it had been mostly bread and potatoes, eggs when the hens had laid, and such dainties as mashed parsnips and an occasional feast of pork when someone in the village killed a pig and generously handed over a parcel of meat to the young couple at the Cat.

Danny and Jenny had worked hard in the pub, and when the snow began to melt they knew they were over the worst and could begin to benefit from the work they had put in that winter, for when no customers could get through they had concentrated quite literally on putting their house in order. They had cleaned, mended, painted and whitewashed, and had frequented any jumble sale they heard about, buying torn sheets, worn blankets, old pictures, wash stands and dressing tables and spending time, as Mrs Harker had put it, 'redding them up', which meant a good deal of work. Jenny, who loathed all forms of needlework, had found herself sides-to-middling sheets, patching blankets and hemming curtains, and had slogged away after the pub closed, determined to have the rooms ready for when customers began to want them. And sure enough, when the weather grew milder they found, as Danny had predicted, that there were visitors to the airfields to whom they could let their rooms, provided they charged reasonable rates.

There was a taxi in the village but Danny got Mr Harker to use their van to take wives and girlfriends to their destinations and drove it himself from time to time despite the pain in his shoulder.

'Well, Jen? What'll we call this dear little yacht? I know you aren't supposed to rename boats, but there's nothing on this one to say what she was called, so I suppose . . .'

'*Kitty*,' Jenny said promptly. 'Because she belongs to the Cat . . . and to us, of course.' She turned to Mr Harker, who was grinning with a great display of pink gums as well as a couple of tobacco-stained teeth. 'What do you think, Mr H? Or should it be something more – more *fishy*, like *Stickleback*, or *Water-skimmer*?'

'Why not *Kittiwake*? Tha's a bird, that is,' Mr Harker said immediately. 'Only I aren't no good wi' letterin', that I aren't, so you'd best get someone else to write it on the starn. But you doesn't want to name her until she're fitted out, which may take longer'n you think for.'

'*Kittiwake*,' Danny said thoughtfully. 'Yes, I like it. And as you say, Jenny, a kitty is more connected with the Cat than if we'd gone for something like *Water-skimmer*.'

Jenny smiled and nodded diligently. 'And it's not just ourselves we've got to please, because we're going to hire it out when summer comes,' she reminded him. 'And *Kittiwake*'s a pretty name, much prettier than *Water-skimmer*, which isn't easy to say. But now the hard work's over, I'll go back to the kitchen and make a big pot of tea and cut the cake Mrs H made this morning. You fellers can come in as soon as you've decided where you want to work on our new possession.' She turned to Mr Harker. 'I suppose it *is* our new possession? I mean, it did belong to the previous landlord, didn't it? And he signed over all that he'd left in the place to us, so . . .'

'Tha's right, my woman. Mr Jameson, he took the sail boat in lieu of a debt what he were owed,' Mr Harker said. 'That weren't much of a bargain even then . . . still, I dessay you'll turn it out bright as a noo penny by the time you've done.'

'We'll put it in the stables,' Danny said, his eyes shining with excitement. 'Boy oh boy, I can't wait to get started! Only I won't rush into things, because one of the lads from RAF Cumber worked in Broom's boatyard before he joined the RAF, so he's going to set me right.'

Chapter Eighteen

'Benny? Bernie? Grandpa's goin' to drive into the village this morning, so if you want you can have a lift, but would you rather go wit' your pals, bein' as how it's the first day of the new term? Only I won't have no nonsense, as you know well. Either you get yourselves ready in good time . . .'

The Muldoon family had been seated round the table, finishing off a substantial breakfast, when Gran entered the room. Benny and Bernie exchanged a quick, surreptitious glance, then Bernie answered for both of them. 'Thanks, Gran, but we've got to do our chores first, I suppose?' She pulled a mournful face. 'It ain't fair. I'm sure you and Mam make us work harder than ever our Daddy did when he were at home.'

Ever since Cormack had joined the British army everyone had had to work a good deal harder, though before he left he had extracted a promise that Dónal would remain on the croft until his return and had also employed Dónal's brother Sam. Now, away in India, he was in for the duration and was so happy that Louisa, knowing protests were useless anyway, had simply accepted the situation and made the best of it.

The twins missed their father but were proud to boast about him to their school friends, though they complained loudly and vociferously when they realised that their list of chores was lengthier now that their father was not around. However, there were compensations. Grandpa was busy, too busy to pay much attention to Benny and Bernie, and now that their mother had Gran scarcely a stone's throw away to run the house, she did a good deal of the lighter work on the croft which might otherwise have fallen to the twins. During the long summer holidays, which had ended the previous day, the twins had helped out when they could not avoid it, but Dónal was an enthusiastic worker and so long as they completed the tasks they had been set he was quite happy to see them go off about their own affairs; probably preferred it, in fact, to their grumbling and reluctant presence.

Louisa, cutting and buttering slices off the loaf, spreading homemade jam and putting the results into a couple of paper bags, shook a reproving finger at her offspring. 'Of course there's more to do on the croft with your daddy off fighting,' she said. 'No grumbling, kids. Now you're back in school, you'll have plenty to occupy you when the dark evenings come: homework and that. But until then, you'll pull your weight and do your bit. Remember, there's a war on.'

'Not here there isn't,' Benny said quickly, before his sister could open her mouth. 'It's not our war, Dónal says so. Only he wishes he could have gone, like our daddy has; he says he's always wanted to see furrin' parts. And don't tell me off for talkin' like that, because it's just what Dónal *did* say.'

Louisa laughed, reached for a couple of apples from

389

the bowl on the sideboard and popped one into each paper bag. 'Remember, young man, you're only half Irish and Gran and meself aren't Irish at all, which is why your daddy went off to fight for us, rather than staying at home,' she said. 'Anyway, you'd best get on with your chores whilst Grandpa puts on his best bib and tucker. Only don't go messing up your good school clothes.'

Gran, who had been buttering a slice of bread for herself, chuckled. 'Telling you kids to stay clean is like expecting the Mersey to flow backwards,' she observed. 'Benny, you feed the pigs.' She put her bread and butter down and went over to the sink, pulling out the two buckets which stood beneath it, both half filled with cooked potato peelings, the outer leaves of cabbage and cauliflower, and other odds and ends of unwanted food. As her grandson got to his feet, she turned to Bernie. 'You can feed the hens and bring me the eggs. And when you've done that, the pair of you can fetch the goats in from the birch pasture. Then you can come back here to wait for your grandpa.'

The twins exchanged covert looks; the last thing they intended to do when they finished their tasks was to return to the cottage, but it would never do to say so. Instead, they meekly picked up the buckets that Gran had pointed out and set off across the yard.

As soon as they were sure they could not be overheard, they slowed their brisk pace and Benny pulled a despairing face at his twin. 'I t'ought we was going to skip school today,' he said plaintively. 'If we've got to go back for our carry-outs, Mam will make us go wit''

Grandpa, and bang goes our chance of a day pickin' blackers wit' Sean and Michael, and makin' some money by sellin' 'em on Sean's mam's market stall.'

'Oh, Benny, you don't *think*,' Bernie said. 'Why d'you think Gran told us to fetch the goats into the stable? It's because she and Mam are goin' to milk 'em, of course. We'll get the goats in, then climb up to the hayloft and hide. You know what them goats is like when they don't fancy bein' milked, and now they've got kids they never fancy bein' milked. We'll watch through the gaps in the planks of the hayloft floor whilst Mam an' Gran are chasin' around and cussin' and that. Then when they take the goats back to the birch pasture we'll nip down and grab us dinners, and by the time they're on their way back we'll be halfway to the O'Hare place.'

'All right; but why does we have to hide in the hayloft? Why can't we just bring the goats in and skedaddle?' Benny asked. By now they had reached the pigsties and he tipped the swill into the troughs and watched whilst his sister fed the hens. 'Suppose . . .'

'Because we want Mam and Gran to think we've gone wit' Grandpa,' Bernie pointed out, with more than a trace of impatience. 'So we have to get our carry-outs from the kitchen. Besides, I like me grub so I does, an' I don't fancy havin' to make do wit' blackers until four or five this afternoon which is what would happen if we just went off. Still, if you don't like me plan . . .'

'Oh I do, I do,' her brother said hastily. It was plain that the thought of existing on nothing but blackberries until teatime was not a pleasant one. 'Has Grandpa gone yet?'

'No, not yet. And that's another reason for keeping well out of sight until we're sure he's left for the village in the donkey cart,' his sister said. 'Wait on while I see if the hens have laid overnight. Oh, and that's another good reason for hiding in the hayloft. If we're caught, we'll say that all the poultry weren't in the hen house, so we were lookin' for any eggs which had been laid astray.' She opened the door of the hen house, then turned to give her twin a wicked grin. 'Good thing you've got me to tell you what to do,' she said, 'else we'd never get a day off school. First day back is always a muddle, so the chances are no one will miss us!'

The Muldoons now had a small flock of four nanny goats, all of which had kids, and one bad-tempered billy, who always did his best to accompany his wives back to the stable when they were taken in for milking. Driving the nannies before them, however, and slamming the gate on the billy and three of the four kids, the twins herded their captives along the deep little lane and were about to re-enter the yard when the postman, hurrying towards them, gave a shout. 'Hi, Benny, Bernie,' he called. 'Save my old legs and tek the post. 'Tis only two letters today, one for you and one for Blackbird Cottage, so you won't be overburdened, but I've got a deal of delivering still to do.'

Bernie took the letters, gave them a cursory glance, and shoved them into her jacket pocket. 'OK, Mr Ryan,' she said cheerfully. 'We'll hand 'em over just as soon as we've got these perishin' goats penned up in the stable for milkin'.'

It was never easy to get the goats to go in the direction

of the stable, but the children managed it, slammed the half-door and then scrambled up into the hayloft. It was a hot day and after only a couple of minutes Bernie shed her jacket. She was pushing it under a pile of hay when they heard Gran and their mother opening the stable door below them. To bribe the nannies into at least a semblance of compliance, the twins saw that Louisa had armed herself with a handful of carrots, with which she fed the goats whilst Gran seized them by their collars before doing her best to keep the animals still for Louisa to milk them. The presence of the kid did not help since it was necessary to crouch on the ground and hold the bucket beneath each bulging udder in turn. The kid, seeing Louisa's inviting back, promptly scaled it as though it had been a mountain, its sharp little hooves causing Louisa to shriek a protest, whilst Gran slapped at the little creature and tried not to get entangled in the rope she had threaded through its mother's collar.

Above their heads, Bernie stuffed her jacket into her mouth to stifle her giggles and she and Benny rolled around in the hay, peering through the planking gaps into the stable below. When Millie, the oldest and most difficult of the goats, kicked over the bucket of milk and tried to butt Gran, who was bending over the kid at the time, it was almost more than Bernie could bear. In fact, she was mopping tears of mirth from her cheeks when she saw something that sobered her immediately; the letters had escaped from her pocket and had fallen down into the stable below.

Bernie gave a gasp of horror, grabbed Benny's arm and jerked a thumb at the gap in the planks. Benny followed the gesture with his eyes, then turned a puzzled face to his sister. 'What?' he whispered. 'Why's you lookin' scared, Bernie? Mam's milked three of 'em, so it won't be long before we can get away.'

'Can't you *see*?' Bernie hissed. 'The letters fell out o' me pocket . . .' She stopped speaking and clapped a hand to her mouth. Below her, there was now no sign of the letters, unless one counted a tiny corner of a blue envelope sticking out of the side of Millie's mouth and the fact that Sally's jaws were moving rhythmically whilst her eyes gleamed with satisfaction. It was pretty clear to the twins that the letters they had promised to deliver had gone for good.

As soon as the coast was clear, the twins rushed across to the cottage, grabbed their butties and set off for the O'Hare croft. Benny wondered aloud whether they should wait and confess that the goats had eaten the letters, but Bernie reminded him self-righteously that there was a war on. 'Mam says letters go to the bottom of the sea whenever a convoy is attacked,' she told her brother. 'That's why Daddy and Mammy number their letters, so they'll know when one or two have gone missing. What difference does it make if a letter's been ate by a whale or a nanny goat? It weren't as though either of the letters was from our daddy, because one were from Claudia – it look like her handwriting and I know she and Mam do write to each other – and the other were just – oh, just ordinary, typed, you know. Probably one of them government forms. So I vote we says nothing.'

Benny thought the matter over as they trudged the two miles to the O'Hare croft and came to the conclusion that his sister was right; there was no point in courting trouble and trouble there was bound to be if the older Muldoons discovered that the younger ones had been mitching off school. 'Besides, Daddy is still very cross with Claudia and would be even crosser if he knew she was writing to our mammy. So you see, he'll be rare pleased with' us for letting the goat eat Claudia's letter,' he said triumphantly. 'And letters get lost crossin' the Irish sea, same as they do when they come from India. So that's all right.'

Bernie gave a long relieved whistle. She knew herself to be the stronger character of the two, but had Benny insisted that they should tell she would have gone along with it, for whenever possible the twins acted in unison. All she said, however, was: 'Good!' and presently, spotting a particularly fruitful bramble, the two children began to fill the bucket they had borrowed from their mother's kitchen. As they picked they chatted comfortably, for neither saw any point in querying their decision to remain silent over the disappearance of two probably unimportant letters. Why spoil their lovely stolen day by agonising over what could not be helped? Indeed, by the time they returned to the cottage that evening they had almost forgotten the event.

A few days later, when Louisa went down to the telephone box in the village for her monthly call to her daughter, and came back to say that Jenny and Danny had taken their new boat, the *Kittiwake*, for her first sail,

Bernie wished aloud that they could have a boat of their own, as the Callaghans had.

'Where would we sail it?' Louisa said, smiling at her daughter. 'Oh, I know the river's quite near, but for a sail boat you need a lake, or the sea. When the war's over, though, Jenny has promised that we can have a holiday at the Cat and Fiddle, and I expect they'll teach you to sail then.'

'Hello, Jenny! No need to ask what you're doing, 'cos I reckon most of the village have either been up here collectin' acorns, or will be comin' up in the next few days.' Mrs Harker, who in common with most of the villagers kept a pig in a sty at the end of her garden, grinned at the younger woman. 'Nice day for it, my woman. And it's easy pickin' an' all.'

Jenny, agreeing, shook the contents of her large bag to show her friend just how well she had already done. It was a bright and sunny day in mid-October, but only the previous night they had had one of the autumn gales which swept across the flat Norfolk countryside at this time of year, hence the number of acorns to be gathered by the country folk as a treat for their pigs. And it wasn't only acorns, either. This wood was rich in oak trees, but long ago someone had planted a goodly number of sweet chestnuts between the wood and some pasture and Jenny meant to gather some of the nuts before she left, for she and Danny loved them roasted on the big fire in the bar.

She said as much to Mrs Harker, who nodded approvingly. 'And there's a deal o' cob nuts in the hedgerows, what'll keep nicely until you're ready to bake your Christmas cakes an' make your mincemeat,' she said. 'But don't forget to leave some for others! Have you gathered any damsons yet? 'Tis hard work, but damson jam is favourite so far as Mr Harker is concerned.'

Jenny admitted that she had not done so, and felt a small pang which she could not suppress as she thought of Fred, who had been one of the many casualties of the recent battle which had been fought by the Luftwaffe and the Royal Air Force in the clear skies of early autumn. Fred had loved her homemade jam . . . but it did not do to dwell on the losses which had helped Britain to gain air supremacy over the enemy, who had been trying to destroy her air defences in order to begin the invasion which they had planned for the autumn, or so it was widely believed.

Mrs Harker, however, clucked disapprovingly, then seemed to recollect herself. 'And why should you collect damsons? It ain't as though they grow in this here wood. No, you have to go further afield. You go through the village, stickin' to the main road for about a mile, then you take a left turn . . .'

Her directions became complicated and Jenny, not wanting to offend, laughed and held up an admonitory hand. 'Don't say any more, Mrs H,' she said gaily. 'Tell you what: next time you're off to pick damsons, could you give me a call? If we go together, I might actually arrive in the right place at the right time. To tell you the truth I've never made damson jam, probably because so far as I know there weren't any damson trees growing

397

near Connacht Cottage. But Mrs Askham at the post office gave me a little pot of hers last autumn and Danny and I both thought it was delicious.' She shot a quick glance at Mrs Harker through her lashes. 'Fred liked it too,' she finished quietly.

Mrs Harker was a typical Norfolk woman, reluctant to show emotion, but she took Jenny's free hand and gave it a squeeze, then bent to pick up her bucket of acorns, which she had placed on the ground as they talked. 'Right, then. When I go after the damsons – it'll be next week I reckon – I'll give you a shout and we'll go together,' she said briskly. 'But now I'd best be gettin' back home, do I'll be late with Mr Harker's tea.'

The two women parted, Jenny to trudge towards the Cat and Fiddle, whilst Mrs Harker went in the opposite direction. As she walked Jenny thought back, with considerable pleasure, over the last six or eight months. Once March had arrived, she and Danny had really got into their stride. As Danny had predicted, their rooms were much in demand, especially at weekends, and as the weather had grown steadily better it was not only their visitors who wanted to hire their row boats, but also men from the surrounding airfields. Jenny had remarked to Danny that she thought the boat trips that they offered did more good than they had ever anticipated, for grey-faced men returning from the battle raging overhead came back after a trip around the fen bright-eyed and relaxed. She had told Danny that their customers might try to forget their troubles over a hand of cards and a couple of beers, but it was the peace and quiet and the wildlife they saw which contributed most to their pleasure in hiring a boat and exploring the fen.

The Callaghans, too, revelled in taking out a boat whenever they had the leisure. They saw water voles, roach, tench and pike, as well as many birds to which they could not put a name. Butterflies abounded: red admirals, painted ladies and the elusive swallowtail. They even caught a glimpse of a shy coypu, creatures which looked like gigantic rats but were in fact vegetarians and harmless, except to the banks of the broads, which they dug into when making their homes. Jenny disliked their large orange teeth, though, as she told Danny, she realised that one should not judge by appearances.

When the *Kittiwake* had been repaired and was usable once more, she and Danny had been taught to sail her and much preferred this method of transport to rowing. For a start they could go much further with a lot less effort, and had actually sailed the *Kittiwake* almost as far as Breydon Water. Jenny had packed a picnic, adding a bottle of beer for Danny and one of lemonade for herself, and they had had a wonderfully carefree day, whilst the Harkers coped with the Cat and Fiddle. They had discussed their plans for the winter, when they would lose the income from the boat trips, but intended to hold quiz and hotpot nights to make up for the lack.

Trudging along with her bucket weighing her down, Jenny thought now that she had never been happier. Sometimes she believed she was only kidding herself, but it did seem to her that Danny's affection was no longer the almost avuncular feeling of a grown man for a child. He asked her advice, often took it, clearly enjoyed her company and was as proud of her achievements as he was of his own.

Then there had been what she now thought of as the nightmare affair. They had had a long and tiring day, with Jenny clearing the gutters at the front of the Cat of an accumulation of leaves which had blocked the passage of rainwater. This had backed up, spilled over and caused a leak over the window of their best guest bedroom. Danny could not climb the ladder because of his injuries, so Jenny had done it. She had never liked heights, but she had been all right when she had gone up to see what damage had been caused when their elm tree had fallen, so decided she would be perfectly all right now if she concentrated on the job in hand and did not look down.

She had completed the task satisfactorily, but when she reached the ground once more and reported that now all should be well, she found she was trembling like a leaf. Danny noticed and had given her a big hug and a kiss on the cheek. 'You're a girl in a thousand,' he said exuberantly. 'When I saw you at the very top of that ladder, leaning sideways to scoop out the leaves, my heart was in my mouth. If you'd fallen – oh, Jenny wren, I dare not even think what I'd do if I lost my little partner.'

Jenny had felt her face grow warm and muttered that at least one problem had been solved, making little of her achievement, but that night she had had a fearful nightmare in which she was once more at the top of the ladder, and below her was not the yard of the Cat and Fiddle and Danny's anxious, upturned face, but a ring of red-eyed and slavering wolves, waiting to tear her – what would be left of her – into a thousand bloody pieces.

She had woken, the scream dying on her lips, sweat trickling down her neck, just as Danny had burst into the room, flung himself down on the bed and taken her in his arms. 'It's all right, it's all right, I'm here, you're safe,' he had murmured, his mouth so close to her ear that she could feel his warm breath. 'You've had a horrible nightmare, darling Jenny; I should never have let you climb that bloody ladder. I'm a selfish swine to take advantage of you the way I do.'

He had kept hugging her, a hand smoothing the hair off her wet forehead. Jenny had sunk back against her pillows, her heart still thumping, but the sweat cooling on her body. She had felt ashamed of her panic and had been grateful that they had had no guests to be awakened by her yells. For a moment, however, she had simply lain in Danny's arms, revelling in his comfortable nearness, before telling herself, sternly, not to read anything but kindness and pity in his embrace. She had then given a deep, tremulous sigh, pushed him away and wiped her tear-stained face with a corner of the sheet, saying gruffly that she was very sorry but no one could help having bad dreams from time to time. 'It was the toasted cheese – cheese often gives me bad dreams.'

Danny had laughed and pulled the blankets up over her shoulders. 'Toasted cheese my foot,' he had said rudely. 'It was that damned ladder. Shall I stay with you? Make sure you sleep sweetly until morning? I could, you know . . .'

For a moment, Jenny had been tempted, but then her wretched common sense had reasserted itself. Pity was no substitute for the love which Danny could not possibly feel, so she had shaken her head. 'It's all right; I'll be fine now. You go back to bed and get what sleep you can,' she told him. Then she had chuckled. 'Good thing tomorrow's Sunday; we can both have a lie-in.'

Danny had gone, looking back anxiously before closing the door, and Jenny had not known whether to be pleased or sorry that she had sent him away, but on the whole she thought she had done the right thing. She would have died of shame had he realised how she felt about him.

Jenny shifted the weight of her bag of acorns from one hand to the other as the Cat and Fiddle came into view. As time passed, the relationship between herself and Danny just grew warmer and more comfortable. In fact, Jenny told herself, a stranger would probably think their marriage was as genuine as they tried to make it appear. And perhaps one day, Jenny dreamed as she neared the pub, one day Danny might realise that he needed her as much as she needed him, and they could . . . oh, they could . . .

On that thought, Jenny pushed open the door of the public bar, took two steps inside and froze. A slim, dark-haired woman was facing Danny, with no more than a couple of feet between them. He was speaking, but Jenny had no idea what he was saying, because before she could even move the girl had flung both her arms round his neck and was hugging him as though she would never let go.

Jenny turned back, blinded by the tears that rose to her eyes, but even as she dashed them away she had recognised her sister. Claudia was here!

She did not think the couple had seen her, but what did it matter anyway? Jenny ran. In seconds she was in the boathouse, jumping into the nearest craft and grabbing the oars. She had to get away, far away, because she knew that she could not face seeing once more that loving couple, clasped in each other's arms.

Desperately, Jenny rowed away from her home – and the man she had always loved.

Chapter Nineteen

Danny was in the bar polishing glasses when someone pushed open the door and came in. He looked up, expecting to see one of the Harkers, or perhaps Jenny, back from her acorn-gathering, and saw a stranger. A slender, dark-haired woman in a dark coat and hat . . .

'Good afternoon. I'm afraid we're closed for another couple of hours – licensing laws, you know – but if you're wanting a room for the weekend . . .' he began, but then the woman gave a little sob and ran towards him and Danny saw that it was Claudia.

'Don't you know me, Danny? Surely it hasn't been that long! Oh, Danny, I've been such a fool . . . I knew I'd made a dreadful mistake almost as soon as we reached America, but then the war started, and no one would tell me where you'd gone . . .'

She threw herself at Danny, clasping her arms about his neck, just as the door to the bar opened behind her. Danny, horribly embarrassed, tried to pull free, but Claudia clung on, pressing herself even closer to him, saying that she had always known, really, that Danny was the only man she would ever love, that her affair with Rob Dingle had been madness, that she had come back the very first time an opportunity had arisen, and had rushed straight to Cumber because someone had told her that she would find him at the Cat and Fiddle.

Over the top of her head, Danny saw that Jenny had entered the room. She was rosy and smiling, but as she took in the scene before her the colour drained from her face, leaving it deathly white. Desperately, Danny opened his mouth to tell her it was all a horrible mistake, but before he could utter a word Jenny had dropped the bucket and backed out of the room, shutting the bar door with surprising gentleness, and disappeared.

Danny would have followed her, but Claudia still clung to his arm. 'If you're worried because you think I'm a married woman, then you're quite wrong; Rob and I never got wed,' she said breathlessly. 'I was a fool, but not that much of a fool . . . And I don't understand why you didn't guess I'd come to you. I wrote to Mam, telling her I was coming home and asking her to tell you I was on my way back to you . . .'

Danny seized her by the shoulders and shook her so hard that she gasped. 'You may not be married, but I am, and the last thing I mean to do is let you ruin my life a second time,' he said brutally. 'I won't have you upsetting my wife, so the sooner you get out of here, the better. You can ring for a taxi – the driver only lives round the corner.'

Claudia stepped back from him, eyes and mouth round with dismay. 'But Mam said you married Jenny and it wasn't a real marriage, just a partnership. You can break it any time; you know you can. Jenny won't mind. I expect she only married you because she always wanted whatever I had. She'll give you a divorce as soon as she knows I'm back. Mam must have told her, and she hasn't bothered to tell you.'

Danny took a deep breath. He marvelled that he had ever thought himself in love with this beautiful, selfish woman, who had no thought for anything other than her own desires. He knew he must scotch this once and for all. 'Yes, I'm married to Jenny. We're very happy and we're going to have a baby, so you must understand that even seeing you might cause her distress, and that I will not have.' He pushed Claudia roughly ahead of him out of the bar. In the yard, he jerked a thumb towards Cumber. 'You'll find the telephone box by the post office. The taxi driver's number is on the front of the book. And don't you ever come here again. Jenny saw you behaving like a loose woman. I've got to go after her, tell her you're nothing to me and never were.'

Claudia began to protest, but even as she spoke Danny had turned away from her and was running towards the boathouse.

By the time she had rowed halfway across the fen, Jenny had begun to think straight. What on earth was she doing, running away? Claudia had married Rob Dingle and gone off to America. Now she, and no doubt her horrible husband, were back in England. She had come to the Cat and Fiddle to see Danny once more and had simply given him a hug, perhaps to apologise for stealing his money, perhaps merely out of old friendship. But whatever the reason, are you truly going to give up without a fight, she asked herself. And now that she was calmer, she remembered the look on Danny's face when Claudia had flung herself into his arms. It had not been delight, let alone passion; it had been a look of surprise, and horror.

He doesn't love her any more, Jenny told herself firmly. Of course I know he doesn't love me either, but I do know he's fond of me. So I shall go back and be perfectly polite to Claudia, and see her off on the very next bus. I won't ask her to stay the night, or to have a meal, not even a drink; I shall tell her politely but firmly to look after her own husband and I'll look after mine. And judging by the look on Danny's face, he'll agree I'm doing the right thing.

'Oh, please God, don't take Danny away from me,' Jenny found herself praying as she turned the boat round and began heading home. Claudia's very beautiful and very clever, but she couldn't look after him like I can. Why, she'd faint with horror if she was asked to dig the garden, feed the pigs or clean out the hens, let alone climb a ladder and clear the gutters. Claudia wouldn't like serving behind the bar, not even if it meant having Danny.

Heartened by this thought, Jenny steered carefully into the boathouse, suddenly aware that she was dreading the encounter to come. What would she do if Danny explained that he still loved and wanted Claudia? Would she meekly agree to a divorce; start working out plans for dividing up the Cat and Fiddle?

But no sooner had she shipped her oars and begun to clamber out on to the catwalk than warm, strong arms enveloped her and she found herself being deliciously kissed; not in a brotherly fashion, she realised, but in quite a different way, a way she had never been kissed before. She gave a deep sigh of contentment and almost timidly put her arms round Danny's neck and began to return the kisses. Then Danny looped an arm round her shoulders and guided her out of the boathouse.

Back in the kitchen, he sat down in one of the easy chairs and pulled her on to his lap. 'You saw who that was,' he said, settling her comfortably.

Jenny nodded. 'It was my perishin' sister,' she said. 'The one you were in love with.'

'Thought I was,' Danny corrected. 'Knew I wasn't when she walked into the bar this afternoon. Told her to get out and leave us alone. Said I wouldn't have you upset. Told her we were having a baby.'

Jenny jerked upright. 'Having a baby?' she said incredulously. 'But – but we aren't!'

Danny chuckled. 'Yes we are,' he said mildly. 'Of course I don't know when, but we are definitely going to have a baby. If it's all right by you, that is?'

Jenny gave a huge sigh, then reached up and kissed Danny's chin. 'My cup runneth over,' she said dreamily. 'Oh, Danny, I've loved you since I was a little girl and I love you still.'

Danny kissed the top of her head. 'I love you too, my darling – oh, Jenny, I love you too.'